Of Grace
and
Courage

Thornhill Veterans Hospital

ISBN-13: 978-0-9994538-1-0
ISBN-10: 0-9994538-1-5

First printing: November 2017

Front cover illustration by Sidney Bailey

Veteran illustrated: Patrick Wade Ret. Major U.S. Army National Guard

Edited by Mary Lewis
Final edit by Stuart Blandford

Published by:

ThomasMax Publishing
P.O. Box 250054
Atlanta, GA 30325
www.thomasmax.com

Of Grace and Courage

Thornhill Veterans Hospital

Barbara D. Duffey

ThomasMax

Your Publisher
For The 21st Century

ACKNOWLEDGMENTS

I'd like to thank those individuals whose undying encouragement helped motivate me to complete this novel. Most of all my dear friends Pat Adams and Martha Phillips who read and reread the manuscript, encouraging me along the way.

This novel would not have been possible without the expert editing of Mary Lewis, also known as the "slasher," who spent hours with me pouring over a huge manuscript in the effort of cutting it down to size. I also want to thank Stu Blandford who edited the final draft with grace, dignity, and positive reinforcement.

The publisher Lee Clevenger of ThomasMax Publishing has diligently obsessed over this work to help create the final product.

Thank you to all the others who have participated in this endeavor, especially my anonymous friend who said, "You've carried this baby long enough. Now it's time to birth it!"

This book is dedicated to all the veterans who spend their last days in Veterans Hospitals. This book is also dedicated to those nurses: RNs, LPNs, CNAs, and aides, who courageously battle heart and soul to deliver good care and devote their life to the service of others. Last but not least, I wish to thank my children, Andrew Fiske and Meghan Duffey, for their patience with me during the months I spent writing this book.

FOREWORD

The Veterans Health Administration is the largest integrated health care system in the United States and serves nine million enrolled Veterans each year.* While Of Grace and Courage, Thornhill Veterans Hospital, is fiction, challenges similar to those in the novel still confront the VHA today.

The author wrote this novel from her experiences working in a number of health care settings as a nurse and nursing administrator. She pulled together hundreds of stories, some inspiring and others demoralizing, to create this account of fiction.

The author hopes that these imperfect and enduring fictional characters may, in some way, give recognition to all those individuals who have fought the good fight to preserve their grace, integrity, and humanity in the face of hopelessness and despair.

She also hopes that this story may be a stimulus to the ongoing efforts of the Veterans Health Administration to improve the care of our cherished veterans.

*Source: Veterans Health Administration   US Department of Veterans

to the One who remembered us in our low estate
His love endures forever.
Psalm 136:23

Chapter 1

As Esther Culver drove up the long drive that led to Thornhill Veterans Hospital in Fayette, South Carolina, she admired the massive live oaks dripping with Spanish Moss that led to the entrance. They did not reflect the irremediable reputation of the nineteenth-century decaying hospital. Several people had told her stories of abuse and neglect about the place, but she didn't believe they were possible now in 2000, with all the federal regulations and inspections. The idea that the elderly and disabled were exploited distressed her, but she was sure the Veterans Administrations had higher standards now.

Esther parked and hurried toward the large brick building with a portico of four columns. Patients lingered in a garden to the left, smoking their cigarettes. They resembled bent twigs, moving aimlessly, ghost-like, silent in the morning light.

Afraid of being late for her appointment, Esther didn't stop to watch the men. She hurried through the electronically-controlled doors into the lobby, feeling thankful to have finally gotten an appointment with the director of nurses for a job. After locating the right office and announcing her arrival, she sat on the oak bench in the hall. Thornhill Veterans Hospital was the last institution on her list. The other medical facilities had refused to hire her because of her suspended Registered Nurse license and impending probation. Thornhill was her last chance.

As Esther waited, she noticed the dirty cream-colored walls and the peeling paint in areas across the ceiling where leaks had penetrated through, exposing the white plaster. Her heart hammered in her chest.

An attractive black woman touched Esther's arm.

"Mrs. Culver. Please come with me," she said. "I'm Mrs. Putnam, the director of nurses." She ushered Esther into a neat office with a tall window overlooking the oaks lining the street.

"Please sit down," Mrs. Putnam said.

Mrs. Putnam pulled a manila file closer, turning a page. The woman's eyes narrowed as they moved down the resume.

Esther fidgeted with the clasp of her black eel skin purse.

Mrs. Putnam finally glanced up from the file, smiled kindly and said, "Why don't you just start at the beginning and explain exactly what happened? I'm concerned that you have been put on probation for six months. Until you satisfy this requirement, you are in jeopardy of losing your license." She settled into her high-backed swivel chair.

Esther gazed out the towering window behind Mrs. Putnam's desk at the massive branches of live oaks. She relaxed, after seeing no impatience or ridicule in Mrs. Putnam's finely chiseled face.

"I haven't worked very much in the last five years because of my two young children, Matt, age three, and Eric, just two. Occasionally, I accepted a home Hospice case for extra money, though. We were living in Maryland at the time. I heard a previous patient of mine was dying of throat cancer. It sounded like a steady case so I took it. I knew the family and felt sorry for them. That was a big mistake," Esther said, pausing to get her breath and trying to calm her frazzled nerves.

"Please go on, Mrs. Culver," Mrs. Putnam said, seemingly unaffected by Esther's distress.

"It turned into an unusual case from the beginning. His children hated their stepmother. They complained bitterly to me about everything from the color of his room to the literature he read. Their criticisms never stopped. That last day, the patient suffered more pain than usual. I had given him all the pain medication the doctor prescribed, but the medicine wasn't working. His wife and children became hysterical about his escalating discomfort so I phoned the doctor for a change in the medicine. Just before I left at 5:00 p.m., I gave him an injection of morphine that the doctor ordered instead of his usual three teaspoons of Brompton's mixture of cocaine and morphine. I explained to the wife about the new dosage and told her if she had any problems to call me at home. The patient had vomited everything we gave him that day, and I thought he wasn't absorbing the Brompton's mixture either because it didn't subdue his pain. His wife was his caretaker at night.

I worried about his declining condition and became concerned his wife wouldn't be able to give him the medicine the doctor ordered. She was eighty-two."

Esther paused and gazed out the window, thinking that this was her last chance to find a nursing job. She loved nursing more than anything. It remained the only means she had to support herself now that her husband was divorcing her.

"At 3:00 a.m., I received a call from the wife saying her husband was dead. She was completely overwhelmed with grief. I told her to call 911. I couldn't get there until the morning because of my boys. My husband was out of town. His children arrived immediately and blamed her for his death. They demanded to know why he died suddenly. Not expecting it to happen so soon. They asked for an autopsy to determine the cause of death. The medical examiner discovered someone gave him an overdose of morphine and cocaine, ingredients of the Brompton's mixture. Three times the acceptable amount was discovered in his blood. His children pressed charges on me.

Esther sighed as she tried to erase the picture of the wife's haggard face at the hearing.

"The verdict was accidental overdose. The judge suspended my license and put me on probation for six months, presuming that I was responsible for the overdose. I swear I didn't have anything to do with it. I never dreamed they would accuse me...even hold my license until the probation became satisfied."

Esther watched as Mrs. Putnam jotted down a few words on the file.

"Believe me, Mrs. Putnam. I never gave the patient anything the doctor didn't order. His wife never admitted giving him the medicine either. I know someone did. He had been vomiting all day and couldn't keep anything down. By their estimates, he received three times the prescribed dose which caused his sudden death. So here I am trying to find a job. I need this job desperately. My husband thinks I'm guilty too. He doesn't believe me. He's a lawyer. When his prestigious law firm found out, they politely asked him to resign. Afraid the scandal would taint their reputation. The family has a prominent name in Baltimore. Word traveled like lightning, that I gave my patient an overdose, killing him. We had to sell our house and move here where my husband's family lives. As soon as we moved, he told me he wanted a divorce and left. I have two preschool boys to raise by myself. I beg you. Thornhill Veterans Hospital is my last chance at a decent paying position. Every other job offers only minimum wage." Esther fought to hold back her erupting tears.

Mrs. Putnam frowned as she scanned the papers in front of her.

Finally, she answered, "I need to discuss this with personnel first. After all, your license is out of state and has been suspended. This makes it quite a different story."

Mrs. Putnam stared in contemplation out the window for several seconds, then glanced back at Esther sympathetically. "I've already checked with our Board of Nursing. They also suggested a probation time of 1,000 hours. If you satisfy their requirements, both your licenses will be reinstated. One for Maryland and one for South

Carolina. This is supervised work. If there is any infraction, you will lose both your licenses completely and forever. Did you know that? This means you will never be able to work as a nurse again.

Esther nodded her head.

"It sounds like you've been through quite an ordeal. I'll see what I can do. I see you worked at Johns Hopkins Hospital. You've gotten yourself into an unfortunate situation here. However, we're in a severe staffing crisis. Maybe, we can use you after all. But, I have to decrease your pay accordingly. Step outside for a few minutes while I make some calls. Please don't leave. If we decide to take you on, you may start tomorrow with a three day orientation."

Mrs. Putnam smiled kindly at Esther, extending her soft hand.

"Thank you. I would appreciate it so much if you gave me a chance to redeem myself," Esther said and cautiously shook Mrs. Putnam's outstretched hand. She quietly closed the door behind her. Her wait seemed interminable. The hallway was busy now with administrative people who nodded and smiled as they passed. Finally, Mrs. Putnam called her back.

"I'm happy to welcome you to our hospital staff," she said calmly. "I've discussed your case with Human Resources. They want you to go to their office now to fill out all the proper papers. I hope we'll see you tomorrow." Mrs. Putnam smiled and patted Esther's arm. "I know this probation has been very difficult for you. Think of tomorrow as the beginning of your new life."

"Thank you so much. I will always be in your debt," Esther said, smiling as she left the office.

Chapter 2

The morning after Esther finished her orientation, at 6:25 a.m., she walked toward Thornhill Veterans Hospital to begin her official first day. The sunlight fanned out, bleeding into the gray sky, painting the clouds in a kaleidoscope of Vermillion, pink, and purple. Esther's legs felt heavy, as she hastened up the dingy, cracked concrete walk toward the hospital entrance. She had already struggled with her two boys that morning, trying to quell their fears of being left at daycare. She felt overwhelmed. She stumbled on an uplifted edge of the concrete. Stabbing pain shot through her foot. She lurched forward, frantically grabbing her thermos, lunch, and purse.

Just take your time, she told herself. She stepped off the walk onto the dirt. A savage, cold, shiver skimmed up her spine and settled around her neck. She reached up and traced the shape of the cross that lay hidden on her chest under her uniform. She prayed, hoping for relief from her fear. She had survived the inner-city hospital of Philadelphia as a student. It can't be any worse than that, she thought. The nurses she met at the orientation seemed nice enough. She knew all the information they learned was up-to-date and on a professional level.

Shrouded in oaks, obscured from view, the entrance to the hospital seemed farther down the lane than she expected. She noticed several patients smoking in the garden to the left. She wondered if they were the same ones she saw the first day.

Yes, we are all castoffs, the forgotten, caught up in fated circumstances, not of our own choosing. She felt strengthened by their beggar-like neediness.

Although her eyes shifted nervously from one patient to the next, she noticed they observed her as curiously as she watched them. They moved toward her so close the heat of their fetid breath surrounded her. She witnessed a curiosity and feeble pleading in their eyes.

Esther rushed on toward the hospital. Almost late for work, she chided herself for watching the men. One man turned and stared at her as if she were a rare bird.

After scratching his head, he said, "Ma'am. There are all sorts of varmints in that ravine beyond the garden down there." He pointed his bony finger toward the lingering mist. "You need to be careful walking up here. We cleaned out that same swamp last year, but no telling what you might encounter."

Beyond a brick wall, Esther saw the deep ravine. In the distance trees laced in bare, gray Kudzu vines partially obscured all but what appeared to be a reflection of water at the bottom. Faint clouds of mist still rose up from the culvert from the early morning chill in June.

She rushed on in quiet desperation.

The same man grabbed her arm. She tried to pull away, but he held on tightly and pointed down the hill to the ravine again. His grasp hurt her arm.

"Miss. Miss. I...a.... I thought you might want to see those graves down yonder. Hundreds of unmarked graves cover that landing. They're nigger's graves," he said, as his mouth twisted in a grotesque, cynical smile.

"This hospital is more 'en a hundred years old. All the niggers came here to be treated. An' idiots too. It was the only place in South Carolina that took 'em in. That's how it got the name, Thornhill. A mighty wretched place it was. Mighty wretched." He bowed a little to her and grinned. "You'll get along okay here. It's changed a lot since then. Since the Veterans Administration took it over." Abruptly, he left her and disappeared into the crowd.

Unmarked Negro graves? It seemed so brutal, so barbaric. It can't be true. It must be a hateful lie. A gesture to scare her. He was just a crazy old man. She pushed the scene out of her mind as she walked on. Whiffs of sweat and old urine forced her to turn away from a few patients walking near her.

Without warning, Esther spotted movement in the thick, verdant blades of grass growing in wild tufts beside the concrete walk. Mockingbirds, emitting sharped pitched cries, swooped down and pecked furiously at a dark form that slithered across the concrete. A snake sought shelter in the rubble.

"Aaaa!" Esther screamed!

The patients raced to the spot where the snake crossed into the garden.

"There it is. I see it," a tall, bony black nurse cried, pointing to the ground under the bushes a few feet away from where Esther stood.

"Shaw, I see you!" another nurse yelled. "Don't get near that thing." The nurse shook her fist at a wheelchair patient rushing to the spot.

The growing crowd craned their necks to see from her side of the walk.

"The serpent is coiled, ready to attack," a patient yelled.

"Chester's caught it!" someone else screamed. "It's a rattler! It's a damn rattler!"

Chester Greese clutched the snake in his powerful, gnarled, red hands and held it high over his head, facing the sun. The serpent writhed in twisted and contorted moves to free itself. Its rattles relayed its fury and sounded like the castanets of a Spanish Dancer. Gibberish rambled from Chester's mouth loud enough to drown out the crowd. It was a mystical sight. His voice hung in the air as if a great wind erupted out of his chest as if he were a famous tenor singing his highest and most powerful note. The man appeared to be in a trance. His eyes bulged wide with excitement.

"Tongues!" someone shouted. "It's the Holy Spirit. It's a sign!" The crowd shrunk back afraid of the omen.

"It's protecting him," another patient cried.

Chester rambled on in an unending tirade. He danced ahead of the crowd still holding the rattler above his head. Beads of perspiration dripped down his face. His biceps expanded and contracted in a rhythmic motion as his body swayed with the snake's. All the time he continued his verbiage. He moved closer to Esther. Abruptly, he stopped his gibberish and stared at her.

"The great power of the Holy Spirit will protect us!" he yelled.

All the others followed his gaze, and their eyes converged on Esther too. She felt caught up in this mysterious rite. She wanted to run, but somehow, she felt transported, transcending her terror. For an instant, she felt as if the patients had lifted her up, imbued her with a tremendous strength.

With one stroke of his arms, Chester cast the serpent to the ground. The snake lay motionless on the concrete at Esther's feet. Its pale belly turned upward. Chester grabbed a brick from the crumbling garden wall behind him and hurled it at the snake, smashing its head. Others grabbed their bricks and crashed them onto the concrete until their target was a bloody mess. The men had become crazy, wild-eyed, and possessed with madness. The patients continued to hurl the bricks down with an intense ferocity as if the reptile embodied all the evil of the hospital, and they had to destroy it. Finished, a cry went up from them all, a resounding victory. They retreated and lit cigarettes. Clouds of smoke rose above their murmuring as if in a peace ritual.

Trembling from the ordeal, Esther hurried on in the dew-filled morning air. She felt the wind pick up. With her, came the first morning breeze that stirred the sparrows to sing from the red azaleas lining the walk that led to the door. Patients and staff rushed too.

It was 7:00 a.m. Esther hastily stepped through the electronically-controlled doors as easily as Alice stepped through the looking glass.

She timidly stood just inside the entrance, hesitating, observing the employees as they entered. She glanced down at her finely manicured nails and soft fingers. She felt her palms tingle. These were healing hands. Yes, the hustle and bustle atmosphere of the hospital stimulated her like nothing else.

A patient she saw earlier, racing in his wheelchair, the one a nurse called Shaw, now sat just inside the entrance in front of her. People nodded their heads in greeting to him as they passed. He acts as if he's the gatekeeper, Esther thought.

A towering, robust, blond-headed man in a white jacket paused in front of her. With relaxed confidence, he saluted and flashed a warm friendly smile in greeting to the wheelchair patient sitting beside the door.

"How's it going, Shaw?" he asked.

The tall man with gentle eyes let his gaze momentarily fall on Esther. He stopped abruptly as if frozen there for several seconds and eyed her with curiosity. His penetrating gaze gripped her, appraised her from head to toe as if to absorb all her essence in one glance.

"Freckles?" he blurted abruptly, laughing quietly to himself. He peered directly into Esther's eyes. "So, you're their green-eyed enchantress," he said in mocking humor.

He smiled broadly, curiosity danced in his sea-green eyes. He assessed her again from the tips of her crepe-soled shoes, paused at her white uniform, and moved up to the edge of her eyelashes as if he had missed something the first time.

Esther withdrew uncomfortably from his stare. He placed his hand on Shaw's shoulder and laughed again.

"Freckles," he repeated.

Esther felt insulted and violated. His amusement abruptly disappeared into a preoccupied and brooding stare. A cold aloofness replaced his smile, as he turned and pushed his way irritably through the crowded hallway. She overheard the others call him Henry. He ignored them rudely as if something had happened to his earlier jovial mood.

Her cheeks burned with embarrassment when he mentioned her freckles. Of all things and at her age, twenty-eight.

A certain wildness in his eyes drew her to him. She bet he was an independent, free spirit. After all that had happened to her, she marveled that this man made her smile, even if she was intimidated by him. Immediately, the caution light flashed, as she felt the pain of her fresh wound. He reminded her of her soon to be ex-husband Paul and wondered why the impetuous types always attracted her.

When she smiled down at Mr. Shaw, she realized he had seen it all. He sat there grinning to everyone with a mischievous Leprechaun's smile. Esther sensed his recognition of her emotion in the twinkle of his eye. Shaw clenched his wet cigarette tightly between his yellow, nicotine stained thumb and forefinger. His tongue protruded from his mouth creating a grotesque picture. Urine dripped through the seat of his chair, escaping the catheter which was loose and dragged underneath. His swollen legs hung down from the seat of the chair, limp from some paralysis, bluish white and bare, resting as if almost dead on the stainless-steel supports. His feet were scarred and bruised from slipping off the footrests and dragged along the floor. Flakes of tobacco and ashes dotted the front of his pajamas like confetti. A pungent odor of feces caught Esther off guard. They should have cleaned him up before letting him sit at the entrance, she thought.

He sits here resembling a gargoyle, those once used in Medieval architecture to ward off evil spirits.

She became caught in the steady flood of employees buoyed down the corridor toward the elevators.

She felt adrift in a sea of black people who wore colorful uniforms, but she noticed their friendliness and camaraderie as they hailed a greeting to each other.

"Hey, baby! I ain't seen you for a while."

"Hey Esther," a nurse called, catching up with her.

Relief filled Esther when she recognized Karen, a black nurse she had met in orientation the day before.

"Well, good morning," Esther said, after dodging the moving employees to cross the hall. The beauty of Karen's soft chocolate skin and fine features still surprised her. Karen's hair surrounded her face in soft, black, even curls. She carried herself with a certain dignity and spoke in gentle waves, high and low pitches of a southern accent garnered from South Carolina. She said she came from the islands, a region whose speech has long been enhanced with a pleasant musical sound. Her immaculate uniform boasted a gold enameled, medallion representing the nursing school she had attended and which she wore proudly next to an honor pin. Esther momentarily regretted safeguarding her own nursing school pin in her safe deposit box with her other jewelry.

The dry heat of the hallway, fluorescent lights, and worn linoleum floors jarred her senses back to reality and stirred feelings of nostalgia for hospital nursing. Yes, she had missed it. It was comforting to think that Karen bothered to hail her, and she relaxed. She didn't remember feeling this anxious in orientation. It must be official first-day jitters.

"It's tough being new, isn't it?" Karen said as she moved her purse from one shoulder to the other.

"It's horrible. I wish I knew what to expect. I guess I'll find out soon enough."

Patients crowded around the elevator. Esther thought how neglected they all looked with unshaven chins, missing teeth, and threadbare gowns.

They were carbon copies of the man at the entrance. Patients had carved their initials in the paint of the green metal elevator door like graffiti in a restroom. The hallway appeared shoddy too, with gouged plaster, peeling yellow paint, and smudge marks marring the walls where hands had groped for support. The two moved onto the crowded elevator. Esther tried to avoid eye contact with the strangers staring at her.

"Do they always let patients loiter around the entrance like that man, Shaw? He was a sight," Esther whispered into Karen's ear.

"He'll be up after us soon enough. I saw him yesterday on our floor, the seventh floor. The second floor will be calling for us to get him cleaned up. That's where he goes to sit with the other men. They stay there, drinking their coffee and watching the nurses who come to the cafeteria for a break. Just try to bring him back to the seventh floor. He will curse you...curse you 'till you give in and leave him there. The whole time you want to leave him there anyway. You want to run away from here as far and as fast as you can. Never looking back," Karen said as a frown was replaced by a look of bitter contempt.

"I won't be here forever. My husband, Terrance, is studying at the university to get his engineering degree. He's very smart and has great scholarships. In exactly nine months, and four days, we will be out of here and on the road to a new life. No more bed pans and bed baths for me. I'm counting the days. Terrance started his final year last week, the June semester. We used to spend the summers at home in Beaufort, South Carolina. We work a small farm with my family on weekends. Whenever we can get away during the winter months," Karen admitted proudly. She smiled broadly, correcting her posture to lift her chin higher. "To us, Fayette, South Carolina, is a big city. It's as big as we've seen except when we go down to Charleston or Savannah. Now, they're cities," Karen said and glanced away dreamily.

"I thought I was the only one who can't wait to get away. Did you see that snake? That man holding the snake?" Esther asked.

"I wasn't close enough. Thank goodness. But I heard him. Tongues! He was talking in tongues," Karen said. "Killed that rattler. Nothing would surprise me here at Thornhill."

"What are tongues?" Esther asked.

"They say it's people talking to God. They say it's the Holy Spirit on him. I don't know that much about it. But my kin always said if you kill a rattler, its spirit will come back on you. Haunt you," Karen said.

Esther shivered at the thought. She felt a kinship with Karen, even though she had only known her since orientation. Esther loved her enthusiasm and optimism. She hoped to catch some of Karen's vitality, hoped to find some cure for her own despair.

"Taking care of Mr. Shaw was my first job yesterday. After you left to go home, I went up to the seventh floor to look around. They were short of help and asked me to go down to the second floor to simply bring him back. When I returned, all the nurses laughed. They had a good joke on me. He cursed me the whole time," Karen said and grimaced. Then, she laughed shyly.

"Somehow, I don't think we can win at this," Esther said.

They both watched the numbers light up above the elevator door. An automatic voice announced the eighth floor, and everyone laughed as the door opened on seven.

They stepped off the elevator and proceeded down the hall.

Chapter 3

The nurses had gathered in the unpleasant, poorly lighted hall for the morning report. Three black nurses, wearing starched white uniforms, stood out against the dreary walls like the last blossoms of summer. They remained patient, silent, standing in a semicircle, waiting for Esther and Karen to join them. A white LPN hung back behind the others, and although her head bent awkwardly away from the two new nurses, her eyes glared at them, intense, suspicious, not missing a single detail. She frowned at Esther with contempt in her eyes, staring first at her finely manicured nails, and then mockingly surveyed her thin frame.

"I guess they dragged you in from the plantation?" the LPN said. "You can call me Shirleen. I work on the north end." The others snickered with deliberate sarcasm and gave Esther the once-over too.

Karen timidly introduced herself and Esther to the others.

Esther felt some comfort as Karen tried to draw attention away from her first impression as a white elite daughter of society. They ignored Karen.

Rudely, they mumbled to each other, "Look at those long pink fingernails. Uh, huh. They won't last long here."

Esther hid her hands from view.

"That's all right. You two take your time like we have all day to wait. I'm Geraldine," a middle-aged black nurse said. She wore a short-cropped, reddish brown wig. Geraldine sighed heavily, then continued, "Just because you're new don't mean you can be late. Now Lyla and Sally here worked last night. They're staying for a while to give you girls a hand with the baths."

Geraldine glanced at Lyla and Sally and smiled. When she turned back to examine Esther again, she said curtly, "But I ain't staying. I refuse to be a slave to this hospital, especially working late without pay. I figure my ancestors took care of that obligation for me. I'll start the report."

Pleased with her sarcastic remarks, Geraldine smiled down at her feet and eyed the two frightened new nurses with disdain. Her orange-brown wig slid off center as she wheezed a little out of breath. She straightened up, squinted her eyes to thin, angry slits, and continued in her high-pitched voice.

"They pay us in comp time and not time and a half for overtime. So, I ain't going to stay over. We're short. They won't let us take our comp time. I call that slave labor. It took me a few months to catch on. I have over two hundred hours of time coming to me. Oh, the RNs get paid time and a half, but not LPNs or CNAs. We're their slaves. I have four little ones to get ready for school when I get home, so, if you have any questions make them brief."

Geraldine began the report. "Room 708, Mr. Fawcett. We call him Buster. His suprapubic catheter is leaking urine all over his bed again. Finally, I gave him some of them blue chucks and told him to clean his self up best he can. I don't have time to wet-nurse sixty patients. If they don't get that tube fixed, he's gonna break down. Then, you'll have a problem. He's so dirty...messes up his bedside table with ashes..."

Geraldine glared fiercely at each nurse.

The other nurses turned away, as if embarrassed. No one wanted to tangle with Geraldine. Esther self-consciously pressed back against the wall to become less conspicuous.

When Esther glanced up, everyone watched her reaction. Glints of mischief shot from their eyes as they punched each other, nodding in her direction.

"710, Bed One. Mr. Hudson still won't help his self. He was turned about an hour ago and cleaned up. His bowels moved," Geraldine continued.

"710, Bed Two, Mr. Moses Rivers hollered out all night. We had to give him Haldol to calm him down. He became angry, complaining that people came in and took everything he owned. He's gonna get 'em. He said we were all sinners and had better repent because Judgment Day was coming sooner than we thought." Geraldine's voice trailed off. She let out a little chuckle. "He's as crazy as a loon on a freezing night in Canada. Kept everyone up all night 'til he got his medicine."

After a while, Esther hardly heard the nurse. They inched slowly down the hall, stopping only briefly as they passed bed after bed housing emaciated, bony, and wretched looking men who smelled like feces and urine. One diagnosis ran into the next in Esther's mind. They all seemed the same, neglected and needy.

The bedside tables appeared crusty with dried spills from dinner the night before. Patients carried urine bags that overflowed onto the floor. They hadn't been emptied since the day before. Geraldine hadn't taken time to measure their output.

Most of the demented or brain-damaged patients struggled in their beds, trying to get up. Their purple-veined fingers roamed and picked at the sheets, gowns, or hair as if minute bugs crawled there. They deliberately picked at a spot, brought their fingers up to their line of sight, examined it, and then discarded whatever it was.

The nurses visited each room, moving down the hall of sixty patients. One patient had taken his clothes off, sang an unintelligible song, and sat naked, twisted in the sheets, soaked in a pool of urine.

Others cursed at the nurses, shouting, "When are you gonna get around to helping us?"

There were so many. Esther didn't know people existed like this. Of all the hospitals she had worked in, this was by far the worst. I only have to last for six months. Then, if I'm lucky, I can accept a position at the University Hospital on the other side of town, Esther thought.

Karen leaned over and whispered in her ear, "After a while, we'll know them all by name. It won't seem so bad." She squeezed Esther's shoulder sympathetically.

Out of the blue, Shirleen yelled at a crying patient, "Oh shut up! I'm sick of your complaining! I'll be in when I get damn good and ready. Do you hear? And not a minute sooner."

"That's telling 'em, Shirleen!" Lyla said smugly. Lyla's huge fish earrings bounced against her long, black cheeks. She wore a purple headband in front of her stringy, black ponytail. Moving her tall, thin form stiffly, she poked her head into the room saying, "Good God."

The patient quickly became silent, retreating further into his ritual-like behavior of picking at invisible specks. The patients reminded Esther of abused children, afraid to say anything or speak their minds.

Shirleen flashed a savage grin.

"These patients will walk all over you if you give them half a chance. Before you know it, we'll be working for the patients instead of ourselves," she said and snickered.

Shirleen pushed her oily, black hair out of her fat, white, pimply face. The bulk of it hung in long, thick unkempt waves halfway down her back, stopping in a mass of split ends. When she raised her arm as if to strike at the patient, brown stains from old perspiration marred her threadbare uniform. The other nurses and staff smiled as if enjoying Shirleen's aggressiveness.

"Shirleen, you might put that one on your list," Lyla said, her fish earrings bobbing cheerfully.

"Good idea," Shirleen responded brightly.

Esther and Karen exchanged glances but remained silent.

The report continued. Then, a curvaceous nurse joined the circle. Her lazy, marine blue eyes squinted slightly, blinking under her strawberry blond curls, and she held her hand against her heaving chest.

"Good morning, Melisa," Geraldine said. Abruptly her tone changed becoming more professional and to the point. Everyone stood up straighter and listened closely to what Geraldine said. Melisa introduced herself to Esther and Karen.

"Hello, ladies. I'm Melisa, the charge nurse."

Melisa glared at the others saying, "Geraldine dear, this floor is certainly a disappointment this morning. These patients smell...ugh," she held her nose. "Whatever happened last night?"

"Miss Melisa. We were short. I only had two CNAs, Lyla, and Sally. I tried to help. Moses Rivers cut the fool. I gave him Haldol. No one's been set up for breakfast. I'll help you before I leave."

"This is the third night this week. I'll speak with Mrs. Shepherd about it today. Thanks for offering to stay, but you need to get home to all your dear children," Melisa said.

"Ladies. Mrs. Shepherd, the nurse manager, suggested I start you out giving medications first," Melisa said and ushered the two to the green steel medicine carts sitting in the hall next to the nurses' station. Some of the patients waited there for their morning pills. Melisa pulled open the drawers and expertly passed out pills to those surrounding the cart. She was so quick that Esther thought she must have memorized what pills each received.

Esther felt unsure about giving out medicines this soon without supervision. She didn't know the names of the patients or where the supplies were kept.

"Esther, you and Karen come with me. If anyone harasses you don't pay them any attention. Remember you both are RNs. The others are only LPNs and CNAs," Melisa said, emphasizing the titles with a snootiness, glancing in the direction of the observing staff.

* * *

Melisa paused momentarily, cautiously giving the new nurses the once over. Karen will be all right, she thought, but the staff is gonna give Esther a fit. She won't last here. They'll chase her off in two days.

If not sooner. She faced Esther and tried to hide her regret. Her warm open manner changed, becoming cold and bitter. She tried to stop herself but had been disappointed too many times before. She remembered the other good nurses who left after their first day, frightened by all the work, the disagreeable patients, and the cursing, insulting staff. If only a few had stayed to improve the conditions, the unit might be quite different. She sighed deeply. She didn't know why she tolerated the shortages and had remained at Thornhill all these years. Nineteen years seemed too long for her to change now. She had become accustomed to it all. The seventh floor was a vacation after her work as a nurse in Vietnam for six long years, but then she loved these vets. That's why she stayed, for the patients.

* * *

Melisa continued, "I...er...I'll go over the medicines with you first Esther. Then you, Karen," Melisa said and patted Karen's shoulder.

"These people need to be fed before we do anything else. When you're more experienced, you can give the meds with the meals. I'll help you today. I think about twelve on this side of the hall need to be fed. I've sent Shirleen and the others to the other side to begin. There are thirty patients on each side. Sixty in all."

Melisa, Karen, and Esther hurriedly retraced their steps down the floor. They changed patients, pulled them up in bed, and set up the trays. One after another, the apathetic men, lying in their crumpled sheets, starred with sunken eyes at the food saying, "I'm not very hungry this morning," or, "Please no more. I think I've had enough." Then, they fell backward onto their pillows, too weak to care. Their teeth clicked together like dead twigs in a winter wind. The nurses tried to hurry, not wanting the food to get cold. As they moved down the hall, Melisa explained the background of each patient. They worked together, and the three of them soon finished the hall.

"If you spit at me again, you'll find out who's boss!" A nurse down the hall yelled, "Don't you spit at me. I'm not gonna feed you anymore. So there."

A gruff masculine voice answered, "Kiss my ass! You bitch!"

Several patients who walked in the hall veered away from the noise and dropped their heads onto their concave chests in fear.

"That was Collins hollering. Don't you think, Esther?" Karen asked.

Esther shook her head not knowing, as she watched another man approach the medicine cart. A gaunt nervous man stood impatiently in front of her. A scaly mass of chapped skin covered the backs of his hands. Scabs oozed dried blood where he had scratched. Psoriasis or maybe even scabies, Esther considered. Her squeamishness melted. She began to see these patients as people, her people.

The man wore a too small, brown plaid, flannel shirt and brown trousers. His hair grew longer than the other patients, but he had combed and parted it neatly. His clean clothes and hair gave him a dignity the others lacked.

Melisa apprehended him as he was about to leave. "Chester. I saw you this morning. You should have been more careful. A rattler! My goodness!"

"Yes, Ma'am. Yes, Ma'am," he answered, shying away a little. He smiled at Esther.

"Chester. I'm Esther, one of the new nurses."

He nodded with a sheepish smile.

"I didn't know you spoke in tongues," Melisa continued. "Everyone's talking about it. You must have been quite a sight."

"Yes, Ma'am. That's what everyone's telling me. But I can't help it. That tongue stuff just come on me. I don't put much store in it. But today, I saw 'at snake was a rattler. It scared me. That's when it came on me. I'm a real sinner. I'm no Holy person. Everyone's ask'en me for favors now. They say'en, 'Chester pray for me.' Miss Melisa I'm going out for the day so I'm ask'en for my pills."

Chester's shy, broad smile revealed broken and missing teeth. "I don't know why the tongues came back. For forty years the Holy Spirit ignored my pleadings, ever since I returned from the war. That's where I felt it most, overseas in the trenches. The first time I experienced the Spirit was when I saw my first rattler about to strike in the bushes near my house. I was just a boy of fourteen, I reckon. The Spirit saved my life that day. Other times, it came close to saving it. But now, why has it returned now?"

Melisa frowned. "I can't answer that question, Chester. I'll let you go out today though.... Until 5:00 p.m.," Melisa said. "But you must be back by supper time. No excuses. Don't bring anything back with you. Do you hear?"

He ambled off down the hall with his head cocked to one side.

Karen and Esther shook their heads with dismay and laughed at Chester.

"You have to watch that one. He brings alcohol back with him," Melisa said. "He has tuberculosis. We keep him here so he can get all his medication. If we discharged him, he'd never finish his treatment and could spread the disease. He's going out for a drink now! The TB is under control. As long as he gets his pills."

"I see what you mean. He really had me fooled," Esther said and thought of Paul and his lies about his drinking.

They stood outside Mr. Markowitz's room and pulled the white cotton isolation gowns over their uniforms. They strung the masks across their noses and mouths to protect them from his Methicillin-resistant staph infection. Esther hardly breathed, wondering how much time it would take to feed this patient. The masks smelled of disinfectant and helped obliterate the smothering, pungent odors of excrement escaping from the room.

Karen tentatively pushed open the door to reveal Mr. Markowitz lying deadly still, staring at the ceiling. His red hair, gray around the temples, tumbled across his pale forehead. Brown old-age spots dotted his face.

"Oh, my God," Esther cried, sucking in her breath.

Mr. Markowitz resembled a corpse, a white sheet covered him up to his chin. When his mouth moved, Esther jumped, startled that he was alive. She tried not to stare at him, wondering if he was close to death. His ashen skin stretched tightly over his bones. His hands lay still on the sheets where they had been placed earlier. His agonizingly expressive eyes glanced down at his rigid fingers, stiff as a mannequin's, frozen into claws.

Esther witnessed the tortured expression of pain and agony in his eyes. His bedside tray table straddled the bed in front of him with his breakfast of scrambled eggs, ham, juice, and coffee just out of reach and cold. A silent torment for a hungry man. She knew he had waited for over an hour for this meal. There were too many patients to feed in a timely manner, she thought, struggling with the futility of it all.

"Mr. Markowitz has been a patient here in this room for the past four years. Haven't you?" Melisa said. "He only leaves the room for treatments with whirlpool baths in physical therapy."

He is a prisoner here, Esther thought. The idea that anyone survived four years of this unending punishment troubled her. We're all in this together. She gently touched his cheek with her finger.

His hand reached slightly. The nurses followed his gaze to the remote control lying on the white sheet just out of reach. They knew he couldn't use it any longer. The disease involved his hands too. The increased tension in his muscles caused excruciating pain whenever he moved.

"You have to be extremely gentle with him," Melisa warned.

His staph infection has spread, eating away one cell at a time almost like cancer, thought Esther. Only, staph moved slower and carried excruciating pain with it.

"Did you want your comfort medicine, Mr. Markowitz?" Karen asked as she gently moved the tray table closer to his mouth. He winced at the slight movement.

"No, not yet today," he said decisively, forcing an attempt at a smile of gratitude.

Karen opened the packages of jelly and butter and spooned the scrambled eggs into his mouth.

The view out the window displayed the tops of the live oaks and the structures of the city beyond, but the filthy window glass placed a gray shroud over the scene.

"Melisa told me you have a daughter. Has she been here lately?" Karen asked, wiping his chin.

"I think it's been about two weeks now. Her grandchildren are sick with colds or something," he replied softly. "Can I have a sip of water please?"

Karen placed the straw from his drink into his mouth.

From a nearby table, Esther collected the gauze, saline, clamps, and irrigation equipment needed to change his dressings.

Melisa supervised saying, "Nurses complete this treatment every morning." She pushed her strawberry blond curls out of her eyes.

As Esther removed the greenish, serious, pus-stained dressings from his buttocks, the stench of decay overwhelmed her, but she assisted Karen in cleaning and packing the raw, deep, red hole in his back the size of a dinner plate.

Karen seemed oblivious to the odor. She turned on the television set to enliven the oppressive atmosphere. They placed the blue, plastic, check bed pads under him to keep the bed dry.

Oprah Winfrey was interviewing a team who just completed its third attempt at climbing Mt. Everest, finally succeeding. Esther felt relieved that the attention had been deflected to something outside the hospital, something normal, and even stimulating.

"Sunny skies are predicted for tomorrow. Two men were shot while trying to rob the Seven Eleven convenience store. All this and more will be featured on the 12:00 p.m. news today."

"I think I'll have my smoke now. If you don't mind," Mr. Markowitz said as he stared at the screen. His smile was a permanent grin created by his retracted muscles.

"Did you ever climb a mountain?" Esther asked in an attempt at some conversation.

"Climb a mountain?" he repeated with little expression. To their surprise, a slight thoughtfulness appeared in his eyes.

"Climb a mountain?" he repeated.

They both waited in silence, watching his lips barely moved in and out.

"I think I'll have my smoke now," he repeated as his voice trailed off. Then, it returned as if from some dark, lost place deep inside. It sounded hollow both in tone and feeling as if all his sorrow had been pushed out and spent, as if it had been replaced by a permanent subjugation, humility, and an uncertain peace.

"Yes. I did," he mumbled. "I climbed a mountain. Quite a large mountain. It was during the war. We parachuted into the French Alps to take out the German border guards between Austria, Switzerland, and France." His words tumbled out now as if each one carried more weight than the last, and the momentum pulled out the next.

"I grew up in Vermont, knowing how to ski." He coughed spasmodically. His thin, chest reverberated to the insults. He glanced around the room, and his eyes settled on the water.

Esther gave him another long sip.

"We took out the border guards. Held the peaks for several months 'till the Germans returned. Refugees escaped through the pass from occupied Austria even before the spring thaw. Assisted by the underground, they passed into liberated France and Switzerland. Many disclosed strategic enemy positions which helped to win the war," he paused, coughed a little, trying to get his breath.

"When the Germans found out, they bombed our camp. I was lucky I lived through that one."

"Oh, it must have been a terrible nightmare," Karen said.

"Do you want me to raise your head a little?" Esther asked.

"A little would be nice. That's where I met my daughter's mother. I escaped the German carnage helped by the French underground militia. She was one of their soldiers. They sheltered me until I reached the American forces. I didn't know she was pregnant when we pulled out. I was sure I would see her again, but the opportunity never came. Before I knew it, I was going home. It was a miracle that Renee, my only child, ever found me. She probably wouldn't have if I hadn't been a patient here. If I had lived somewhere else. The Veteran's Administration has a record of each hospital I've lived in for the past six years. Since I got this disease. Seeing her is my reward in life, although I don't deserve it." A thoughtful warm expression replaced his blank stare.

"Oh, I was young then. I could do anything. When you're young...." His voice trailed off again. Sadness and a deep melancholy appeared in his eyes.

Poor man, Esther thought. The only one in the world to care about him is his daughter. He didn't know she existed, and now she visits every week, trying to replace some of those lost moments before it's too late. Life is filled with bitter ironies.

Esther prepared his smoke. The cigarette holder was an odd contraption of long green tubing attached to a mouth piece. The end of the tubing was perched on, and fixed to, the ashtray and held the cigarette. The device enabled patients to smoke safely without needing hands. It reminded Esther of the contraption used by the caterpillar in Alice in Wonderland, only Mr. Markowitz wasn't blowing out green smoke. Esther deftly placed the lighted cigarette in the holder and the mouthpiece in Mr. Markowitz's mouth. After several puffs, his facial muscles relaxed, and he nodded in appreciation.

"You girls...live every moment you can. Look at me. Now, I can't do anything. I have to wait for someone to feed me, clean my privates, and even scratch my head." His voice cracked, as the corners of his mouth trembled with emotion.

Esther rubbed his forehead. His face moved back up toward her hand, like a puppy asking for more caresses.

"Okay, Mr. Markowitz," she said, feeling compassion for his humanity. "We'll be back in a little while."

The air in the hall smelled of urine, but it was a relief to Mr. Markowitz's room. "He's one of the better ones. At least, he can talk," Karen said.

Chapter 4

Karen and Esther's relief was short-lived. Melisa waited for them at the medicine cart.

"You're late," Melisa said, scowling. "You need to get busy and pass out these pills. Most of the patients going to physical therapy have already left. It's 9:00 a.m. These should have been given out by 8:15 a.m. I went ahead and gave some of them their meds."

"We're sorry Ma'am. Mr. Markowitz took so long," Karen said apologetically.

"Well, you've got to be faster than that around here. Esther, you start with Mr. Gunther in Room 704. I'll come with you this time. Karen, you take the other cart and go over to the Rooms 714-722. I'll come down and spot check you on your meds when I'm finished with Esther."

"That's fine with me," Esther answered and shrugged her shoulders meekly.

Melisa filled the small, clear plastic cups with pills. Then, she quickly disappeared through a patient's doorway. She didn't give Esther a chance to help her. Esther followed her, self-consciously watching Melisa move from one patient to the next. She didn't know where to start, afraid she might do something wrong.

Some patients ambled up and down the hall. The demented and severe stroke victims strapped in wheelchairs, sat along the walls, agitated, and yelled at Esther in meaningless gibberish. They tried to escape like so many Houdinis. Even in their demented state, some skillfully performed surprising feats, gaining their freedom.

The men eyed Esther with hard vacant stares and drooled as they hollered, screaming randomly like tortured souls not to be comforted. Lights above the doorways flashed on, one by one.

Melisa returned to the cart, rubbing hand lotion into her palms and fingers. "What are you gaping at?" she rudely asked Esther. "Get busy!"

"Melisa! Can't you give these men something to calm them down?" Lyla yelled from the nurses' station? "They sound like fighting alley cats fixin' to breed." Lyla laughed. "Those old buzzards will go on forever. I knowed that one's a KKK veteran. Came from that town in Georgia, Terrenceville. They were all KKK people in that town."

"Yes. We'll get them in a minute," Melisa answered, a weariness masked her face.

"I was waiting for you to explain how the medication system works," Esther answered as casually as possible.

"Oh. Didn't they teach you that in orientation?"

"We went over the forms a little, but that's all. No one has name tags. I don't know one patient from the next."

While Melisa impatiently showed her how to identify the patients by their pictures, a black face hung out of the third door down the hall.

"Honey, you'd better get in here 'cause your Buster is refusing to eat. He says Melisa's the only one who can help him. An' I'm glad to let you take care of him. The way it is now...you have him spoilt rotten." Lyla flashed a broad grin and disappeared back into the room.

Melisa's shoulders drooped in disgusted resignation.

"Can't they do anything right for these patients? Do I have to do everything?" she said, glancing irritably at Esther as if a sword had pierced her heart. "You might as well come with me."

Ignoring the flashing lights and undelivered pills, Melisa turned abruptly and limped into the eight-bed ward. Buster picked his head up a little as she entered, complaining in his whiny southern voice.

"I've tried to feed myself, but I just can't. I can't move these fingers to pick up the spoon. Those girls know that. I can't move my arms. I can't move my legs. I try. God knows, I try to move what I can." Buster let out a deep sob. "My legs haven't been moved since last night. Pain is shooting through my hip," Buster cried.

"If you asks me, he's nothing but an uppity bag of bones," Sally said. She continued making the bed next to him. "He says, 'Melisa knows how to fix me...just call Melisa. You don't have to worry about me.'"

Lyla turned a pouting face toward Melisa and gave her a hard look.

"If you asks me, Melisa, he won't accept help from any of us. We don't have time to deal with that kind of attitude." She grumbled, as if insulted, then left the room in a huff.

Melisa shook her head with dismay saying, "Lyla! Lyla! Lyla! What difference does it make if I try to do what the patient needs? That's our job. It's not gonna hurt you to try."

Melisa whispered to Esther, "They don't want to help him 'cause he has a few delicate requirements. They know what to do, but they just won't take the time. If he were black. Whew! They would drag out the red carpet and dote on him hand and foot." Melisa surveyed his predicament. He put on his most pitiful expression for her benefit, and she bought it.

"Oh dear! It's no wonder you can't eat. Let's pull you up in that bed," Melisa said, motioning for Esther to help her.

"Esther, grab his arm and be careful not to move him too hard. These girls jerk the patients up to the head of the bed and rip their arms out of their sockets. That's how they must have treated their dolls, pulled their arms and legs off limb by limb." She stopped for a second, fussed over his sheets, took a dirty pillow out from behind his head, and replaced it with a clean one.

"I tell them to be careful with these fragile patients, but no one listens."

She paused, then gently picked up his leg and moved it carefully to another angle. Then, she moved the other leg parallel to the first, but his leg muscles spasmed and both knees drew back together, shaking in a scissoring action.

"How's that now?" Melisa asked, disappointed that his legs refused to obey her placement.

"When we finish feeding you, Esther will help me bathe you, and maybe we'll get you up." She patted his arm and picked up the tray of food to be warmed.

"Okay. Buuut my legs hurt when you move them," he cried out.

When they finished Buster, Esther resumed the medicines and watched Melisa limp down the hall. Her tightly fitted, white slacks enhanced her thin legs and rounded hips. She had certainly kept her hourglass figure, Esther thought. She was sexy in a plain, unintentional way. Her walk was unique, with its minute halt never graduating to a full limp, not the result of an accident, but the harsh remainder of a defect from birth.   She had been born with a clubfoot. The surgeries were successful, but the right leg remained shorter than the left.

Melisa was the pulse of the floor, a regular, consistent, enduring beat, personifying its heart. The patients knew her, trusted her, and depended on her judgment and nursing care. She hardly spoke with the patients. Occasionally, she nodded or answered yes or no, but never in a judgmental way. She cared for the patients needing the most difficult nursing procedures or the terminal ones. She worked tirelessly, completing each task as needed. She loved her work, and her love spilled over to these destitute patients.

Esther knew Melisa was a hard taskmaster because she heard the other nurses complain bitterly, "We have to do everything exactly the way she wants it."

Melisa never raised her voice. She didn't have to. The look on her face or the way she pulled a patient up in bed was how she corrected Esther's work. The other nurses were sensitive to it too. She might reposition a limb immediately after someone else finished, unconsciously insisting her way became the best way.

"I've worked at Thornhill for years...watched the politics come and go...and the nurses change from good to bad, but the patients always remain the same—needy," Melisa said.

Esther continued passing out medicines. When she approached Mr. Kroger, he huddled under the covers.

"I have cancer. I have CANCER! I don't need any pills! I'm going to die anyway!" Mr. Kroger proclaimed. He clutched the covers up to his chin and refused to let go or sit up.

"You must take this medicine. It'll make you feel better," Esther said timidly moving back. "Your cancer is curable. Didn't you know that?"

He withdrew under the sheet-like a turtle into his shell.

She patiently peered at him, considered his infirmity, and waited for his response. He advanced a little. At first, only his upper face and lip were visible. Then, his words tumbled out as if a dam had broken.

"No, they didn't tell me that. They haven't told me anything. All they do is give me this chemotherapy," he stammered. His face curled up like a child who was about to cry.

The medicine had taken his hair and left his skin a ghostly pallor. He sank back down under the covers until the top of his bald head was the only visible sign of life. His lips twitched uncontrollably. At first, Esther thought it was some kind of palsy, but she soon realized the twitching was a side effect from his medication.

"Oh, leave him alone," Mr. Marshall said. He was the black-haired patient with black-rimmed glasses in the other bed. "He goes on like that day after day." His left leg was a stump resulting from a below the knee amputation. A flaming red scar at the tip outlined the flap. "What can I do about it? Nothing...that's it. Nothing. Who are you? I haven't seen you before. Oh...another new nurse." His belongings surrounded him. Brown paper bags filled with books, papers, and dirty clothes lined the walls. Their contents overflowed onto the floor.

Shying away from his raised, clenched fist, Esther stepped back quickly. Melisa had warned her about his volatile behavior.

Clothes hung from the overhead, orthopedic bar spanning his bed from head to foot. His leg prosthesis stood propped against the wall.

"Look at me," he continued. "What can I do about my state? I'm sick. Very sick. Diabetes," he snarled. "I have nowhere to go. No place to live. No one to look after me. The state put me in here...I might as well be locked up. Imprisoned."

He laughed a rather cynical laugh. "But I look after myself. I do my own laundry, feed myself, and change my bed. I even give myself my own medicines. I have all my pills right here." He pointed to four or five medicine bottles on his tray table.

"I'm all right unless someone bothers me, then look out." His brown eyes became enlarged and bulging. "Don't bother me," he shouted again, while precariously standing up on his good leg and holding onto the overhead bar.

Mr. Kroger retreated under his sheets again, totally covered.

Esther playfully tapped on Mr. Kroger's forehead. "I'm going to pry you out of this shelter," she said smiling.

Glancing back at Mr. Marshall, she said, "I've heard about you. I won't bother you except I must see if you're taking your medications. What was your blood sugar this morning?"

"I didn't check it," he answered. "But I will before lunch. I promise."

Without warning, he sat back on the bed and popped his head down hard on the pillow. His mouth pushed out into a pout.

"Okay. If you don't check it, I'll have to stick your finger myself," Esther scolded.

Sheepishly smiling, he complained as she was about to leave the room.

"Nurse. My stomach hurts. I need a laxative or something to move my bowels. I've asked every day, but no one's helped me. I'm all bound up."

"I'll check with the doctor when he comes by this morning," Esther promised.

Stopping to wash her hands, Esther groaned at the filthy sink and stench of the dirty, yellow tiled bathroom.

Melisa leaned out of Mr. Markowitz's room and called to her, "Esther, we need your help to get Mr. Markowitz on the stretcher. They've called for him in whirlpool therapy."

Esther brushed the loose strands of her auburn hair back over her ears and quickly slipped into the isolation gown and mask. Her hands felt chapped after washing them all morning in the harsh soap. She sighed as she watched the call lights flash on again down the hall. She ignored them and entered Mr. Markowitz's room.

To her surprise, Lyla, Shirleen, Karen, Sally, and Melisa stood in position just waiting for the last person to balance the move and prevent any fractures from his severe osteoporosis.

As they were about to lift the patient from the bed to the stretcher, the towering, golden-haired physician's assistant poked his head into the room.

"Melisa, has Mr. Markowitz been weighed today or any day in the past two weeks? Since I've been gone?" His rabbit smile exposed his two front teeth and communicated an expression of 'I caught you', as he glanced from one staff to the next. "You should have weighed Mr. Markowitz every day to see if he was losing weight, but I guess you forgot."

Each squirmed self-consciously. His gaze fell on Esther and rested there, again, curiosity covered his face. She averted her eyes, trying to avoid his burning stare. The aroma of his aftershave mingled with the pungent odors of the cloistered room. A spark of interest shone from Mr. Markowitz's eyes.

Melisa fluttered her hands in the air in exasperation and stuttered, "Uh. Uh. Uh. Girls. While we have everyone here…. Sally, get the stretcher scale. We'll weigh him now."

Her back stiffened as everyone groaned in protest.

"So, Melisa. It might have been nicer in the islands if you had decided to join me. I might have enjoyed rubbing your back and thighs," Henry Seward quipped. He hesitated ever so slightly. A smile played across his sun blistered lips and around his eyes.

The faucet dripped in the silence. Mr. Markowitz wheezed loudly, but not another breath moved in order not to miss the anticipated flattery or even possible disclosure of unrequited love.

Henry continued mischievously, "And treated you to the vacation of your dreams...the life you were meant to have...not this drudgery day after day...night after night…." His voice trailed off.

Melisa blushed and her head twitched in silent pleasure that he singled her out. "Oh, Henry dear. If only I weren't married," she managed to answer, smiling at the idea.

Esther watched the girls grin and titter to themselves. Even Mr. Markowitz chuckled and offered a wager for the next opportunity Henry might have to lure Melisa away.

The dream still afloat in the room, the nurses moved Mr. Markowitz to the long stretcher scale and then back to his bed. It took three to hold him on his side like a log. The other three, on the other side of the bed, attended to the gaping, oozing, raw hole in his back exposing the pelvis bone. The stench was unbearable, even though they had dressed it that morning. Dead cells and dead skin, thought Esther.

The nurses didn't complain or retreat, only waited for Henry as he inspected the huge, red wounds on the patient's back and hip.

His expression grew grim as he used the probe and knife to excise dead tissue from the bedsore to prevent gangrene.

When he parted the pink flesh, the bone lay at the heart, exposed, white, hard, unaffected yet by the disease. When he removed the probe, Mr. Markowitz let out a cry of pain. Henry gently replaced the dressings. Their faces grew solemn and serious. They all knew his tissue died a little more each day, and soon the last day would come.

As they moved the patient back to his previous position, pink fluid shot out of a hip socket hole like a ruptured pipeline. As hard as they tried to keep his leg straight, it was loose, free-floating. The nurses all stared at Henry for an explanation. He merely shook his head with resignation and whispered, "The hip joint is gone. Eaten away by the disease."

All the time Mr. Markowitz lay there with his face in Esther's bosom, displaying his frozen permanent smile. A solemn, pained expression of tolerance and wisdom escaped from his eyes as they absorbed the meaning of all the people working on him at one time and the significance of their compassionate expressions.

The nurses perspired ever so slightly above their masks from the stuffy heat of the room. The color differences between the staff seemed lost, for now, lost in the heart of the bosom of the deep South's root: Mammy's tending to their babies' needs, mother's enduring self-sacrifice for their families' good.

The nurses' expressions of compassion, in the face of despair, softened their otherwise angry faces. With a sense of purpose, they focused their attention not on prejudice, or hatred, or past grievances, but on the art of healing, the act of providing comfort in an effort to set the death clock back one more day. It was all here, Esther witnessed.

Yes, it came alive here in this room, she thought. The qualities that were necessary to create an excellent environment for patient care of any kind had been obscured under the cloak of exhaustion, stress, and anger. The previously hidden components of love and caring emerged in those few moments, transcending all previous obstacles, and glowed in this room for Mr. Markowitz. Yes, at that moment love, compassion, and peace beamed from everyone, illuminating the room with its purest light and gave Esther hope and promise for the future.

Just as quickly as it appeared, it disappeared, as if it had been a dream. When the door opened, one by one, the nurses walked out, only to retreat again under their mask of intolerance, anger, and bitterness. The girls glanced back at Esther, wearing their previous searing scowls. She felt hurt again, and for no reason.

When she returned to the hallway, Melisa walked towards her laughing. It was one of the few times Esther saw Melisa relax. Next, to her, a tall, muscular, black man casually laughed back at some remark she made. He stretched his thick neck and his loose muscular body into twists and turns mimicking Michael Jackson's moon-walk.

"Esther," Melisa said, pointing to the man capriciously moving across the hall. "This is Jewels. If you need anything, ask for Jewels. He is in charge of supplies. He stocks and restocks and tries to cheer us up, don't you?" she said, peering affectionately at the now gyrating man and tried to give him a tender pat on his back. He was too swift for her and slid gracefully away from her outstretched hand, laughing at himself, and at his own impishness.

"Just beat it...Beat it...Beat it...." Jewels sang, slip-stepping across the floor, and moving his head from side to side. He continued the rendition of Michael Jackson in the middle of the hall for everyone's delight. His expertise ignited enthusiasm from the nurses and others, giving them all a much-needed break.

"Right on brother," the ward clerk shouted.

Jewels became serious saying, "If you need help Esther just ask me. Yeah. An' say Jewelllsss, please help me!" He mimicked a female imitation of a request in a feminine, high-pitched voice. His large black eyes danced in his square handsome face. His thin line of a mustache moved to the smiling line of his mouth, mimicking his gyrating body.

Esther laughed at him saying, "Thanks, I will."

She watched with the others who had congregated to enjoy the scene. Jewels loved every minute of the attention.

"Esther, you have a phone call," Lyla yelled from the nurse's station and raised her eyebrows in a snooty expression when Esther grasped the receiver from her hand.

Esther thought of her two sons in daycare. She worried something might have happened to them. To her surprise, though, the voice was Mark's, her brother-in-law.

"How's everything going on your official first day?" he asked with enthusiasm. It was as if he were asking how she faired in a Siberian prison camp. She couldn't hide her weariness.

"It's been hard," was all she said.

"I called to check on you. I'll stop by tonight. If it's all right. You can tell me everything then."

"Thanks," Esther answered.

Chapter 5

Several days later Esther was late again giving out her medicines. It was after 1:00 p.m., and her pills were due at 12:00 noon. As she filled her pill cups, she watched Melisa leave a patient's room with an arm load of soiled linen. A few minutes later Melisa pushed a patient down to the showers. She became a reassuring familiar sight and never seemed to stop for a moment's rest. She pushed on like an automated doll; her only resemblance to humanness was her barely perceptible limp.

"Esther, can you help me with Mr. Markowitz again?" Melisa called.

When Esther entered Mr. Markowitz's room, she wasn't overwhelmed by his condition this time. Now, she saw the person and not his disintegrating body.

Melisa and Lyla waited for her. They held him on his side for Melisa to replace the soiled pads and sheets at the same time. A Mideast scent of incense tainted the air whenever Lyla moved. When Melisa finished, she rubbed Mr. Markowitz's skin with Aloe cream to prevent it from breaking down.

"Do y'all remember the movie, Love Story? It was on TV last night. Did you see it?" Melisa asked. "I missed it at the movies."

"I settled myself down with popcorn and sweet tea to relax for the evening. I couldn't wait to see that movie. When my big Italian husband, Tony, came home, I had only seen the first half hour. He changed channels the rest of the night. I begged him to stop. He laughed, touched his revolver lying on the table, and grunted. He's a policeman. I was furious at him. I knew it was the end of the discussion. He's gotten so testy these past few months. Whenever he visits his mother, he returns in a very ugly mood." Melisa continued rubbing Mr. Markowitz's skin only a little harder now.

"Mr. Markowitz, you're lucky you can watch anything you want."

The nurses turned him to the other side. They continued in silence until the door opened.

Henry entered, a nervous mischievous smile swept his face as if he enjoyed interrupting their work like an impudent child.

Esther's stomach churned at the sight of him.

Contrary to the isolation rules, he didn't wear a protective gown. He must think he's immune to the deadly germs, Esther assumed. His white trousers and hot pink, madras plaid shirt made her eyes dance in the grungy room.

"Well, I see you're back again. Where have you been? Mrs. Shepherd has searched for you all over the hospital. Your vacation is over, I thought. There's a meeting you need to attend," Melisa said, color rising in her cheeks.

Esther noticed a deep glow radiating from a burning fire in the center of Melisa's marine blue eyes. The same light gleamed from Henry's sea-green eyes.

She ached for Paul and wondered what her future would be like without him. Love isn't everything, but it makes life very complicated at times, times like these.

"Yeah, I'm back," he answered, not taking his eyes off Melisa. As the two gazed at each other, tense electricity moved around the room.

He turned toward Esther. She felt magnetically drawn to him. She sensed a ravenous desire from him as unmistakable as a cat in heat. The intensity of his stare frightened her. She turned away to avoid him, but when she looked back, he continued staring at her.

"How are you doing Mr. Markowitz? Appears you've kept them busy," he said.

"Yeah. I try," Mr. Markowitz answered and wheezed, "I try."

Melisa fidgeted by repositioning the same limb three times. She gave Henry an imploring stare.

Henry, I don't think you've met our new nurse, Esther Culver. This is her third day in the hospital." Melisa flashed him a don't make any waves expression.

With irritation, she turned to Esther saying, "This is our illustrious physician's assistant, Henry Seward. He's just returned from a South Seas expedition." She threw her head back and laughed. "Yes, he returned several days ago, but he has eluded us temporarily." She glared at him. The fire in her eyes was gone.

"It's nice to meet you. The patients are asking me about you," he offered.

"The patients are constantly asking me where you are," Esther said.

He nodded his head. "They want to complain about their medications or some such thing."

Melisa stood up straight saying, "Henry was born with a silver spoon in his mouth. It's still there, tarnish and all."

"Now wait a minute. Do I deserve that? I don't think so."

He turned to Esther and said, "It wasn't the South Sea Islands. It was the Governor's Cup sailboat race from Miami to Nassau. It was quite an arduous journey. Something I really wouldn't call a vacation. And I wasn't born with a silver spoon. It's just that I have friends who have silver spoons in their mouths," he laughed.

He scrutinized Esther again, closer, oblivious to the silence in the room. A sheepish smile played across his lips.

"Weren't you here the other day helping to turn Mr. Markowitz? I remember you now."

"Uh huh," Esther said and smiled. She knew he had noticed her that afternoon, but she was flattered that he remembered.

He glanced back at Melisa saying, "I'm here now. Just don't overload me with work. Not for today anyway. Actually, I have been here for several days in meetings. They're trying to change a few things around here." He nodded to her and abruptly left the room.

* * *

When Henry reached the pile of charts in the nurses' station, the glare, from the overhead lights, was still too bright for him. He grabbed a chart and moved into the nurses' lounge at the oak table, thinking he shouldn't have stayed out so late last night. The writing on the pages blurred in front of him.

The phone rang, and he answered.

"I'm looking for Henry Seward," the voice on the other end replied.

"Ha. Ha! I suppose you found me again, Melisan. You do seem to know all my haunts."

"I've missed you. I thought you dropped off the end of the earth in that race down there in the Bahamas. I'm glad you're home, Sugar. Charlotte is having a small get together tonight. We haven't seen your face for some time. We'd love to see you at 8:00 p.m.," she said with a hesitancy in her voice.

"I can't make any promises. I'll try." Henry hung up abruptly, stretched, and felt his ego bolstered a little. Melisan wouldn't leave him alone, and he knew it. If he attended the party, his presence would tell her he was interested again. But he liked the company. He'd wait and see what the day brought.

* * *

Esther returned to distributing meds, conscious they were late again. She tried to speed up her delivery system. I mustn't linger so long in each room, she thought. The patients are needy, and it hurts to cut their conversations short. They have no one to help them. As she moved around the hall, her shoes stuck to some spilled substance on the floor. It's probably dried urine. It usually is, she thought as she entered Jessie Taylor's room.

"Ah, you're nothing but an asshole," Shirleen yelled at Jessie Taylor and pushed rudely against Esther on her way out. Esther dropped his pills and glared fiercely back at Shirleen.

"Hey! Watch where you're going!" Esther said, but Shirleen ignored her.

Jessie was distraught. He was a black man who had so many pink blotches all over his skin it was difficult to tell whether he was white or black. A pout sprouted out around his thick lips as he tried to conceal a sob. His basin of cold bath water sat on the bedside table too far away for him to reach.

"I hate that bitch. I just hate her," he cried, oblivious to Esther's entrance.

"I hate her too. Anyone who doesn't, I think is a little crazy," Esther said.

Jessie stared at her in surprise, and they both laughed.

"Look at this," he said. "She brings in the bath water and says, 'Do it yourself, Kid.' She doesn't give me any towels or soap. I can't even reach the water. I haven't had any towels all week. I can't get out of bed 'cause of these fluids. Every time I see her, my blood pressure soars. This isn't a hospital. It's a torture chamber. Some kind of rite for purification like fraternity hazing. Maybe we got to go through it before we die. If you asks me I've had it. My wife is leaving me. I'm stuck with this disease for the rest of my life. What else can happen? I got that bitch for a nurse."

"I just dropped all your pills. Tell me what you need, and I'll be right back. Do you need anything for pain?" Esther said.

"You're the first person who's asked me about pain this week. Usually, Melisa does. She's the only one. That bitch, Shirleen, will never ask me if I need anything."

"Well?"

"Yeah. Give me everything I can get. Maybe it will last for the rest of my life."

After giving him his pills, Esther went to the linen room for more towels, gowns, and sheets for Jessie.

Jewels, Jason, and several other black men stood around in a circle laughing at some joke. When she entered, they stopped their conversations and watched her. She felt uncomfortable as their eyes followed her when she moved from one shelf to another. Their silence scared her. She brushed past Jason, the ward clerk, to reach for the rubbing alcohol, but he didn't move. She had to press between his back and the shelf. She retreated quickly, trying to ignore their off-color comments.

The door opened, and Mrs. Shepherd, the nurse manager, a short, heavyset black woman, stepped into the storage room.

"Uh huh. I see ya'll in here. Why ain't you men doing what you is supposed to be doing? That's what I wants to know?"

"Come on, Mrs. Shepherd. We're taking our break," Jewels said.

"The way I see it...you is always taking a break. I'd like to see some work. Jewels we need irrigation trays and more fluids. Here's a list for you," she said and glanced cynically at the others.

"The rest of ya'll just git out of here. If I see you loitering in here again today I'm gonna put you on report." She studied Esther curiously and marched over next to her.

"Alcohol? What do you plan to do with that...girl? Drink it?" She glared at Esther the same way she eyed the others.

Startled by the fury in Mrs. Shepherd's eyes, Esther answered, "I...was gonna use it to clean the tray tables and the bedside stands. Everything's so filthy. I don't know whose job it is to clean. Nothing's being done. I can't work in this filth. The tray tables are covered with old food and drink spills. The bedside tables are sticky and marred with ashes and old cigarette butts. I'm cleaning as I go." Esther didn't wait for an answer and moved toward the door. She wondered why Mrs. Shepherd didn't make the other staff tow the line like she did these men.

Mrs. Shepard grunted and glared at the black men who were still standing around listening. They jammed their fists into their trousers and filed out, disgruntled, mumbling under their breath, and laughing to themselves like a group of guilty boys.

Esther rushed back to Jesse's' room with linen and medicine. She wasn't surprised to see him staring out the window. His sheets were a rumpled mess. IV fluids still dripped antibiotics slowly into his veins.

"I'm back. I have everything you need. Towels, washcloths, pajamas, and something for pain," Esther said and smiled warmly. He didn't look up. He continued to stare out the window. She replaced the cold water with hot and gently bathed his arms and body. All the pink blotches covering his skin amazed her. Esther couldn't hide her shock.

"It's the disease. Scleroderma. Leukoderma. It's the white man's disease. My great-grandmother was raped by her white owner and passed this genetic weakness down the generations until it erupted with me. The blotched monster."

"I'm so sorry. I didn't know Scleroderma was a white man's disease."

"Yeah. It's not a pretty sight. My nerves are involved now and although I graduated from college, I can't work anymore. My nervous system is damaged. I will never regain the use of anything," Jessie said. "I served in the first Iraqi invasion. They say it came from some chemical they used to try to kill us, but I know it's the devil white man trying to erupt. The man who raped my great-grandmother.

Esther didn't know what to say. On his bedside stand sat a picture of his family. "Are those two girls yours?"

"My wife's divorcing me and taking my twin girls. I love them so, but I'll never be able to watch them grow up. I don't know why she's doing this to me. I will be chained to this bed for the rest of my life. I'm only thirty-five. I'm too young to go through all this. The rest of these men are in their eighties, or older. They have lived their lives. I have only started to live mine."

"Hey, Esther. I see he suckered you into bathing him. Mighty smooth Jessie. Mighty smooth," Shirleen said. She withdrew as quickly as she popped her head in the doorway. They heard her cynical laughter as she moved down the hall.

"Oh, don't pay any attention to her. She's trying to get to you. Ignore her. You'll be a lot better off."

"I'll never forget the day it started. This pink color began to emerge on my shoulder here as a tiny spot the size of a dime. Everyday, I watched it grow until it spread across my back. It was as if the devil himself ate away the black pigment in my skin. I had nightmares of that bastard trying to get out. That white bastard...who was my great-grandfather, destroying my black skin so he can shine through. I rode my bicycle twenty miles every two or three days. I was in great shape. One day I had trouble wheeling the twenty miles. The effort became too hard. I was reduced to only fifteen at one time. Then, my ability diminished to ten miles at a time. I got the hint and went to the doctor. He discovered I had this disease. It didn't take them long. A few tests, that was all. They calculated how long Scleroderma will take to involve all my limbs." He glanced up at Esther forlornly. "God has no pity. I have been a good person all my life."

Esther returned to her medicine cart worrying about all the work she had left to do. She felt like crying too. Not only about Jesse, but all the morbidity depressed her, especially not being able to do anything about it. They have no hope. She felt further behind.

Henry sat in the nurses' station next to the chart rack. Mrs. Shepherd stood over him and grimaced as she gave him the run-down on each patient.

"All right Florence I get the picture. All these men need miracles and all the doctoring I know can't give them one," Henry said, as he opened another chart. Esther watched his shoulders sag from the futility of it all.

"No, Henry. All I want you to do is do the best you can with what we've got. They just need to be comfortable," Mrs. Shepherd said and sat down hard in the rolling chair with a disgruntled, "Humph."

I guess I'm not the only one behind, Esther thought, feeling somehow comforted, knowing she wasn't alone. She was in a race with the clock too. From the moment she arrived every second counted and was tallied at hourly intervals. It became the same for the patients. They were in a race with the clock to live as much life as possible in the time they had left. Their medications, meals, and treatments were given at exact time intervals. Even their projected stay became calculated in days and months. The question of whether they would be discharged to home or die here in the hospital, alone, had already been decided. They forgot about one thing: God's time. They can't predict God's time. Her heels ached and the throbbing rose up into her calves. She wished she had worn her tennis shoes, at least they were designed for comfort. She needed them now, especially on these hard, unforgiving, linoleum floors.

Shirleen swished by with the new admission in a wheelchair, an elderly black man who had suffered a stroke. His wife walked beside him. Esther vowed she wouldn't let Shirleen intimidate her again. As Shirleen moved down the hall, Esther felt a new hardness, a new determination, and a new courage infuse her soul.

Shirleen swung her hips from side to side, speaking in low tones directly into the man's ear.

"Hey, boy. Let this be a word to the wise. If you know what I mean. Don't call us. We'll call you. We don't like patients who are always asking for something. Don't expect anything and you'll be a lot happier. Don't bother us, and we won't bother you."

Shirleen shoved the wheelchair in wide, audacious jerks of unbridled fury. An evil smile curled and uncurled her puffed up mouth. The man hunched over, ashamed. The force of her thrust almost threw him out of the chair onto the floor several times. Esther held her breath, knowing that she'd soon be Shirleen's next target. Shirleen never took her eyes off Esther.

Anger raged through Esther like a cyclone, but it didn't have anywhere to go. She wanted to grab Shirleen and drag her down to the supervisor's office, but this was only her third day. She tried to repress her anger, but the tempest continued to erupt until it touched the center of her being, her integrity. Acid gnawed away at her insides, forming a ball between her breasts. Esther ran to the kitchen to get a carton of milk. She was determined to face Shirleen down.

The new patient must think all the nurses are like Shirleen. Shirleen's abuse is a bad reflection on the whole floor. Visions of the Nurses' Board meeting after her trial and the face of the Hospice patient's wife haunted Esther momentarily. She grabbed the medicine cart for stability. I've got to hang on and not get so upset. How did I ever let myself get involved in this predicament anyway?

Chapter 6

It was almost lunchtime when Esther watched the patient's return from physical therapy. The paraplegic patients, stroke patients, and amputees raced their wheelchairs down the hall, cheering each other on. Their spidery fingers clutched at each other in an innocuous, playful manner. There was a desperation about it as if they tried to recapture life's essence and meaning by participating in the sheer sport of contact. It was as if they stopped their jiving and punching, they would die. They yearned for the true meaning of life. In the past, they filled this hole with drink, or sport, or some business endeavor. It was too late for that now. There was no drink, or sport, or business to fill the void, only pain, suffering, and loneliness. They lacked a strong spiritual base. They depended on each other though, and this became their one common bond. They were each other's family.

Esther saw their needs, plain as day because they became her uncle before he died. She tried to talk to him about God and Jesus, but he only laughed at her and patted her head. She had deep faith and believed that the Lord helped her every day.

Her uncle had always indulged her by saying, "The Bible is filled with fairy tales. They are nice stories for little girls, but not for men. Miracles just don't happen the way the Bible says they do. It might be nice if they did, though."

When the patients passed her medicine cart, they slowed down, let out a rebel yell, and banged the metal sides for effect as if they were touching base.

Using the hall for a runway, Patrick Shaw was the first to slam his chart on the counter so hard and fast it slid halfway across the nurse's station.

"Hey, knock it off boys," Jason yelled.

"You almost got a strike, Shaw," Simon shouted. The others laughed. The landing strip ended in the day room where the patients zoomed into place at the ashtray to get a smoke before the lunch trays arrived.

Esther watched the men fight over lighters and jam the cigarettes into their mouths. Their animations appeared grotesque like comic burlesque caricatures. Several days of bearded stubble covered their ruddy chins and their hair had grown down to their collars. They bantered with each other and vied for attention with the most exciting tale of the morning. The room filled with smoke. She wondered how anyone could breathe.

The patients suffering with lung conditions like chronic obstructive lung disease, emphysema, or cancer appeared oblivious to the din. They still smoked with the others or just hung out. Patrick Shaw sat in the middle.

Mr. Marshall, the black-haired amputee wearing black horn-rim glasses, interrupted her, "These men are disgusting, aren't they? Just look at them smoking away their life in that filthy room. They're probably drinking too. Filthy no-accounts. It's a saloon. I'll never go in there. No. Not on your life." He sneered in their direction and gave them the Italian curse sign. Then, he disappeared into his room like a disgruntled cockroach.

Esther carried the medicine cups to the day room. The sun filtered through the gray smoke. Dust particles sparkled and danced in the rays as the smoke rose into large swirling circles above the ashtray. Maybe the sun will sterilize the spots on the floor where it rests for a few minutes, Esther thought. Cigarette burns and holes marred the yellow vinyl upholstery and linoleum floor.

"What's this guys? Adult education?" she asked jokingly of the six men circled around the ashtray. Their raucous voices reverberated out into the hall.

"Hey, it's nurse Good Body!" one of them yelled. They all cheered.

One by one they took their medication. They already had cups of water and added to them with the pitcher full of ice water they passed around. They complained of being so thirsty from physical therapy. Some of them laughed at that idea.

Esther wondered why they were so jovial, too excitable. Esther spotted Chester. He had returned early. She watched him slip a brown paper bag quickly into his pocket. The rest of them jeered at her.

"Where've you been all my life? I ain't seen you around before."

Their grimy fingers reached up toward her and even grabbed her uniform. Her feet stuck to the besmeared floor stained with a mixture of spilled coffee, ground in ashes, and soda, and the odor of dead cigarette smoke hung over the room.

Once back in the hall, Esther called to Jason, "The cleaning fellow left his cart in the middle of the floor. He's been gone for over an hour. Can you call housekeeping and find out when he's coming back? The day room is a revolting mess."

"Just because I sit here don't mean I can do everything. If you want the place cleaned you call. Take care of it yourself. I don't know how everyone gets the idea I'm the one to do these things. Look at these charts piled everywhere. Now leave me alone." He turned away and sat down hard in his chair shaking his head.

"All we need around here is another white Miss Prissy. Let her do it herself," Jason said under his breath, as he threw the charts into a pile on the counter.

No one cares about anything but doing the least amount of work, Esther thought.

"Oh, they're doing all right," Mrs. Shepherd chimed in. "They do the best they can. The cleaning staff is short of help just like the nurses. The janitor is old, and he can't clean every room every day, Esther."

Mrs. Shepherd sat down sharply in her padded chair dismissing Esther as if she had just vanished.

"I haven't seen you here for a while, Ben," Mrs. Shepherd said to the pharmacist who checked a medicine cart in front of her.

"Hey," he said. "I've been on vacation."

"Oh, that's nice," she answered absentmindedly.

Mrs. Shepherd looked exhausted, but the other nurses didn't seem to notice. All morning, one by one they petitioned her attention to unload their complaints of too much work, aching muscles, personal problems, or patient worries. Esther watched a steady stream enter and leave Mrs. Shepherd's office.

"Just do the best you can. That's all you can do," Mrs. Shepherd told first Geraldine, Sally, and even Shirleen.

"We are in a staffing shortage. We can only do so much. Two nurses for thirty patients is too little, but we have no choice. We have sixty patients on this floor, and they all need to be seen about."

"I'm aching all over. All I do is take pain pills for my pulled back. I have to return to this floor every day. I don't get any rest," Sally pleaded. A frown grew across her face.

"We're supposed to get new nurses in a few weeks. If they stay. That's the question. If they stay?" Esther overheard Mrs. Shepherd say to Jason.

"What are you still doing here, Mrs. Shepherd," Lyla hollered from the hall. "I told you I'd stay and try to help out today. You should go home. You can't work every day and every night."

"I had too many loose ends to tie up before I left. I'm on my way home now. I promise," Mrs. Shepherd said and laughed. "I just love this place and can't stand it when I'm gone."

"Sure, I hear you. I feel the same way only I love to eat. That's the reason I stay," Lyla said. Her tall thin figure strode off down the hall leaning forward on her too long legs. She resembled a crane with her hair pulled up into a high unkempt ponytail. Her full, wide, black lips led her body in a headlong dash.

Mrs. Shepherd discarded her lab coat, revealing a tightly stretched, bright pink sweat-shirt barely reaching over the waist of her brown, straight skirt tightly hugging her hips. The kick pleat was torn. Mrs. Shepherd lumbered from one end of the nurses' station to the other in anguish like a giant over-burdened bear. For that moment, she appeared lost and fell into a kind of pacing. Her joints creaked with each step. Her dark, despairing expression was emphasized by the dark circles swallowing her black eyes. They cast a shadow over the rest of her distended face. Her hair escaped its set and shot out, helter-skelter, in short, black tufts around her head. It seemed when she discarded her lab coat, she slid out of the shell that disguised and protected her from the intense exhaustion she suffered. As she rounded the corner to the elevator, she passed Henry returning from some errand. Esther watched her stop and give him directions.

When Henry approached Esther, his usual carefree expression was replaced by irritation and contempt. He stopped briefly, eyeing Esther with angry calculation.

"Hey, I presume you're single...er...no sign of a ring or anything?" Henry said off-handedly, grinning a teasing smile. His strong aftershave aroma filled the area.

Esther still stood at the medicine cart and calmly glanced up at him; although, her insides churned oddly.

"Yes, that's correct. No sign of anything. But there are scars. Divorce scars," she answered indignantly, feeling as if everyone were after a chunk of her emotions today. A little here and a little there and nothing will be left. Her cup felt empty.

"Oh, I'm so sorry to hear. Has it been recent?" Henry asked. A surprising gentleness covered his irritation.

"Yes, too recent. Only one month. Actually, the divorce won't be final until July. Otherwise, I wouldn't be working here," Esther answered, feeling uncomfortable from the stares of Lyla and Sally who entered the nurses' station. She nervously continued to pour her medications, spilling several pills.

"Looks like you're busy. Why don't you have dinner with me tonight? We can talk about it over Strawberry Shortcake?"

He leaned over her and breathed his warm breath licentiously onto her neck. She shivered but didn't move. Her mind raced ahead. She thought of her brother-in-law, Mark and her two sons. Half of her wanted to run off, forget this place, and everything else, and lavish in a night out with this extremely attractive male. Her other side reminded her of all the responsibilities including the effects of a painful aftermath. God was forgiving, but it was too soon for her emotionally to become involved again, and she knew it.

"I'm sorry. I know you mean well. I have two boys to pick up at daycare. They need dinner and bedtime stories. Maybe some other time. I appreciate the offer though."

"Sure," he answered with disgust and stomped over to the charts waiting for his attention. He picked up several and slammed them down, cursing under his breath. His attitude didn't help Esther's mood.

Cries erupted from the other side of the hall.

"Help! Help! Help! Someone, please help me! Why can't anyone feed me? I need help," the panicked voice shrieked on in an unending tirade.

The staff in the nurses' station starred in the direction of the yelling, but no one left. Esther had already learned to stay out of situations on the other side of the floor. The black nurses clung together like a gang and stuck up for each other to the point of retaliation.

Henry cursed under his breath, threw up his hands, and glared at everyone around him who refused to go see about the patient.

The tirade continued. Esther couldn't stand it any longer. She ran into the room on the north side and immediately the feculent smell of feces and urine hit her in the face. Mr. Pearlman lay naked in the middle of his bed, soiled with excrement from head to toe, rattling the ancient iron bed rails with all his strength, screaming at the top of his lungs out of desperation, and trying to pull loose from his arm restraints.

"What's the matter?" Esther asked softly.

"Everything's the matter. Look at me. I'm naked. No one's cleaned me up today. They've taken all my things and sold them. Even my house. I don't know what's happened to my dog. Tears streamed down his cheeks. They've hated me for years. Now, they're taking out their revenge." He strained at the restraints trying to free his arms.

"Who's doing this to you?" Esther asked.

"Who else? My daughters. My spoiled daughters. They think I'm dead. Ohhhhhh...Help me. Help me," he cried, writhing in his bed, sounding lucid and confused at the same time.

Drawn to his pleadings, Esther hesitated, wary of the other nurses. They didn't like her to interfere with their patients. While he screamed, she retrieved the wash basin and filled it.

Gently, Esther washed his face, arms, and upper body as he quieted down.

"They've sold me down the river. Thrown me into this horrible place. Children. I rue the day I had every last one. They're the devil's disciples."

Esther quickly finished scrubbing his limbs which were each still tied spread eagle on the bed. She knew she had to untie his arms to dress him.

Mr. Pearlman begged her, "Please, ma'am just untie my arms so I can bend them. I'll be good. I promise."

She sorted through the sheets piled on the chair for a gown and found a threadbare, torn one with missing tie strings. Disappointed, she decided to use it anyway. She didn't want Mr. Pearlman running through the hall naked. She untied his arm and pulled it through the sleeve.

"Oh, yeah. That feels so good. Let me keep my hand out for a few minutes. Get the circulation moving."

Esther smiled at his relief and released his other wrist. He frantically rubbed his hands together, touched his face, and scratched his body all over.

"Ohoooo! Ma'am! Free my legs. I'll be good. I promise," he cried and reached for his legs.

Esther hesitated, observing for signs of a dangerous nature, but she didn't see any.

After Esther released his feet, he instantly caressed his sore ankles. She smiled sympathetically and reached for his wrists to apply hand lotion.

In a split second, he pulled away, as frightened as if she carried a knife. He stood up on the bed, jumped frantically from side to side, squealed and laughed at each foiled attempt she made to catch his leg.

He wasn't playing. She realized too late he was having a catastrophic reaction. He didn't understand that she wasn't going to hurt him. One minute he was clear as a bell, and just as quickly he turned into this crazy, out of control patient, who was paranoid about her intentions.

"Noooooo...Nooooo! Don't do that," he squealed, as she tried to grab his feet. "Don't do that. Don't do that!"

Esther was scared he'd fall and injure himself. He had no fear. His foot hit the bed rail, but he was oblivious to the pain, still laughing hysterically.

Esther moved his lunch tray closer and tried coaxing him to sit down and eat. She even held a spoonful of potatoes up to his level for him to reach. He hit the spoon out of her hand and kicked the tray sitting on the bedside table with his foot, dumping coffee and food all over her uniform.

Esther retreated, pressed the call button and yelled, "Help! Help!"

The call light blinked off and on, but no one came.

"Stop this! Sit down," Esther yelled.

He stammered, "Uh oh! Uh oh! Uh oh...." He stopped his actions in mid-air.

Esther, hysterical, turned to see the gaping mouths of Lyla, Sally, and Shirleen staring at him. Henry stood behind them wearing a wry smile. Mrs. Shepherd pushed in between the others.

"What's going on in here?" Mrs. Shepherd said wearily.

"I untied him to change the bed, and he took off," Esther answered.

"Uh huh," the nurses said in unison, never taking their eyes off Mr. Pearlman.

"Maybe that'll teach little Miss Goody Two-Shoes to keep to her own patients," Sally whispered.

They circled the bed, and with one invisible signal, they each grabbed his legs and arms and wrestled him down to the bed. As he sought a way to flee, his frightened eyes darted around the room.

When they finished restraining him, they glared at her and grunted. Then, everyone laughed.

"That's the first time I've ever seen him do that," Lyla said.

"Yeah, I wonder what got into him. I didn't think he could stand up," Sally said amazed.

It was Shirleen who said, "I guess little Miss white Prissy decided to free his butt. I guess this gave you something to think about. This ain't all fun and games. Is it?"

"He was filthy, lying in his own excrement. Crying out. I did just what...anyone would do," Esther explained. "He scared me to death. Thanks for the help." Esther fled the room.

* * *

Mrs. Shepherd returned to the hall and waited for the elevator. She reviewed her day of trying to keep Henry from skipping out on his charts, of the new nurse questioning everyone's actions, and Shirleen acting more aggressive than usual.

A young man wearing a white coat shouted demands in her direction. He called to her, but she didn't hear him. Thoughts of her daughter absorbed her. Her daughter had gone to the doctor for tests that morning, worried she was pregnant.

"Mrs. Shepherd," he shouted again, "I have to transfer two patients up here to your service." The young man stood directly in front of her, towered over her, and yelled at her.

Her eyes focused on his young, impudent face.

"This is geriatrics, doctor. We have no more beds," she answered.

"I have two patients I have to transfer. You can do something about it," he demanded.

Mrs. Shepherd continued to glare at him with a steely don't push me around attitude.

Realizing that force wouldn't work, he settled down a little and asked with a more imploring tone, "When will you have another bed or two or three?" He followed her as she returned to the nurses' station.

"Do you see that sign," She said and pointed to a small blackboard hanging on the wall over the telephones with a heading DEATHS in bold white letters.

"Yes," he answered sharply.

"When that sign shows two or three room numbers, then we'll be able to answer your requests," she said. "And not before," she shouted as if she had just slam dunked a basketball into the hoop to win the game.

She paused and examined the infuriated man with her hardcore black eyes. She grinned in a brutal, don't push me any further way.

"You see, the only ways people leaves here is either to go home, or to another nursing home, or to die. We won't have any beds for a while."

He fidgeted, trying to escape Mrs. Shepherd's penetrating gaze.

"I guess I'll have to think of something else."

"Now, let me tell you how it is," Mrs. Shepherd continued, as she grabbed his shoulder with a grip of steel to thwart his escape. Two spear-like rays of fierce energy shot out from her eyes toward him, as if they contained all the anger, frustration, and fury she endured these last few days.

She held on as if nothing at all had happened.

"I've worked here about seventeen years. I've seen everything. I've witnessed a number of upstarts like you who think that because I'm black you can push me around. We're in a staffing crisis. I've just worked three shifts myself as a CNA. I'm needed at home right now. Most of these nurses worked last night. When we have a few beds come free, I may decide to freeze those beds until we get more help."

"Yes Ma'am," he answered.

"When patients come to this floor, life becomes a waiting game for them. Some reach their peace sooner than others, maybe without so much suffering. Others leave, go back into society a little changed, maybe for the better. Our job is to take what comes and do the very best we can with each one. It's God's job to take those whom he thinks is ready for the other side. I advise you to fix up those patients you are so eager to be rid of and recycle them into society because there is a long waiting list for our floor. The seventh floor, geriatrics, and rehabilitation.

Mrs. Shepard sighed deeply, almost like the death sigh itself. Her stature shrunk a little as if air had been let out of a bag. She sagged from the weight of it all, the floor, the patients, the nurses, and the impudent doctors.

"I will...Ma'am. I will," he said, cowering backward, anxious to get away.

Mrs. Shepherd still hung onto his shoulder. He tried to pull free.

"I hope so, boy, for your sake. Otherwise, you might just turn into one of these unhappy tenants."

She released the doctor saying, "Jason, I'm fixin' to go home now. Please don't call me till tomorrow."

She patted the doctor on his shoulder.

"Do the best you can. Just do the best you can."

On the way down the hall, she stopped to speak with Esther.

"I've asked a couple of the nurses to take you under their wings and help you find your way around. If you have any problems just hold them until tomorrow when I hopes I will return." Not waiting for Esther's reply, she ambled on to the elevators.

Her thoughts returned to her daughter. She prayed Valorie wasn't pregnant. She was only in her second year of college at Emory University. It cost the whole family a lot for her to go there, even with scholarships, but Carver, her husband, had his heart set on one of his children graduating from Emory. She has to get out of the small town of Fayette, South Carolina, he pleaded.

"After all," he always said, 'Fayette ain't the only place in the world, and we're members of the world.'" Mrs. Shepherd said out loud.

Valorie had studied so hard to attend Emory, and to have to leave because of a pregnancy was a disaster. Somehow, she saw her own girlhood stretching in front of her. She hoped and prayed Valorie didn't have to have an abortion the way she had to when she was in her teens. Only hers wasn't legal.

Mrs. Shepherd stepped onto the elevator shaking her head and sighing, "Um. Um."

Chapter 7

A week later, Esther witnessed Shirleen and Mr. Shaw arguing at the end of the hall. His bulbous tongue stuck out of his mouth grotesquely. His eyes glowered at her with wild ferocity, and his garbled speech pelted her as if each sound were a bullet.

"If you think I'm gonna clean you up, you're crazy. Clean yourself up, you shit. Take a shower! Stop bothering me!" Shirleen hollered.

Mr. Shaw cursed her in his unintelligible guttural speech.

"Same to you, man," Shirleen yelled with contempt. She saw Esther watching her.

"What are you gawking at? He ain't nothing but scum. Mind your own business," Shirleen said. She stalked away and disappeared into the nurses' lounge.

There he sat, the man behind his masquerade, exuding his hoarse, garbled sounds in Esther's direction, pointing to his lap. He wheeled so close the stench of feces made Esther gag.

"Clean up," he pitifully garbled, as his soft eyes caught hers. "Please," he said with short, puppy dog grunts. Esther saw an intelligent person hiding under the disguise of this stroke victim who was unable to articulate his words clearly.

Feeling resigned to all the unacceptable sights on the seventh floor, she patted him on the shoulder and left to gather clean pajamas and linen from the utility room. When she returned, he was waiting.

In the shower room, she assisted as Mr. Shaw showered, shaved, powdered, and dressed. He remained silent during the ordeal, but afterward, he said clearly and with sincerity, "Thank you," letting the words fall ever so carefully in front of his usual garbled, Jabberwocky syllables like deserters silently falling into the muster line. After his last remark, he left. With his two immense, gnarled hands, he pushed the wheels swiftly down the hall to the elevators and disappeared. He was on his way to the cafeteria to be with his own kind.

"Shirleen surely is a mean one, isn't she?" Esther overheard Melisa tell the ward clerk.

If Melisa realizes it, why doesn't she fire her for abuse? Esther thought, feeling enraged. Shirleen and her black cohorts escaped to the nurses' lounge or the cafeteria, while Melisa picked up the slack and raced to wash and feed those patients left.

Frustrated, Esther decided to slip away herself for a cigarette. Once in the nurses' lounge, she watched one CNA sewing needlework. She moved to a corner chair, lit a cigarette, and breathed a sigh of relief.

"You think this work is hard?" Sally said. "You're still in orientation. Just wait till next week or the next when you are the only one taking care of thirty patients by yourself." Sally stood over Esther, glaring contempt down at her.

"That's right Sally. You tell her. The new ones don't last long around here. Afraid of real work," Lyla said.

"Afraid of an honest day's work?" another black nurse spit out, sharp and taunting. She sat behind Sally. Esther hadn't seen her before.

One by one the nurses unleashed their anger on Esther as if she were the cause of their agony. They took turns assaulting her and backed away like a pack of wild dogs. Esther was furious, unprepared for such a siege.

Sally smiled as if she enjoyed watching Esther press back against the wall in retreat.

"Look at the little, white thing. She's not tough enough to work here," Sally whispered to Lyla who stood up to join Sally.

Lyla stared at Esther with hate in her eyes.

Esther grappled for words, words that might pacify them, rectify whatever hurt she caused to warrant this attack. "I don't know how you care for all these patients by yourselves and continue to do it day after day. I really don't know whether I can work as hard as you," Esther sputtered meekly, extending them credit for all their labor.

Sally interrupted, "Yeah. You white nurses...you RNs.You think you're entitled to an easy assignment. Well, you can think again because around here the RNs, LPNs, and CNAs are just the same. We're all killing ourselves. On a good day, we're lucky to have three staff for thirty patients. Usually, we have only two nurses on a side. Sometimes only one. Baby...you should consider yourself lucky the other nurses are gone. They were witches. We are pleasant by comparison. Until about six months ago, this place was evil. After moving some around the hospital, conditions have improved, but not much. The hospital expects you to bust your ass." Sally pursed out her lips indignantly, breathed hard, and stalked out.

Shirleen chimed in, "Yeah, and if you don't like it, you can leave now before we finish training you. Leaving us short again."

Esther refused to withdraw. I'll not grant them the satisfaction of seeing I'm scared stiff.

"Humph," Shirleen said. She turned abruptly and left the room. The others filed out behind her, grunting their fury at Esther.

Esther scrunched up her trembling face and said, "Same to you too."

She withdrew another cigarette, lit it, exhaled, and bit her lip. I'll never last here. Mark was right. What am I going to do if I quit? Six months is too long to even think of working here. This place is a disaster.

Esther tried to choke back her emotions, but her tears flowed down her cheeks like Niagara Falls. She couldn't stop crying. It's no use. I have to tough it out one day at a time. I have no other choice.

She let out all the pent-up anger she had repressed. Her tears flooded on, "I can't seem to do anything right," she moaned. "Somehow, I should have been able to stop their attacks."

Esther tried to think rationally. She had always tried to do the right thing. She attended church regularly and had deep belief that God would help her. This calamity was beyond anything she ever dreamed. If only the Board of Nursing hadn't suspended her license. It was too late now. She was forced to work at Thornhill. She never wanted a divorce or imagined raising her two sons without a father. Her life had spiraled out of control.

"God only you can help me now," she pleaded. "Please help me, Jesus. I can't do this without your help." She patted her face with a cold, wet, paper towel.

Esther returned to the hall to finish feeding her patients. She felt faint and dizzy from not eating herself. Her fifteen patients were on bed rest and needed everything. Good care was beyond her physical ability. No wonder this unit can't get help or keep it. She knew why the nurses were angry. She was upset too. This was only her ninth day, but at least she knew them all by name now. Their faces stood out clearly in her mind, their diseases, and the wars they so valiantly fought. Yes, the names and places were becoming so familiar, too familiar: World War II, Vietnam, Korea, The Gulf War, Afghanistan, Agent Orange, Normandy, Guam, the death camps.... These men were the survivors. Their stories inspired her, and she knew she had to be strong for them. She tried to compose herself and go on.

Melisa spotted Esther leaving the nurses' lounge. "They've gotten to you, haven't they?" Melisa said. "I know what they're doing. They're trying to scare you off just like they have every other nurse who tried to stick it out. All they want to do is sit around. If we get any decent nurses up here, they know they won't be able to. I'll be damned if I'll let it happen to you. I'm too old to carry this load alone anymore."

Melisa's hand trembled when she grabbed Esther's arm. By the grim look on Melisa's face, Esther knew it had been difficult, delivering good care while fighting the staff to complete their work.

"Are you all right?" Esther asked, glancing at Melisa's chest where she held her hand.

"I keep having this chest pain. I think it's from lifting all those patients alone," she answered.

"Ask me. I'll help you. Don't try to do everything by yourself."

"Damn it, you bitch...I'm gonna get you if it's the last thing I do...you're nothing but a witch...Satan herself," a man screamed, filling the halls with echoes.

Everyone in the nurses' station stopped short. It was Jessie Taylor who yelled at the top of his lungs. Immediately, after the barrage of foul language, they heard dishes crashing to the floor."

Esther ran to his room. Shirleen almost knocked her down running out, coffee covered her uniform.

"Jessie Taylor scalded me! He threw his hot coffee at me! Scalding me!"

Before Esther could enter the room, another dish crashed against the wall across the hall. His soup spattered onto the floor. She stopped short, not wanting to invade his firing range. Shirleen made him hysterical. His reaction didn't upset Esther. She even wanted him to continue, hoping the tirade helped him release his fury. Maybe cause Shirleen to think twice about cursing out a patient. Hooray for Jessie Taylor, Esther thought.

Jessie hurled his entire plate of food at the wall in front of her. It hit with a tremendous force, leaving potatoes, tomatoes, and creamed chicken on the dirty wall and broken dishes on the floor.

Within seconds, Melisa and Lyla came up behind Esther, waiting for some sign the tirade had ended. Henry rudely shoved past the women, turned, and screamed at them.

"Stay the hell out of Jessie's room. Haven't you done enough damage already?" Henry slammed the door behind him, barely avoiding slipping on the spills.

All three waited silently in the hallway, shaking their heads in astonishment, and burst out laughing. They knew Henry intended to take care of the situation. He was the patient's advocate, and they trusted him.

Esther finally finished passing out all of her medications. She watched Karen wearily staggering out of one of the patient's rooms, carrying a load of dirty linen, and losing her balance for an instant.

"Are you ready to go to lunch yet?" Esther pleaded, still shaken from Jessie's tirade.

The expression on Karen's pale, drawn face reflected Esther's feelings.

"Yes, I'm starved and tired too. Let's go," Karen said and glanced at her watch. "I didn't know it was so late. We have to hurry before the cafeteria closes."

They saw Mr. Shaw, Chester, and a few of the other men congregated around the vending machines in the hallway near the cafeteria. Mr. Shaw waved to Esther as they passed, and she smiled in return.

"Didn't I tell you they'd be here?" Karen said and laughed.

When they finished lunch, Esther whispered to Karen," Have you noticed how abusive some of the nurses are to the patients. They mistreat them and have no compassion.

Karen smiled kindly at Esther. "I know what you're asking. I don't know how to answer you. I see what happens, and I don't like it either. What can we do about it? We are so short of staff. If they go, there's no one to replace them. All I can do now is ignore it until I can do something. I learned a long time ago to mind my own business. That keeps me out of trouble. I try to do the best I can to help these poor people. Someday, we'll get to the bottom of it. When? I don't know."

The two laughed at each other's sigh of relief to have escaped, even if for a short time.

"From what Sally said, this floor has had a bad reputation for years," Esther said.

"Oh, it looks as if it still has a bad name. Just mention the seventh floor to anyone and watch their reaction," Karen answered.

"If that's the case, why doesn't anyone do anything about it? Why do they let it continue?"

"Come on...I'll show you. On our way back, let's get off on the ninth floor. It's the medical floor," Karen explained.

When the nurses stepped off the elevator, the hall smelled clean with the linoleum brightly waxed instead of their dull, grimy one. The walls had been papered with a cheerful, washable, textured covering. The ninth floor reflected the type of hospital unit Esther expected to find everywhere. Attractive pictures hung on the walls in several places along the corridor. The day room was decorated with lovely, green plaid upholstered furniture, and green drapes hung at the shiny, clean windows. Men sat comfortably in their robes, talking to family members or just reading. What a contrast to the seventh floor where the families don't visit.

Plants and flowers decorated the window sills or bedside stands. No one on the seventh floor ever received flowers. The difference was like comparing the Upper East Side to Harlem.

"I suppose it's like having slum landlords for the poor and appreciative landlords for the wealthy. One tries to deprive the poor tenants to keep as much profit as possible. The richer areas provide more amenities to attract the higher paying residents," Karen said to Esther, who felt disappointed after realizing the discrepancy.

"I grew up in the more affluent areas of town where people didn't accept anything but the best," Esther replied, shrugging her shoulders.

"I know all about slums. I grew up living on a small farm plot in one of the poorer sections of the Sea Islands. We always had trouble getting the owners to provide repairs. Homes just disintegrated around us unless we made the repairs, paid for them ourselves," Karen lamented. "Now my family owns their own land and house, but daily living is still a struggle.

Karen sighed saying, "Part of the reason for poor care is because some of the nurses and CNAs never learned how to deliver good care. They are exhausted by short staffing problems. When they grew up, they received rough handling, cruelty, and even abuse. That's all they know."

"I don't believe they're that ignorant," Esther said. "These nurses are mean. You're using their past as an excuse. Why doesn't someone tell them...show them? Teach them how to deliver excellent care? What about the ninth floor? The nurses and staff work together to create a safe and clean environment. Those patients won't stand for anything else."

"I don't think you understand. It's second nature for some of them. It's how they survive. They will have to tap into their emotions to care, to love, and to do right. They have to risk too much of themselves. You see. Some of them are more comfortable with anger and hatred. That's how they grew up...defensive. Especially by white people. That goes for Shirleen too. She's living with a black man who abuses her. Anger consumes her. Right now, it's all she has to give. It's her protection against exposing her vulnerability. I really don't think she knows any better," Karen explained and turned her own anger toward Esther.

"You whites think we have control over our behavior, our lives. You think all we have to do is study hard, work hard, and be kind to climb out of our environment. It isn't that way for us. At every turn, doors are shut in our faces. Whatever you think, it's always the survival of the fittest, the fastest, and the most cunning. There's no room for compassion. Here at Thornhill, it's the same. The hospital holds staff over to work another shift if someone calls in. Everyone is overworked. There's no relief. They don't get overtime either. They get comp time...no money. The staff is exhausted, hostile, and some of them are sick. It's slave labor. The modern day kind. These girls may only get one weekend off a month. All the other weekends are split with one day off. What about their children? They don't have time to see about their babies. They leave parenting to surrogates. When the Justice Department comes to inspect for accreditation, everyone is paid overtime, but as soon as the inspectors leave, the system reverts back to comp time."

They both fell silent, having reached a road block neither wanted to attempt to move.

When they returned to the floor, Henry angrily paced back and forth in the nurses' station.

"Where's Mrs. Shepherd? Have you seen her? I've been looking all over for her."

"I think she left for a meeting about an hour before we went to lunch. Yes," Esther replied and thought for a second. "It was just before Jessie Taylor's tirade."

"Uh oh," Karen whispered into Esther's ear. "He's out to get someone. I've never seen him like this."

"How's he doing now?" Esther asked. She noticed Henry's blistered lips had healed, and his sunburned, peeling face had faded into a soft tan.

He didn't seem to notice her sensitivity or even Karen's. He merely glared at them.

"He's doing damned horrible. I ordered Ativan for his anxiety, but

I don't know how long it's gonna take him to calm down. I'll tell you one thing. I'd like to punch the shit out of her. She's the vilest bitch I've ever seen up here, and I'm not putting up with it anymore. I'm gonna do whatever it takes to get rid of her," Henry said, pounding the counter of the nurses' station with his fist. "Shirleen told him she saw his wife with her lover walking in the mall. They were kissing and hugging each other. She told him no one would want to be married to him the way he looked."

"She loves to torment Jessie and the others too. She's crazy. How can she get away with it? That's what I want to know? How?" Henry lamented.

He walked over to the water fountain, drank in deeply, returned to his seat, sat down, and propped his legs up on the counter. Abruptly, he dropped his feet angrily to the floor, as if he'd just recalled something else, leaned over, and slammed his fist into the metal desk drawers at the end of the counter. The sound reverberated in the hall, but no one said a word.

"If you see Mrs. Shepherd, have her page me," he yelled, glaring at the two nurses who were afraid to move. He disappeared around the corner of the hallway, heading for the elevators. The silence turned heavy.

Shirleen's hysterical laugh echoed off the bare walls and startled Esther and Karen. She had hidden across the hall in a patient's room and heard Henry's entire tirade.

"Sooo.... Mr. Henry thinks I'm a bitch. He wants to punch the shit out of me. We'll see who does the breaking this time!" She left the room in a fury, releasing another cynical tirade of laughter.

"We'd better warn Henry," Esther said. "I'll page him. You try to page Mrs. Shepherd. I think that this is one time we need to do something."

Esther and Karen placed their calls to Henry and Mrs. Shepherd. They charted in some of their patients' records in the nurses' station while they waited. After ten minutes with no response, they hurried to their patients' rooms to complete their afternoon chores.

One way or another, Esther vowed to warn Henry before Shirleen did something evil. Shirleen's savage fierceness frightened her.

Chapter 8

Two weeks later, Karen and Esther walked casually down the hall of the ninth floor. They had just completed the hospital's course in CPR.

"I'm amazed the hospital goes to all this fuss about resuscitation when the conditions here are so terrible," Esther remarked. "I've never had to resuscitate a patient in all the years I've nursed." The idea terrified her, although she knew the steps.

"I haven't either," Karen replied.

Karen's face glowed when she answered, "I can't imagine I got a hundred on that test. I'm still amazed I did it." She laughed softly to herself, shaking her head.

"This place is a horrible mess...isn't it? Oh, the regs stipulate we become certified every year...no matter what happens here. It seems that the hospital wants to maintain a good front with the licensure board. It's good though, we need it. We need more. Everyone needs to pass the CPR test and become certified," Karen said and glanced at Esther with regret. "I worried all night about that test. That's all I need now is to lose my job because I failed a test. Maybe every day is a test, a test of stamina, a test of compassion, and a test of perseverance. A test devised by Almighty God. That's what my grandmother says, 'Darling, God is just testing you. Always do your best. Do your best for God!' " Karen's face glowed.

"I think she's right," Karen said and pointed to the door that led down the stairs.

"Sure why not," Esther answered. "We need the exercise...don't we?" She laughed. "I prayed half the night that I would pass the test too. I pray every day for the Lord to help me get through. He's helped me too. That test was so easy compared to what we face every day. We've been here almost a month now. Can you believe that!"

"We are surviving this mess, aren't we?" Karen said. "I guess it's been that long."

"All I saw was Terrance hating me for the rest of my life for failing. There's nothing at home for us but sea oats, sand dunes, unemployment, and poverty."

Karen's happy expression dimmed at the mention of her home. She thoughtfully looked up at Esther saying, "If only there were some other industry in Beaufort. Some way the blacks could make a decent living.

The blacks who have owned their own land for generations are losing it to increased taxes.They can't make the inflated tax payments for their small parcels of beach front property. The white speculators are moving in, just waiting for their death like vultures. The prize is the anticipation of tourism and trade with condominiums. These families have worked the land all their lives. Raised their children. Buried their dead. It's all they have in the world to give them dignity and freedom. I hate it for them. It breaks my heart whenever I think about it."

Esther felt sorry for Karen's family's plight, knowing Karen was struggling just as hard to better herself as she was.

"It's been a long painful history of determined people," Karen confessed with deep emotion. "The first Africans who inhabited the islands were slaves, Gullah's, which means 'a people blessed by God.' Cemeteries still anchor the islands to the slave trade days by inhabiting the bluffs over the beaches facing Africa. Slavers buried the dead there to prevent the spread of disease. Sometimes, hundreds of bodies were buried in one grave. People who died of Yellow Fever and Malaria. Slaves who spent their lives working in rice paddies. My grandfather said the cemeteries faced the ocean because in death Gullahs were finally free to reach back over the Atlantic to their homes in Africa. There's still pain over slavery," Karen explained sadly. "The blacks harbor as much anguish and regret about their slavery heritage as white Southerners bemoan the Civil War."

They both became pensive. When they reached the door to the seventh-floor stairway, Esther opened it and held it for Karen in an attempt to compensate for some ghost from the past that had tormented her new friend.

Esther was overwhelmed at all the racial hatred that still lay festering under the surface. It seemed as if each black nurse and CNA carried all the past grievances of the entire black race on their backs, in their hands, and in their hearts. When one person said a word even in innocence about their plight, the ugly monster reared its ferocious head, exaggerating even the smallest, most innocent comment out of all proportion.

Esther felt helpless. She didn't grow up with prejudice. Her family entertained black people. She was never aware of the ugly root. It seemed as if the wounds grew deeper and more ugly as the years passed, instead of healing and bringing peace. The black nurses have turned against her just because she was white. Her own ignorance in the matter upset her. She never thought about race or being black before. Growing up in the North allowed her to be open-minded, free of the provincial disease. The vitriol from prejudice completely absorbed some southerners.

As Esther held the door for Karen, irritation and intolerance erupted inside her. She didn't want to take the blame for centuries of oppression, but it felt as if she was the chosen scapegoat, and she resented it.

Karen smiled apologetically at Esther when her eyes froze at something beyond the door.

"My God! My God! Look! Call for help!" Karen yelled.

Esther recoiled when Karen bounded down the steps. Esther followed her but stopped short on the stair above her. Karen bent over a patient lying in a crumpled heap on the landing in a pool of fresh blood, with a wheelchair on top of him. The side of the wheelchair had splintered under the pressure of the fall. Pieces of jagged wood punctured his neck like a spear, severing the jugular vein, carotid artery, and pointed back through the other side of his neck. He lay upside-down, impaled there by the splintered arm of the chair. His gaping mouth hung open in mid-scream. His bulging, horror-stricken eyes stared at the pool of fresh blood below his body. A red stream ran across the concrete to the edge, where it dripped to another puddle below. Esther turned away from the gruesome sight. The patient was Jessie Taylor.

Karen checked for a pulse and pressed her stethoscope against his chest under his bloody green shirt. Esther tried to pull him up so Karen had better access to his chest, but she couldn't move him.

"I'll go for help," Esther whispered.

"Jessie Taylor's dead," Karen said in disbelief, still moving the stethoscope across his chest and back.

Esther ran up the steps to the seventh floor and down the hall to the phone in the nurses' station. "Code Blue...Code Blue...Code Blue," she yelled into the phone. The noise blared out over the hospital through the loudspeakers. "Code Blue...seventh-floor stairway," she repeated.

The nurses' station was empty.

"Where is everyone?" Esther yelled.

She ran into the nurses' locker room, it was empty. She banged on Mrs. Shepherd's office door. No answer. Almost everyone attended rounds with the sick patients every morning. The entire treatment team.

The hall speakers didn't reach the patients' rooms with the doors closed. Esther raced back to the intercom system, pressed the buttons and paged, "Mrs. Shepherd...Melisa...Henry...there's an emergency in the back stairway! I've called the Code!"

Esther stared hard at the box for several seconds, waiting for a response. The short lapse of time felt interminable. She became frantic.

The antiquated brown intercom machine with one corner broken, and the buttons often sticking, wasn't working, Esther thought. None of the patients answered as they usually did saying, "She's not here."

Esther pushed the buttons again, and again, and again in an attempt to get the machine to work. Finally, she pressed down the white plastic button on the end of the box again, and again, and repeated her call for help. This time Mrs. Shepherd answered.

"We hear you," Mrs. Shepherd replied with a high pitched voice. To Esther, the screech sounded like music.

Esther raced back to the stairway and yelled to Karen, "I finally reached Mrs. Shepherd. She's coming. What can I do to help you?"

Karen tried to turn Jessie over onto his back again, but he remained impaled under the wheelchair. He was too heavy.

"Don't move him," Esther shouted. "Maybe we should just keep him in that position and let them see how he was when we found him. What do you think?"

"We should try to resuscitate him. If we can. I think it's been too long. He's lost too much blood. There's no way we can bring him back after losing all this blood. Where are they? What's taking them so long?" Karen yelled, as she stopped her struggle and stared down at Jessie Taylor. "You know his discharge was tomorrow. I wonder what provoked him to suicide? He's so young. So much younger than all the others."

The door at the top of the stairs opened. Melisa reached them first. Relief flooded Esther the minute she saw her.

Melisa, Mrs. Shepherd, Jewels, and Henry all stood motionless, paralyzed, in shock on the steps above them.

"Jesus! Jesus!" cried Mrs. Shepherd, flashing a searing glare at Esther and Karen. "What happened here? Do either of you know?"

"He's dead," Esther said flatly. "He was like this when we found him...only minutes ago." She stared at Jessie's gaping mouth and dripping blood. "We think it's suicide. Maybe an accident?"

They all began shouting simultaneously, giving directions to each other. Their voices ricocheted off the concrete walls and echoed in the cold stairway.

Jewels and Henry pushed past the nurses. When they reached Jessie, they gently maneuvered the shattered wooden wheelchair until they were able to lift it free. Part of the splintered arm of the chair remained impaled in Jesse's neck.

"Where in the hell did he find this antiquated mess?" Henry whispered.

They untangled Jessie's twisted body. At first, Jewel's hands trembled. Then, large, uncontrolled jolts overcame him. Tears filled his eyes and spilled down his cheeks, but he struggled to continue in his task. He had spent much of his time in Jessie's room the last few days, jiving and carrying on his usual break dancing antics, desperately trying to cheer Jessie up.

Henry and Jewels lifted the limp, cumbersome body free of the chair in one swift motion and carried him up the steps. Melisa, waiting at the top of the stairs, wrapped a blanket around Jessie's head and neck so his blood didn't drip out onto the floor.

Esther and Karen watched frozen, silent, in shock, as the others performed their duties in their ghost like rhythms.

Mrs. Shepherd sighed deeply when they disappeared through the door. She grabbed Esther's arm in a strong clutch.

"It was good you two didn't move the body before we got here. I'll call the coroner. Now, we have all these witnesses for the inquest. I've only been through this once, but it was horrible." She paused, trying to get her breath.

"First I want you to come with me to my office and tell me exactly what happened. After that Karen, I want you and Esther to go to the bathroom and clean the blood off your uniforms. Maybe go home after you dispense your medications. Put on a gown or something to cover the blood you can't wash out. I think there's some Hydrogen Peroxide in the stockroom. She struggled to breathe now and grabbed onto the railing for support.

Chapter 9

"It was a suicide? Don't you think?" Esther asked, but didn't like the perturbed contemplation in Mrs. Shepherd's face. Her skin had taken on that grayish cast she always wore when something happened. Fear and panic reflected from her eyes, as she moved the snuff under her lip back and forth nervously.

"You don't think someone tried to murder him. Do you?" Karen added, her voice shaking.

"I don't know any more than you girls. Just tell me what you saw. I'm sure the administration will probe all the possibilities." Mrs. Shepherd leaned back in her chair. Her breaths erupted in short wheezes.

Esther and Karen described verbatim what happened, mirroring each other's words. Esther became nauseated in the stuffy room. Vertigo overpowered her from the stress of seeing Jessie and trying to remember it all. She glanced around at the piles of papers stacked haphazardly in the corners and on top of Mrs. Shepherd's desk. Boxes of holiday decorations had been shoved under one side of a shelf. Esther thought the room resembled a closet with a path cleared from the door to the phone. A schedule sheet lying on the desk was marred with crossed off names and others written in their place. A dirty, ceiling vent exhausted hot, dusty air onto the nurses through blackened cobwebs. The phone interrupted their recounting several times. When they finished, Mrs. Shepherd abruptly ushered them out.

"Now don't say a word to anyone about this," she said as an afterthought. "We can't keep it quiet, but if you see a reporter just ignore him. Say you don't know nothing."

The two retreated to the locker room to wash Jessie's blood from their uniforms.

The nurses in the lounge were already recounting Jessie's suicide. Lyla who had just returned from lunch was talking with Selysia, who had been called in to help with the patients before the suicide so Lyla and Sally could go home. Lyla and Sally had worked since three o'clock the previous afternoon. Almost twenty-four hours. They looked exhausted but didn't seem to mind working overtime because they were finally allowed to get overtime pay as long as the Federal inspectors were in the hospital to renew their accreditation. News of the suicide traveled like a wildfire in a field of dry grass, growing out of proportion until it became a raging inferno. Esther wondered what the surveyors would say about it.

Violet, a nurse from the ninth floor, stuck her head in the door saying, "I heard about Jessie Taylor. I'll help if I can. We'll be down here in half an hour. You poor things. I can't imagine what it was like."

"Thanks," Karen said, still trembling.

Selysia stood in front of the yellow, steel lockers, changing from her black spiked heels into her white, crepe-soled, nurses shoes.

"I wonder if those white folks Jessie always said were trying to take over his body will be at his funeral. Them white folks that owned his slave relatives," Selysia quipped, squinting narrowly at Esther. "He has a whole white family somewheres who don't know about him." Selysia laughed and gestured to Lyla. The two convulsed in laughter.

"Hush up, you two. I can't believe what you're saying. He's our brother now," Karen scolded.

Esther huddled in the corner praying the conversation skipped her.

"Yeah honey, you're right! We shouldn't go on like this. It must sound just terrible," Lyla said and shot a wicked grin to Selysia saying, "I don't know what gets into us, do you Selysia?"

"No!" Selysia shouted. "We shouldn't say them things about our brother. But, he's Esther's brother too. Now ain't that a turn of the coin. We ain't talking about our black brother, are we?" She laughed. "But her white brother what's inside of him. Her diseased side. Her hidden side." Selysia chewed harder on her new gum making it crack. She cracked it and cracked it until Esther felt like screaming.

"Oh you're heartless," Karen broke in, "If you'd seen him the way we found him, you wouldn't be mocking him like this. I'm still shook up. He was so young."

"You're all being cruel. What about his children? His wife? What about them? Don't you have any pity for them?" Esther said, trying to hide herself in the corner of the dingy, yellow room. They continued to laugh and joke as if Jessie was a side show at the circus.

Esther washed her hands until they felt chapped. She had taken off her uniform and tried to clean the blood stains. She gulped a swallow of her tea, singeing her tongue. But she didn't care. At least, she felt something. The hot tea warmed her body from the inside out and permeated her nerves one by one, relaxing them, soothing them.

Mrs. Shepherd stuck her head into the room and surveyed the sullen faces.

"Karen, come out here and talk to these detectives. All you others get yourselves out here, and get your work done."

Esther breathed deeply, thankful they didn't want her. If she and Karen hadn't stopped to talk in the stairwell on the ninth floor, they might have discovered Jessie before it was too late. But he must have been in the stairway long before they entered it. Only seconds of time ebbed between his life and death. Oh, she had to push the thought out of her mind. What about the other nurses on the floor? Yes, what about them?

Karen returned shaken by the questioning. "It isn't too bad. They're calling for you. The detective is just asking questions about what happened."

"I can't go yet. My uniform is still wet. I haven't been able to get the stains out either," Esther said.

Sally asked, "Is the Medical Director out there checking over the situation?"

"No," Karen answered meekly. "I didn't see anyone else."

"I'm not surprised. You'd think he was the Czar of all Russia the way he treats us peasants," Sally said.

"I'll tell them for you, Esther. Just take your time," Karen said.

* * *

Karen had already dressed in a patient's gown and waited for her uniform to dry when Esther left the room. Everyone sat silent for several seconds after the door closed. Karen washed the blood out with hydrogen peroxide and hoped it wouldn't stain, but a slight brown hue to the fabric remained. The vision of Jessie Taylor hovered, fresh in her mind. She didn't want to argue with Sally.

"Come on, Karen, tell us what they wanted?" Sally demanded.

"All they wanted was what I told Esther. The detective wanted to know whether we thought it was a suicide or not. That's all."

"Well, what else could they be thinking?" asked Lyla.

"What do you think?" Karen replied.

Murder? Oh, my God!" screeched Sally. "It couldn't be murder. Unless. Shirleen...."

"Oh, she's a mean one all right. She'd never do anything like that," Lyla blurted out in defense.

Sally shook her head no, "Shirleen's too scared to murder anyone. She's all talk."

"Well, where was the Miss Shirleen anyway? I saw her earlier at breakfast in the cafeteria. I haven't seen her since," Sally said, squinting her eyes at the stunned faces.

Melisa opened the door and moved quickly to the chair in the far corner next to Karen. Her thin hand fluttered to her chest.

"I don't know how I'm ever gonna get over Jessie's death. I never thought he was suicidal," Melisa said.

"Oh, you will forget about him soon enough. Just like we all will. It's just another day on the seventh floor," Sally shouted.

"Now this is what I tell my babies and mark my words if I'm right. We are wandering in the desert looking for the Promised Land. We be thinking that it's just over the hill. We get to the next hill, and guess what, we ain't there yet. All our lives we are struggling to reach the top of the mountain...so we might as well make the best of it. Maybe when we retire, we'll be in the Promised Land. But, you know what I think? The Promise Land is Jesus when we die. Hard as we try, we won't see it till we die. So cheer up. Don't look so glum. Cause," Sally paused, peering around the room at the still, pensive faces of Karen, Lyla, and now Melisa focused on every word. A triumphant grin exploded on her lips, and she declared with a wiggle of her hips, "Cause ladies, Jessie Taylor is in the Promised Land, and you ain't!" When she left the room, the aroma of her sweet perfume lingered.

Lyla became lost in her own thoughts and strode out. "It's pay day!" she quipped back smiling.

* * *

"I hope I don't have to go through that again," Esther said, as she returned to the nurses' lounge and dropped into a nearby chair.

Karen reached out and touched her shoulder affectionately, but faced the others saying, "I don't know what his black part is doing, but his white part is flying around the room watching everything that's going on, wondering which way to go," she said and laughed. "For some reason, I still feel his blood's warmth on my hands, as if his life is still here. I kept washing and washing but still couldn't get rid of that feeling. It's as if Jessie is still reaching out, not able to release my hands." Karen shivered.

"I feel anxious too," Esther said. "I still have my medications to give. Not too many though. Why didn't Shirleen come in and offer her two cents?" Esther asked the silent faces around the room. "Is she taking an extended afternoon lunch? The detective asked me where everyone was at the time of the discovery? Can it happen again to someone else? Will other patients want to kill themselves from this tragedy?"

"I was wondering that myself," Karen said, shaking her head sadly.

"Sally said the police took pictures of the steps, the body, and even the wheelchair. They took samples of the blood on the steps and fingerprints on the door to the stairway. They've questioned everyone who was on the floor during Jesse Taylor's death, even the patients."

Later that afternoon in the day room, as Esther finished distributing her medications, she overheard a patient, Hugh McCaffrey, talking about the suicide to the others.

"I know just how Jessie felt when he went over the hill. Sometimes now I feel that way too. I feel like I did in those days. During the Second World War. In that prisoner of war camp. Kind of like going around the bend. Just like Jessie. That's what they called it at the camp – going around the bend."

He gazed around the room at the men's blank, staring faces as if he were analyzing them. He laughed softly to himself. He ran his fingers across his stubbled chin and squinted his hazel-green Scottish eyes as he continued, "Several boys lost it and ran out of control. They deliberately ran like crazy dogs into the fences. Got shot to smithereens. A machine gun can do nasty things to a man's body. I remember it plain as if it were yesterday. At the German prison camp, I resided in a barrack surrounded by huge barbed wire fences. You know, similar to the ones you've seen in the movies. With machine guns. Yes, just like the ones in the movies." He reached down and adjusted his paralyzed legs in his chair.

"It makes me feel better if I pick them up and move them around." He took a moment to light another cigarette, as he took a cursory view of each face glued on him. "I was in the prison camp for four-and-a-half years. The men in our group were British pilots. I enlisted in England in the British Air Force. The Krauts captured me at the battle of Dunkirk in 1940 and incarcerated me for most of the war."

He paused momentarily to take an angry drag from his cigarette, then blew out the smoke. "You might think we were lucky to be there instead of in the air or in the trenches, but we didn't think so. I was in the First Air Division Squadron. My plane got shot down over Germany. I crash landed in a field just a mile from the Belgium border.

My co-pilot died in the crash. I was injured here on my legs but crawled away from the plane. If it hadn't exploded, I might have escaped across the border. The explosion attracted Krauts from every direction. I guess we were lucky to be kept alive. I don't know why they didn't shoot me. I guess it was because I was an American. They might easily have incinerated us as they did millions of others. We weren't worried a bit. I always imagined I would make it home. I never thought for a moment of being killed. Almighty God watched over me. Most of the others felt the same way. We were just kids then. I was only twenty-two. Imagine. Sent off to war like it was a lark. They always put the young, green boys on the front lines. The boys were too naive to recognize the danger. Too gullible to be scared."

"Sure, we know what you mean," Chester said. "What did y'all do to prevent yourselves from going nuts? I know exactly what you mean. I was one of those green ones at the battle of Normandy. I fought in the trenches with Patton's Army clear through to the death camps in Germany. Liberated them too."

Hugh continued. "We all know you fought till the end, Chester. It was commendable too. But we didn't have anything. We just sat there waiting in Stralsund, Germany, up near the Baltic Sea for almost five years. There were fourteen or sixteen men in each barrack. Yeah, we were crowded. They captured us at about two-hundred plus pounds, and when the GIs freed us, we only weighed about ninety or a hundred pounds. Maybe less."

"Hey, brother. You were lucky to be alive," said Williams, a stout, brown-faced, bald rehabilitation patient sitting in a wheelchair, patting his stomach.

"Yeah, I guess you're right. We were lucky to be alive. There were millions of Jews who died." He shook his head in affirmation then coughed spasmodically on the smoke.

"The earth was wet, black sand and collapsed when you dug down even a foot. We tried to dig out every night anyway, supporting the earth with anything available, a chair, a post, a trash can. Every third or fourth night, we'd make it almost under the fence. Somehow, the guards seemed to know exactly when we reached that point. There must have been a stool pigeon. Never found out who it was. They assaulted us just before going under the fence and threw those covered in sand into solitary for weeks on end.

"Hey, McCaffrey, take your medicine," Chester interrupted as

Esther held a cup of pills in front of him.

McCaffrey continued after swallowing his pills. "You could buy Europe with a carton of cigarettes during the war. The Red Cross distributed cigarettes as part of the Geneva Convention's treatment of prisoners. Goodies from home. The Germans couldn't get the cancer sticks," he laughed again. "We traded them for everything. We named our guard Bear because he was huge and muscular. He was pretty fair. It wasn't his fault we were there. His other name was Bastard." He paused deep in thought, contemplating the memory. His lips became thin and pursed; a tremor ran over his body.

"Yeah, some of them went around the bend similar to Jessie. I'm getting quite tired now. I think I'll take a rest." With that he wheeled himself out of the room, a gray pallor masked his previously jovial face.

"I wonder what got into him?" Williams said.

"He's got some ghosts too, I bet. Yeah. We all have a few terrors hanging around," Chester said. "My varsity football team from high school all left on the same day. Only half came home. They couldn't wait to fight. They didn't imagine for some it would be their last."

"Oh, that ain't nothing," said Mr. Gunther who entered the day room to see why everyone was staring at McCaffrey. Gunther was exercising with his new right leg prosthesis, taking a walk with his new arm cane, trying to keep his balance. He laughed loudly. His black, beady eyes glared at all the men through his black horn-rimmed glasses. He wore his usual dress of a khaki safari shirt with khaki Bermuda shorts.

"You want to hear some stories? I was in India during the war. Course, then it was under British rule. We were there for protection. They didn't have any of those 'Save The Children Charities' then either. Men, women, and children died like flies. The caste system is how they governed themselves. A primitive leftover from an ancient Hindu religious society. The Untouchables were everywhere, starving to death. You were forbidden touch or help them. We tried to bring in troop trains, and they threw themselves on the tracks to move on to the next level of the caste system. They died to come back as a rich man." He laughed sarcastically, standing a little taller, noticing he attracted everyone's attention.

"The cow is sacred to them. They don't eat meat. They're vegetarians. They starve to death while the cows run wildly through the streets. Mother Teresa had plenty of people to practice on. Starving people, beggars, ragged children, flocked toward you just to get a small coin. No one ever tells you about the Hindus. All they talk about are the Jews. They had difficulty removing all the dead bodies off the streets before daybreak. Diseases of every kind plagued Bombay: cholera, typhoid, diphtheria, dysentery, even smallpox. No vaccinations you see. Why Bombay was teeming with every imaginable infirmity. No medicines. No doctors. For the British...yes...but not for the Indians. Get the picture? Life wasn't worth two dead flies. You got used to it after a while."

Mr. Gunther leaned against the wall for support, holding his stainless steel canes in one hand and pulling out a cigarette with the other hand. "Can I get a light?" he said, laughing to himself, laughing at the sight of the men's faces, and laughing at his own precarious position.

Chester came to his rescue. He puffed deeply on the cigarette.

"I guess we aren't worth more than that these days now, are we?" Mr. Gunther quipped, laughing again, rubbing his clean shaven chin and cheeks.

"Oh shut up. I've heard enough of that garbage. What about your money? You haven't given me the money yet for the booze," Chester whispered in Mr. Gunther's ear. Chester twitched irritably, jammed his hands impatiently into his ragged pockets and pulled them out again. His arms protruded beyond the edge of the sleeves of his white shirt.

"Yeah. You're right," said Gunther. "Well, last time I didn't get as much as you promised. So, I got a better source."

"You're making a big mistake, man," Chester said, stopping abruptly when he realized Esther overheard their conversation.

Lyla impudently stuck her head in the doorway and pulled a shy, new patient into the day room. Then, she gave him an audacious shove. "Go on in there and sit a while till you get your fill. If you stay too long, you might become one of them deadbeats," she said smugly and left laughing.

Esther grew eager to escape. She had only two more medications to dispense. *Will I ever have peace?* The image of these destitute men struggling to regain their life, searching for salvation, and fighting for their last breath, haunted her now and even changed the way she saw life. Her life became entwined with theirs because their struggle was her own. She felt alone, destitute, and defeated too. She fought with herself every day to be able to climb out of this quagmire against submitting and surrendering. In a way, the patient's courage inspired her strength, gave her power to defend her sons, fueled her energy to get up every morning, come to work, and persevere to try to change the conditions.

Esther watched Chester move from one patient to another, trying to get money for alcohol. She hoped they'd all get roaring drunk. She laughed to herself at the thought of the scene.

"Esther," Melisa called from the nurses' station. "You have a phone call," she yelled with irritation.

Esther picked up the receiver and said, "Hello!"

Mark's voice sounded wonderful to her.

"I'm glad you called me back. We've had a suicide here. Can you pick me up earlier? They've given me the afternoon off, and my car won't be ready till tomorrow."

"I have a few loose ends to clear up. Then, I'll be free. We can go out for a short drink before we need to pick up the boys. I'm happy you called because I've had a difficult day myself. They're still trying to set up the stock options for this company. I've just had it. I'll see you in thirty minutes," Mark said and hung up.

She retrieved her purse from the locker room and passed Mrs. Shepherd on the way out. She merely waved that she was leaving and acknowledged Mrs. Shepherd's nod.

The hot, July fresh air and sunshine soothed her as she waited for Mark.

To her surprise, Henry, Chester, and Shaw were in the garden area next to the hospital, joking, and passing the time of day.

Esther knew the men watched her. She self-consciously glanced away, not wanting to talk to them, and hoped Mark arrived earlier. She knew she'd be waiting for a while, but she didn't care. Minutes had slipped by, but no Mark.

"Hey. Can I offer you a lift somewhere?" Henry's soft voice startled her. He appeared different out here in the sunshine, away from all the misery and death, more relaxed and even happy. Golden glints flashed through his hair, and a soft aroma of aftershave aroused her senses. She witnessed his vulnerability today. His compassion after Jessie's suicide. Shivers skimmed her spine at this sudden microscopic view she had captured about his character. All the misery and desperation must get to him too.

"No. I...a...I'm waiting for my brother-in-law, Mark Culver. He's picking me up."

"All you have to do is let me know. I'm taking off now. Listen. Do you like jazz? A group of us are meeting downtown at Green's for a drink Friday night. Maybe you'd like to join us? Several nurses from the hospital will be there. I didn't have a chance to tell you before, but I thought you did a great job today...with everything that happened. I've been meaning to tell you, I think you're courageous to stick around here in this Hell hole."

"Oh! There's Mark's car now," Esther said and waved in Mark's direction. "Thanks. I appreciate the encouragement."

Henry touched her elbow affectionately and opened the door of the freshly waxed, black Ford Mustang. The horror of the day was diminished by the expression on Mark's face when Henry leaned his golden head into the car and said, "Take good care of her. She's been through a tough day."

Then, Henry gently assisted her as she sat down in the front seat.

All the way home she felt the imprint of Henry's hand on her elbow and shoulder, warm and reassuring.

Chapter 10

The next morning Mrs. Shepherd obsessed over improving the nurses' station by washing the chipped counter, torn chairs, grimy telephone, and even the charts with alcohol in a futile attempt to try to erase the effect of Jesse Taylor's suicide. She ambled back and forth, checking and rechecking to see if everything was in order.

She wore her best, blue, polyester dress under her new white lab coat with her name stitched in red script across the pocket. She tried to prepare herself for anything. She knew the administration would be interrogating her for the suicide again. Maybe now they'd reconsider hiring more staff for the unit. Mrs. Murphy had to see their dilemma. Everyone suffered working short. She'd warned them a tragedy like this was possible, but the responsibility ultimately fell on her. She needed this job, especially since her step-daughter was pregnant. If the hospital fired her, she'd lose her retirement. She girded herself with what remnants of strength she had left and prayed.

"I need your help Lord, today," she said.

Mrs. Putnam had phoned to say she hired a team of professionals to debrief the staff about the suicide. Mrs. Shepherd wondered what all the fuss was about? The administration officials still pestered them about the facts. She thought they'd talked to everyone already.

The Medical Director stood around for a couple of hours the day before to assure Henry filled out all the proper papers correctly and notified the family. It was the longest time he stayed on the floor in the past month.

She sighed as Henry rounded the corner from the elevator saying, "Uh, huh."

His shoulders drooped with resignation, and his eyes peered out of dark circles from sleeplessness. She knew his moods just by a glance.

"Henry, I need to have a word with you in my office."

"What do you want now? Haven't I had enough meetings?" he replied gruffly, anxiety showing in his eyes as he frowned down at her. He glanced around the nurses' station and inhaled deeply. A half smile played on his face. "It smells as if someone has been drinking...heavily."

She jammed the bottle of rubbing alcohol on his chest saying, "I'm trying to clean up a little."

He brightened, and nodded his head in agreement, "It needs it."

Florence Shepherd promised herself to be on her best behavior to everyone today, even Henry.

"Henry, I'm impressed I didn't have to chase around the hospital for you," she said softly and laughed.

"Oh, lighten up Florence! You knew I'd be here. Quit giving me a hard time. What's up now?" He picked up an old coffee mug and turned up his nose at the day old coffee. "Looks as if you were here late last night again," he replied softly.

He dropped into a chair. "Jessie's suicide should never have happened. Where was Shirleen all day yesterday? I never saw her after morning rounds. After we found Jesse. I want to wring her neck. She drove him to it. I know she did. I'm going to prove it too," he scowled.

She ignored his outburst. "They're sending up some people for a debriefing this morning at nine. Have you ever been through this before? I have, but I was hoping you might have some ideas, what to expect?"

He sat hunched over. A deep grief swept across his face, a vulnerability she had never seen before. Any sign of fragility had always been obscured by his anger. His voice sounded agonized, husky, and gruff.

"I was in Johns Hopkins Medical School at the time. My wife of two years, Christiana, died only several weeks before of Hodgkin's Disease. Her death overwhelmed me. I grieved deeply. I barely maintained my classes. I noticed a friend of mine, Brian, was losing it too. He missed classes and failed assignments. He even failed labs. All the warning signs were there, although no one spotted them." Henry took another deep breath and sighed deeply. "Somehow, I considered it acceptable for me to fall behind. I no longer had the discipline needed to study. When Christiana died, she took all my drive with her. She took everything, even my desire to live. The school board was unforgiving. Death or no death, the administration expected me to make my grades."

Henry glanced at Mrs. Shepherd with a timid smile as if trying to see if she understood. She leaned forward, stupefied that he divulged this personal information right now.

Henry stood up to stretch his legs. Mrs. Shepherd knew this memory was too painful for him to remain sitting. He had to stand up and walk around to be able to talk about it. She glanced at her watch; time was running out before the debriefing.

He continued, "Brian had no excuse except the unrelenting, savage pressure inflicted on us to learn another table or slide or disease. Johns Hopkins was just too much for him, and he had been drinking heavily. Everyone noticed his vagrancies, but they were afraid to report it. They didn't want to get him into trouble. Exposing his dilemma guaranteed putting in jeopardy the work he had already completed."

"When Brian didn't appear for class, I rushed to complete the lab because I sensed something was wrong. We had been working with rats and vitamin deficiencies. I raced through the feeding and the charts. This time my suspicions about Brian escalated. I ran to his room to wake him so he wouldn't miss the next class. Brian had already missed more classes than allowed. The day before the Dean had called him down for it. When I reached his room, the door was locked. I pounded it hard, trying to wake him, but there was no answer. I spotted the janitor down the hall and bribed him for the master key to open Brian's room. He went with me. When we opened the door, Brian was hanging from the water pipe. He was dead. The weight of his body shattered his neck and pulled the pipe from the wall. If only that damn pipe had broken, he would be alive today."

Henry shivered, disgust covered his face. "That was my last experience with suicide." He studied her reaction. "Brian's suicide occurred ten years ago, and yet, it feels like yesterday. I've been here at Thornhill ever since. Ever since I passed the physician's assistant boards. It amazed me how easy they were."

"There are just some things you never forget. It was after the debriefing that I left town. I realized then some things in life are just futile. At that point, my life in medical school was one of them."

Mrs. Shepherd regretted that he divulged this personal tragedy to her now when she didn't have the energy to respond. Her focus was Jessie's suicide. She didn't have time to react. She knew he had attended medical school, but didn't know the circumstances that led to his leaving.

All she managed to say in reply was, "What about the debriefing, Henry? Do you remember the debriefing?" Mrs. Shepherd stared into space, pushing out her lower lip in contemplation, exposing the pink flesh hiding just inside the brown. "You know suicide is a sin. It is a forgivable sin. The Bible says it is not a mortal sin. I found that out long ago. The Lord will forgive them." She let out a deep sigh.

Henry reached out and touched her shoulder. "I know you try to do a good job here. I don't blame you for anything." He gave her a feeble hug. "I still wonder if the worst nurses and CNAs were fired, and new ones hired, the conditions would improve for all these men."

"Debriefing, Henry?" she repeated. "The conditions here are too harsh and bring out the worst in everyone. No one wants to work with the dying. New staff has to be trained, and they leave even before they finish probation or fall in step with the ones we fired. No one comes in to see these patients." She took a deep breath and shook her head. "Debriefing, Henry?"

"Yes, I hear you. They had a debriefing," he sighed deeply. "They didn't really know what to do." He ran his fingers over his rough, whiskered chin and across his eyes as if trying to erase the sight.

"The whole thing was barbaric and inhuman as I remember. The administration brought all the students together to talk about our feelings. They called it a psychological autopsy. It was a debriefing. The more we talked about it. The better we would feel. Some tragedies you never feel better about, and that was one of them."

"So, that's all it is? Just talk. They just want everyone to talk about what happened and what led up to it?" She smiled relieved. "I didn't know what they meant by debriefing, especially with a suicide."

There was an urgent knock at the door. Mrs. Shepherd opened it. Shirleen stood there, silent, even shrinking back a little, not her usual defiant self.

Mrs. Shepherd's back stiffened. I'd like to see you burn for this, she thought. There was something different about Shirleen today. She was trembling, forlorn, and overcome with fright. The other nurses stood behind her, watching for Mrs. Shepherd's reaction. Mrs. Shepherd sensed an unusual wariness pervading among the group.

Uh...huh. Mrs. Shepherd thought. They are scared, really scared. Maybe this is what we needed to get these women straightened out. She felt the power she held over them, and she intended to use it for all it was worth.

"Where were you yesterday?" Mrs. Shepherd asked Shirleen bluntly.

Mrs. Shepherd glanced at Henry who stood beside her seething.

Shirleen stuttered a little, "Didn't Jason tell you? I...a...had an appointment." She appeared pale, ashen, and perspiration broke out on her forehead.

"Henry was just leaving. Weren't you?" She shoved him out the door past Shirleen and pulled Shirleen into her office before Henry attacked her. She slammed the door in the other nurses' faces. It was already 8:30 a.m. She wasn't in any mood for more confessions.

"Did you know Jessie Taylor committed suicide yesterday?" Mrs. Shepherd asked Shirleen.

"I didn't know until just now. Sally told me when I came to work this morning." She squirmed uncomfortably in her seat. For once, her long, stringy hair appeared clean, pulled back into a ponytail, and tied with a red ribbon. "I didn't have anything to do with it. So, don't blame me."

"No one's blaming you. I want to know where you were yesterday, especially since I expected you to work the entire day," Mrs. Shepherd said. Her voice sounded smooth and silken and didn't betray her fury at Shirleen's impudence. "All right. What's going on, Shirleen?"

"Please. Whatever happens? I can't lose my job. I left yesterday morning to have an abortion. I was only eleven weeks, but I just couldn't have that baby. Not now. You see my husband is black. He's a trucker and gone most of the time. When he returns home.... Well, he's abusive. He's so jealous. He thinks I'm running around on him. He beats me." Shirleen began to cry. "I will never have that bastard's baby. Never!"

Mrs. Shepherd still hadn't softened. This wasn't the only thing wrong. It's Shirleen's neck she's worried about. Not her baby's.

"That's not all," Shirleen continued. "Look, Mrs. Shepherd, I've been on drugs too. That's why I didn't want to have that baby. The girls told me there will be a drug screening today. We all have to comply. If they take my urine specimen, they'll find out."

The confession threw Mrs. Shepherd into a tailspin. Drugs? How can she be on drugs, and no one knows it? That explains why the patients aren't getting their medications. Was she taking their pain medications? That also explains why she's always so angry at the patients and staff. Was she in withdrawal? That explains why she's so timid now. She appeared terrified. This was her chance to get rid of Shirleen. The chance she had been praying for. If she had tried to fire her before, Shirleen would have reported Mrs. Shepherd to the Union Shop Steward and filed a grievance.

Although with Shirleen gone, the entire lower end of the hall, fourteen beds, wouldn't have a nurse. Weekends were the worst. They depended on Shirleen for all those baths and feedings. She was a fast worker if she wanted to be. Drugs? I never in this world expected Shirleen to admit she was on drugs, Mrs. Shepherd thought.

"You have really gotten yourself into a pickle," Mrs. Shepherd said with irritation. Although inside she felt a huge burden lifted. Shirleen's time on the unit was limited. She had real ammunition now with just cause to let her go.

"You have made us all suffer for your habit. Maybe even caused Jessie's suicide by tormenting him so much. You enjoyed his anger, didn't you?" Mrs. Shepherd's black forehead wrinkled. She began to see her own errors of not getting Shirleen fired earlier, letting Shirleen get away with it all, letting Shirleen bully her and everyone else on the floor. She glanced at her watch; it was 8:50 a.m. It was time to get started with the debriefing. It's gonna be all right, she told herself.

"I did a little. Neglect him a little too much," Shirleen admitted and glanced up at Mrs. Shepherd with a contemptible smile. "He always said his white side brutally attacked his black side, Scleroderma."

Mrs. Shepherd rose to leave her office, "I'll try to do the best I can. I can't promise you anything." Shirleen appeared vulnerable, but she guessed it was all a show. Shirleen was trying to save her neck.

Shirleen grabbed her arm and pleaded, "Please, Mrs. Shepherd. I'll do anything you ask. I have nowhere to go. I'm leaving my husband."

Chapter 11

When Mrs. Shepherd entered the conference room, the nurses were already sitting at the oak table. She nodded in greeting.

A young man at the end of the room stood up with his hand outstretched toward Mrs. Shepherd.

"How do you do, Ma'am? My name is Hank Prescott. I'm the psychologist. This is Julie Small, my assistant and also an RN, Nurse Practitioner," Hank said pointing to the lady sitting next to him. "We are the debriefing team called in to handle this unfortunate situation." Hank scanned each of the faces in the room with an accusatory expression.

Mrs. Shepherd stood at a vacant seat next to Esther and Karen and introduced herself. Glancing around the room, she caught her breath and nodded when she saw the Director and Assistant Director of Nursing.

"I think we should begin by introducing ourselves. Karen, why don't you begin?" As staff members gave their names and positions, they appeared scared and intimidated.

Hank Prescott stood up to preside over the meeting, but Mrs. Putnam stood up too, motioning for him to wait and directed her comments to Esther.

"I think we owe you some thanks. This unit shows a caring from the nurses that it didn't have before. First, it smells wonderful, better than ever. The patients are clean and bathed for a change. I think you are partially responsible for this. Esther felt her cheeks redden with embarrassment. She didn't think anyone noticed her efforts.

"Thank you," Esther replied and smiled self-consciously. "I don't deserve all the credit. Mrs. Shepherd has tried hard to staff the floor while we're so short. We're all trying hard to do our jobs well."

She felt the icy stares of the other staff bearing down on her. She heard their sighs and "Miss Goody Goody Two-Shoes…" echoes. She sank in her seat. Someone must have told the Director she treated the men like human beings and not animals, but she wasn't the only one. What about Melisa, especially Melisa?

When Esther looked up, Henry smiled down at her. His eyes met hers, and Esther felt their intense warmth radiate through her. This time, however, she didn't turn away so fast. Being admired felt good.

The Director of Nurses sat down gracefully, leaving Hank Prescott standing alone to face the disgruntled staff. He nervously pulled at his kelly green tie, checking its position. He frowned as he pushed his tortoiseshell glasses back up his long sharp nose with his thin fingers. His sickeningly sweet aftershave lotion infiltrated the air.

Mr. Prescott laughed smugly and said, "Ladies and gentlemen. Let's get right to the point. A patient by the name of Jessie Taylor died yesterday. We want to find out why. What led up to his apparent suicide? What drove him to this tragic end?" He cleared his throat and produced a large whiteboard to write on and set it on the easel in the front of the room.

"If you don't mind, I'll use this board to demonstrate where his room was in relation to the stairs."

The board slipped and fell off the stand onto the floor. Everyone laughed. They quickly regained their composure while he replaced it.

The hot, dry air in the room became suffocating from the ancient radiators, while the staff waited in anxious anticipation for some abhorrent disclosure. Esther noticed Shirleen perspired heavily around her ashen face and struggled to stay awake.

"Ladies. Did anyone observe anything odd about Jessie? Anything at all during those few days prior to his death?" Mr. Prescott asked as he paced back and forth.

Selysia commented first. She pushed out her full Vermillion lips and shook her head in disgust. "Well, I thought it was mighty strange for him to want that hideous, antiquated wheelchair his brother brought in for him to use. He practically guarded it with his life. Rode in it everywhere even though he could walk. It was his grandmother's. He said she had used it for years before she died. If it was good enough for her, it was good enough for him too." She watched everyone's reaction.

Selysia shrugged her shoulders and continued softly, "We tried to get him a chair from central supply and rehab, but they were out. We put in a requisition for a new one for him. He became impatient waiting, so his brother produced that old wooden one...until his came in. In the evenings, he hung his IV medication on that steel pole and wheeled himself around and around the hall from one end to the other until I thought he'd be dizzy."

Sally interrupted, "That's true. Only he stopped at Moses Rivers' room for a while, and then continued on his way." She smiled sweetly and folded her hands in front of her as if she were praying.

She's putting on quite a show, thought Esther.

"Oh," sighed Melisa, as she glared at the two with tired frustration. Her thin fingers fluttered at her chest. "Jessie wasn't odd in the least. He was a very sensitive young man. Only thirty-five. Everything was against him from the start. He's been suffering from Scleroderma. His skin turned white in patches like a spotted dog. The disease insulted and violated his delicate self. He imagined he had absorbed all the hatred and anger from all the white folks in his life, and the evil erupted on his skin. The disease was his own savage Satan erupting, passed down from three generations when his great-grandmother was raped by a white man. The devil was destroying his nerves."

Melisa demurely shook her head in affirmation. Her eyes teared up.

Esther glanced around the room at each face reflecting proper remorse. They didn't fool her for a minute. Her own cynicism shocked her, but it felt warranted. Mrs. Shepherd sat next to her adjusting her weight anxiously.

The Director and her Assistant rose from their seats, smiled at the staff, and left the room. Everyone breathed easier and chatted amongst themselves.

Mr. Prescott stood up to regain control.

"Maybe Jessie died the way he wanted his life to be: a dramatic, unforgettable, spectacular melodrama. Maybe he wanted to shame everyone else, provoke the feelings of guilt in those who wronged him. Maybe he wanted to end his own misery in his own drama of life with a simple act in which he intended no malice."

Hank scanned the room with his sinister eyes.

"All right. I know you're thinking this wasn't your fault. No one is blaming you. It's merely my job to point out what the other people are thinking. I don't want you to say anything. Just try to remember those little events that stand out most in your minds."

Esther was about to burst. She'd had enough of this psychological stuff. Trying to get the picture of Jessie Taylor's face out of her mind was hard enough. Not his real face, but his suicide face.

Mr. Prescott turned on a portable radio and set a timer on the table ticking away.

Jessie Taylor became a bomb ready to go off. They didn't see it coming. They should have. Their training included preventing a suicide. They were too busy to even think about Jessie taking his life.

Everyone squirmed and perspired even more. Mrs. Shepherd

snorted impudent breaths. Karen's brown face had taken on a whitish cast. Melisa cried softly dabbing at her eyes with a dainty handkerchief, trying to stifle sobbing hiccups. Shirleen trembled and perspired profusely. Selysia merely ran her Vermilion nails over the table in a rhythmic fashion, beating out the tune playing on the radio. This was just like Selysia, thought Esther. Henry leaned haphazardly back on two legs of the antiquated metal chair. A smile played on his lips as he surveyed the others and zoned his angry, tormented gaze on Shirleen.

Henry is enjoying everyone getting their comeuppance, Esther thought. Jewel's head rested in his hands.

Lyla watched Shirleen like a cat, waiting for something to happen.

It was Karen who broke the silence, "This air is getting too stuffy for me. I...ah...." Karen lurched out of her seat and bounded out the door. No one followed her. The staff flashed accusatory glares at Hank. No one said a word.

Mrs. Shepherd stood up and said, "These girls have work to do. I don't understand what all this is getting to. I thought this session was to help everyone release tension. This debriefing is only raising anxiety levels." She frowned and scanned the room. "Maybe some of us can leave and come back later?"

No one left.

Mr. Prescott sketched a picture of Jessie's room, and the stairs, drawing an arrow from his room to the stairs. "Now what do any of you remember about Jessie yesterday morning? Who had him as a patient?" He glanced casually around the room. All the eyes focused on Shirleen. She retreated. Her usual defiance gone.

Shirleen reluctantly answered, "I did, sir."

Esther watched Henry. His complete attention was focused on Shirleen.

"It was a usual morning. I gave him his bath water. He complained and didn't really care for his bath. So, he pushed the bath water away. That's all I know. I was busy giving medications. I didn't really pay any attention to him after that," she answered meekly.

"Well, I did," Melisa broke in. A perturbed tone erupted in her voice. "I went in to see Jessie. He received a phone call from his brother. I went in to tell him. Jessie became very upset. He said no one cared about him. No one helped him do anything. Shirleen just threw his towels in the room and left. His wife was getting the divorce, he wasn't. She was afraid and couldn't watch him die a little each day. She knew his pension from the insurance company provided enough to support him. The disability policy became the only good thing to happen to him in all his life. He said he purchased the policy on a whim, never dreaming he'd need to use it. It paid all his bills even here at Thornhill."

Melisa raised her hands in the air helplessly, and continued, "Yes. He acted very upset." She glanced around the room and let her gaze rest on Henry.

"I put a note on Henry's list about it. I hoped Henry had time to go in to see him." She looked at Henry to see if he wanted to respond, but he didn't. He appeared deep in thought, evidently oblivious to what she said.

Hank picked up the conversation. Popping up, like a tin figure in a shooting gallery, he appeared cold, callous, and indifferent, thought Esther.

"Yes. You people definitely cared about him. We're not here to point fingers at who's fault it is, if anyone's. We only want to get the facts. So the rumors are squelched. To help you unburden yourselves of any anger or feelings of guilt."

The last comment became too much for Henry. He jumped out of his seat.

"Well, I'm here to point the finger. I've waited a long time for this. It's making sense now. Melisa, you put that note on my pad, and I saw Jessie. I saw him an hour before he died. He was crying. He was devastated. I ordered a dose of Ativan to calm him down. He said he needed something to calm him when his wife arrived. She said she had the papers for him to sign. He said Shirleen had just left and tormented him again."

Henry stood up straight now, pointing at Shirleen. "This woman needs to be fired. I'm gonna see to it. Jessie told me Shirleen confessed she saw his cute wife hanging all over her lover in the shopping mall the night before. Shirleen told him his wife was having an affair with the man. She lied. I called his wife yesterday before she came to see him and asked her if she was having an affair. She denied it. She said she felt anxious about Jessie coming home, but she wanted to see him and help him as much as possible. I suggested she wait for another day to bring the papers. I explained to her about Jessie's depression, delusions, and anxiety. She agreed and confessed she didn't really know why she had the papers drawn up. His illness scared her so much, she didn't know what else to do. She admitted she felt afraid to manage his disease day in and day out. She knew she was running away by getting a separation and divorce. She felt trapped and didn't know what else to do."

Henry resumed his seat. His face drew down in an agonizing frown. He glowered hatefully at Shirleen.

Esther sensed the tension building in the room. All the eyes glued on Shirleen. She was clearly not herself. She refused to face them, appearing ashamed, and guilt-ridden. She avoided attacking Henry with a verbally abusive defense and denial of his alleged accusations. She remained silent. Lyla punched Shirleen to get a rise out of her, but she merely pulled angrily away, motioning for Lyla to leave her alone.

It was Florence Shepherd who broke the silence when she rose and walked to the door. "I think I've had enough for now. Hank why don't we takes a break for lunch. I don't think that this is getting us anywhere." She smiled sweetly at all the nurses.

Henry slammed his fist down on the table. "I'm not ready to leave, Florence. Someone died here yesterday, and it was her fault," Henry yelled angrily at Shirleen. "Are you gonna let her get away with it? She provoked him every day with her sly insults and lies. She tormented him to the point of committing suicide. She took away all his self-respect and demoralized him. Is there no justice here?"

"Henry! Henry just calm yourself. This kind of outburst won't get us anywhere. She didn't kill him. There's nothing we can do except report her for neglect and abuse. I intend to do that, but we must let this go for now," Mrs. Shepherd said and motioned for Henry to drop it.

Esther had never seen Mrs. Shepherd so distraught. Something is brewing. Esther followed everyone else out of the unbearably hot room, stopping momentarily to watch Mrs. Shepherd pull the resisting, fuming Henry into the sanctuary of her office.

Chapter 12

After the meeting, the staff quickly disappeared. Esther assumed they went to the cafeteria for lunch. Curious to see which staff had taken their place during the meeting, Esther hurried down to the end of the long hall. The patients seemed content enough. In Mr. Kroger's room, she saw two strange nurses talking with Karen. Mr. Kroger hid under his sheet, as usual, only allowing his one eye to peer out at the ladies to see what they were doing.

Karen motioned to the two new nurses. "Violet and Carol came to help us from the eighth floor. Are they finished?"

"Yes, thank God. You look as though you need some lunch. Come join me," Esther said.

"You're right. That must be why I feel so tired. I have been working seven days straight with no break. Maybe lunch will do me good."

"Yeah. Come on. We don't have much time before they continue," Esther said. She didn't really care about lunch that much. All she wanted to do was smoke a cigarette. Her legs felt stiff and ached from sitting all morning.

Once in the cafeteria, they grabbed a table near the walled garden where sparrows hopped around to salvage a crumb. Esther lit her cigarette even before they both sat at the table. She felt instantly relieved.

"I'd like to punch somebody. Our anger is internalized with no outlet making us frustrated and tired. The nerve of that supercilious man. He acts as if he has all the answers. And Shirleen. She has taken over without saying a word. Everyone knows she caused Jessie's death," Esther said, relieved to be able to complain to a sympathetic ear.

"Jessie Taylor's dead, and we are accusing each other. He died because he wanted to die. All the talking can't bring him back. I worked here all last weekend, and he was miserable. His entire family complained to him because he was sick as if he were able to do something about it. Hank was right about one thing. Jessie took charge of his life for once and committed the act himself."

"I thought you went home to Beaufort last weekend."

"No, we didn't go. I had to work. Terrance had to study for his exams. His mother criticized us for not helping her more. She said the beans needed to be picked. I don't understand why we have to do all her work too...even clean out the hog pen."

"My mother-in-law never offers to help with anything, Esther said. I've been living here now for about three months, and she hasn't been to see me. I suppose since Paul left she feels awkward visiting her grandchildren. But, they are still her grandchildren. It's a ten-minute drive to get to our house from hers. She always has a bridge game or tennis or some other pressing engagement. Mark, Paul's brother, is the only one who helps me. He drops in for a visit and takes the boys to the park or the ice cream shop. They really love him and mind him too. Better than they ever minded Paul. Mark will make a great father."

"I'm pregnant," Karen blurted out and shied away from Esther's reaction of shock.

"Pregnant and working here at Thornhill?" Esther said and felt empathy for her. How is she going to do all the work? It's hard enough, even too hard, with a healthy body, but pregnant? She'd need a miracle.

"Oh, my. That's wonderful news. When did you find out?" Esther said and managed to smile through her shock.

"Oh, you don't think that," Karen answered, looking defeated. "I don't even think that. Not now. Not as long as I have to work here at Thornhill. When I went to the doctors, he said about four months. Maybe the Lord has some reason to pick now, of all times, when my husband's in college. We tried for two years back home. I've suffered through two miscarriages. I don't know what caused them. Maybe lifting on the farm. We were always disappointed. Let's face it. If we had two children to support, we'd never be able to even think about him going to college. I waited to go to the doctors because I thought I'd have another miscarriage. But not this time. Life turns out the way it's meant to turn out." Karen laughed to herself. "I had to leave this morning because I felt like throwing up. It would have been rude, puking on Mr....What was that word you used? Supercilious Hank Prescott. I don't know what it means, but he surely is that just the same."

Esther felt this change in Karen's life sapped her own energy. It reminded her of her own pregnancies when she became more vulnerable, emotional, and sensitive.

Esther glanced at her watch and realized it was time to return. She detested leaving the peaceful patio, its warm, rich sunshine, and its peace. Karen avoided any conversation about the suicide. It appeared to be too much to handle coupled with the shock of her untimely pregnancy.

* * *

"All right, Florence," Henry said when they were safely in Mrs. Shepherd's office. "What's the big secret this time? Why are you covering for Shirleen?"

"I'll tell you. Shirleen wasn't here yesterday. She left soon after giving her medications to have an abortion. She left her abusive husband and has promised she will not cause us any more grief. She begged me to keep her on here. That's all. It wasn't her fault that Jessie killed hisself. He killed hisself because he wanted to die."

"What are you doing? You are surrendering the prime opportunity to rid yourself of the black widow herself. If you don't let her go now, you will certainly regret it later. All right, Florence. What does she have on you? I can't imagine why you're being such a pushover."

"Another thing, Henry. Stop trying to make Jessie's suicide a Federal case. If word gets out that we have indeed neglected him, we can all be sued including you, especially you. Even after all your moralistic attempts to soothe that man, his family can still sue. They can sue whether it's our fault or not. Just keep quiet. That's all I'm telling you. Another thing, let this be a word to the wise. Let me handle Shirleen. She's okay. Just let me handle the situation."

Florence had already decided not to tell Henry about the drug dilemma. If he discovered Shirleen was on drugs, she would deny ever having known about it. He was angry enough probably to press criminal charges against Shirleen for vindictive harassment, abuse, and illegal drug usage. While Shirleen deserved every bit of it, the process would destroy the unit, her, and the staff who have worked so hard.

"Florence, you're sweeping the dirt under the rug. Protecting this hospital. The facts always boil down to what's best for the unit, the administration, and the hospital. Save the administration at all costs. Make them look good under the worst circumstances. No one really cares for the individual patient, do they Florence? That's why I left medical school. Watching the administration cover up my friend's suicide made me sick. And Jessie's makes me sick too. It's gonna come back to bite you, Florence. I've seen it before. It still hasn't played itself out and won't until something's done." Henry left her office in angry despair.

* * *

They all stood outside the door not wanting to be the first one to return to the debriefing. Each staff member had their own excuse.

Hank Prescott returned as chipper as usual. What does he know of problems, thought Esther. Supercilious was a good description of him. She'd like to see him in one of those wheelchairs with his legs flaccid appendages and submerge him a few times in the whirlpool bath. She laughed to herself. I bet that'd take some of the starch out of him. What does he know of men and women losing their dignity, their possessions, and all their security? What does he know of being caught helpless and vulnerable with your own baby growing inside your body? Maybe Karen was right after all. Jessie Taylor fought back at life with all the willpower, anger, and courage he had on reserve, until in the end, killing himself seemed the only way to retaliate without losing his self-worth and have everyone pity him. She'd just figured it out. Actually, Karen realized it first, or maybe, it was Frank Prescott.

Yes, Jessie touched every one of their lives indelibly by his final act. Esther knew of all the deaths she had seen or will ever see, Jessie's will stand out. As long as she lives, she will never forget seeing Jessie Taylor lying there in the stairway, dead.

Hank Prescott impatiently tapped his pointer on the table as they all filed in and took their seats. He cheerfully greeted each one as if they were his long lost friend. Esther already hated him. She abhorred this entire day. Henry appeared haggard and overwrought. They hadn't heard from Jewels, Jessie's closest friend.

Mr. Prescott banged his pointer on the table for attention. "Now, ladies and gentlemen. Let's get to the meat of the discussion. Let me inform you, anything discussed here is strictly confidential. You are free to express any point of view here without retaliation from anyone. This debriefing is designed to help you rid your mind of the anxieties, anger, and guilt related to Jessie Taylor's death. Who found the body in the stairwell?"

He glanced around the room letting his eyes fall on each one momentarily. He was obnoxiously cheerful and condescending, Esther thought. She felt his expectant gaze fall on her, and all the other eyes followed his. Their stares attacked her like hot pokers goading her, taunting her, setting her up for the next sacrifice. Their eyes waited like vultures ready to jump on any and all morsels she threw out. With the exception of Melisa and Karen, the staff yearned for any evidence of her failure to tear her apart. They loved to twist and turn everything she said, then return it as vicious attacks to sabotage her credibility, her respect, and even her self-worth. Yes, she knew in her heart they were all waiting to find out what it was like to be the first one to find Jessie.

Esther glanced self-consciously over at Karen who had retreated in her seat, not wanting the eyes to fall on her. Tinges of guilt began to erupt inside of Esther. If only. If only they found him sooner. If only they had been on the floor.

"Karen and I went to the CPR course, and when we returned to the floor, we found Jessie Taylor dead in the stairway. He fell down the steps in his wheelchair, and the splintered chair sliced through his neck rupturing all his major vessels. I'm sure he died almost instantly," Esther said.

Her voice echoed flat, unemotional, even apathetic in the silent room. It didn't sound like her voice at all. Her heart raced in her chest. The pounding became exaggerated and magnified in her ears from her nervousness. Her own fear shocked her. Then, a new thought broke through like the sunlight on a stormy afternoon.

"Hours may have passed before anyone found him. If we hadn't decided to walk down the stairs." With that bit of previously unmentioned morsel, the others groaned, chattered amongst themselves, and seemed to be very pleased with their newly discovered prize.

"Why, of course. Why hasn't anyone acknowledged that before? It was quite by accident that the girls found Jessie," Mr. Prescott echoed in his contemptuous manner.

Jewels raised up his puffy, agonizing face from his gigantic black hands, and glared at all the nurses, even Esther. She hadn't seen him this way before. He frightened her. He had always been light hearted, joking, playing tricks, and hiding out in the dirty utility room. But not now. This was a side none of them had ever seen before. He stood up. His immense body filled the corner at the opposite end of the room. His raging black eyes scanned the room, finally resting on Shirleen.

"It's all your fault. Jessie Taylor's death is all your fault, and everyone knows it. You killed him as sure as if you deliberately pushed him down them steps." He pointed his finger at her, almost touching her face. He slashed the air in front of her white insulant face as if his finger were a sword. It frightened her too. She backed away, cowering.

Esther felt thrilled, exalted, even vindicated to see someone else, besides Henry, finally attack Shirleen. But, the other staff became intimidated by Jewels' unexpected outburst. Hank Prescott squirmed uncomfortably in his chair. With every attempt he made to speak, he received a raging hateful rebuff from Jewels.

"You never let up in your tirade and attack on Jessie. He was your private scapegoat. Every time you walked down the hall you ran in and told him, 'You're nothing. Your wife loves someone else. She never loved you. You're just an ugly nigger. Your great-grandmother deserved to get raped. Who cares about you anyway? You're no good. You deliberately drove him crazy. Oh, I can continue. You killed him as clearly as if you shot him with a gun. He was a friend of mine, and I'm telling you now watch out because I'm gonna plague you like you plagued Jessie."

Jewels breathed hard. He was in an evil frenzy as if all the hate he had ever felt for anyone came out here at Shirleen.

"And I see the rest of you every day out here as if you own the universe, telling these patients to go to hell. Who are they to ask for something? Who are they to expect excellent care and attention they deserve? You women think you are something special. Well, think again. Your men don't like you. They all hate you because all their lives you've torn them apart limb by limb. Castrated them of every male vestige, including their penis. You want us to provide you with your hearts' desires. When we do, you treat us like shit. Like we're no good and don't deserve anything. Yeah, you women get exactly what you asked for. It's no wonder your husbands beat you. Who was the last person who was kind to them? Not you! Do this...Do that...You're stupid...You're a dummy because you don't do anything all day. Your daddy was a dummy too. He's never been here either. You're evil just like your daddy.

Shirleen sat in the corner crying. Hank Prescott rose and shouted, "I think we have had enough today. Meeting dismissed!"

"We don't appreciate you blacks attacking our white folks here. Let that be a warning to you," Hank said, directing his comments to Jewels and the rest of the staff.

Mrs. Shepherd pressed her body between Hank and Jewels and glared at Hank until he turned away.

"Ladies. Ladies," Mrs. Shepherd called. "Remember, we need urine from every-one of you for a drug test. Now. Today. Stop in my office before you leave. Violet is there to help you." Mrs. Shepherd watched in silence as Shirleen slipped out the door unnoticed.

Later that afternoon, Mrs. Shepherd discovered Shirleen had left the floor before having her urine tested for the drug screen. She felt furious and decided to call the abortion clinic.

"Hello. This is Mrs. Shepherd from Thornhill Hospital. Did a Shirleen Dander come in yesterday afternoon to have an abortion? I'm her boss, and she told me she was at your facility all afternoon."

"Why, yes. We can't divulge confidential information, but she signed permission to inform you if you called. She came in yesterday afternoon about 3:00 p.m. She didn't leave until after 7:00 p.m. She was our last case. Is there anything else I can help you with?"

"No. That's all. Thank you."

Shirleen lied to me again, thought Mrs. Shepherd. She wasn't at the abortion clinic at 10:00 a.m. "Um...Um," she mumbled. "Where was she?"

Chapter 13

Several days later, Chester Greese sat by the window in the day room deliberating about how well he was recovering from his tuberculosis. He watched the smoke from his cigarette circle into a thick gray haze illuminated by the two beams of sunlight that ended on the grimy, coffee stained floor. Smoking didn't seem to bother him anymore now than before his diagnosis, he decided. He wasn't wheezing or even out of breath.

Oh, the doctor told him to quit and told him that his TB could kill him if left untreated. The doctor even told him that cigarettes would kill him one second at a time with each puff.

"Naw," he mumbled and shook his head. "It doesn't matter if I quit or not."

"How's it going?" Chester said to Williams.

"Humph," Williams said, as he glanced down at his paralyzed leg, in agony. Frustration showed in his eyes while he positioned the chair as close to the ashtray as possible. His face bore a resigned reflection of the tired old compliance he had endured all his years of life only to face this now. Chester imagined anger rising like smoke from Williams' head as his gnarled fist fell exhausted in his lap. With futile jolts of thwarted attempts, Williams fumbled with his twisted hand again, groping in his shirt pocket for his cigarettes and lighter.

"Thank God, it's time for lunch," Chester said to himself, as he looked away, not wanting Williams to see his half smile. Chester smiled, not at Williams, but at the futility of it all, the futility of all their struggles. "The sufferings of life always catch you off guard," he said to himself, shaking his head in affirmation.

He had been waiting for something to happen, anything. He regretted watching the patients like Williams working so hard for so little. It made him feel more helpless. It made him feel as if he should be struggling all the more.

They'll all be returning now, he reminded himself. He pressed out his cigarette in the ashtray and stood against the wall just to watch them enter the day room one by one. He knew the rehabilitation patients returned exactly at 11:30 a.m. He knew that if the morning hadn't been productive for them, they'd exhibit hostile, angry moods like Williams.

He stared down at his rough, scaly arm and scratched an itch. Without a watch, one day melted into another, and the end of the morning activities punctuated the afternoon. Meals and medications were the only real timekeepers, although the pills were sometimes delayed an hour or maybe two, depending upon the nurse. Today, his memory lapsed, and he didn't remember getting his morning meds – not that it mattered. But to his great satisfaction, he counted on lunch, and dinner arriving punctually at twelve noon and 5:00 p.m. He set his clock by them, and today, he again hoped to.

Chester marveled that the nurses finally got smart and placed the ashtray out in the middle of the room, several feet from the wall. Now, the patients reached for it without burning themselves, each other, or the floor. He lit another cigarette and waited. He blew a fresh cloud of smoke into the already thick air and coughed to clear his throat. He walked over and mashed out his new cigarette in the ashtray, blowing out the last bit of distasteful smoke. His mouth felt hot. He didn't know why he had kept it up all these years. Just habit.

"Need some help?" Chester mumbled to Williams who struggled to light his second cigarette with one hand, while the other lay paralyzed in his lap.

Williams grumbled something inaudible.

Chester reached down with his lighter and lit William's cigarette with one stroke. He examined his own two healthy hands wondering if he'd ever be paralyzed. He rejected the thought immediately and started to leave the room.

Suddenly, Williams' face became that of Jessie Taylor's. Chester fell back to the security of the wall.

Lately, he was plagued with visions of Jessie Taylor and thoughts of his suicide. That's all anyone else thought of too, even Shaw who never thought of anything much except getting a snort of whiskey. Chester had been as shocked by the act as anyone.

He thought Jessie Taylor the least likely of all the men to commit suicide. Why Jessie dared to talk back to Shirleen. He even dared to throw things at the walls. I'd love to toss my meals at the walls every day, but I don't. I just accept the way things are. I've quit fighting. "Yes, I hate to admit it," he said to himself,"I've quit fighting everything." All I want is a quiet life, go to the AA meetings, stay sober a while, tie one on a while, get sober again. Just a quiet life."

"Hey," Shaw said and raised his fat, white arm in greeting as he sped to the ashtray. He ran his chair into Williams' chair almost knocking over the ashtray.

Williams responded angrily at Shaw, "Watch yourself, Buddy. You're not the only patient in this God-forsaken place."

Chester didn't miss the mischief in his eyes. Shaw loved to aggravate everyone; Chester concluded. If only to raise some emotion out of them.

Nancy, the physical therapist, an energetic sprightly young woman with long blond hair, stuck her head in the doorway and yelled, "Hey, Williams. I'm watching you. You left before you finished all your exercises this morning. Tomorrow, I want to see you for twice as long. You've got to get that arm moving. If you don't, you will lose it."

She chuckled to herself. Then, she flashed a brilliant smile, saying, "Shaw, I missed you too this morning. You didn't even come down to the rehab center. Where did you go? Were you playing hooky? Do I have to send a note home to your mother?"

Shaw retreated into his chair. A sheepish expression crossed his face. He whispered to Williams, "Hay, Williams. You gotta stay out of sight like me. That's the only way they'll leave you alone. Otherwise, they'll make you do all that crap. Exercising. Walking. They can't make me do any of that. I'm too old, too tired, and too smart. Ha! Ha! Ha!"

Chester puzzled over how Shaw had declined physically and mentally in the past few months. A little bit each day. Maybe, he was more confused. So what if he couldn't hold his urine. He figured it was just a phase. Shaw would recuperate soon. He detested the thought of something happening to Shaw. He remembered when Shaw never soiled himself at all. He'd get real embarrassed if you told him he smelled. Shaw's decline had been too rapid.

"Hey, Chester, got a cigarette?" Shaw begged. "I'm all out." His leprechaun face curled up into an amiable smile...all except for his tongue. Chester marveled at how he could smoke with it sticking out the way it did, but he managed.

Reluctantly Chester handed him the cigarette saying, "Henry said he's going for cigarettes today. Did you ask him?"

Chester stared out the one grimy window to the trees below and the pond in the distance. Was the same deterioration happening to him too? Was he on the slide of downward mobility like Shaw? Was he slipping into the doomed with declining memory, and disintegrating organs?

Threading his bony fingers through his neatly slicked brown hair, the word death echoed in his mind, disheveling its order. The word death evoked scenes of his own mother's and father's death and funeral. He glanced down at his threadbare, plaid shirt from the Good Will. It reminded him of his poverty. He caressed with newly found concern his rust colored pants, noticing the torn pockets, and frayed hem. This image of himself summoned pangs of shame.

Chester laughed with astonishment, thinking of himself for the first time as pathetic. Why hadn't he ever thought of himself as dead before? He saw his life in a microcosm of activity. It was almost poetic in a way of eating and crapping, soiling and cleansing, sinning and repentance.

"Don't you want a whirlpool bath, Chester? Come on you'll feel better. You'll feel like a changed person," the nurses tried to coax him.

Maybe they're all Baptists, trying to get all the souls to heaven before that last gong rings. Dunking them in the whirlpool tub. Yes, it seems like the spirits got to cleanse us before the end. Like the last purge. Wow. By golly! I never thought of it before. This is the last quest for immortality. A purification rite for salvation. The image terrified him. Tongues. He'd spoken in tongues the first day the nurse Esther arrived.

"Yes. God and purification are right around the corner," he said to himself. He laughed at himself for conjuring up the preposterous idea. The scene of each patient dunked into the whirlpool tub invaded his thoughts and underlined his summation. Yes, in the end, it was a baptism of sorts.

Chester remembered the snake and the Power that had been on him that day. The Power hasn't been back since, though. He knew he was speaking in tongues immediately when the sounds erupted from his throat. His father and uncle believed in the Holy Spirit of Pentecost and always claimed to speak in tongues. He hated his father. He hated his father for many things, but most of all because he knew his father didn't believe in all that malarkey. He knew his father was lying to everyone about having the Spirit. He didn't really acknowledge the Spirit himself until he received his own transformation.

He always figured everyone was having a fantasy. All except for that time when he ran out to the barn to escape his father's wrath. His father had taken the strap to him for some reason. He didn't even remember now what he had done. He lay crying in the corner of the barn when this great warm cloud surrounded him. It covered him with an overwhelming and penetrating love, an uncommon peace, and reassurance. He immediately realized that it was the Spirit. It had come and gone so fast that he wondered at the validity of the vision. But he overheard the others talk about it too. He knew it, all right. He heard everyone in his family speak in hushed tones about the cloud, all except his father.

Chester sighed a deep grieving sigh. Maybe that was why his father acted so angry all his life. Because he never really had the Spirit. He felt left out, shunned by all the others.

The Spirit that came to him that day in the barn appeared also on many other occasions, but it disappeared when he refused to go to church anymore. He thought they were all hypocrites. His parents and the others...they said they believed, but they didn't act like it. They were cruel, angry, and stabbing each other in the back.

He had to admit the Spirit returned to him weeks ago...when he found the snake. Why the snake was a rattler. He didn't know what possessed him to grab it. It just seemed to be taunting him, egging him on, and for some reason, he refused to resist it. Maybe he was losing it too, like Shaw, and everyone else. Maybe he had too much to drink the night before.

Out in the hall, he heard the tap, tap, tap of the white cane of Mr. Sylvester Street and the continuous demands broadcasting from his alcohol-demented brain, "Call my social worker, call my doctor, call my wife. I know she'll take me back today. Observe me, all fixed up. Look at me boys. Do I look ready or what?"

What a demented jerk, thought Chester, watching Sylvester's entry. He couldn't help but laugh.

Sylvester Street filled the doorway of the day room. Sanguine smiles crossed almost all the patient's faces as they watched Sylvester strut into the room with his arm linked through Esther's. The nurse bathed, powdered, shaved, and wrapped him in a blue and white striped bathrobe. He wore brown paper slippers. He pranced around gracefully like a French poodle, as proud as if he received the Best in Show award. He was a picture all right as his churchman chin pointed toward the ceiling. His roaming unseeing eyes danced back and forth in his face like the broken eyes of a doll as he walked. He held his stick pointed in the air as if he didn't know which direction was down, instead of fixing the end of the cane irresolutely to the ground.

"If he isn't careful, he might decapitate someone waving that cane," Chester said to Shaw.

Esther walked Sylvester to his usual spot on the vinyl sofa next to the ashtray and TV channel changer. Cigarette burn scars and ground in soda-ashes marred the varnished finish of the table, but he didn't see this and merely shouted, "Just put my coffee down here." He felt into the air for the top of the table. Eventually, he lowered his hand until it reached its destination. Smoothing his palm over the flat surface, he smiled with satisfaction.

Esther gingerly placed the coffee on the scarred table top as directed. Sylvester sat down, smacking his lips and let his cane slide under the couch.

Men who had just returned from physical therapy gathered around and enjoyed Sylvester's manipulation of the nurse. All the other nurses would have told him to go to hell and shut up by now, but not this one. Esther patiently and slowly guided him around as if she didn't have another thing to do. No one spoke. They all watched in astonishment as she withdrew a cigarette out of her own pocket, placed it into Sylvester's mouth, and lit it with her own lighter.

Shirleen stood in the doorway. A gleam of sadistic pleasure crossed her face.

In an instant, the patient's' shoulders shrugged up in resistance and their backs curved over instantly as they cowered in painful resignation. Quickly, they shuffled away from the sound of her abusive voice. Their eyes darted fearfully, scanning the room. Esther stood there in silence, watching Sylvester. His head twitched with palsy, and the grin on his face exposed his yellow teeth grinding together in resistance to Shirleen's voice.

Esther wore a soft, compassionate expression. Her auburn hair glowed in the smoke-filled sunlight. The beam surrounded her at just the right angle to completely engulf her with rays, giving her a certain spiritual essence. For that moment, she became a vision, a bright star, a Phoebes, and radiated a brilliant luminescence.

Shirleen witnessed the sight, and with unbridled fury, she strutted over to Esther and screamed so everyone could hear, "Well, honey! I see you found you a new boyfriend. I didn't think you would pick one from this passel of brats. I guess I was wrong.

No one said a word or dared to glance in Shirleen's direction, afraid Esther'd be her next target.

Esther refused to be intimidated, and merely shook her head with exasperation, saying, "Can't you see the humanity occurring here?

Can't you see this is the end of their lives? It is our job to see to it that these patients pass through this time with empathy and dignity. If we don't do this. We will fail at our task. This is the task that God has given us."

Esther stared boldly back at Shirleen, ignoring her fury and merely let the words fall at Shirleen's feet. The words fell simply and gracefully as if each was a treasured diamond that had been presented expressly for Shirleen's examination, but Shirleen missed it.

Startled that anyone dared talk back to her, Shirleen snarled, "Honey, I hate to tell you this, but you can't make an Arabian stallion out of a jackass."

Chester immediately told Williams Shirleen was wrong, because that was exactly what Esther had done with Sylvester.

Chester thought Esther appeared saddened for a second, then she let out a sigh of frustration. Without another word, she left the day room too. She left exuding a certain graceful dignity and undiminished integrity. The men sat there in a daze as if frightened for themselves and for Esther. Chester was afraid Esther might have provoked a severe retaliation from Shirleen, something so cruel as to destroy Esther. He knew Shirleen would never stop attacking Esther until she broke her down as she did them.

Sylvester, oblivious to the confrontation, continued talking on to no one and to anyone about his wife taking him back. He yelled out his demands to the ceiling, sipped his coffee, and dragged on his cigarette, "Call my social worker! Call my doctor! Call my wife."

No one noticed Patrick Shaw in the back of the room frantically pulling on Chester's sleeve and grabbing his arm tightly with both hands. He gripped so strong that he dragged Chester down into his face. "Come on, Chester. Now's the perfect time. Take me with you. No one'll miss us. Please, take me with you," he pleaded with every power of coercion that he possessed. Shaw chased Chester with his wheelchair from one corner of the room to the other.

Chester watched him pound the arm of the wheelchair in protest. Shaw struck his paralyzed legs with his fists repeatedly like a savage.

Shaw's actions got to Chester, and he felt sympathetic again. There was no place to escape. He experienced his own craving for whiskey. A burning in the pit of his stomach that Patrick Shaw voiced. Every nerve ending reached out and screamed for the foul-tasting, burning Jack Daniel's Tennessee Fire that transported him to another time, another state of being, another realm of being free to choose to be one of the good old boys. Whiskey transported him to a realm without the confines of the hospital, its regulations, its AA meetings, and its ball-busting nurses standing guard to castrate him of every male vestige.

"Yes," he had finally relented. "Yes, just this once I'll take him," Chester said to himself. The face of Jessie Taylor skipped through his mind, leaving him convicted in his determination.

"Live before it's too late," he whispered to Shaw. "After all. I hate to drink alone anyway. Okay, come on. I give in," Chester said, laughing softly to himself. "Just this once. If you tell, I won't let you forget it."

Shaw glanced furtively up at Chester, his face filled with awe, even cherub-like wonder at the idea that Chester was finally including him.

After dinner, Patrick Shaw's eyes sparkled as he flashed his mischievous grin.

"Wait a minute Shaw. Wait!" Chester whispered as he stopped, disappeared into a patient's room, and stole two styrofoam cups from the bedside table.

"Okay. Let's take the back elevators. They'll be empty this time of day," he cautioned.

The two moved stealthily down to the elevators and out the back entrance of the hospital. No one stopped them. The air outside felt nippy, cooler than Chester anticipated. A slight drizzle forced Chester to hesitate for a second, as he wondered if it weren't too cold for Shaw.

"What are you waiting for, Chester?" Shaw demanded in a hushed voice.

"Nothing! Nothing!

He ambled in long loping strides and shivered from the cold air. He glanced up into the sky at the clouds forming a storm front.

"No one's gonna come out in this mess!" Chester remarked, glancing back at Shaw for a second, thinking it's pretty cold for July. Chester pulled the collar of his sweater up around his neck against the chill. He watched Shaw huff, puff, and pull the wheels until they sang with speed across the macadam of the parking lot.

Shaw's hands appeared stiff and weak after pushing his chair wheels all the way out to the graveled path around the lake. He pushed steadily on, only stopping now and then for a moment's hesitation to open and close his fists to regain the circulation.

Chester felt for him and took over pushing the chair.

"I don't like the looks of this, but we may not have another chance." He patted Shaw's head affectionately. "Wait here! I'm gonna search for the bottle I stashed!"

Ducks and geese swam over to the two men begging for handouts.

Chester tried to scare them into the lake but had little luck with several large ones. They were fearless and chased him wherever he ran.

Chester kicked up the piles of pine needles and leaves surrounding the larger oak trees. He ran faster and faster, from tree to tree in a frantic, crazed panic, searching for his alcohol.

"Chester. Chester," Shaw yelled, trembling from the cold. "Chester, wait a damn minute. Come here and maybe we can figure this thing out." Thunder clapped in the distance. Clouds overhead grew thick and black.

"Okay. Okay. I'll start again," Chester shouted as he raced over to Shaw, terrified suddenly at Shaw's shivering, and struggling for air, a bluish cast flooding his face, neck, and hands. He touched Shaw like a fretting mother. He ran back and forth several times from the woods to the lake saying, "Don't worry Shaw. I put it under a pile of pine straw at the base of a big, old, oak tree. I can't remember which tree it is. Don't worry. I'll find it!" Chester retraced his steps from the day he hid the bottle.

He returned,"It is no use. The bottle's lost."

Shaw's face and mouth shook spasmodically from the stinging rain.

Chester grabbed Shaw's shoulders shaking him to rouse some recognition saying, "Come on, Shaw. Don't fail me now. We're almost there. A spot of brew will take these shivers away." Chester took off his sweater and wrapped it around Shaw. "Just you wait and see."

He pushed Shaw's chair quickly now, around the lake, talking to him all the time to calm him down. The two had become cohorts and pals, partners in sin.

"I see it. I see it. This is the spot!" Chester ran into the thicket of shrubs again, stumbling to maintain his pace.

Shaw's guttural sounds erupted louder and burst into screams of Jabberwocky. His body shook in tumultuous jolts.

"Hold on, Shaw! Hold on!" Chester screamed.

He ran to the base of the largest oak and hysterically dug into the mound of compost. His hand hit the hard smooth surface of glass, and he yelled triumphantly, "I found it." His heart pounded.

He held up the bottle, screaming, "Where're those damn cups. Where are they?"

Chester felt behind Shaw searching for the cups. Shaw was soaked from rain and putrid-smelling excreta. Underneath his back lay the crushed cups.

"Oh shit!" Chester screamed. He fought his squeamishness of sharing the lip of the bottle with Shaw and took the first swig of whiskey himself. Immediately, he felt the liquid burn his throat down to his stomach, warming his body from inside out.

"What difference does it make," he said and swallowed another deep swig of the rich whiskey. Its warmth radiated throughout his body infiltrating and invigorating the nucleus of every cell. Immediately, his tensions relaxed, exactly as he had yearned for, and anticipated.

The rain stopped. The clouds parted, and a lingering sunset hung on the horizon.

"Okay," Chester declared, as he grit his teeth and bolstered his nerve. "Come on, Shaw. Take a big draft to warm your innards."

Chester patted Shaw's cheeks and face, trying to bring him around. It didn't help. All the time Shaw kept uttering those guttural sounds of Jabberwocky. Finally, Chester slapped him hard on each cheek.

"Shaw! Shaw! Come on! Come on! I have the stash. It's here." Chester watched Shaw's over exposed body convulse in shivers. His psyche had withdrawn from too much stress. His cheeks turned purple. He didn't respond, only squealed like a hysterical animal, unable to record the message.

Chester shouted, "Damn it all. Stop those noises and look what I found!"

Chester turned frantic. Not knowing what else to do, he poured the whiskey slowly over Shaw's tongue and held Shaw's cheeks together to form a small opening. He let some trickle down Shaw's throat. When the whiskey hit the back of Shaw's windpipe, it ricocheted, creating the deepest gag reaction Chester had ever seen. The whiskey absorbed instantly. When Shaw's brain registered the content of the abrasive stimuli, he stopped his gagging sounds. His eyes bulged open. His face flushed red, and although he struggled to get his breath, a twinkle shot forth from his eyes.

With all the control he could muster, Shaw ceased all coughing, rasping, choking, and even breathing for a split second, and another, and another until his face turned almost black from a lack of oxygen.

Chester panicked. With all his might, he drove home a blow with his fist to the area between Shaw's shoulder blades. The force of that blow knocked all the air from Shaw's lungs with one stroke. Along with the air, shot out the remainder of the whiskey that had entered the wrong pipe. It all shot out with such might, the force of it sent the chair backward almost two feet, treacherously close to slipping into the lake. Chester reached out and grabbed the back of the chair, saving Shaw from a swim. The geese and ducks circled again. Finally, Shaw's coughs spasmed out.

Paralyzed with fear for Shaw, Chester stared at him in silence, overcome by the scene, thinking he could have died right here in this Godforsaken park.

Chester took several more deep swallows from the bottle, never taking his eyes from Shaw.

Shaw's recovering, Chester thought and breathed a sigh of relief.

He prayed finally, "Thank you, God. Thank you, God. Thank you, God," until the final spasm ended.

When Shaw recovered, he reached and grabbed the air for the whiskey. They both let out a tremendous hoot, laughing uncontrollably at each other's fumbles and recoveries.

"Take it easy. Take it easy!" Chester said, and helped Shaw take a slow drink. "I thought you were gonna choke to death right here at this lake."

Chester eyed Shaw intently and noticing his shivers hadn't subsided, he said, "I gotta get you in. You'll get pneumonia from this if I don't."

He shook the whiskey around again in the bottle and helped Shaw with another slow draught. Chester watched Shaw's shivers subside. A pink glow appeared around his nose and cheeks. He remained vulnerable, childlike, trembling like a wild animal caught in some steel trap.

"You almost died. You almost choked to death here in front of my eyes. Why didn't I think twice about bringing you out here? You jerk," Chester mumbled.

Chester saw Shaw again in another light. He saw Shaw's body crumpled up and slowly degenerating, eroding away by years of hard life. Now, without provocation, Shaw still suffered a continued wear and tear like the Egyptian Sphinx, curled up on his frozen lion's body and feet, watching and knowing all, but never changing, only wearing away slowly like paint on a board fence. His mind came and went, almost gone now.

Chester thought of himself and imagined he was a twelve-year old again, addressing his puberty. It was their club; their boy's club. Chester and Patrick Shaw exchanged rights and blood and stash and butts like brothers in the right of passage.

Shaw moaned coherently now, "Look, Chester, can't we go somewhere else? Do we have to go back to that hospital? They'll crucify me if they find out. Those black nurses will come at me with a vengeance."

"Shaw, we've set our mark. It's just you and me now. There's no one who wants us or who will take care of us," Chester explained gently to himself as well as to Shaw.

He laughed softly. "We are at the end of the line. There's no return on this train. Oh, I got my daughter who I ain't seen in twenty years. I don't even know where she lives anymore. So who do you have...no one? All we have is each other and that's that. We ain't got no money either. I guess all we got's is the good Lord looking after us." Chester remembered the Holy Spirit and repeated, "We have the good Lord. That's who we got."

Chester shook his head realizing the nurses were gonna be pretty sore if they discovered this escapade. He threw his cigarette into the lake. "It's ok. Just be cool. Don't let on. Don't egg them on either or let them know you've been out? You'll be all right."

Chester sighed deeply, glancing at the brightly lit hospital ahead of them. He felt a headache coming on. He figured he'd drunk too much too fast. He didn't care because it helped obliterate all that was to come, all that was to be, and all that he'd left behind.

Chester took another swig of whiskey and twisted the top tightly onto the bottle. He gazed into the twilight. Without warning, he opened the cavern filled with forgotten and repressed experiences lying deep inside, experiences seething, boiling up, and erupting with the force of a volcano. They were so powerful Chester lost control and bemoaned memories he had forgotten existed.

"Shaw, it was dark, cold, and pouring like this. The rain pelted hard clouding the sight of the beach when we landed at Normandy on D-Day. I had hidden stash here in my water canteen. I figured I needed the extra boost on a morning just like this. We zig-zagged across the beach. It was dawn, and I was damn scared. So scared, I shit myself and didn't even feel it until the next day. Men puked from fear when they fell flat, avoiding the enemy fire, and got up to run again, run right into the bullets, and keep on running if they didn't get killed."

Chester took another deep swallow, whiskey overflowed his mouth, running out the corner. He continued oblivious to the sting of the drink. "The rain pelted at us like today, only it mixed with the smell of gunpowder, sweat, blood, shit, and puke. I reached the shelter of the first dune and hovered there catching my breath, trying to steady my shaking knees. With the rain came the continual shelling from the Germans on the cliffs above."

"I pulled out the canteen and swallowed a big draught. The whiskey energized every muscle, and I grabbed the grenades, climbed the hill without fear, and took out the gun overhead."

"Yes," Chester said, staring glassy-eyed through the bottle. "You've been my best friend through thick and thin. You saved my life that day. Without you, I would have lost the nerve to go on." He turned and glanced in Shaw's direction. Shaw sat there with his head bowed slightly, listening, just listening, a frown crossed his face. He shook his head. Shaw responded to the feelings more than the story.

"Shaw, we started with thirty men in our unit, only six survived. I watched their heads get blown to bits right next to me. My buddy James was running behind me. He had two children and one on the way. I glanced back long enough to see him crumple in the surf, blood circling his body. It could have been me, easily. I have always wondered why it wasn't? Why he got it, and I didn't. I was single. Even then, I was the party boy, wanting no responsibilities. Not even taking care of myself. All these years I've been running from responsibility, running as fast as I can. Why I wonder? I still don't know. Maybe I'm just yellow, scared of life, scared of death, and scared of everything in between. Just yellow inside and out. Facing old Gertrude isn't the worst thing I've ever experienced. Come on, Shaw. Let's go in."

Chester swung the bottle around his head. A sanguine smile emerged on his red bloated face. He released the bottle to fly into the air saying, "Goodbye, old friend."

The bottle flew high over head like Flyer I from Kitty Hawk until it reached its summit, and then out of gas, it began its descent, spiraling down, down, down, spinning like the house in the Wizard of Oz, until it landed with a splash right in the middle of the lake. The geese swam swiftly toward it, thinking it was food. But, it just bobbed there up and down. The circles grew larger on the surface of the water, fanning out to the edge of the lake from the dead soldier floating on the tide.

Chapter 14

Chester turned Shaw around and pushed him in the direction of the lights from the hospital. They started to sing.

First Chester, "The old songs. The old songs. The old songs." Then, Shaw joined in with his slurred guttural sounds, trying to utter the syllables. They didn't remember the words or the melodies, but they sang anyway with revelry of theatrics, a remnant from the past.

They continued until they reached the door. No one was about, and the two were unnoticed, except by the guard as they opened the door and entered. Chester tried to silence Shaw's noises as they sped along the hot, brightly-lit corridor to the elevators.

Weary and somewhat scared of the repercussions, Chester pressed the buttons. When the door opened, he put Shaw on and immediately stepped off the elevator to let Shaw go up alone, hoping Shaw had enough sense to get off at the right floor. Chester snuck around the hallways to the back elevator and got on. When Chester reached the sixth floor, he stepped off, intending to climb the steps. His lack of energy came as a shock to him because he had felt so bolstered so energized. He moved on silently to the stairway, stopping there momentarily to get his breath again. He tried to stifle a spasmodic cough. He climbed the stairs with difficulty, hoping no one discovered him.

The floor was quiet. "Shaw hasn't arrived yet," he mumbled.

Mr. Letters, a cancer patient laid in his bed wheezing, struggling to get his breath. Chester's bed was next to his.

"I bet you'd love a snort too," Chester said in the direction of Mr. Letter's thin, black body lying in the crumpled sheets, tobacco flakes dotted the white here and there. The milky tube feeding dripped into his stomach. Mr. Letters smiled weakly. The opening in his mouth was a large cavern eaten away by cancer. Yet, he chewed tobacco still, and spit occasionally in the cup on the bedside table.

"A snort for the road. Huh. Your last road, I suspect," Chester said while quickly tearing off his wet clothes and preparing for the shower.

"Cold night. Huh!" Letters wheezed with a weak attempt at a laugh.

"Sure is. I'll be here tonight now," Chester said under his breath, as he disappeared into the shower.

The elevator doors opened, and Shaw moved his chair out and

headed down the hall, militant, aggressively mouthing the words, "The old songs," in his guttural sounds, leaving a trail dripping behind him. He was stolid and stoic like Odin riding above the wheels of a litter carrier, majestic in his charade.

Stepping out of the shower, Chester felt disappointed at hearing the guttural sounds of Shaw still in revelry. He dressed quickly. Peeking out to see what was happening, he wanted to see which angry eyes stared out of the severe cold faces of the evening nurses. Years of rigid frowns creased Anne's cheeks permanently with ugly, deep wrinkles pulling at the edges of her mouth.

Anne, an obese white nurse who smiled with her mouth, but not her eyes, was in charge. A blood-red lipstick painted her mouth curving above the natural lip line to form a heart shaped configuration which made her lips appear lopsided.

When Shaw rolled his chair past the nurses' station, both Feran and Anne stared at him in disbelief. Simultaneously, their backs stiffened, breasts heaved, and glancing at each other Anne said, "I'm not cleaning him up, are you?"

"Lord. Lord. Where has he been? Get a whiff of that smell," Feran sighed, resting her bony elbows on the counter.

"It'll knock you over. Maybe if I put him in the shower, he'll calm down, and no one will discover his condition. If you know what I mean."

Anne smiled at Feran, raising her eyebrows with delight. Chester knew what that meant. It wasn't good. He waited for a couple more seconds and then returned to the ward following Shaw.

Shaw reached his ward in the back and pulled his soap and toiletries out of the bedside table. Luther, a black man tied to his chair, clapped his hands, winked his good eye, and grinned at Shaw.

"It was great guys. Just the way I thought it would be."

Even Henderson, a stroke patient, paralyzed on his left side, and unable to talk, banged on his tray table, applauding Shaw's escapade. Instantly, Shaw transcended reality and catapulted into the role of hero. Silently, he gazed around the room at each patient; his pajamas soaked, his hair dripping, his torso still blue and shivering from the cold. Heedless of his physical aberration, Shaw proudly held up the sign of the victorious V alternating with the thumbs up.

One by one the veterans, tied into their chairs, banged on their tray tables. Their grins exposed toothless gums. This was their victory too.

The men refused to be ignored no matter what the price.

"Sound off. Sound off. One two...three...four."

Anne's frame filled the doorway. She smiled cynically with her blood red lips.

"Hey. Hey!" she shouted. "Knock it off. Solitary confinement!" she threatened.

The racket became clamorous, resounding around the room, and out into the hall. The other patients gathered at the doorway, banging on their tray tables on their wheelchairs with whatever utensils they salvaged from the unit.

Standing behind Anne, Farren quietly declared, "You babies with tube feedings is gonna miss your dinner tonight if you don't hush up. Cause...I ain't gonna feed you. Now, we's gonna shower Shaw and put him to bed, like the bad boy he is."

They both ignored the ruckus and pushed the grinning Shaw into the shower room.

It wasn't long before the men heard screams of "You bitches. You Satan worshipers. Torturers. Turn it off! Damn it! Turn it off! Cold. Too cold! Hurts! Yeooooo!"

They had turned the shower on full force. The water shot out so hard that it stung and even hurt on the sensitive parts. Shaw returned to the room clean, dry, powdered, and submissive.

The two nurses laughed toward each other, "Nothing like a cold shower to take the starch out of a man."

"Don't it beat all," Feran laughed. "Anyone else want one?"

The men retreated again into themselves, leaving only the Parkinsonian-like twitches of the head or limb. The faces returned their withdrawn, grim, glassy stares of defeat. Occasionally, a tiny twinkle shot out from the still burning embers that lay at the heart of their eyes.

"All right, Bard. Let's get 'em back to bed." Feran motioned to a giant, black man standing over six feet. Bard, the other evening nurse, wore a spotless, white uniform, and his skin shone like copper from many lubricants. His muscles curved in waves, bulging out his shirt like a Notre Dame halfback. When he lifted someone, they moved smoothly and without a hitch.

"Don't Shaw remind you of that there KKK representative we saw picketing the other day at the courthouse?" Feran baited Bard with her poison grin.

"Shore does. I don't know why I didn't see it myself." He raised his eyebrows. After placing Shaw in the bed, Bard laid a punch to Shaw's groin area. The only noise was a stifled groan from Shaw as he whimpered in pain.

After several more blows, Bard retreated, saying smugly, "That ought to take care of him. Now, the blacks don't take kindly to the white robes. You oughta pray they stay out of our area."

Outside the ward, Williams, the black paraplegic from the day room and rehabilitation room, turned in his wheelchair and grabbed Chester's arm.

"Chester. Chester. That Bard fellah is giving it to Shaw. Got him good in the groin." Williams motioned for Chester to do something.

"Yeah," Chester winced. "I saw it. I can't do nothing. What can I do?"

"Maybe if you go in the others won't get it too. You know...for that banging and stuff," Williams pleaded.

"Feran said that none of them is gonna get their tube feeding dinner tonight just cause of the noise. Gawd. They ain't letting the men have any fun at all. What kind a place is this anyway? I ain't seen such cruelty! You white! Man! You gotta do something!"

Chester sat down heavily on the chair next to the door, running his hands through his hair. His elbows cut into his knees, and he curled into a fetal position. His hands fended off the pleas of Williams. Inside, he felt that old scared feeling of helplessness cover him like a thick fog obscuring every light and vision, a thick fog magnifying the sounds of the pleas of warning that came falling over and over again like a foghorn.

He got up and walked back to his room and told Letters what happened.

"Go find Henry. He's down reading the x-rays. He's working late tonight," Letters said, struggling with his wheezing. He spat a huge gop of tobacco into the styrofoam cup on the bedside table. The tobacco mixed with blood.

"All right! I'll go and get Henry!" Chester meekly promised. The whites of his eyes grew too big and his broad shoulders hunched back against the fear he was finally challenging. The old fear that recurred over and over in his mind. The same old fear he felt as a child when his abusive father was on a drinking binge and lit out at anyone within reach. He saw himself, a boy hunched under the covers in his bed, hoping and praying his father didn't drag him out of bed and beat him for something he had forgotten to do.

Then, his old recurring fears from fighting as he marched with Patton's army through France and into Germany came back. His body shook from his memories of trudging on from trench to trench, not knowing if the next bullet was for him. Even the overwhelming fear returned from the stench that he remembered from the death camps he liberated. After all these years, the ghosts from the past still haunted him.

Williams withdrew his wheelchair from Chester's room. He rapidly turned and sped down the hall to Shaw's ward.

Headed in the opposite direction, Chester sneaked down the stairway in pursuit of Henry.

The x-ray room appeared empty and dimly lit except for several lights illuminating films of chests and skulls. From the office, Chester heard laughter and Henry's voice.

* * *

"Too bad you missed the match. We beat them 6:0, 6:0. Yes, Carla was there too. She asked where you were. I lied and told her you were working overtime. Look, Man. I wish you'd tell her the truth and not keep her hanging on."

Henry sat with his feet propped up on the desk, brushing crumbs from a pizza off his rumpled yellow trousers. He pulled his loosened tie off and threw it over the other chair. His posture relaxed. His grin broadened in a teasing way.

"I'm not covering for you anymore. This is it. If you don't tell her you're seeing Susan. Then, I will. No. I don't want to lose you as a friend, but maybe I'd like to date her myself. I'll call you back later. Gotta go." Henry glanced up still grinning. "What's up, Chester?"

"You gotta come up to the seventh floor. Anne and Bard are at it again. They ain't gonna give anyone no tube feedings cause Shaw came in a little drunk and set all the others to banging on their tables, making a lot of noise."

"Where did Shaw get the stuff? Are you sure he's drunk?" A tentative frown replaced Henry's smile, and his worn, drained feelings of futility returned. He withdrew into a shell of protection to shield himself from knowing the haunting atrocities delivered to these men in their final hours.

How many times have I tried to help them? He grabbed the last bite of his pizza, his lab coat, and motioning toward the door with a large swoop of his arm, he grumbled, "Come on. Let's go."

His giant stride was long enough to take the stairs two by two. Chester followed slowly like a dog at his heels, wheezing louder with each step, quickly falling behind.

"Hey, Buddy. It's not gonna be that bad. Is it?" Henry stopped his climb long enough for Chester to catch up. He squeezed his arm reassuringly.

Chester glanced up at Henry with the eyes of a cowering hound. "Naw. I guess not. I've seen worse."

The wheels began to turn in Henry's head, a smile played on his lips, then erupted into a full grin.

"I thought you stopped drinking, Chester," Henry stated simply, sniffing his breath.

"I tried. I really tried hard. I thought one little snort a time or two shouldn't hurt."

"Ah. Huh. What about Shaw? Did you pass Shaw a little snort too?"

"Well. He begged me and begged me. He was such a pitiful sight, sir! I couldn't refuse him."

"Ah. Huh. So, you and he went out to the lake and had a couple of snorts?"

"Yes, sir!"

"I'm beginning to see the picture. Then, the men cheered Shaw when he returned."

"Uh huh."

"Okay. Don't worry. I won't report you, but make this the last time. I don't think the others can stand another night like this one. Do you?" Henry laughed.

"Na! I don't, sir," Chester replied, while he pretended to stare sheepishly at his feet and shift his weight from one foot to the other.

Opening the door to the seventh floor, the two parted company when Chester sought refuge in his room, and Henry proceeded down the hall to the nurses' station. The front desk was deserted. Henry flew down the hall to Shaw's ward and overheard some commotion behind one of the curtains. The other patients remained in bed huddling under their sheets. He stood behind the curtains silently for several seconds, witnessing a very unusual scene.

"You no-account, white bastard. Don't think that you can go

around cheering for someone acting out. I'll teach you. You get no dinner and a bonus from Bard here."

Henry heard groans and screams. He ripped back the curtain. His weight pushed Feran into the wall. He witnessed Bard push the patient's stiff legs high up in the air toward his head, causing excruciating pain. Before Bard realized Henry's presence, Henry heard the cracking from pressure on the brittle bones.

Hudson screamed.

At that moment, Feran dropped the patient's hand which appeared inflamed from the hyperextended pressure on the wrist.

Instantly, Henry knew why there had been so many fractures on this ward. "All right! This is it for you two!"

"What are you doing here? This ain't none of your business. So, just get yourself out and let us continue getting Mr. Hudson in bed." Feran pushed toward Henry with all her weight.

I saw it. I saw everything. Now, I think you two had better wait at the nurses' station."

"Help me, Jesus! Oh, help me, Jesus!" Hudson cried repeatedly.

"They ain't nothing wrong with him. Now, you go on. He's just mumbling about our moving him back to bed," Feran said softly. Her tone quite a contrast to the caustic, angry, and accusatory malice of the previously overheard conversation.

"Is that right, Hudson? Or is something wrong with this hip?" Henry shook his head and gestured toward Hudson's pelvic region.

Hudson cried out in agony when Henry tried to touch the place where he witnessed the tortured flesh becoming black, blue, and swollen.

Henry continued questioning Feran about Hudson's condition. "Did he have a good dinner tonight? Did he have a good appetite?" Henry examined Hudson's eyes and mouth closely as he off-handedly continued his questioning. Hudson's head twitched continually from some undiagnosed, nervous malady or palsy. His teeth were missing, and the gums displayed several ulcerated areas on the bony ridges. His gray skin clung stiffly to his bones.

"This looks like malnutrition," he glared at Feran. "Has he eaten anything today or any day lately?"

"I don't know what he ate today cause I wasn't here. His dinner was okay. He ate slow. With ten patients to feed if they eat slow..."

Her eyes left Henry's, glanced down to the floor, glared at Bard, and then back to the patient. "I guess they don't get as much."

Did you eat today, Hudson?" Henry asked.

"No." Hudson shook his head. Henry ignored the glares from Feran and the fuming signs of her heaving breasts.

"Where's his dinner?"

"They done took it."

"Well, get it back."

"I ain't gonna feed no more patients, and I ain't gonna order any more trays. If you wants to feed them that is up to you. It ain't my fault we don't have enough help, and I ain't gonna kill myself for these dead beats." Feran flashed a lethal sinister smile.

"Okay, Feran," Henry said. "Then either I will, or I will find someone to do it."

Henry glanced around the ward. All their eyes fixed on watching his reaction.

Feran stalked out in a huff with Bard following. Their attitude of stiff aggressiveness bent slightly against the resistance.

The eyes of the men flashed back and forth from Henry to Hudson. The only sign of life in the gray, drawn faces was the movement of their large bulging eyes. They were too weak to complain.

Henry saw it and couldn't do anything about it. But maybe now was the time to make his move. Now he had proof. It was such a delicate situation because many of these patients acquired fractures by just being moved or hitting the bedsides because of their severe osteoporosis. But tonight he witnessed it himself, first hand, with no mistake. Now the job remained to convince enough people the suspected abuse was even more widespread and force the administration to change the staff.

"So are you going to feed those patients or am I going to have to call Nursing Service?" Henry demanded as he faced the three nurses: Bard, Feran, and Anne, who all wore indignant expressions on their faces.

"Honey, I don't know what you're talking about. I personally fed half of those patients, and I know Ruby fed the others," Feran quipped.

"Yeah, they don't remember. That's all. They plainly don't remember. Can't even remember their own names most of the time. Huh, Feran," Anne said.

"Anne is right. They can't remember anything...so what's you worried about? We ain't gonna feed them again and that's that,"

Sapphire, an evening CNA said, and grabbed two charts off the counter next to Henry, jamming them into his leg as she retrieved them.

"Sorry, honey. I didn't mean to touch ya!" Sapphire said and laughed a little. The others grinned too broad, toothy grins and shook their heads in agreement, as she replaced the charts. "You need to be careful, brother."

Henry picked up the phone and pushed the buttons.

"Hey! This is Henry on seven. I need someone to come down and help these nurses feed some patients. They say they're too busy." He stood there quietly for several seconds waiting.

"Sorry, man. We're short on all the floors tonight. I sent the two extras to the unit. I'm sorry. I can't help you," said the evening supervisor, who was one of the only black male nurses in the administration.

"All right. Play your little games. Starting now, I'm gonna order tube feedings for each of the patients in that ward except Shaw. I will personally check them every day. Have all the equipment ready, when I get back from x-ray," Henry said and glared at each nurse sitting in the nurses' station.

Bard, Feran, and Anne were still smiling with sadistic, contemptuous grins. They watched Henry's every move, waiting for his next strategy.

Their attitudes became even more insolent because they knew he had no choice but to accept their terms of care. There was no one else to care for these patients. Even if they hired new nurses, it would be quite a while before they became oriented. Two weeks or more at least. They had him, and he knew it. But, he had one chance; if Mrs. Shepherd agreed to have these patients transferred to another floor where there was more supervision.

Even though it was 10:45 p.m., almost time for the change of shifts, Henry called Mrs. Shepherd. He called the Director of Nurses. *I'll get them all out of their comfortable beds and homes.* He intended to end this abuse once and for all.

Later that evening the white shadows of Hudson's hip x-ray dimly lit the room. The message was unchallengeable. The x-ray displayed a clean hip fracture at the head of the femur. The break meant only one thing - the pressure on the area had to be forced and with considerable impact to cause such a clean crack. His bones were heavy enough to resist any mild injury or accidental impact, but not brute force. That was it. Bard had used brute force on Hudson's legs and fractured his hip. The images from the x-ray proved it. Henry was sure this evidence was strong enough to hold up in court as proof. He knew he had a legitimate complaint to bring to the attention of the administration. He sat in the dark room, contemplating what to tell Mrs. Shepherd when she arrived.

Henry leaned back in his chair with his feet propped up on the desk. The phone rang.

"Hello," Henry answered, still contemplating the state of the hospital.

"Henry, is that you?" asked the caller.

"Hey, Jeff. What's up? Henry replied in his all-American, nonchalant voice, shaking the shroud of contemplation and the tragedy of inhumanity he witnessed.

"How about some tennis tomorrow afternoon? I have time on my schedule and can meet you at the club at around 3:00 p.m.

"Super. Sounds great! How about 2:00 p.m.?"

"Henry...er...some problems? I've been trying to get a hold of you all evening. Sounds like midnight oil to me. You need some excitement in your life. I've got just the blond as in BLOND."

"Yeah. I...a...well.... I'll talk to you about her tomorrow. How's that?"

"Sounds great."

"Okay. See ya' tomorrow."

Chapter 15

It was 11:55 p.m., that same evening when Mrs. Shepherd sat in her office, staring at the ceiling, shaking her head. The black fullness of her lower lip protruded into a disgruntled pout. Occasionally, the sight startled Henry as the soft pink flesh that lay just inside the wrinkled brown skin of her lip push itself out like an opening flower petal. Tonight, Mrs. Shepherd obsessed over the accusation, and in an expression of deep remorse, she frantically moved her snuff, hidden under her lower lip, from one side to the other. The bulge resembled a giant jawbreaker hiding just inside the brown flap of skin that made up her cheeks.

"I'll tell you again," Henry declared, "I saw Bard push Hudson's legs so hard the head of his femur broke. They've been having a field day, taking their anger out on these patients."

Henry stood up unable to sit any longer. "I'm losing my patience with you, Florence. What are you waiting for? Why don't you immediately call in some of the other nurses? I put feeding tubes in five of the patients in that ward, all except Shaw. They're not eating, and no one is feeding them. I'm going to fight this disaster. I'm changing it now."

Mrs. Shepherd watched Henry pace back and forth. Her tone pleaded for leniency. "Henry, maybe the patient just screamed while they moved him. Maybe that's all it was. You know how they do? The least little thing could set them off. I just can't imagine Bard and Feran would do anything like that deliberately. They've been here for five years now. They're reliable. I've never had any complaints. The night shift is here now, and Bard, Anne, and Feran will be going home soon."

She glanced at her watch. "It's 12:14 a.m.," she said and winced painfully from her arthritis. A heavy weariness surrounded her again Henry noticed.

"Look, Florence. Dead people don't talk. There're plenty of patients who suffered various kinds of fractures over the past five years. It's never occurred to us what was happening. I began to be suspicious in the last few months when we lost so many too soon. In February, we lost twenty-five patients. Don't you see? This is the first proof? What more do you want? Another death. More deaths resulting from fractures and starvation. This is not a hospice ward."

She peered thoughtfully at him, as if examining his mood, his anger, moving her snuff from one side of her mouth to the other, only slower this time as if trying to figure out what to do.

He never took his eyes off her. "You remind me of a baseball coach who tests the waters before deciding what to do. If that's true why did his hip fracture? Examine this x-ray and see for yourself. Look! You can ask any of those men in that room. They'll tell you. If you don't believe me then..."

Henry stopped abruptly and glared at her pomposity and ignorance. Suddenly, he hated her. He hated all the times she acted as if they didn't have any control over the situation. He hated her passivity. She was scared. He saw it in her face. She was the boss. Why was she so scared of those two-bit nurses? They didn't have any control over her. She acted the same way just the other day when she refused to get rid of Shirleen. It was the perfect chance. Shirleen was already tormenting the patients again. She was even more cantankerous than ever before. What's going on?

Henry stood up and towered over her defeated form, which had slumped down into the chair. She avoided his intense glare in passive defiance. She remained silent.

"No!" he screamed at her. "Now, I'm telling you! I'm going to the Director of the hospital and reporting this incident whether you do something about it or not. Get some good nurses in here. I'm sick of feeling helpless, watching these patients die because of negligence and even abuse. This is a felony offense!" he screamed. "I intend to see that they are charged. What about Melisa and Esther and a few others who are working as hard as they can? They can't fight all the others' abuse either. They are at risk of being charged too when they've done their best. It's the condition of the floor, the staffing, the supervision. You've got to do something!"

He felt his blood pressure rise, as blood flushed into his angry cheeks. He felt his face bulge out from his torturous feelings of agony.

"All right Henry. All right!" Mrs. Shepherd cowered, pushing her chair back into the corner, hitting the wall. "I'll put them on probation until we get this incident straightened out."

He knew what she was thinking...another inquest. Then, he remembered that Chester and Shaw had caused all the ruckus in the first place. The administration will attack the floor for that breach of conduct for lack of supervision. It all reverted to her. She was the one responsible. It didn't matter if they had a staffing deficit or not. She became the one at the heart of the problem.

Mrs. Shepherd displayed only resignation. Her great hulk of a body heaved a recalcitrant sigh. She stared up at him. Her face clouded with pain.

"I don't like this, Henry. I don't like this at all. What's gonna happen to everyone if they prove that this abuse is true? What's gonna happen to us?"

He stood there in silence looking at the boxes of holiday decorations under her desk. How many Christmases and Easters and other holidays had come and gone, and their remnants had been stored here in her room. He wondered how many other secrets had been aired here and kept hidden. He was sure there were many. He tried to hold in his triumphant smile. He had her now, and she knew it.

A victorious jolt of adrenalin charged through Henry's body. For once, he stood up to her. Stood up to Mrs. Shepherd, the queen. Why had it taken him so long? He had suspected these two nurses for a long time. Now, he was taking control. Proof...yes! It was this proof that convinced even him beyond a shadow of a doubt.

"We'll all lose our jobs," Mrs. Shepherd said in a small stricken voice. She smacked her lips indignantly and sat up straighter, "I had no way of knowing this sort of thing was happening. What about the nurses who aren't responsible? What about the nurses who care in their heart, and soul, and deliver good nursing practices? What about Melisa, Esther, and Karen? What about them and the others, Sally, Lyla, and Selysia who always do their best?"

"Is that what you're worried about? This has nothing to do with them...or me...or even you...for that matter. This has to do with feeding the patients regularly and not injuring the patients in any way. It has to do with these veterans who fought for you and me. It has to do with them. Giving them the good care that they deserve! Helping them in any way we can!"

"Oh, come on Henry. The patients are fed regularly. We all do the feeding. We do all their care."

"What about the ward on the east of the hall? I think you should see Hudson. He hasn't had a good meal for weeks. He's a perfect case of malnutrition." Henry leaned down into her tormented face saying, "If he dies from the hip operation tomorrow morning...they will be charged with murder."

Mrs. Shepherd jumped, startled at the mention of the word murder.

Stunned by the reality, she blindly groped around for the phone. It was a full minute before she responded.

"All right, Henry. I guess you've pointed out to me all the ramifications. I'll call the Director of Nurses immediately. We'll take care of the situation. Did you actually contact the surgeon? Do you think Hudson can tolerate an operation? I wonder if he is in too bad a condition physically. You know some of these men have been here for months, simply wasting away with old age. First, one system shuts down like the kidneys or immune system, and then another until they are in a coma and death soon follows. But, we don't want to take things into our own hands and hasten death. I think these nurses are just too tired and angry. You're absolutely right. We need about five new nurses. This is the last straw, isn't it?"

Henry smiled for the first time. He felt relieved. He patted her shoulder sympathetically, saying, "I knew that if you saw the entire picture you would take the right approach with this. I want you to take the steps to have all the nurses who are abusive dismissed...including Shirleen."

He had said it. He forced her to get rid of Shirleen. He knew there would have to be another inquest. He abhorred the process as much as she did.

Henry left Mrs. Shepherd's office feeling light headed, free for the first time in ages. Yes, he was free of the weight of stewing about the abuse and its consequences. It was difficult enough not being able to cure the patients, but seeing the angry nurses abuse them for kicks was beyond his endurance. How had he tolerated it for so long? Esther was the one who's caring stood out like a beckon in the dark against the others' anger and apathy. Yes, this all started with Esther, he concluded.

The dim lights in the long hall cast eerie shadows as he walked toward Hudson's ward. His footsteps echoed loudly. He felt masterful as he passed Mr. Kroger's room, Mr. Markowitz's, and the others. Yes, he thought, these patients were his family, the children he never had. He had certainly become their guardian.

Geraldine was working tonight. He heard her huffing and puffing as she pushed the medicine cart, with its squeaky wheels, down the hall from room to room. The noise sounded comforting to him. She had many faults and even a mean temper, but she wasn't an abuser. He knew that for a fact. Just too old for the job, and the job, too big for her.

He guessed they already finished bed check. At 11:00 p.m. every night, the nurses changed every soiled bed and replaced the attends, adult diapers. He knew they had to be dedicated to continue this care day after day. It was difficult to imagine two people changing sixty beds and attends every four hours, plus handle any other emergency and feed twenty-five of those patients on tube feedings. Yes, he knew the work was overwhelming, even impossible. But, they were expected to complete it without complaint. That's why they were getting paid. This was nursing.

Filled with relief that he didn't have to worry about poor nursing care anymore, the words, "They'll all be fired," resounded in his head.

He paused for over a minute outside of Hudson's curtains and listened to his soft moaning. Henry knew he hadn't given him enough pain medication. He didn't want to order him too much because of his age and malnutrition. Startled, Henry shook his head in disbelief seeing Shaw, sitting in his wheelchair, patting Hudson's hand for comfort. He debated whether or not to go in.

Henry didn't like the expression on Shaw's face and pushed past him to the head of Hudson's bed. Hudson's breaths moved, in short, quick drafts between his moans. Shaw shook his head as if to say Hudson wouldn't make it. Henry grabbed his wrist and felt for a pulse. It appeared weak and thready, barely palpable. Henry hastily moved the bell of his stethoscope up and down Hudson's chest. His skin palpated cold and clammy from the shock of his injury. Henry panicked for a second, thinking if Hudson died all his proof might die with him. Then remembered the x-rays. It was a touchy thing now. Should he order him a stimulant or let him go in peace?

He decided to try for it and ran for the cardiac cart. He returned to Hudson's bedside to find life barely hanging on to Hudson's tormented body. He gave him an ampule of Sodium Bicarbonate hoping to counteract the acidosis of shock. Then, he injected a cardiac shot of epinephrine.

Henry listened through the bell of his stethoscope as Hudson's heart rallied, finally, for a few seconds, but it soon stopped, again. He decided to dispense another bolus of Sodium Bicarbonate followed by the epinephrine. He didn't wait for the medication to work. Henry immediately started the resuscitation efforts. He speeded up the IV fluids. Shaw sat beside the bed, quietly mumbling to himself, as Henry tried to bring Hudson back.

"Look, Shaw, I did the best I could. I'm sorry. It doesn't look like he's going to make it."

Henry gave up. He stepped back from the bed. He heard the sounds of a prayer come from Shaw. Henry realized why Shaw treated the nurses with abuse now, cursing at them, and expecting them to clean him when he could clean himself. Henry smiled, thinking how manipulative Shaw had been. All that gobbledegook was just a show protecting Shaw from having to conform to the nurses' demands. That's how he got away with everything, Henry thought, and laughed.

Without warning, a tremendous sigh emanated from Hudson as he returned from the dead and took a deep breath. Henry didn't wait. He was on him in a second.

Henry produced his stethoscope and listened to the bounding leaps of Hudson's heart. He changed the IV and increased the drip rate to fast. He attributed Hudson's sudden return to life to the effects of the epinephrine that took longer than usual to finally kick in. But he doubted if Hudson would live through a surgery. After several minutes, Hudson's hand groped around on the sheets and squeezed tightly when it found Shaw's.

"Can you hear me, Hudson?" Henry asked softly, checking Hudson's pupils with his flashlight. A soft and caring expression crossed his face.

"Yeah.... And get that thing out of my eyes," he whispered with a raspy voice, pulling his head away from the light.

Henry and Shaw laughed at his sudden consciousness. Staring down at him, Henry marveled that Hudson's meager thread of life had returned with so much energy. He didn't wait for a second.

"Hudson, I have to ask you this. Can you give me a verbal account of what happened last night so I can tape record it? I'll get Mrs. Shepherd down here so she can hear it too."

"It seems so long ago. I guess you're talking about my hip. I don't have anything to lose now. I'm not afraid of 'em anymore either."

"Good. I was hoping you'd say that. I'm going to find Mrs. Shepherd, and we're gonna nail those two, Feran and Bard," Henry said, as he folded up his stethoscope and stuck it in his pocket.

"Thank you, Jesus. Thank you, Jesus!" Hudson called out and as if to summon the Almighty.

Henry returned down the hall thinking this was Providence. He didn't really believe in supernatural intervention, but if there ever was a time he needed it, it was now. He decided not transfer him to intensive care. The last thing Hudson wanted was to be kept alive indefinitely on a respirator.

Henry knocked at Mrs. Shepherd's door hoping she hadn't left. He glanced at his watch and realized it was 3:45 a.m. He was about to leave when the door opened, and Mrs. Shepherd stuck her head out saying, "What's the matter now?"

Her eyes appeared bloodshot and puffy from not enough sleep. Her red jersey skirt and white blouse were wrinkled and disheveled, obviously slept in.

Hesitating, Henry explained, "Hudson arrested, but he's all right for the present. I want you to come down and witness his testimony of what happened to him before he dies. I don't think he'll last the night. Do you have a tape recorder?"

"This has been a nightmare, hasn't it? It's one thing after another. Sure, I'll get it. Hold on." She disappeared behind the closed door.

Twinges of guilt tormented Henry after his previous outburst of anger at Mrs. Shepherd. She was obviously trying to do the best she knew how.

"All I have is the nurse's report recorder. It'll work for this one time. Come on. Let's go," she said with a sympathetic smile.

She ambled her large body down the hall. "Hey, baby. Wait a minute," she hollered after him.

Henry obsessed over saving this evidence on record. They almost lost Hudson and all the evidence for abuse. Why didn't I do it immediately? He chided himself now. If he lost the proof of Hudson's suffering, his accusations of abuse will fall on deaf ears.

Keeping the vigil at Hudson's bedside, Shaw still held onto Hudson's hand, affectionately. Henry noticed that Hudson's breaths heaved in quick short blasts now. "We need to get this over in a hurry," he said to himself.

Mrs. Shepherd followed him. When she saw Hudson, she stopped short. The pathetic image of this emaciated man in excruciating pain startled her. Henry motioned for her to come over closer to the bed. She moved past Shaw, excusing herself. Shaw nodded off to sleep occasionally, but still held tightly onto Hudson's hand.

Henry didn't waste a second. He placed the tape recorder on the bed next to Hudson's mouth, pushed the button, and said, "Mr. Hudson, Mrs. Shepherd and I, Henry Seward, wish to ask you some questions."

"Now, I know you have had a rough night and since you fractured your hip, you are in great pain." Henry held the mouthpiece up to Hudson's mouth.

"Yes, I'm in pain," Hudson mumbled.

"Hudson, just tell us in your own words what happened."

"I don't rightly know what happened first except Shaw came into the ward in a good mood and everyone was cheering. Then, the nurses came in yelling at us to shut up. The next thing I know, they is come'en at me. They said I deserved to starve and Bard that huge, black, male nurse, shoved my legs...so hard...." Hudson couldn't hold in his emotions any longer and cried uncontrollably. Finally, he restrained himself and continued, "I didn't feel the pain at first. I heard only the crack. Then, I couldn't move my leg. The pain is unbearable. Feran bent my hand until I thought it was gonna break. That's when Henry pushed around the curtain. Jesus! Jesus! What would've happened if Henry hadn't come?"

Henry patted Hudson on the shoulder after shutting off the tape recorder. "I think that's all we need. Isn't it, Mrs. Shepherd?"

Mrs. Shepherd's face seethed with anger, her eyes clouded with emotion.

"This is just a mean plot to get back at Feran and Bard for trying to keep order, isn't it? He never hurt you. He just put you back to bed. Bones break all the time this way. These men have brittle bones, and they just break for no reason at all. They call it osteoporosis. I've seen it a million times. Turn that thing on again."

She grabbed the tape recorder out of Henry's limp hand. He didn't comprehend what she said. Maybe she had lost it or something. He had to stop her somehow before she upset Hudson too much.

Puzzled and confused, he pulled the tape recorder back.

"Now wait a minute, Mrs. Shepherd. I don't know what your plans are, but I'm not letting you badger this patient anymore. I think he's been through enough."

"You're all angry at us because we is black. I know what you're doing. I'm going to tell the Director of Nursing and the Director of the Hospital too. Trying to falsely accuse us of abuse. I can see it now in the headlines...."

"If you counter me on this one, I'm gonna report you, Mrs. Shepherd. Do what you like, but...." He grabbed the tape out of the recorder and put it in his pocket.

"Look, Henry. No one is gonna believe you and him against me, Feran and Bard. They've been working here too long."

"You want a fight? I'll fight you. I'm gonna check every patient who ever acquired a fracture up here and investigate who worked when it happened or when it was reported. If you don't back me on this, I will implicate you too. You forget one thing. I caught them in the act. I actually saw Bard push his legs up high toward the wall and heard the bone crack!"

"Maybe he was just changing the chucks or something," Mrs. Shepherd pleaded. This'll ruin both of them...their entire careers."

"They knew what they were doing. Face it! They all know what they are doing. Trouble with this place is the staff accepts violence and abuse. There are no limits here. I take back what I said last night. This is our fault for not setting an example, even if the work is too hard."

"Ever since that new nurse, Esther, has been here, I've watched all of you load more and more work on her. Shirleen refuses to wash her patients, and Esther finishes doing it because she doesn't want to see them suffer. You let these other black nurses sit around while she is filling water pitchers. Melisa is running her little tail off, and here you are just sitting in your chair talking on the phone or going to some meeting. I don't see you pitching in while we're in a staffing crisis."

Henry felt exasperated. All he cared about now were the men. All these years. Yes, he had been here for nine years. He had put up with it all this time, trying to do the very best he could. For the men and women who reside here to die because they didn't have any place better. He tried to rally himself to stand his ground...not surrender. All he wanted to do was go off and play tennis as he always did. Somehow that made him feel better. If you can't change it, forget about it, he always told himself. But now, here was his chance to change everything. He refused to submit. No matter what it took.

Mrs. Shepherd, infuriated, stood up straight to her full height to continue her accusations. "The story's out. It's black against white all the way. Henry, you're splitting this floor right down the middle. I'm gonna remember this and when you need a favor...forget it...just forget it. You hear?"

Mrs. Shepherd left the room in a huff, and Henry stood there in silence for many minutes staring after her. He tried to get his breath from getting so angry. He heard murmurs of defense from the veterans directed toward him out of the dark.

"Go get em, Henry. You're right, Henry. Don't let her get you down, Henry."

He wanted to cry like Hudson was, whimpering like a kicked dog, but he grabbed another chair and sat down next to Shaw to wait through the night at Hudson's bedside while he died.

"Prepare to meet your maker, Hudson," Shaw said quietly and began his prayers.

This was new for Henry. This was the first time he sat through a night prayer vigil. He never expected Shaw to be the one praying.

Shaw said softly, "Our Father, who art in heaven. Hallowed be thy name. Thy kingdom come. Thy will be done on earth as it is in heaven...." Hudson followed him carefully and didn't miss a word, coughing now and then between syllables.

After several prayers they were all quiet, resting, and contemplating. Hudson's condition seemed to have stabilized for the present. His vital signs improved. His heart beat increased and sounded regular. Henry debated again whether or not to send Hudson to the small intensive care unit the hospital had on the ninth floor but declined the idea again. He felt calmer now, and more adamant about defending Hudson's case.

His watch said 5:00 a.m. He tried to doze off, but sleep eluded him. All the events of the past few days sped through his mind again. What happened to the floor anyway? The order of the floor had been upset. The nurses were angrier. The patients were rebellious too, ever since Jessie Taylor's death. It seemed to upset everyone's equilibrium, even his.

He leaned back in his chair and noticed Shaw was wide awake too, staring out into space. They watched the light glowing on the horizon through Hudson's window, a gray haze before sunrise. The window was ajar about an inch, and Henry heard the chatter of birds singing their prelude to morning.

"So, Shaw. I bet you can fill my ear about what's happening around here. Everyone thinks you are demented. Here, you are saying prayers. What a farce you are," Henry said, laughing softly to himself. That's what he loved so much about this job, expect the unexpected.

"I've fooled them, haven't I?" Shaw laughed too. "I even fooled you, Henry."

"All right, Shaw. What's your story? I've been wondering about you, anyway." Henry was enjoying this, but he didn't want to let on how much.

"Look at me, Henry. I had this stroke which made me paralyzed, and they gave me all these medicines to calm me down. I didn't take any of this lying down. The Veterans Administration stuck me in this hell hole of a hospital where they knock you if you step out of line for a second. I decided to act dumb and ignore all their rules and regulations. I can't stand to stay up here all the time and watch these patients die slowly day after day. I loathe it. So, I run down to the cafeteria and outside. The morning air is good for me." He let out a sumptuous laugh.

"I can't imagine how you have fooled everyone," Henry said. "Wait till they find out. We'll have a good laugh on 'em, won't we?" Henry said amazed at Shaw's charade. He adjusted his weight on the two legs of the chair that he was balancing.

"Look, Henry, I intend to keep my masquerade going as long as I can. So, I'd appreciate it if you wouldn't say a word to anyone. They'd give it to me as bad as they gave it to Hudson if they discovered it. I didn't tell you before, but Bard threw a punch to me last night too. For going out and getting high on the few snorts of whiskey Chester let me have. Just act like I don't know nothing. That I'm a bother and a jerk. That's what they all think except Esther. She is different. Quite different. Even intuitive somehow and knows I know what's happening." A thoughtful expression played across his face. His devilish twinkle returned.

"That explains part of your deception, but religious?" Henry shook his head, bewildered. "You don't strike me as the religious type."

"No, I don't. But I come by my name honestly. Patrick Shaw, Irish Catholic, at your service. I was an altar boy as a kid. I didn't pay too much attention to religion until World War II. I served in France as a cameraman, and my job was to take pictures at the front for the Associated Press. I was in trenches and bunkers with wounded men close to death. No priest or chaplain around, only me. So, I'd say a prayer with the men or for a dying one. Several times I even baptized a few just before battle. I never wore a cross or anything else to let them know. They always seemed to come to me for help. Still do. Selling real estate is a strange profession. People come to you from everywhere for you to help them relocate. Sometimes they are all broken and stirred up. Many times they need a prayer or two. That's just the way it is. One of these days, I'll be the one who needs the prayer."

Shaw coughed to clear his husky throat. Then, he sipped some of Hudson's water.

Shaw rubbed Hudson's unresponsive hand for several seconds and seemed to understand Hudson's labored breathing.

Forlorn, he glanced up at Henry and continued, "This is the second go round in the trenches for me. Pretty soon, it'll be my turn to travel up to the old Man upstairs. But until then, I'm the only person close to a priest, chaplain, or minister here at Thornhill. Oh, we have our token preacher. All he does is come by and place those pamphlets face up on the tray tables. They're especially useful in those rooms where the patient is comatose. He never prays or even speaks to the patient."

"You can say that again. They go into Mr. Markowitz's room, although they aren't supposed to and put that flyer on his table with the picture of Jesus on the front. Maybe all they think people need is to see Jesus's picture," Henry replied and laughed.

"Yeah!" Shaw laughed too and continued, "Then we have those well-wishers. Lay people come to visit and simply walk in and walk out of each room like a roaming ocean tide, never taking the time to stay and talk or even offer fresh water to drink. Half the time, they move in and out of the rooms so fast, the demented patient doesn't even know anyone has been here." Shaw shook his head in disgust and sighed with resignation. "I guess all this die'n, and misery scares 'em."

Henry chuckled. "You're right Shaw. It does scare them. It scares me too. When I started working here, every time someone died it reminded me again of my wife dying. That gut wrenching pain has never left me. Even now, even tonight, when Hudson arrested, it came back with full force. I imagine that grief will stay with me forever. I see her in the casket. I see her in the last stages of Hodgkin's disease in the hospital. I undergo the same passion, and misery I lived through that first time. I see it all over again. I must admit even though I experience it repeatedly, as the years pass, the wound is bearably sensitive. No longer agonizing."

Henry sighed and dropped his head in his hands, still wondering, after all these years, why such a terrible tragedy happened to him and the woman he loved so deeply.

The two men settled down, slumped in their chairs, overcome with exhaustion. The glow on the horizon had grown bright enough to cast light in the ward. Small bedside night lights glowed around the walls, and the room seemed to warm up. The slow even breaths of the men in the ward acted as a hypnotic, lulling Shaw and Henry into drowsiness followed quickly by sleep.

Henry was the first to awaken. It wasn't the familiar clamor of the breakfast trays being passed out, or the strong aromas of coffee and syrup, or the moans of common complaints from the patients, or the smell of aftershave and soap from those cleaning up for the morning that woke him. No, it wasn't any of those things. His eyes rested on Hudson whose breathing had ceased.

Esther stood opposite him on the other side of Hudson's bed. Henry watched her silently. Esther, unaware he had awakened, listened for Hudson's heartbeat. He saw her generous chest heave a sigh of resignation and the gentle compassionate expression in her eyes as she reached down and pulled the sheet up over Hudson's head. She closed her eyes and prayed, "Dear Lord, please receive your humble servant, Mr. Hudson, into your loving arms and keep his soul safe from suffering. In the name of Jesus, I pray, Amen."

It's official, he thought. Sudden panic rose in his gut. The urge to run out of the room and yell at the top of his lungs, "No. No. No! Not Hudson! Not another one!" overcame him. But, he reined himself in and opened his eyes full, absorbing Esther's gentle countenance as she turned and moved slowly and thoughtfully away.

"Thanks," he said in a low raspy voice. "We anticipated it and even waited for it, but in the end, we fell asleep."

Startled, she gazed at him, shaky from Hudson's death. She appeared timid and even afraid, like a startled deer, as if he were going to yell at her.

She returned several steps and whispered, nodding over at the still sleeping Mr. Shaw, "I'm sorry, I didn't mean to wake you. I heard all of you had a very tough night. Just rest. I'll call the morgue and anyone else who needs to know. Does he have any family?" she asked, glancing quickly away as if not wanting to hear that Hudson was alone too.

Henry couldn't bear to tell her that he didn't have anyone, so he just said, "I called them last night. They live out of town. They'll be making all the arrangements. Thanks for helping out."

He wanted to touch her and embrace her suddenly for his own reassurance, but he merely watched her walk out of the room and listened to her footsteps as they faded away down the hall.

Tomorrow, he remembered, was the annual Fayette, Fourth of July marathon. For the past two days, he missed his practice. His arms and legs moved stiffly from a night of dozing in the folding chair. After making his rounds this morning, he intended to go home and train. He wanted to run far and fast, hoping to lose some of the painful desperation he felt for these patients and himself.

Chapter 16

"They've fired Bard and Feran," Shirleen exclaimed, astounded, as she flopped into a chair in the nurses' lounge."

It was the Fourth of July, the day after Hudson's death. The staff had waited all morning for the news. Esther's bad mood deepened as Shirleen sat across from her. She had a difficult time, trying to find a babysitter on the Fourth of July Holiday and begged Mrs. Shepherd for the day off. She refused, saying they still had a staffing crisis.

Shirleen shot Esther a taunting smile saying, "It's all your fault." She pointed her finger directly at Esther. "And I intend to prove it's all your fault. You're the one who's gonna burn and not them. What do you think about that, Missy?" Shirleen twisted her mouth into an evil, cynical grin.

The others in the room, Lyla, Sally and Selysia merely listened, overwhelmed with fatigue.

Finally, Selysia, glancing up from her Chinese lunch of fried rice and egg rolls said, "Look, Shirleen, lay off Esther now. It's not her fault, and you know it. Just let it be."

Selysia kept eating and licking her fingers. Her full lips glowed with the Vermilion lip-gloss. Black curls framed her thick neck and cheeks, creating a resemblance to Miss America.

Esther felt pleasantly amazed that Selysia stood up to Shirleen for her. Esther always marveled at how she stayed clean, pressed, and spotless after a day of washing patients and making beds. Esther watched her wash five patients on the stretcher in the shower, one after another, without so much as receiving a chipped nail or misplaced curl. Today, Selysia wore a kelly green, silk blouse under her white, spotless lab coat, a gold chain circled her neck. She wasn't even an LPN, only a CNA, but she was a better nurse than anyone Esther had ever seen except maybe for Melisa.

"Don't tell me what to do, Miss Goody Goody...Miss Selysia. Just because your girls are in college don't mean you can tell me what to do."

Shirleen stood up glaring at Selysia and Esther. Her eyes glowed with fury and shot evil glances to each of the other nurses watching.

"I heard that, Shirleen," Lyla said, pushing out her full fish like lips. "But I heard Bard and Feran broke Hudson's hip, and now he's dead. Don't you think it's about time you realized you can't push everyone round? You're lucky they didn't fire you because of the way you treated Jessie Taylor. I've had enough of this," Lyla said as she left the room.

Esther knew they were scared. Esther felt sorry for Shirleen, always trying to be the tough guy, always trying to hurt someone. She was astounded at the others who were on her side for a change, even stood up for her.

"For your information, I have proof. I had a long talk with Mrs. Shepherd about you, Esther." Shirleen raised her eyebrows, a gleam of satisfaction emanated from her. All the faces in the room stared at her wide eyed, expectant, even excited at the thought of hearing new gossip. She smiled slowly, savoring every second of their anticipation until finally, she continued.

"You were the last one to see Chester and Shaw leave the floor yesterday. You let them go, knowing full well they intended to go out and get drunk. If they hadn't gone, Hudson would still be alive. It's all your fault!" Shirleen glanced around the room with delight. The staff shook their heads in affirmation.

Sally questioned Esther quietly, "Is that true? Why, ever since Jessie Taylor's death, no one's allowed to leave the floor without written permission. Didn't you know that?"

"Of course, I knew that. I didn't know Chester and Shaw were going to leave the hospital. I gave them their medications, and I went home. I never knew anything about it. Besides, they were at dinner that night. They didn't leave till after dinner, and I left at 3:30 p.m." Esther answered, angry and defensive.

Oh God, Esther prayed silently. Shirleen is trying to set me up.

Esther rose from her seat, shot Shirleen a seething look, and strode out of the room. Once outside, she felt defeat surround her as she returned to her medicine cart. The accusatory expressions on everyone's face as she left the room followed her. She yearned for the day when she could walk away, leave all this suffering behind.

What happened to the day? Esther wondered as she poured her medications. She pushed Shirleen's accusations out of her mind. Her thoughts flooded back to when Mark called last night. He said Paul was getting married to his childhood sweetheart. He asked if he could bring some legal papers over tonight for her to examine and sign. Their divorce will be final next Friday, July 11th.

"Who's Victoria?" she had asked Paul repeatedly, but he only retreated from her, paled, and gazed forlornly out the window. He never answered her. Then one day he said simply, "Just an old friend."

From the moment she heard the mention of Victoria's name, all the little questions she asked herself about Paul's behavior were answered. It was too late. She married a man who had always been in love with someone else. All his polite remarks and actions of affection lacked some igniting spark. She pushed the idea out of her mind, but it repeatedly came back to haunt her.

It wasn't until they moved back to South Carolina that all his strange behaviors finally made sense, developed into a pattern. She never forgot the day they all lunched in his mother's garden. Agnes invited several of his old and dear friends to celebrate their arrival home, their move to Fayette, South Carolina. Her mind raced on despite all the work she had to do. The cruel scene painfully invaded her thoughts.

He waxed his Corvette, shined his shoes, and chose carefully his most expensive linen shorts and matching monogrammed shirt. There was an invigorating fire in his eyes that she hadn't seen before, even a mysterious longing. He pranced around like a young stallion. He picked her ugliest dress for her to wear, the most inappropriate. She puzzled over his remote attitude and tried to hide her hurt feelings.

Esther glanced at her watch, as her preoccupation with Paul cost her precious minutes. She had difficulty shaking her oppressive, melancholy feelings. She tried to fill Mr. Kroger's cup with pills, knowing he had to go for his nitrogen mustard treatment early today. She shuddered at the idea they still used this archaic treatment for cancer. She pushed that potential conflict out of her mind for the present.

Once in his room, Esther poured out Mr. Kroger's water and handed him his medication. His attention remained fixed on the television.

"Why don't you sit down here and join me, Esther?" he asked. "I'm watching the movie, Dr. Zhivago. I love the snow scenes." He patted the chair next to him, motioning for her to sit down.

The invitation made her smile, even bestowed on her a sense of comfort that he wanted her company. She yearned for any kind of respite. She sat down for a minute in the cushioned straight back chair.

Mr. Kroger smiled with pleasure and gazed longingly at the screen saying, "They're going to make love any minute now."

Both Esther and Mr. Kroger peered into each other's eyes and laughed sheepishly. Then, Mr. Kroger asked, "Do you believe in God, Esther?"

"Yes, you know I do."

"Then, so do I," Mr. Kroger answered, sitting back into his chair with delight and peeked a look over at her several times, pleased with her company.

Unable to fix her attention on the movie, Esther's mind wandered back to the day in the garden when she knew her marriage was over.

It all began when they entered Paul's mother's house. Agnes whispered something into Paul's ear and caused his face to flush red and produce a nervous smile. From that moment he completely ignored her.

Esther remembered the Jasmine was in bloom, and the green vines, covered with the tiny white fragrant, star-like flowers, climbed lattices along the walls surrounding the garden. The scent caught her off guard, and she reveled in the miraculous odor until she realized they weren't alone. Paul had already become mesmerized by the figure of a striking blond lady who stood in one corner of the garden, basking in the sunlight. Her long hair flowed down her back in soft, waving curls. Her round face shined like a pearly, iridescent moon with her blue eyes as two precious jewels. She wore a beige Belgian linen, cut-leaf dress, with embroidered flowers detailed across the bodice, and along the hem. Tiny linen slippers had been died neutral to match the dress, and Esther marveled that her feet were so small. Victoria smiled with a shy, yearning hesitation, and timidly reached out her equally tiny, delicate hand to greet Paul.

Esther watched as Paul and Victoria silently groped each other with their eyes, becoming spellbound. Their magnetism was out of her control. Their bodies remained separated only by the strict code of ethics they learned from birth, southern propriety.

Finally, after Esther walked over, grabbed Paul's arm, and demanded as politely as possible to be introduced, Paul said, "Esther, this is my old friend…Victoria!"

Victoria glanced up and sweetly took Esther's outstretched hand.

Esther stuttered a meek, "It's nice to meet you," before Paul said gruffly, "Don't you have to check on the boys for a minute?"

She watched helplessly as Victoria's charm dragged Paul willingly out to sea with a great surging tide and undertow. Where had Victoria been all these years?

Now, Paul wanted a divorce to marry Victoria.

The movie droned on, and Dr. Zhivago's, Laura, was whisked away in the colonel's sleigh never to see Zhivago again. Tears filled Esther's eyes. She ran from the room, patting Mr. Kroger's head on the way out. She had to stop thinking about Paul and Victoria. She had too much work to do.

She moved deep in thought from one patient to the next, as if she were drugged, barely hearing their complaints or requests.

Later that evening, after she put her boys to bed, Mark arrived just as he promised. She brought him a hot cup of coffee and set it on the table in front of the sofa as he opened his leather briefcase.

"I'm sad that I have to be the one to bring these papers to you. Anyone but you," he said, sighing deeply as if feeling her hurt.

"What happened Mark? What did I do wrong? I can't imagine my nursing license probation was the cause of all this,'' Esther pleaded.

"I wish I could spare you all this."

He met her eyes finally, and spoke softly, "Southerners are clannish people. They take pride in their names and heritage. People think this isn't true anymore, but they are mistaken. Sadly mistaken. Victoria and Paul were betrothed to each other in marriage before they were born."

Esther dropped her cup. It spilled before she hastily picked it up. Mark grabbed a napkin and immediately blotted the accident.

"Their mothers are best friends. They promised each other their children would marry. From infancy, the two spent almost as much time together as a brother and sister. Call it sorcery or magic spells - whatever it took - Paul and Victoria never had their own choice. The families raised them as the little prince and princess.

Mark surveyed Esther's reaction as she cringed in horror.

Her marriage had been a mockery from the first second, Esther thought.

"Paul was the one who came to Baltimore and courted me," Esther said defensively. "I met him while he attended Hopkins University. Now you're saying he didn't have a choice. He married me against his mother's wishes?"

"Yes. He married you because Victoria had already married someone else. She married the son of a Texas oil magnate. The marriage ended disastrously. The man, whom she married out of spite to her own mother, drank heavily and abused her. So she divorced him and returned here to Fayette last year. My mother had it all planned when she insisted you and Paul move back here. My wonderful mother orchestrated the entire setup. Paul has always loved Victoria, and when she married, he discovered you on the rebound. You had no way of predicting this. You were the innocent bystander. They have no mercy. If you don't mind me using the old cliche', you were a 'babe in the woods' when he met you." Mark produced the documents and pointed to the blank lines at the bottom of the page.

"But what about our two sons? What about Matt and Eric? Didn't he ever love me or us?" Esther cried in desperation.

"I'm sure he does in his own way. He grew up thinking Victoria was to be his queen. His entire inheritance is legally tied up to the productive consummation of that match. All my father's inheritance was left in a trust to Victoria and my father's blood grandchildren, meaning Paul's and Victoria's children," Mark revealed in a screeching inhuman voice. "She is to receive a sizable monthly income, and the residual will be dispersed when the grandchildren if any, turn twenty-one."

Esther jumped up and ran to the French doors on the other side of the kitchen. She banged her head against the glass, sobbing. What about her children? Mark said her sons were considered illegitimate according to the will. Paul's father was still alive when Paul married her. They must have disowned Paul immediately, but he never said anything about this to her. He held it all in. He never revealed to her that his family disapproved.

Mark continued, "He left his sons out too, Esther. Both Paul and me. How do you think we feel about it? Twelve million isn't anything to sneeze about. We're only hoping mother will divide the balance of her estate between each of us." Mark held his head in his hands, shaking it slowly from one side to the other as if he still had difficulty accepting the contents of the bequest.

Esther's mind raced on. Out of no fault of her own, her children became disowned, and her marriage a hoax. She never saw this coming.

She turned and screamed at the cowering, somber Mark. The man who had known all along.

"And you Mark. What about you? Where do you fit in this maze of deception?" She asked gruffly. Why had God let this happen to her? She always prayed and believed. Now, Paul cast her away like a used overcoat, without a second thought. He rejected his own precious children as if they had never been born. "Yes, Mark! Where do you fit into the family?" she asked again.

"Esther, I know exactly how you feel," he said groping for words and staring forlornly up at her. "I was always the second child. The second born has to pay homage to the first. I never counted. I was raised by Ruby, the black maid. My mother loved Paul. She never betrothed me to anyone. I suppose they thought I would pick someone from a good family, maybe to replace my own lost fortune."

"Oh, this is so medieval and so barbaric. I can't imagine anyone rejecting their own child," Esther said fuming, still crying softly to herself.

Exhausted, Esther slumped down on the couch next to Mark. Now, all the little lies made sense. All the devious methods and conniving his mother used to manipulate them made perfect sense to her. She felt so dumb to have missed it. All the time, she thought they moved to Fayette because Paul lost his position in his prestigious law firm. What a charade. He used her probation as an excuse. She knew Victoria would never work either. Now, what should she do?

"Look, Esther, if you sign these papers, it'll make it easier on all of us," Mark said, retreating uncomfortably from her anger.

She glanced over at Mark, seeing him in a new light. "Oh, you poor thing. Why do you stay? Why do you continue to take their rejection day after day? You have a profession. You can leave and venture out on your own. Why do you stay?"

"I don't know. Maybe one of these days mother will have a change of heart. Maybe she will see I'm the one who loves her the most and not Paul." He glanced at Esther with a childlike innocence and with a strange, vulnerable hopefulness.

"What?" Esther said. She didn't believe her ears. He merely waited around for crumbs from Agnes's table. This realization made her more furious. The good are the ones who are hurt. Well, maybe Victoria deserved Paul. At that moment, Esther decided she wasn't waiting around for anyone ever again. It wasn't worth it. She had to find her own niche in life and surrender Paul forever, give up on lost causes altogether.

She glared up at Mark. "This is gonna cost Paul," she said emphatically. "He must be ready to pay anything for his freedom. I'll sign, but first I want five hundred dollars a month child support for each child and a trust fund for college expenses for each child. I also want a thousand dollars a month alimony...no, make that three thousand...to help supplement my income. He's a prominent lawyer. He can afford it. Especially with Victoria's trust. Without that, there is no deal." She got up and walked back to the kitchen, grabbed the half empty bottle of wine in the refrigerator door, and poured herself a giant tumbler full.

Mark rose, came over to her, and drained the last of the Merlot into a small glass. "Let's drink to blood," he said with resignation. "Our blood. They're feasting on our blood. Aren't they?"

"Yes. They've conquered us. How can they be so cruel?'

Mark gazed down into her red tormented eyes.

"I don't know," he answered. "I guess they grow up walking over people. They never learn anything different. They never suffer the consequences." He held Esther's hand affectionately.

"I need a break. Maybe I can take you and the boys to a cabin in the mountains this weekend. After the papers are signed on Friday. There's a wonderful spot in the Smokey Mountains I know you'll love. I promise it'll be strictly friendship." He laughed to himself. "Yes, friendship from your ex-brother-in-law."

"I don't know, Mark. All this has hit me pretty hard. Not only the divorce but everything else. This Victoria business and all." Esther slumped into the chair, feeling haggard, and spent. She wanted to go to bed and forget it all.

"I think this will be just the diversion you need to help you recover. Look, I know it may take years to forget Paul, but for now, I'm looking for small breaks to help you survive the tough spots." He peered affectionately into her eyes.

"All right, Mark. You win. I think I'd be dumb to pass up a chance like this. We'll be packed and ready. The boys really need a new amusement too."

She raised her glass of wine and toasted, gazing deep into his eyes. "To Friday. The beginning of the rest of my life!"

Chapter 17

Mr. Letters rose up on his elbow and spat into the Styrofoam cup sitting on his tray table. Esther moved about the room in a fog, deep in thought about her impending divorce. Was this siege of bad luck ever going to end? She remembered the tiny lump she had palpated in her left breast that morning.

Esther mashed his cup of pills to add to the tube feeding. She marveled at the finesse Mr. Letters used to retain a wad of tobacco in the only intact pocket left on his cheek. Cancer had eaten away the other side of his face. A delicate pink graft of skin covered the huge, hideous hole. His chest rattled with each breath, a slow rhythmic gurgling.

"Have you seen your family lately?" Esther inquired. She wondered what led him to this gruesome point in his life, as she filled the tube feeding.

"Naw. I haven't," he gasped.

"Should I call someone now?"

"They live up north somewhere," his voice trailed off. "Too far to come," he whispered, then wheezed with thick congestion. His cough grew into an enormous spasm. Esther suctioned him. He lay in his bed, silent, and with dignity, bore the pain.

It was almost time for the 2:00 p.m. medications, and Esther hadn't finished Mr. Letters' morning care. Catching the sight of Henry turning the corner to the elevators, she raced to grab him for advice about Mr. Letters' wheezing.

"Henry, wait a second," she called after him.

Aggravated, he turned to see who had interrupted his escape. "Okay," he grumbled, begrudging her a half smile.

"It's about Mr. Letters. He's so congested, I wondered if you wanted to order oxygen or something. I've been suctioning him all morning to keep him comfortable. The intern, Solomon, ordered a High, Hot, and Heavy enema for his constipation, but I think it's too much for him.

"It figures. Yes, give him oxygen. I'll order it. Give him his morphine and a Fleets enema. All he needs is morphine now." He glanced down at her sternly, not really listening to her words, only guided by some past experience. "GIVE HIM HIS PAIN MEDICATION," he shouted.

"All right. All right," Esther replied. "What about the enema? Can you give me a directive?"

"I told you all he needs is a Fleets. Look, he's not going to last much longer. Just keep him comfortable, as comfortable as you can." Henry took in a deep breath as if trying to calm himself. He gazed at her more thoughtfully now. He touched her shoulder lightly. "You're doing a good job. Continue the good work."

He brushed her cheek softly with his finger. He turned abruptly just as the elevator arrived, leaving Esther standing there groping for words.

Everywhere she turned death lurked in the corners. How do the others do it? Maybe that's the reason they just seem to ignore all the agony because it's inevitable.

"But I can't," she said to herself. "I just can't submit like the others." At that moment she vowed to find some way to make dealing with the dying easier and more tolerable.

She leaned against the wall for support and remembered the lump she felt in her own breast. In the morning confusion she had forgotten about it. It felt like a little spot of hard tissue protruding from the rest. She must stay calm about it and not let herself become carried away. The sight of Mr. Letters always haunted her. His throat was one large lump of cancer spreading. She had marked the hard cancerous tissue from the soft normal skin. The invisible plague marched on one cell at a time, and she watched it move a little more each day.

Fear gripped her. She begged God for relief as she walked reluctantly back toward Mr. Letters' room.

She secretly sought comfort at the window in the far corner of the darkened room.

Rain pounded the earth outside. Gray clouds hung over the horizon. The July storm pelted the parking lot below, washing off the dust. She felt safe here and allowed her tears to mirror the overdue drops of rain on the dirty window glass. After several minutes, she heard a voice.

"It used to get to me like that too. But now, I just accept it. I just accept it all and try to hang on long enough for just one more day," Mr. Letters said.

"What for? What for Mr. Letters?" she asked.

"No matter what I do, I can't let go," he wheezed and coughed, but continued. "No matter how bad it gets, I can't abandon that rope. So I just hang on and pray that I have another day."

"What difference does it make if you just let go? The end is coming anyway. Like that man who fell down the stairs, Jessie Taylor. Let go as he did. Before all the suffering and pain attacks you."

"Once you let go honey…that's all there is. Then, nothing is left. Even in experiencing the pain you know you're alive, and that's the way I like it. Alive. You'll never see me at the bottom of those stairs," he said quietly and spat another gop of tobacco into the cup.

She held his bony, thin black body upright, comforting it through a coughing spasm. She gently laid him back onto the pillow. She suctioned him again.

"I'm going to wait awhile to fix you up. After you have an enema, I'll put you in the whirlpool tub for a good soak. We'll get you feeling better."

"That sounds just fine," he said weakly.

"Chester will be amazed at how good you look."

"Yeah. We'll surprise Chester," he said quietly, playing along with the game, although they both knew it was just a game.

She returned with the Morphine and injected it into his buttocks. Neither one flinched. She felt grateful to be able to give him something for comfort. He was thankful she brought it.

Passing through the nurses' station, Esther saw Mrs. Shepherd talking with Lyla and Karen.

"I ain't never gonna feed that man again. If you want him fed, you go in there yourself. Look at my uniform. He spit a whole mouthful out at me and that does it," Lyla fumed, her tiny yellow baseball cap bounced on top of her hair with each gesture.

Mrs. Shepherd sat there smiling at the two nurses and answered, "I hear you, and I hear him too."

The patient yelled at the top of his lungs, "Get me out of this place. I don't belong here. Send me home. Come back and feed me…."

"Well, you'll have to fire me cause I ain't gonna feed that bastard," Lyla said, as she stormed into the locker room.

"He's just demented and don't know what he's saying. He just doesn't know what he's doing," Mrs. Shepherd said, calling after her in a pleading voice.

"That man isn't demented, Mrs. Shepherd," Esther said. "Listen to him. He sounds pretty clear to me."

"Hush up," she whispered, shooting a dirty glare at Esther.

Esther watched her eyes follow the other nurses into the locker room. Mrs. Shepherd glanced back at Esther, silently shaking her head no in frustration.

In seconds, the indignant man wheeled himself out of his room with his one crippled hand and over to the nurses' station shouting, "Look at me. I'm a man. I'm a human being."

His penis hung out of his pajama pants opening, gray and limp. The nurses didn't see it at first, but then it caught their attention. Esther saw in him all the male humanity calling out for attention. His last vain attempt at masculinity before death. A pert, elderly woman with decaying features passed by the nurses' station, eyed him with horror, then escaped to the elevators.

"I'm a man," he hollered again. "I'm a man. Don't you see! I'm not crazy."

Mrs. Shepherd answered, "Yes, we know you are." She hastened over to him and covered his lap with a towel. She turned his chair around and pushed him into his room. Then, Esther heard her tell him calmly, "Come on, now. You need to finish your lunch."

Esther sighed in sympathy and entered the locker room to retrieve her purse. She was going downstairs for an afternoon break.

Lyla, Shirleen, and Karen were in the nurses' lounge when she entered. They stopped talking and watched her every move. Withdrawing her purse and checking for her money, Esther discovered the ten dollars she put there that morning was gone.

Frantically, she painstakingly removed everything in her purse to check the bottom and the other pockets, but they were empty. She saw smiles on the faces of each of the girls, except Karen. She sank inside. Now, what was she going to do? This was all the money she had until the end of the week.

She fumed silently. I'm quitting, and I don't care what happens. Unwilling to let on to the others, she went into the bathroom and locked the door. Once there, her sobs erupted, and for a long time, she cried uncontrollably. She ignored the rattling of the doorknob by the others wanting entrance. How can God let all this happen to these men, she wondered. Eventually, she dried her eyes and left the shelter of the bathroom. The others were in the nurses' station when she emerged. Their huge brown eyes followed her as she approached Mrs. Shepherd who sat at the far end of the station talking to Jewels.

"Mrs. Shepherd," she said softly, trying to keep from being

overheard, "Someone has taken ten dollars out of my purse."

Mrs. Shepherd's eyes bulged, and she peered into space for several seconds. Her posture bent in defeat, as she said, "Honey. Didn't I tell you not to keep any money in the locker? Nothing is safe here." The worried look grew into a mask across her face. "Are you all right?"

"Can you lend me some money for a snack for break until tomorrow?" Esther said flatly. Now, she knew what defeat felt like. They had beaten her finally, cleverly out maneuvered her, and kicked her when she was down.

"Sure. Here's five dollars. Pay me back when you can," Mrs. Shepherd said.

"Thanks. Did you know Shirleen shared my locker with me today? Er...she insisted...even forced me this morning. I tried to talk to you about it, but you were too busy with Henry. In a conference or something."

"No, I didn't know that. I see what you are saying. Try to hang in there a little longer, and maybe we can come to the bottom of this situation."

Later that afternoon, Esther bathed Letters in the whirlpool tub and dressed him in new pajamas. Chester returned from his search for his daughter, stretched out on his bed, and napped as soundly as a cat curled up on a rug.

"Look at him, Letters. Doesn't he remind you of an angelic child?" She laughed at Chester as she helped Mr. Letters transfer from his chair to his bed.

Mr. Letters smiled with a few wheezes. He shook his head in agreement.

Chester's one eye slowly opened and scanned the two. A small smile emerged across his spidery-flushed face. The whites of his eyes were bloodshot and heralded the past day's excursion of over indulgence of alcohol. She and Letters laughed at Chester's meek sheepish smile. The smell of alcohol permeated the air and filled the room.

"Did you have any luck, Chester?" Mr. Letters inquired, his coughing returned, and Esther suctioned him a little more.

"No, I didn't," Chester sighed. "I called all the numbers the social worker collected. It has been a few years since I talked to my old lady. Oh, she's probably married to someone by now or moved away. Who knows where my daughter is?"

He laid back on the bed, puzzling the question with his arms bent in above his head resembling wings.

Chester raised up slightly, enough to stare at them straight, saying sadly, "You can't go home again, once you leave. Well, everything and everyone changes. They all grow old like me, only I didn't see it cause I ain't around. Oh, you think they're the same and sometimes you even expect them to be the same, but they ain't. They'll never be the way you see them. At least, that's what I think. So I gave up and had a few snorts at the Bunker. What difference does it make if I found her after all these years? She won't want to see a loser like me."

"Come on. Don't talk like that. You aren't a loser. Just down on your luck with this Tuberculosis," Esther said. She and Letters laughed a little to themselves. Esther knew it was like him to go out and get drunk. He didn't need an excuse.

Letters rose up on his bony elbow saying, "It all started when I left to join the Navy. I never turned my head back to look. Couldn't."

Letters let his voice drop and whispered on in small, distinct words, "My mother died when I was twelve, and after that, I lived with kin. No, I never wanted to look back," Letters wheezed. "Chester, why don't you ask the social worker if she can help you find your daughter? She might be able to. They have their ways." Letters coughed spasmodically. Then, he spit his phlegm into the cup again.

Esther wretched a little when she noticed the bright red blood he coughed up out of his lungs. She discreetly turned away from him and felt for the little lump in her breast. She felt scared. Really scared.

"Sorry Ma'am," Letters whispered, he noticed the expression on her face.

"Do you believe in God?" she asked.

"I haven't thought about it in all these years," he smiled with one side of his mouth. "You worried about my soul, girl? I know I don't have much longer. My mother was always worried about my soul. Maybe that's why I haven't thought about it. My mother worried about my salvation, dragged me to church. My wife too. Oh, I used to drink just like Chester here. It irritated my wife. You know, I think after she died, I just plum lost the taste for it. It just didn't taste the same," he took some time to get his breath.

His thickened wheezing frightened Esther, and she suctioned him again, pulling out pinkish red, bubbly mucus into the bottle on the wall.

He said, "I guess I have faith in God, that is…." He seemed

anxious to talk despite his congestion. "My mother did. She always talked about angels and those cherubim and Jesus. She sang in the choir. Sang spirituals around the house. Why, I didn't have to go to church. I had it right there in my own house every day. No, I'm not scared at all. I'm amazed too, 'cause I thought I would be. But now, I think it'll be just fine."

He laid his head back on the fresh white pillow and dozed off quickly, only his chest continued to gurgle and rattle with each expiration. He hadn't even taken time to put his feet under the covers.

Esther gathered his blue and white seersucker robe and paper slippers and opened the beige metal locker at the foot of the bed. To her amazement, she discovered two-fifths of whiskey hidden in two brown paper bags. She knew they belonged to Chester. She glared angrily at him.

His eyes focused on her hard, followed every movement she made.

"The hospital rules forbid you to bring alcohol into this institution," Esther said, glaring at Chester long and stern. Letters slept peacefully now. The scene aroused a certain sympathy, a certain feeling of compassion for their situation. Then, she remembered Hudson and Chester's escapade with Shaw.

Without a word, she quickly hung up the robe, dropped the slippers into the bottom of the locker, and retrieved the whiskey. She retreated in her mind and thought what harm would it do if she let him get away with it again? They were dying anyway. They were all dying a little each day. She smiled. The alcohol didn't cause Hudson's death, Bard and Feran caused that.

"I think Letters is right, Chester," she said. "You should ask the social worker again to search for your daughter. It can't do any harm. Don't forget. You're the only father she has ever had or will ever have. Why don't you try again?"

She dropped the bags of alcohol on his bed and said, "Please dispose of this discreetly." Smiling, Esther left the room not waiting for an answer.

Out in the hall, Sylvester Street hung on the telephone, with his white cane propped precariously on the wall. He puffed on a nearly burnt out cigarette. Esther paused long enough to take the cigarette out of his hand and mash what was left in the ashtray.

"I can come home now Mable, any time you want. The doctor says all you have to do is come here to get me. I promise I'll be good. I won't cause you a moment of worry. Just ask my doctor or social worker. Doctor! Doctor! Social Worker!" he yelled. "They'll be here soon. Wait, here's the nurse. She'll tell you," he said, as he grabbed Esther's arm before she got away.

"Hello, Mrs. Street. I'm the nurse. Yes, Sylvester is doing better. I don't think he understands that you can't take him home anymore. I'll try to explain that to him."

"Okay, here you go Sylvester. She wants to talk to you again," Esther said, patting him on the back. He swayed back and forth from one foot to the other expectantly. His teeth ground together behind a big smile with his lips puckered out.

Esther continued on down the hall toward the nurses' station. It was almost time for her to go home.

"Hey, did you give that patient the High, Hot, and Heavy I ordered?" Solomon, the new intern asked when Esther passed him on her way to the nurses' lounge.

"Er. No. I didn't."

"Ah...why didn't you? I ordered it!" he laughed cynically.

"Because I got a directive from Henry for a Fleets instead. That worked just fine. The HHH enema was too much for him."

"I certainly hope Henry wrote an order or you will be in trouble girl," Mrs. Shepherd broke in. She laughed too.

"Well, that big enema probably would have killed Mr. Letters. So, I used my judgment," Esther said, hoping that Henry had remembered to come back and order it. This is all they need to get me fired, she thought. Both Mrs. Shepherd and Solomon glared irritably at her as if they enjoyed giving her a little trouble. She was intimidated, but she tried not to show it. She briskly walked over to the chart rack and pulled Mr. Letters' file.

Sure enough, the large scrawled signature of Henry Seward, written in fat, curved, black letters, undeniably followed the order: O2 and Fleets enema PRN. Esther handed the chart to Mrs. Shepherd and strutted into the locker room. She felt stronger, more confident, and even more energetic.

Yes, she had gained strength. Was it from Mr. Letters or the fact that Henry, for once, followed up? She didn't know. But she knew she was able to depend on his support.

All the way home, Esther wondered if Mark had talked to Paul and if they settled on some amount of child support and alimony. They had a time limit. Thank goodness something was on her side. Paul wanted to marry Victoria immediately, so maybe he'd agree to her terms without a fight.

She vowed not to give in to anything less for her children or herself. She had to be strong now for them. This was their only chance for a higher standard of living. She pushed the vision of the lump out of her mind and concentrated on something positive. She wanted to take the boys out to dinner on payday at the end of the week. Yes, that's what she wanted to do. Then, she remembered Mark said he wanted to take them to the mountains.

Chapter 18

The next Monday morning, Esther glanced up from her deep thoughts to see Karen step out of the crowd, waiting for the elevator, and move closer to her.

"Did something good happen? I hope so!" Karen asked.

"No," Esther answered. "But, I had a wonderful weekend. I mean the boys and I." Esther smiled, remembering the experience. "Mark, Paul's brother, took us to the mountains over the weekend. I guess to cheer us up. Paul and I signed the divorce papers on Friday. My divorce is final now." Esther turned away from Karen's gaze, trying to avoid showing the pain she felt.

"Mark borrowed a friend's cabin, and the boys loved it. So did I. We hiked two miles to a beautiful waterfall on Sunday and cooked out. Both Matt and Eric walked the entire way. I discovered if you want to tire out your children, just take them on a hike. The boys climbed trees, fished, and enjoyed the change of scenery. The air was so crisp and clean smelling."

Esther noticed how drawn and pale Karen appeared and was reminded of her pregnancy. She pointed to Karen's stomach.

"It looks like you stuffed a throw pillow under your dress. You're growing fast, aren't you?"

Karen patted her belly lovingly, "It sure feels like it. I'm still sick every morning. I hate this stage."

The nurses in the nurses' lounge locker room passed the time joking and laughing, but Esther ignored them, lost in her mountain retreat. She locked her purse behind door 203. Remembering Shirleen had taken her ten dollars, she refused to share her locker with anyone today. Her mind wandered through report as one might jump from rock to rock to cross a mountain stream. Mrs. Shepherd had assigned her to the ward at the opposite end of the floor, the end designated for the rehabilitation patients. Shirleen usually worked this ward.

"Hey, Cutie! Did you hear the news?" Shaw whispered in his slurred speech when she entered the large sunny room. Everyone within earshot echoed his exuberance. Esther smiled too, shaking her head tentatively no, not knowing what they were talking about. She watched as the men skillfully transferred to the wheelchairs, washed at the sink, and dressed without help. Now, she understood how Shirleen finished her work so quickly. She always had time to hang around and harass everyone.

"Hey Blondie," four of the men repeated in unison. "Where have you been all my life?"

Esther laughed, thinking I'm not blond.

Shaw rolled his chair up close to Esther and whispered in Jabberwocky under his breath, "The Wicked Witch of the West is dead!"

"I must apologize. I don't know what you're talking about," Esther replied.

Shaw had bathed and was freshly shaven.

"Yes. The Wicked is dead," they chimed again and laughed.

She felt cheated, put upon, and resented the men's jokes and tricks this morning. They kept on teasing and joking with her. They enjoyed her innocence, naivety, and played it for all it was worth.

Lyla walked into the ward, drawn by all the laughing and joking. She appeared as confused as Esther.

"What's all this commotion about? What's going on?" Lyla said.

"They keep yelling the Wicked Witch is dead!"

"Well, I know why they're excited! Mrs. Shepherd fired Shirleen Sunday. She won't be back." As the words left Lyla's lips, everyone cheered.

Lyla veered backward from the impact of all the revelry.

Esther's thoughts raced, caught up in the incredulousness of Shirleen being fired, especially now, after all the incidents she had successfully evaded.

"Shirleen fired!" Esther echoed softly, as if Shirleen's ghost was still there, hiding behind every door, skulking in the corners, and intimidating every soul determined to make a fuss or complaint.

"All right what happened? Is this a joke? How did she get fired?" Esther queried, suspicious. "Nothing can be this great."

Lyla's tone softened and her attitude became penitent, even sweet by comparison to what it was when Shirleen was queen.

"Shirleen pulled a muscle in her back on Friday and was allowed to go home on sick leave. Imagine that? The schedule had assigned her to work this weekend, but Mrs. Shepherd and the doctor told her to take time off with pay. Someone saw her working at the Meadowbrook Nursing Home Friday night, Saturday, and Sunday and told Mrs. Shepherd. Mrs. Shepherd went out there herself on Sunday and witnessed her working just as fine as you please. So, I guess that's the story. She let her go on the spot."

"All I can say is that God answers prayers," Esther replied.

The men listened and answered Esther's comment with their own.

"Amen, or Praise the Lord, or Glory Be."

Williams said, "That's sure the work of the Lord cause it's too simple to have happened any other way."

"Ya'll can be as thrilled as you want to be. One thing remains. Who will replace her?" Lyla scolded. Her thin, stick-like body stiffened, enormously offended.

"That's easy, Lyla," Williams retorted, unmoved by her nebulous threats. "No one! Because she didn't do any work."

The others laughed as he drew in a deep breath.

Marty, a right leg amputee patient, continued, "Ya'll and Melisa completed her work, or we did our own bathing and stuff. What we couldn't do, the others helped us. We helped ourselves. Maybe the beds. She made a few beds. Melisa did most of the work when she finished her other patients." He sat up straight in his chair and enjoyed being the center of attention for a change, without the witch cursing at him under her breath.

"Humph," Lyla grunted again before saying, "We'll see." She strode off down the hall.

Esther imagined a great raging force of changing tides flood over the seventh floor just like the great cloud of Passover floated over Egypt. It had protected and delivered all the houses covered with the Lamb's blood.

Yes, they knew the pain of bondage well, but at least now they had a chance to choose their own direction without Shirleen's cruel criticism.

With a new sense of exhilaration, Esther delivered medicine to the men before they limped off to physical therapy.

A tall, wiry man with coppery skin, wearing a blue uniform jacket, pushed a wet mop at the end of the hall. The others, Jewels, and Wills scrutinized the man they called Clay as he mopped and laughed, mopped and declared, mopped and disclosed.

He glared at them with glints of defiance shooting from his determined black eyes, all the while dodging the patients' and staffs' disgusted stares with the exceptional agility of a frequently convicted man. All the time, they knew he laughed at them, pitied them, and mocked them for their simple-minded adherence to the rules of life.

"Yeah," Jewels laughed. "We hear you. You ought to be glad to get this job. Mrs. Shepherd is good to us. You'll see."

"She can be just great. But get me away from these dead people. I can't take this kind of work," Clay admitted.

The others laughed, scoffing him as he mopped.

"The judge frowned at me, black as thunder, and said, 'Now Clay. This little girl needs a father. Her mother needs more money. She is your responsibility. You are bound by the law to make up the money not paid for child support in the past. She needs you.'"

"I said yes, your Honor." Clay laughed and flashed a mischievous broad grin in the men's direction. "Yes, your Honor," he continued. "But just you wait. I'll be out of here in a couple of weeks. I'll go home, sit down, smoke myself a little joint, have a few beers, watch football games, and smooch with my girlfriend. That's all I want in life. Is that too much?"

"Yeah," Jewels said. "I've heard that before. The judge will put you in jail if you don't obey. He's got you by the balls. That's clear!"

"Yeah," Wills said. "You won't have any of the things you like to do. No joint. No beer. An ain't no gals in jail. That's for sure." He rubbed his wooly hair, and tied up the rest of the dirty linen bags and threw them on the metal cart.

"Well. I got one over on her...my ex-old lady. The judge gave me visitation rights, and I'm going to use them. I'm taking my little girl to the circus, to the library, and anywhere I like. That old lady ain't gonna have no say in the matter. You'll see. I'll be daddy to that girl."

"Yeah. You'll be daddy if you live long enough. Stop this gabbing and get to work. You're new," Mrs. Shepherd said, as she inspected the floor he just finished mopping. "Now get yourself into that day room and mop that floor until you can see your face in the reflection. You hear me?" She laughed, as she peeked into the rehabilitation ward at the end of the hall.

"What's your name again?" Mrs. Shepherd called back to the man.

"Clay," he said. "Clay Jarrell." He sheepishly and humbly grinned from ear to ear, enjoying the attention.

"And what's this I hear about dead people? We don't let no dead people stay around here long now do we, Jewels?" She smiled.

"No. Not for long anyways," Jewels answered, cowering at the thought of a dead body.

Shaw sped by in his wheelchair. Mrs. Shepherd pointed at him saying, "There's one who's half dead, but we just let him go now, don't we? He don't count, does he Jewels?"

"No, he don't."

They both laughed as the expression of fear crossed Clay's face momentarily, soon replaced by his easy mischievous grin. His eyes, however, studied Shaw's precarious movements as he whirled down the hall.

Esther completed passing out her medicines. She sighed a breath of relief when the last patient wheeled down the hall toward the elevators for the 9:00 a.m. physical therapy appointments. As Jewels disappeared into the utility room, Esther remembered when he threatened Shirleen. He warned Shirleen he'd get her for what she did to Jessie. She wondered if he was the one who reported Shirleen to Mrs. Shepherd. She intended to find out before the day was over.

I have all this time left on my hands, Esther thought. The patients won't be back until noon for lunch. I guess I'll go in and see how Mr. Letters is doing and of course, Chester.

Her heart felt uncommonly light since she finished her new assignment. She checked again each bed and bedside table to see if every top glistened and all the toiletry items grouped together. Fresh blue and white seersucker spreads covered beds.

She strolled past the other rooms where Lyla, Melisa, and Karen frantically worked, still feeding and bathing patients. Their faces flashed with irritation and contempt when they spotted her.

Esther overheard Lyla say to Karen, "It looks like she has a nice easy spot now that Shirleen's gone. I imagine you have to be white to get any respect around here."

"Looks like it. Don't it?" Karen answered.

Esther ignored their comments and escaped into Mr. Letter's room. She returned to the hall to see the number of the room. She rushed back in realizing another patient slept in Mr. Letters' bed. The brown eyes of the emaciated replacement stared blankly back at her when she said, "Where's Mr. Letters?"

"Huh?" he answered.

Chester came out of the bathroom all showered and cleanly shaven, smelling of aftershave lotion.

"Where's Mr. Letters?"

"Come on over here, Miss Esther," Chester said as he sat down heavily on his bed.

She took the chair next to him.

"He's dead," Chester said softly and evenly without a crack in his voice.

"Dead?" She stared silently for a few seconds at the patient taking Mr. Letter's place.

"It's too soon. What happened?" Tears filled her eyes.

Chester rubbed his hand over his forehead. He finished buttoning his clean yellow shirt and frowned slightly in contemplation.

Finally, he answered, "Well, no one fed him and no one gave him anything for pain all weekend. Yesterday, he just died."

"Fed? All they had to do was fill his tube feeding. That's all. Who do you think did it? Which nurse?"

"There were only two on this side this weekend and for twenty-eight patients. Oh, I don't know." He shook his head in disgust and shrugged his shoulders. His eyes stared forlornly at the floor.

Esther stumbled over the words in her mind. She didn't know what to say anymore. She tried to maintain her composure. She felt as remorseful as he did.

"Well, did you find your daughter or even look for her this weekend?" she asked irritably.

He stared at her with surprise at the change in tone.

"No, I didn't get a chance to call anyone. I think that I'll let the social worker help. I can't seem to think on anything else but Letters. Not yet anyhow."

"What about his family? Did anyone come for his things?"

"I guess his niece came to see about his body. That's all I know." Chester laid back down on his bed and closed his eyes.

"Look, Chester. I know you're upset about Mr. Letters, but don't let that stop you from looking for your daughter. I bet she'll want to know about you too." Esther smiled at Chester who avoided her words, didn't meet her eyes. He covered his face with his arm, watching her out of the corner of one eye.

"Miss Esther, she ain't gonna want to see me. It's been too many years. I don't know. I just don't know about it anymore."

"I know what you mean. You're scared. You've got to pray about it. God will help you find her. I just know it. He really works in mysterious ways."

"He doesn't care about me, I'm sure of it. I'm not really a

Christian. I'm a true sinner. He doesn't care about me."

"Chester," Esther said softly, touching his bent shoulder. "God loves you as much as He loves me and everyone else. He wants us to love Him and come to Him for help. Look homeward means look toward God. Search for him. He gave his Son to forgive us our sins. He loves you."

"I don't know about that, ma'am."

"Oh yes, you do. What about that snake and other times. The Holy Spirit will help you when you least expect it. He knows even before we do what needs to be done.

Esther tried to repress her remorse about her father, rose, and tiptoed over to the new patient sleeping peacefully in Mr. Letter's bed.

"Well, what's your name?" she asked, trying to stifle her irritation and shock at Mr. Letter's death. She knew he was with the Lord now, and knowing that gave her comfort.

She straightened up this man's bedside table. Even though the top of the cold aluminum table shined brightly, she still envisioned Letter's Styrofoam cup and tube feeding equipment sitting there. She glanced at the wall for suction equipment, but the nurses had removed it. The change was unsettling. Remorse gripped her. She wanted to run, but she merely stood solemnly staring down at the new patient, experiencing less empathy. He evoked no emotion from her. Her feelings died with Mr. Letters.

"James Otis," he said withdrawing from her, barely drawling out the words before he retreated back under the covers.

"Where did you come from?"

"I was at the Lovely Manor Nursing Home for awhile I guess. I don't know why they sent me here," he said, his voice echoing in his chest, sounding hollow. It was the deep sound of emptiness Esther knew so well. It was the sound of hunger, an emotional hunger as well as physical. It was the sound of air bouncing off the inside of worn out lungs. His arms appeared so pitifully thin that his tendons and veins bulged out from his bones only restrained under a thin layer of lackluster tissue. She touched him softly on the shoulder.

"Can I check your back a second for sores?" She turned him over with only a push of her finger and discovered his coccyx area flushed red from pressure all around the bony prominence. There was a raw area in the center from extended chafing and friction from sliding him across the sheets. This skin opening bore testimony to his poor nutrition and negligent turning. No matter what you do, they end up like this emaciated specimen.

"I'm gonna get some patches to put on your back to help it heal. You'll have to stay off your back for awhile now." She knew it might take a month to heal this bed sore.

"Okay, Ma'am," he said, glancing up at her as innocent a compliant child.

Still examining him, Esther noticed little sores, open and oozing, surrounding his neck and spreading across his back.

"Do those itch?" she asked, pointing toward the sores as she tentatively moved away. Scabies she thought, trying to remember if she had touched him there or not. All I need is a case of scabies, she mused. She carefully examined his few thinly-growing, black hairs, brushed back to cover a shiny bald spot of a scalp.

"Yes, there they are. I knew it," she said to herself. "Lice. Has your head been itching Mr...er...er...Mr. Otis?"

"Well, I guess a little last week," he answered, glancing curiously up at her. "Sometimes, I itch all over. Other times, I just itch here and there."

This poor soul doesn't even know where he is or why he's here. All he knows is that he needs to be washed and have three meals a day to live. By the looks of him, it won't be long. Lice too. Esther laughed at the futility of it all.

She glanced at Chester. He had already dozed off and snored in his contentment. Well, this is home for him too. It's the only place he can count on for three meals and warmth.

She left the room and bumped into Mrs. Shepherd walking toward the nurses' station.

"Did you know this new patient, Mr. Otis, has lice and scabies. He's as emaciated as a little bird."

"Aren't they all?" Mrs. Shepherd said indifferently. "And I'm not surprised about the lice. That nursing home, Lovely Manor, isn't as lovely as them people declare. We get them back in bad shape, keep them until their insurance is renewed, and they are back on their feet again. We return them to the nursing homes fixed up and in good health only to have them come back with some infection of one kind or another. The nursing homes won't keep them if they get sick. They say, they aren't hospitals only nursing homes. What do you think of that? Frankly, I don't think there's much of a difference."

"Mrs. Shepherd, these floors are still so dirty. The other floors aren't dirty like this one. I get nauseated when I wash my hands. I don't understand why some rooms are dirtier than the others. It's a wonder all these men don't get sick."

"Well, honey. All these men have built up a good resistance to these germs. You know what I did last week?" Mrs. Shepherd leaned down close to Esther's ear and whispered, "I just happened to be standing near the Director of housekeeping at a big meeting and told Melisa real loud that I was tired of having my floors be so dirty. I'd really like to see the hall floors shine like they do on the other private floors. She agreed with me in a loud voice. So loud, in fact, quite a few people heard and turned around to stare at us. Old Rory just can't clean these rooms like they need to be cleaned, anymore. I've tried to help him along because of his arthritis, but these floors really need a good scouring and waxing. Maybe, that's the reason they sent us Clay. Maybe, he'll come every day. God knows, we need him." Mrs. Shepard raised her eyebrows, shook her head in disgust, and laughed.

"I wonder how long Clay will stay, Mrs. Shepherd?"

"If we're lucky...for a while maybe. They just called me from personnel. We have two new nurses coming on Wednesday. Tell the other nurses I want everyone to treat them as if they were royalty. For the first couple of days anyways."

Back in the nurses' lounge, Esther opened her patient's chart as Karen came in and slumped into the folding metal chair next to her, exhausted.

"I hope I can last the next three months. My legs throb with pain now." She reached down and rubbed her swollen extremities with gentle strokes.

"You're not lifting any patients, are you?" Esther asked, wondering how she'd be able to avoid the heavy work. Even turning some of the patients from side to side involved strenuous stretching and pulling.

"Not much! Thank goodness. The staff has been great. I'm only to give medications and pass out water pitchers now. Isn't that wonderful? But I'm giving all the medicines for the whole side. Thirty patients. Which means I'm on my feet practically all day." Karen rolled her eyes and then smiled sweetly. "I never expected to be having a baby. This baby will be born when Terrance only has one semester to finish. Then, we'll be able to go home. He's excited now, too. When I first told him, he acted as if our whole life was over. Now, he's even talking about it in a positive way. I only wish he wanted to do the grocery shopping. I'm afraid to do all that lifting. But you know how men are. He says all he can do is study." She drank her cup of juice in one swallow. Then, she poured another one.

"I get so thirsty here. Do you?"

"Yes. I guess it's all the running back and forth we do." Esther smiled excitedly up at Karen. "I just heard we're getting two new nurses on Wednesday."

"That's wonderful."

"It means each side will have one more hand," Esther declared with great satisfaction.

"Well, I think they'd tell you anything around here just to get one more day's work out of you. I'll believe it when I see it," Karen admitted, but grinned excitedly and affectionately patted her stomach.

"Imagine, everyone's workload will be lighter."

Jewels sheepishly poked his handsome face around the corner of the door, "Now what's you two ladies doing on this hot August summer day? Just passin' the time." He side-stepped his immense body into the small room and danced pirouettes on heels and toes. He danced around several chairs even using one as a partner. The nurses held their breath as he leaned this way and that, just missing falling into the wall or a group of chairs at the end of the stuffy, cream colored lounge.

Abruptly, his mood changed. He pulled up a chair and sat next to Karen with elbows on the table and his head in his hands.

"I just don't know what to do about this problem I have," he said cautiously, glancing up. Worried brows shaded his brown tormented eyes.

"Oh, he's just playing with us," Esther said. "I've seen him do this before. Come on Jewels. You're teasing us."

Karen appeared insulted, "No. No, he isn't. He's serious this time. Aren't you Jewels?" Karen affectionately patted Jewels' immense brown hand.

Esther concentrated on Jewel's coy smile and deep, complicated, fooling eyes.

"Jewels," Esther said, presenting her very best smile." It was you...wasn't it?"

"Me? What?" he answered coyly and laughed.

"All right Jewels. Tell us how you caught Shirleen," Esther said.

He didn't move a muscle or an eyebrow. The expression in his eyes changed to a pool of pleasurable acknowledgment.

Karen brightened, "You caught Shirleen?"

The voice which responded wasn't the stock manager, and it wasn't the clown-impersonator. It was the voice of a man who had struggled in long desperation to vindicate a friend, to uphold integrity, and to ensure the rights of another. He struggled for something he had vowed to accomplish and succeeded by a peculiar twist of fate to finally avenge himself and his friends.

"Jewels, we're waiting," Karen said.

"It happened quite by accident," he said casually. "She fell into my lap...as if Jessie Taylor guided me...as if he told me what to do next. Calla, my girlfriend, begged me and begged me to go over to Meadow Brook Nursing Home. She had some pajamas to take to her aunt. Her sister didn't want to go. I hate going over there. I gotta get away sometime. Anyhow, driving her there wasn't enough. She wanted me to go in with her. So if I knew what was good for me I'd better do it. Even against my will, I went in. Immediately, out of the corner of my eye, I see Shirleen in her uniform giving a patient a hard time. Only there, she acted sort of quiet. Hunched over the patient. Whispering kind of. I knew what she was saying."

"She didn't see me so I hurried to Calla's aunt's room and back, hoping she didn't find out I saw her. I was afraid for Calla's Aunt Hattie. Well, I asked her aunt who is crippled but not demented. She said that white girl worked there every week. She was as mean as a hickory stick. I knew she meant Shirleen. I knew this was my lucky day. So I left. Only on the way out, I stopped to make sure. I asked the supervisor if Shirleen was a staff nurse there. When she said yes, I asked if she'd be scheduled on Sunday?"

Jewels laughed to himself.

"That was quite a coincidence. Wasn't it?" Karen retorted.

Jewels smiled at the two, puffing out his chest and boasting, "I knew we had her. I planned a big surprise for her too. I called Mrs. Shepherd right away. She decided to go over first thing on Sunday morning before church. That's all," he flashed a sheepish grin.

"Wow. You can't imagine how thrilled I felt when I heard Mrs. Shepherd had fired her. She stole ten dollars from my purse. No one did anything about it either. She intimidated me so much that I'm still scared of her."

Jewels shook his head in affirmation. "You're not the only one who's afraid of her. We all are. She had something over on all of us. I didn't care anymore what happened to me. I wanted to get back at her no matter what it took. I intended to punish her for what she did to Jessie and everyone else. No one is safe around her. She is still intimidating patients at that nursing home." He leaned back in his chair with victory beaming across his face.

"Yeah, I got her for now!"

When Esther left work that day, she carried with her a new found enthusiasm, bolstered by the knowledge of the new nurses arriving, Shirleen's demise, and Mark's genuine show of affection for her and her sons. For the first time in months, she felt euphoric at the idea of beginning a new life. She experienced a freedom she never imagined. The weight of her albatross was lifted from her neck. Jewel's retaliation against Shirleen represented a success for all of them.

Chapter 19

A week later Esther enjoyed her lighter task of work with the men in the rehabilitation ward. She poured medicines for each patient quickly so she'd have time to help them get ready. She realized how hard the men struggled with morning care, rushed to finish their breakfasts, and labored at the final stages of dressing in order to arrive at physical therapy on time.

Painstakingly, they fought their own hopeless frailties, attempting to button the buttons on their shirts with their feeble paralyzed hands. They balanced precariously on their one good foot as they tried sometimes in vain to pull their trousers over their other limp, lifeless leg without falling. Esther encouraged them all one by one. She helped pull a sleeve on for one and cut the last piece of pancake for another. The patients began to rely on her eager assistance.

These men possessed a deep courage so powerful it ignited a willpower and determination to return to their past life no matter what the cost in time or energy. Their future existence depended on their success. They talked of God a lot. They cursed Him and then apologized. An innocent hopefulness consumed their daily struggles.

She wondered if Mark would stop by tonight. For the past couple of nights, he talked about contesting his father's will for her two sons. He contemplated suing his father's estate for his and Paul's share of the inheritance. She didn't understand his persistence, feeling he opened himself up for more rejection. She figured their father sealed the will with iron clad, invulnerable clauses, fortified with years of unquestioned judgments. The thought of it all made her cry. The will not only caused her divorce but forced her to sue her ex-husband's father's bequest. She didn't want to go along with it all, but Mark insisted to the point of frenzy. Esther wished for an end to all this vindictiveness.

"Esther," Melisa called impatiently and waved her dainty arm. "Esther, come over here and meet our new nurse Violet Gray." Melisa's strawberry blond curls bounced in her enthusiasm, as her head trembled slightly with excitement.

When Esther approached, Melisa yelled proudly, "She's a member of the new Bleeding Hearts Team." Melisa beckoned for Esther to hurry.

Esther's first impression was embarrassment when she saw Violet.

"I've seen you before. You've come to the seventh floor several times to help us out.

Violet was fastidiously dressed in a crisp, white uniform. Looking down at her own soiled skirt, Esther hastily tried to hide the spilled trace of the iridescent yellow, Potassium Chloride medication streaking the front of her uniform. She had tried to wash it out, but the effort only spread the stain.

"Er...a.... The Bleeding Hearts Team? I haven't heard that name before," Esther said.

"Yes," Melisa exclaimed. "It's all Violet's idea. She's put together this team of nurses who move all over the hospital from floor to floor, making beds, giving baths, shaving patients, and giving emergency help to the floors who are short of staff. They named it the Bleeding Hearts Team because "bleeding heart" means a person who is usually tender hearted to those in extremely unfortunate circumstances. Don't you think that's a wonderful name?"

"Yes, I do. It's nice to see you again," Esther said, gracefully extending her hand.

Violet returned Esther's smile and shook her hand with a strong grip.

"Melisa tells me you have already set a good example for the floor to follow. She says your nursing care is excellent," Violet said."

Esther smiled again and said, "Thank you. But so is Melisa's and the others."

"Yes, it's all Violet's idea!" Melisa said brightly for the second time, obviously proud of Violet's endeavors.

"Please continue, Violet," Melisa said.

"I'd be happy to explain. We're like the Red Cross. It is a neutral party moving from floor to floor to help out wherever we can. We've been here all morning."

"I don't think we can get along without you now that we've discovered you," Melisa said. "I'm sure we'll grow to depend on you. Won't we, Esther?"

Finally, Esther thought, the patients will get adequate care. That's if this group consists of well-trained nurses. She found the idea hard to believe.

"I'm surprised it's taken this long to figure out some way to supplement the nursing staff. Maybe if you helped us here earlier we wouldn't have had so many problems," Esther said, remembering Jessie

Taylor and Hudson. She couldn't bear to think about the others.

Melisa fidgeted with the papers she carried, acting as if she'd like to move on.

"We hope you'll stay and feel satisfied working here," Melisa added, trying to smooth over Esther's rough edges.

"Thanks," Violet answered. "I hope so too. How was it where you came from?"

"For the past five years, I worked private duty and took time off to have my two boys. I really don't know what staffing problems are like now. I've never seen it this bad though. We had thirty patients on each floor, but only five patients to each nurse. At least, that's what I'm accustomed to."

"Whew. It sounds like heaven. Imagine that. You'll never see those numbers here," Melisa interrupted, irritated. "We can always hope now can't we?" She inhaled a shocked, deep breath at the idea, then as if a cloud overcame her, taking away her joy, her face returned back to the previous mask like an expression of sadness that Esther knew so well.

When Melisa continued her voice sounded stiff, defensive, "Well, Mrs. Shepherd said just this morning we're expecting two new nurses on Wednesday as soon as they finish orientation. Esther, dear, I hate to change the subject, but I have work to do." Melisa smoothed her hair in a flutter. "I must go see what Buster is up to."

Melisa turned to Violet saying, "Thanks for the help. We really need anything you can do."

Without waiting for Violet to finish, Melisa flew off down the hall like a nervous little sparrow, having tarried too long away from her nest.

Jewels stopped in mid-breath, sucking in his wind as if truly moved by Violet.

He turned his startled gaze on Esther, saying on a more serious note, "Esther, remember if you need anything you can't find here just page me, and I'll come running. Running as fast as I can." He dramatically swooped over to her, towering beside her, grinning from ear to ear.

"Come on, Esther. We hear you, Jewels," Violet said, and pulled Esther with her as they escaped down the hall. "He's too much for me."

Immediately, however, their smiles were replaced with expressions of horror. Mr. Brimley sat strapped in a wheelchair beside the utility room door, thrashing about in his usual uncontrolled palsy-muscle spasticity, when Esther realized his restraints had been applied so tight they cut into the skin of his wrists. His hands protruded from the sleeves and dangled like blue gloves, discolored from lack of circulation.

With each awkward rotation of his spastic head, he groaned and slammed his head back against the wall hard to arouse attention. Quickly, they pulled at the ties to loosen the grips, but the restraints remained too tight. The girls let their hands follow the strips of cloth along the back of the wheelchair, trying to figure out how to untie the tangled mess. Mr. Brimley didn't stop banging. In a nervous frenzy now, saliva spewed from his mouth with each turn of his face from one side to the other. Saliva flew out and dripped down his chin, becoming a frothing mass in front of him, a collar, from his chin to his chest. It resembled the bubbles exuded by a crab left out of water too long. It was produced by his deep inexpressible hysteria.

His chest, posy-vest ties tangled around each other several times and ended in tied knots under the chair. The wrist straps intertwined and became knotted with the loops from the chest restraints.

"What a mess. I wonder who did this?" Esther said groping with the ties.

"I'm getting some scissors." Violet raced back into the clean utility room.

Sally indignantly strolled over to the two, towered above Esther and Mr. Brimley, and glowered down at them saying, "What do you think you're doing? Did I ask you to untie him? He's an escape artist, and he'll get free from everything."

"These restraints are cutting off the circulation in his wrists."

"There's nothing wrong with his circulation. That's how they always look. He has poor circulation. Haven't you been told to mind your own business? Now is a good time to start."

"Look! I don't know what you're doing, but this man needs these restraints loosened. I'm not walking away until they're properly replaced," Esther said, stood up, and glared back at Sally.

"I know the difference between right and wrong, and I'm going to do the right thing every time. You can count on it! So, maybe you'd better think again."

Violet bolted through the door and brandished the scissors.

Sally reared back like a startled colt. Violet shot forward still waving the blades triumphantly in the air. Sally, afraid she might be the next target, recoiled in retreat, backing away slowly like a conquered foe, never taking her eyes off the two.

Violet wasn't fooled for a second. She caught the mood and gave Esther a cautious, I think I missed something look, all the time slicing away the straps of Mr. Brimley's prison. Sally watched with fury boiling inside, but never said a word.

They freed him in no time. His spastic arms flung themselves on the sides of the wheelchair. Once freed, he slid down, almost to the floor, but the two nurses grabbed his arms and tried to pull him back up into the chair.

"Gosh! What have we let loose here?" Esther said, all the while knowing Sally and her friends observed every movement they made from the room across the hall behind the door.

"Don't worry. We'll get him tied back and safely!" Violet reassured her. "Let's put on this new posey and get him sitting upright in the chair first. He has Lou Gehrig's disease and knows everything that's going on here. It's such a pathetic way to go. His body is quickly disintegrating, and now he's lost his ability to talk. Soon, the nerve damage would affect his lungs, and he will suffocate."

"You know everything. Don't ya' Mr. Brimley?" A broad smile crossed his open mouth as he attempted to make some comments, but only unintelligible frustrated grunts erupted.

The two fought to keep him in the chair, finally grounding him, and tying the straps across and underneath the back of the chair. Violet whipped skin lotion out of her pocket and gave Esther a squirt of the white pearly substance, smelling of a flower bouquet, into her palm. They rubbed the raw slashes on his arms with the lotion. Within seconds the color returned to his hands and fingers.

"Now, that's much better isn't it, Mr. Brimley?" Violet turned to Esther saying, "This is the way these restraints should be applied. I think someone got carried away and didn't pay attention to what they were doing. Don't you think?" Her eyebrows raised, and she gestured toward the hidden eyes across the hall where Sally and the others still watched from behind a door.

"I'm sure that's all it is. You don't think this was deliberate do you, Violet?"

"I'll get him some water," Esther said.

Mr. Brimley quickly drank all the water Esther gave him, nodding his head in appreciation.

"Look at this. I'll get you some more, Mr. Brimley," Esther said.

He emptied the second cup, but Esther decided to wait for another, not wanting to overload him with fluids.

Violet sighed and said, "Some days we go from room to room and give drinks of water to those patients who can't reach their tables. You'd be surprised how thankful they are for just that one kindness. Come on. Let's go down to my office and take a break."

Esther loved their little rabbit hole of an office. As she left, she anticipated escaping there in the future. Running to the elevator, she allowed her fingers to palpate under her breast once again and felt the lump which seemed larger. This morning in the shower she discovered another minute lump next to the first. She relaxed a little remembering that she scheduled an appointment for tomorrow afternoon.

Maybe Mark will go with her? She knew if she asked him nicely he'd try. It seemed to her that he'd do almost anything she asked of him. Mark's sense of responsibility carried over to her for some reason, and she grew to depend on him for many things.

The elevator door opened, and she returned to the seventh floor. In exactly one hour she could go home. She counted the minutes. The white Formica top nurses' station loomed in front of her, a great white albatross, directing her through her storm.

When Esther neared the day room, the rich, deep, tenor voice of Jeremiah's singing greeted her, "This is my Father's world...."

She spotted Jeremiah Moses standing solemnly in front of the window, just gazing out, still singing. Other patients had gathered in groups of five or six in the opposite corners. One by one their faces turned toward his voice. They peered longingly at him, loving his nostalgic music, as if he were a prized canary, not wanting him to stop. Others shook their heads and pointed to him yelling, "There, he goes again."

Some of the others joined in and sang along with him. Chester stood up, went over and put his arm around Jeremiah Moses' huge shoulders and began singing too. Tears erupted from Chester's eyes and splattered unheeded down his cheeks.

When Jeremiah Moses finished the song, he didn't stop, but continued on singing, "We are climbing Jacob's ladder...soldier's of the cross."

Jeremiah's powerful, rich notes vibrated with such captivating intensity that they rattled everyone and everything in the room.

Sylvester Street stood there too, and he began to sing as well, only he prayed along with the words saying, "Lord, please touch my loving wife so she will find it in her heart to take me home. Ooooh, I want to go home."

Jeremiah finished singing and began to preach, "L'Lord," he stuttered. "Tttthese men are poor mmmiserable sssinners. Pppplease find it in your heart to ffforgive them and shower them with your loving grace. Yes, Lord. Shower them with your loving grace and forgiveness."

By this time, a crowd had gathered along with Mrs. Shepherd, Clay, and Jewels. Henry arrived for a meeting of some kind, quickly stuck his head in the day room, and then retreated laughing, shaking his head in amazement. "What's next?" he said to Esther, who stood to his right.

But the patients ignored the onlookers and echoed, "Amen...Amen...Amen," in unison after each prayer Jeremiah Moses delivered.

"Since my people are crushed, I am crushed. I mourn and horror grips me...."

"Amen! Amen! Amen! Brothers!" the people echoed.

"Oh, that my head were a spring of water,

And that my eyes a fountain of tears,

I would weep day and night for my lost people.

Oh Lord, where have you gone. Help us back to the fold."

"Amen! Amen! Amen!" the people echoed.

Jeremiah walked around the room touching first Chester on the head saying, "Bless you. Bless you." Then Sylvester, "Bless you. Bless you." Then he touched Shaw whose eyes were closed while he mumbled his garbled speech. "Bless you, brother. Bless you," Jeremiah said softly. Jeremiah made the rounds until he'd touched every head in the room. Then he cried, "We're here, Lord. Come get us. Take us into your fold." Then he sang in powerful rich notes, "Amazing grace how sweet thou are to save a wretch like me...."

The others joined in and sang in unison. Before long, they were all singing whether they knew the words or not.

Jewels leaned over to Mrs. Shepherd and asked, "Ma'am, do you want me to collect Jeremiah and take him to his room?"

"No," she whispered. "I think I'll leave him be for today and see how far he goes. Maybe he'll settle down soon. We've put him on some new medicine lately. But thanks anyway."

Jewels smiled to himself saying, "If you listen to him, he doesn't sound as crazy as he used to...does he? Maybe the medicine's working."

Esther turned and gazed up at Henry. "This man is giving me chills. Just listen to what he's saying. Would you?"

"He's not missing anything, is he? You know...I think his history said he was a minister before he started having hallucinations. It doesn't seem like he's forgotten anything, does it?" Henry shrugged his shoulders, then straightened again, appearing to throw off the sermon.

"Henry, what faith are you?"

"Who, me?" He glanced down at her a little baffled. "I...a...don't know. I don't pay too much attention to any of this stuff." His expression grew sheepish. He shied away from any more questions as if expecting a barrage of criticism to follow.

He turned around and gently grabbed Esther's hand, pulling her to him. "How about having dinner with me tonight? I think there's a full moon. You could get dressed up and...it will be so sweet." His face moved so close to her, she felt his soft cheek rub hers, his breath was warm and inviting, and his other arm caressed her back. She tried to pull away, but he had her wedged in the corner by the door so no one else could see.

"No. Not tonight Henry. This isn't a good time. Maybe later," she whispered in his ear. He didn't back away, but held his position, leaning into her body with a gentle movement. When the others approached the door from the day room, he pulled away and resumed his casual demeanor with a deep twinkle in his eye and a smile playing across his lips.

Without warning, Chester dropped to his knees and stared up at the ceiling with tears streaming down his cheeks. Slowly he began to pray, "Father, forgive me for all my transgressions. I'm new to this praying stuff, but I feel as penitent as your worst sinner. Please help me find my lost daughter, and please look around for Mr. Letters 'cause I know he's one of your new arrivals. I miss him. I promise in front of all these people that I will quit all my bad ways...and...you know what I mean. And I will do...ah whatever you want me to do. Thank you. My name is Chester."

"Amen, brothers. Amen, Jesus. Hear this miserable sinner,"

Jeremiah said softly.

"Glory be! I bet all those other men looking shocked over there in the corner are a little sorry cause their gofer has just died," Mrs. Shepherd remarked, as she hardly stifled her choking laughter that was followed by the others: Henry, Jewels, Clay, and Dr. Solomon who just joined them.

Lyla walked by pulling the linen cart and hollered to Karen, "Looks like Jeremiah is holding an old time prayer meeting."

Karen ran over and poked her head in the room. "Well, what do ya know? I never expected to see that."

Sylvester Street fell down on his knees with his blind eyes looking toward Heaven. His teeth clicked and ground back and forth, and with his hand raised to the ceiling, he called, "Lord...Lord...Lord. I'm waiting for you to help me down here. I called my doctor, my social worker, and my wife, but they are all busy. Now I'm calling you to help me out. Lord, why can't I go home? Please, let me go home."

"Amen, brothers. Amen," Jeremiah yelled again, still humming to the tune of Amazing Grace.

Esther wiped the tears out of her eyes in spite of the other's laughter.

Two women walked up to the nurses' station and asked the ward clerk where Sylvester Street's room was. One appeared a little younger and bore Sylvester's course features. The other one looked like a sweet, gray haired lady who appeared well dressed and finely manicured.

Esther watched the two women walk toward the day room.

"That's Sylvester's wife and daughter," Henry whispered. "I wonder what brings them here. I haven't seen them for several months. They won't return my calls. I guess they have had just about enough abuse from old Sylvester. He spent years as a bad alcoholic, you know, before he became institutionalized. He's suffering dementia from his alcohol abuse."

"Oh, I didn't know that."

"Yeah. I bet that lady endured plenty of abuse over the years and that daughter as well. Course, in those days, no one talked about it. No one ever mentioned what went on behind closed doors. Some of these vets have been alcoholics. Lost their families...money...homes...and everything."

"I think it's so sad. They're all so pitiful looking."

The two women glanced over at the crowd and smiled when they recognized Henry. "He's in there," Henry said, pointing to the day room.

"Esther," Jason the ward clerk hollered. "Your admission is here." He pointed to a frail looking lady parked in front of the nurses' station in a wheelchair.

I'll be there in a second," Esther said, determined to meet Sylvester Street's wife and daughter. His wife stood in the doorway and waited. His daughter smiled and darted her blue eyes from one individual to the next.

They all waited expectantly to see Sylvester's reaction when he greeted his family.

Mrs. Shepherd gasped in shock and nodded a greeting as she moved back from the doorway.

Sylvester still on his knees praying, alternated with crying and pausing, now singing again, didn't know they were there.

His wife and daughter stood in resigned silence, watching Sylvester pray, no sign of emotion erupted on either one's face. The others in the room stopped crying and praying. A hushed silence blanketed the patients, all except for Sylvester. When he realized that the others had ceased their outcries, he stopped too.

"What's the matter with everyone? Why's everyone so quiet?" His blindness prevented him from seeing his wife and daughter standing quietly in the doorway, but he knew something was different. He groped around the floor until he found his cane, then he stood up. He felt the air with his hands saying, "Mabel, is that you? Is that you?"

She smiled softly as she walked into the day room and put out her hand touching his. Then, she gave him a big hug.

"Glory! Lord Jesus! You've done it! Thank you. Thank you, Mabel. I love you. Take me home."

Cheers rang out all over the room, and each patient raised their face to heaven and prayed, "Thank you...Lord Jesus!"

Esther ducked her head out of the room and realized she'd have to rush to finish up. Then, she remembered her admission.

The new admission waited in the hall just behind Esther. She was a tiny contortion of wrinkles and bones, fragile in every way. The lady sat perfectly straight in the wheelchair with her arthritic hands folded in her lap, a smug frown pouted out on her lips, but exceedingly kind eyes caught Esther's attention the second she approached the counter of the nurses' station.

"Young woman. Young woman. I have been sitting here for quite a while. I don't know how long because they've taken my watch. But I hope you can help me into my bed and unpack my things. I've come here to die," she remarked, dropping her head as if ashamed.

She gazed at Esther with pleading eyes and continued, "I've been sent by relatives because they've tired of me. They say I'm too much for them. So, I hope I'm not too much for you!"

Esther laughed to herself thinking this tiny lady is such a dear sight, even a breath of fresh air. Thornhill was just the place for her now. Esther envisioned everyone loving her. She will rejuvenate the floor if she didn't drive everyone crazy.

"Doddie MacIntosh," she said. My relatives originated from Scotland. But you can just call me Doddie. All my friends do. They're all dead. They're the lucky ones." She pinched Esther's arm gently as she smiled up at the ceiling.

"All my children think I'm tight with my money. I'm Scottish by genetics, but my tight money genes must be recessive. My lawyer said all my money's gone. I should have been more Scottish. Maybe, I'd still have my money. Dear me. It's rather cold in here, isn't it?" She glanced at Esther with resignation. "You look like a sweet girl. Can you take me to my room now?" She sat in her wheelchair stoically, like a queen. Her arms rested casually on the armrests of the chair. Her white freckled hands, covered with protruding veins, dangled freely to point in the right direction.

Several large, expensive looking, brown leather monogrammed suitcases occupied the floor behind her chair. "Who brought you?" Esther asked, picking up one of the bags and realizing it was too heavy.

"No one brought me. Augusta, my daughter, sent me here in a taxi. She said life was just too short...blankety, blankety, blank, blank. Anyway, I'm here. I guess I was too much for her. I had one of my temper tantrums last night and hollered out as loud as I could all night, but it didn't make any difference. All I wanted was a glass of water and to go to the BR."

Esther knew her room was on Sally's side of the floor and worried how Sally and Doddie would fare. She imagined lots of sparks flying. All the way down the hall Doddie talked and talked as if no one ever listened before.

"I never dreamed I'd be a patient here at Thornhill...of all places. I guess I have reached the all time low you hear everyone talking about nowadays. Like the Great Depression."

"I always thought I'd end up in one of those old age homes boasting grand expansive grounds partitioned off with wide concrete paths for wheel chairs. Immense oak trees and magnolias planted far enough apart to grow, but not to look too crowded. Down the end of a gently sloping hill, I'd see a lake stretched across to the horizon like rich, gray satin shimmering in the dying, evening sunlight. Ducks, geese, and even swans might take a swim with their young ones. Then sun themselves on the banks." She glanced up at Esther, continuing, "I guess I got that wrong."

Esther stopped halfway down the hall and turned into the only private room on the floor reserved for females.

"Look, Doddie. Look out this window. We have a lake here. With ducks and geese too. There are paths to ride on. But you must be accompanied by a staff. The hard part is getting a staff member to take you. They are so busy. Maybe someone will take pity on you and take you out there." Esther pulled down the sheets.

Doddie kept motioning for Esther to take her to the BR as she called it. Esther rolled her into her large bathroom accompanying the spacious private room.

"Okay. I have your transfer belt. If you just hold on to that bar, I'll help you move from one seat to the other," Esther said.

"That would be all right except I can't move from the waist down. My legs are frozen stiff from arthritis." The lines between her eyes deepened into furrows, and she sat quietly in patient humility. "I guess old age teaches us everything about patience and dependence. I must trust in God for everything now. Even this."

What am I gonna do? Esther worried, knowing she couldn't lift her by herself, even as light as she looks. Esther went to find someone outside in the hall to help her. She knew most of the nurses were probably angry at her because of Mr. Brimley's restraints, but she tried anyhow.

To her surprise, Clay mopped the gray linoleum just outside the door. The smell of fresh floor wax jarred her nostrils and caused her to exclaim, "Wow! What do we have here?" Esther walked up and down the floor gushing over the change.

"This is a miracle, an absolute miracle. What have you done?" Esther said. The entire hall floor was Spic & Span clean and shone with a lustrous glow.

Clay merely stood at attention with his hand on his hip. He wore an immense grin across his long narrow face, exposing beautiful white teeth.

"Clay," Esther said sweetly, "I was wondering if you can do me a favor. I'm in a bind."

"Yes, ma'am. I'm happy to do anything you ask. You hear?"

"I need some help getting this new patient to sit on the commode. Can you lift her for me? She can't stand by herself." Esther smiled cautiously and felt like she'd asked him for a million dollars. The words were out. They had rushed out quicker than she expected, and she dreaded the moment he politely declined.

"Why, yes ma'am. Just show me what you want me to do. Clay here will help you with whatever," he replied as if pleased to talk to someone.

With absolute perfect grace, he lifted Miss Doddie to the commode and waited patiently in the hall for her to finish. He deftly placed her into the bed and pulled up the sheets. Doddie directed the process like an expert and told Esther where to place each tiny, embroidered pillow.

"Thank you so much Clay," Esther said. "You've saved my life."

"Just call me anytime. You shouldn't be lifting these heavy people anyhow. Just call Clay."

When Esther returned to the nurses' station, the phone rang.

"Hello," she answered.

"Esther! Is that you?" Mark asked.

"Yes. It's me. You're lucky you caught me. In a few minutes, I'll be on my way home."

"Guess what? I've filed an order to contest the will in the names of Matt and Eric. I've decided to represent them for you for free. I called to say I can't come over tonight. I'd like to change it to tomorrow if that's all right. I'm swamped with work."

"Sure," Esther answered wearily. "I'm tired myself. I'll talk to you tomorrow. Thanks for everything."

Just hearing his voice gave her a boost of energy. He proved his reliability to her every day, and now she relied on his affection more than she knew.

Chapter 20

The next day, Esther was anxious to complete her work early because of her doctor's appointment at 4:00 p.m. Esther organized the patient's treatments. The suffocating, South Carolina, August white heat radiated through her body from the morning outside. It lingered uncomfortably, and she still felt parched even within the confines of the air conditioned hospital. Her polyester uniform stuck to her damp body as she hurried down the hall, oblivious to the morning confusion of complaining patients and harassed nurses.

When she spotted Melisa hanging out of Buster's room, searching for someone to help her, Esther felt like ducking into a nearby doorway to avoid her. She admitted to herself how scared she was of the lump in her breast. She intended to breeze through the day, avoiding conversations with everyone, if possible, afraid she'd break down.

Melisa saw her, it was too late.

"Esther," Melisa called, impatiently waving her arm. Please help me pull Buster up in bed," she pleaded.

Melisa looked thinner and wearier than Esther had ever seen her. Melisa frowned, appearing downcast. Shaking her head in desperation, her eyes fixed on the floor as if deep in thought, waiting for Esther to join her. Her contemplation concerned Esther. Melisa always kept everything to herself and trying to discover the problem was futile. Today, Esther felt too upset about her breast lump to think of anything else.

When Esther reached Buster's room, the packed suitcases took her by surprise.

"What's going on?"Esther asked, noticing Buster had already been shaved, bathed, and dressed in a blue and white hospital sear-sucker robe. His legs, crippled up like a pretzel, spasmodically scissored as his knees rubbed together, revealing his anxiety.

"They're sending me out today to Riverview Nursing home," Buster said with a recalcitrant sigh. "I guess my insurance money came through again. In six months, it'll run out, and they'll send me back. At least, I'll have a change of scenery."

The devastation Melisa felt was evident in her darkly circled, downcast eyes. She fidgeted by adding extra aloe cream to his elbow joints and hands. She positioned his legs first to the right and then to the left, soliciting Esther's help and pulled him up in the bed twice. Buster winced in pain, irritated by all this fussing. Melisa collected his comb, toothbrush, and hand feeding device, wrapped them deftly in a wash cloth and placed them in the suitcase. But at the last minute, she retrieved his black comb and styled his hair for the third time.

"Don't worry about anything, Buster. I've given complete directions to the nursing Director about your care. They'll be so much nicer to you than some of these girls here," Melisa said, stretching her long neck to its full length, trying to stifle a pout.

Buster merely glanced down in disgruntled submission, and let his stiff outstretched hands fall limply to the bed.

"I'll be all right, Melisa. It won't be the same without you."

"I know. There now," she said as she pulled up his sheet and patted his head. "You're gonna be just fine."

Melisa smoothed the hand lotion over the backs of her own hands, through her intertwined fingers and back again. The expression on her face remained stiff. Her meager attempts at a smile were strained. She continued to fuss over Buster until the ambulance drivers arrived.

A bald-headed man, wearing a white shirt and black pants, gruffly pushed open the door to the room and handed a clipboard to Melisa.

"Monroe Fawcett," he said. "Ah...Buster?" He examined Buster and frowned when he pulled back the sheet saying, "Is that you?"

"Oh yes! Here he is," Melisa said, bending down over him to adjust his glasses. Then she pointed to his pile of belongings saying, "These are his bags."

She smiled triumphantly through her sadness, and her eyes twinkled with pride in him. She adjusted his collar as if he were her child going to his first day of school.

In seconds the two men moved him to the stretcher, covered him up, and carried him down the hall. The other nurses followed the stretcher to say goodbye and good-luck as they moved Buster to the elevator. All the usual joking and teasing they had used to torment him was gone. Their wishes appeared genuine as they waved a final goodbye.

Esther felt a twinge of sorrow at seeing Buster leave. He was one of the lucky few who left still alive. She didn't miss the tears in Melisa's eyes, as she waved her delicate hand goodbye.

Even Henry shook Buster's outstretched hand, congratulating him on beating the odds and outliving the poor nursing care. All the nurses laughed good-naturedly. The door opened and within seconds Buster was gone.

Mrs. Shepherd walked up to the crowd of nurses and staff, grinned a mile wide, and pointed at the two strange women with her saying, "These ladies are our two new nurses."

Everyone gaped at them as if they were oddities and touched their hands and clothes to see if they were real.

Pointing to the short, pleasantly-plump, oriental woman with a kind face, on her right, Mrs. Shepherd said, "This is Sakiko Smith. She and her husband moved here from Okinawa, Japan," Mrs. Shepherd proclaimed with delight, "Her husband is a Baptist Minister."

Sakiko bowed to each one of the nurses, as Mrs. Shepherd gave her their names. Her short, black bobbed hair edged her cheeks, and the thick perfectly trimmed bangs stayed put as she flashed her wide smile, showing off her many gold fillings.

She said, "Hi," each time she bowed. She resembled a Japanese doll.

Pointing to the other nurse, a younger, black woman, with her hair cropped short in an afro style, Mrs. Shepherd said, "This is Tristina Jones. She just moved here from Atlanta, Georgia. She is an R.N. and worked in a nursing home there."

Tristina wore a red plaid jumper and resembled a college student. Her red stockings were a surprise, ending in her comfortable brown loafers.

Mrs. Shepherd proudly surveyed the two nurses saying, "I know you are as excited to have them as I am. At 2:30 p.m., I'd like to have a conference in the nurses' lounge."

Everyone groaned testily, wondering what this meeting was all about. The only time they held a meeting was if some rule or code had been broken.

"Don't worry. It's just a meeting."

Mrs. Shepherd sported the new nurses around the floor for everyone to admire as if they were two rare, prize ponies. It had certainly been a long time since they hired new nurses. The big question was would they stay? Conditions had to improve with the added help. If no one left, and other new nurses joined the staff, the patients would get excellent care, thought Esther.

All the nurses filtered back to their various tasks including Mrs. Shepherd followed by the new nurses.

Esther was surprised to see a very tall, shapely, blond standing next to the nurses' station. Volumes of shimmering curls rested on her shoulders, and she wore a daringly tight, red suit embellished with a large, white linen collar. The vee neck at the bodice was cut too low exposing the tops of her full bosoms and extended down into her cleavage.

"Can I help you?" Esther asked.

"Why yes, Sugar. I'd like to see Mr. Henry Seward. He told me he worked up here, and if I ever needed him, I should call him on the seventh floor."

The lady placed her small, red, clutch bag on the counter, and tapped her sculptured, red nails across the white Formica just to pass the time of day.

Well, what have we here, Henry? Esther thought, surveying the lady from head to toe. Esther pondered the origin of the woman. Was she really here to see Henry? Pangs of jealousy rose up inside Esther's tightly clenched stomach, surprising her. She tried to quell the feelings, thinking maybe this woman was his long lost sister. Somehow she didn't imagine Henry having a girlfriend, even though she frequently caught him talking on the phone to someone.

"Well, I'll try to page him, and see if he's still in the hospital. Er...is he expecting you?"

"Actually, no he isn't. I thought I'd surprise him. I know he'll be thrilled to see me again." She let her sky-blue eyes scan the ceiling.

Deftly, she opened her purse, took out a small bottle of perfume, and dotted each temple and each side of her neck with the overwhelmingly sweet scent. "Is there some place where I may wait for dear Henry?"

"Certainly. Why don't you sit down here in the nurses' station? You must have just missed him. He was here a minute ago. I think he went down on the elevator with a patient who was discharged."

The woman sat down in the old swivel chair, crossed her long slender legs, and arched her feet which were cradled in dainty, red, four inch, spiked heels. She heaved a captivating sigh.

You'd better watch out, Henry. Her claws are showing, thought Esther, as she glanced down at her broken nails, and sexless bag-like uniform. She gave up on her repressed infatuation with Henry immediately, thinking she'd never have a chance against a siren like this one. Henry has a wonderful, compassionate side, but his other side looked like bad news. He was the image of Paul, a party boy. A party once in awhile is great, but not every night.

Esther returned to help Melisa clean out Skipper's room.

"I hate saying goodbye to any of these patients," Melisa said. "Buster has been the most difficult in a long time. He isn't well. He appeared more pitiful and helpless today than when we admitted him. I've tried my best, but no treatment we used has worked."

She bagged the dirty linens and searched through the bedside table again.

"Oh, Esther, look what I found." Melisa pushed her strawberry blond curls out of her eyes with the back of her wrist. "We searched for his watch for days and here it is. I was sure someone stole it. Well, I guess I can just send it to him. Maybe I'll go visit him in the nursing home."

As Melisa held the gold watch in her hand, the soft, wrinkled skin of her palm surrounded the timepiece as if it were an egg in a nest. It was as if she cradled his broken body in her hand, willing it to be healed with all the energy she possessed.

Esther gazed out the window at the too bright, white August sunshine, thinking how stifling hot it was, in the high nineties. August seemed to linger on forever, never giving a single moment's breath of reprieve to the heat.

"For some reason, my sister, Jennifer, has been on my mind all morning, "Melisa said, deep in thought. "It was such a long time ago. That day began and ended just like today. I remember standing at Jennifer's bedroom window the summer she turned sixteen. Only that day, I held Jennifer's gold locket in the palm of my hand instead of an old, worn-out watch. I found it in the back of my sister's bedside table drawer after my mother and father carried Jennifer to the hospital. On that hot August day, we had no air conditioning in our Kansas home. Jennifer suffered from Rheumatic fever. I spelled my mother for two months bathing, feeding, and trying to infuse life back into her weak lifeless limbs. In the end, it was no use. She died anyway. She died the very next day after they took her to the hospital."

Melisa squinted her eyes in an effort to hold back her tears, but one broke loose and dripped down her cheek. She dragged a white linen laundry bag to the door of Buster's room. She collected all the surplus soap, lotion, alcohol, and other things and placed them in another bag to discard. She sank down in the straight chair beside the bed.

Esther noticed the veins on the back of her worn hands had begun to protrude in waving bulging green lines under her wrinkled tissue paper skin.

"If only Jennifer had lived," Melisa said. "They sent me away to my aunt's house after the funeral. I never understood why I was sent away, and my sister Julie wasn't. If Jennifer had lived, my life would have been better even if we were poor. My daddy drowned his sorrow and grief in drinking, causing him to run off the road into the river. His death and Jennifer's death haunted my family for years and perpetuated our poverty in every way. Yes, she robbed everything from my family when she died."

"Why does God inflict so much devastation on us? I've never understood. I never forgave God after that. Maybe never will. I kept my sister's locket and still have it. This time I will give Buster back his watch." Melisa half-heartedly got up, picked up the bag of trash, and turned to Esther.

"My heart pounds in my chest sometimes so hard I struggle to get my breath. A ringing noise in my ears drowns out the sound of my heart," she said. "I never dreamed my only son would be killed in a motorcycle accident with a tractor trailer truck. Life never lets you in on the tragedies it has in store for you."

"Are you all right?" Esther asked as she gave Melisa a hug. "I'm so sorry. I never knew you lost your son. I don't know what I'd do if I ever lost my sons. I know I'd never get over it."

"Yes. I'll be all right," Melisa said, turning her face away momentarily. "I guess seeing Buster leave got to me a little." She smiled sadly at Esther, appearing still overwrought.

"Here, I'll help you with that." Esther reached down and picked up the bag without much effort. She sighed at the sight of the empty room where Buster lived for several years, noting the blank walls, the exposed mattress, the shining aluminum bedside table, now a generic hospital room. Her footsteps echoed off the empty walls as she picked up the last linen bag and carried it out.

"Come on. You look like you need a break. Besides I need to talk to you about something. On the way to the lounge go to the nurses' station and see the girl who's waiting for Henry. I'd like to know if you've seen her here before or not?"

Melisa smiled obediently and passed her handful of leftover trash to Esther.

Esther watched her pause at Mr. Kroger's room on the way and decided Melisa never knew when it was time to stop. In a split second, she returned to the hall on her way to the nurses' station, smiling with mischief in her eyes.

She's just as curious as I am about this girl. The hurt indignant expression on Melisa's face when she returned caused Esther to wonder again if Melisa had had a relationship with Henry.

Esther had already lit a cigarette and poured her cup of tea from her thermos when Melisa came to the nurses' lounge. Sally and Lyla sat in the corner eating scrambled eggs and sausage. Sally looked upset. Usually, Sally appeared to be on top of the world most of the time.

"Hey, Sally. How's Doddie doing?" Esther asked, knowing Doddie gave her a hard time.

"Oh, that one. It took me almost an hour to finish her up this morning. She still wasn't happy. There's no pleasing her," Sally scowled, gave Esther her black look, and resumed her highly animated, highly charged conversation with Lyla.

"I worked all last night at the nursing home, and I'm exhausted. I can't seem to get my breath. I need the extra money for my daughter and grands. I was held over last evening too. I've been up for twenty-four hours," Sally confessed, clutching her chest.

"Sally, ask Henry to look at you. He will, you know. He can tell you if something is wrong past exhaustion," Esther offered. "Don't you know it's against the law to work more than sixteen hours? How do you get your sleep?"

"That's kind of you, Esther. I think I'll ask him as soon as I see him. I know all I need is sleep. Thank God Mrs. Shepherd didn't send me to the nursing home today. I sleep here and there. I need the money, and $8.75 an hour doesn't bring it home." Sally slumped in the corner of the nurses' lounge, continuing her conversation with Lyla.

"If I can help you in any way, please don't hesitate to ask me. I've helped you before, and you know it. I've tried to help you a lot," offered Esther.

"Thanks. I know you have, Girl. Yes, you have. And I haven't forgotten it either," Sally said, hanging her head.

Melisa joined her finally, carrying a cup of coffee, a rare occurrence for her. Usually, she drank juice or ate an orange. She dropped into the chair, deflated, beaten down, and worn out. "Already it's 10:00 a.m. and my feet are killing me. I can't seem to get rid of that pain in the middle of my chest."

"Have you gone to the doctors about it?"

"Yes. I've gone so many times he's tired of seeing me. 'Stop lifting,' he says. He says my body is too old for all this physical work. I can't quit. I just can't quit. Only two years left until I retire. I know it doesn't sound like much when all these men are dying, but my time here is coming to a close. Let someone else take my place, I tell myself every day. I still come back though, but I feel as if I've paid my dues in more ways than one."

"Someone has helped you," Esther said. She smiled at the image of Melisa working so hard all these years, trudging up and down these unforgiving halls with her minutely perceptible limp, her fine, dainty hand fluttering on her chest, and delivering the loving words of encouragement she generously lavished on each of her patients. She knew she had to have a helping angel. "I think the Lord has been with you every day to work miracles."

"No. I don't think so. It's just hard work. That's all," she sighed and glanced up at Esther with curiosity. "You are so funny about your faith. You think God is helping everyone everywhere. You are so naive. God has bigger things to do than help us."

"I hope he's helping me," Esther answered. "I'm depending on it. I'm glad you came in here for break. I've been upset too. I found a lump in my breast and I'm scared to death it's malignant." Esther dropped her eyes avoiding Melisa's intense stare and nervously lit another cigarette.

"Well, I'm sorry to hear that," Melisa remarked, sitting up straighter and examining Esther closer as if she were seeing her for the first time.

"I know one thing for sure. You'd better stop smoking those things or else. You see what happens to these men up here who have smoked all their lives." Melisa leaned over and gripped Esther's arm hard, bit her lip and said, "You poor thing. Do you have someone to help you? Who is going to care for your boys?"

"Mark is going to take me to see the doctor this afternoon. If I didn't have him I guess I would be doing this all by myself. At least, we have the new nurses, and I have taken Shirleen's end," Esther examined her rough hands and frowned at their dryness. They mimicked her emotional wasteland right now. She grabbed the bottle of hand lotion from the table and squirted a gob into her palm. She massaged the white cream through her fingers and felt a tiny sting, then she remembered cutting her finger on the edge of the starched sheet this morning.

"Did you see the girl who's waiting for Henry?"

Melisa's eyes grew into two immense saucers, and the heat rose in her white cheeks, creating a blush.

"Oh! I sure did. How could I miss her?" Melisa laughed softly to herself. "He has so many girls no one can keep count. I kid him about them. He knows I don't approve of his antics. I think he needs emotional help. A psychiatrist! He really needs an intervention of some kind. Girls call day and night for him. When I chastise him about it, he just laughs it off. As if it were nothing. He's hurting all those poor girl's hearts, and he knows it. He's just a heartbreaker. I'm glad he hasn't gotten to you yet. I'm telling you right now don't fall into his web of lies! His trap!"

They both laughed at the thought of Henry seeking emotional help for wanting to see a different girl every day and night.

"Did you know that Mr. Letters died because he didn't get anything to eat?"

"No. Who told you that?"Melisa replied, her voice squeaking with a high horrified pitch. A tortured frown replaced her sumptuous smile.

"Chester confided in me. He said no one replaced Mr. Letter's tube feeding all weekend. That's why he died."

"I'm not surprised. These girls just won't do what's right. Although Mr. Letters was just hanging on when I left on Friday. Even if he had or hadn't been fed, I don't think it would have made any difference. His cancer had already won the battle. We knew it would be any time. But I'm sorry to hear that. I'm hoping he was mistaken. Sometimes, I just want to give up." Melisa threw her hands into the air, shaking her head vehemently.

"I know it sounds horrible, but we're lucky to have the nurses and staff we do," Melisa said. "They're only LPNs and CNAs. They don't have the knowledge that RNs do. The staff doesn't want to do the dirty work anymore. They're too interested in the lights and glitter of life. They don't care about these old people. It's just a job to them. We've got to put a stop to all this abuse and neglect. I'm trying to think of a way to get to the bottom of it."

Esther bit her lip in consternation, trying to not feel the pain of having Mr. Letters die that way. It could have been her. If this lump turns out to be malignant, her life would be in jeopardy of slipping away. Her cheeks grew hot from her own anxiety. She panicked momentarily to the point of not being able to think of anything else.

The door to the nurses' lounge burst open and Henry towered above the two with the blond on his arm. A resurgence of heartache rose up inside Esther as if Henry's actions were assailing her personally. This woman reminded her that she wasn't good enough for him. The sight of her evoked Esther's deepest fears of loneliness and rejection. Stop this, she told herself. You don't even like Henry. Her pangs of jealousy remained just the same. They were like the same stabs she endured when she saw Paul with his wife to be, Victoria.

Henry pranced into the room, smiling, teasing, and even taunting the two nurses.

"Have you two met my old friend, Camille?" he said flippantly. As if all the jokes and puns directed toward him in the past about his illustrious life had just come to a pleasant fruition with this female.

His attitude disgusted Esther and amused Melisa. Melisa played along with him and with the use of Camille as his scapegoat. She acted as if didn't see anything wrong with it.

Esther became embarrassed for Camille, even though she seemed to enjoy being linked with the illustrious physician's assistant as well. Esther felt as if Camille had been accused of loose behavior in the effort to exploit Henry's reputation as a stud. Esther realized her disgust was to no avail. Henry appeared determined to see this act through and sat in a nearby seat with Camille on his lap, laughing, joking, and making silly small talk for everyone's benefit.

Sally and Lyla stuck their heads in and waved to Camille. This bit of action confused Esther, further entrenching her feelings of alienation. They acted like they knew her.

Oh, I wish I were a man, she thought. I'd prance around with several women in an effort to break every woman's heart who has ever denied me.

"So, Henry. Did you and Camille meet here at the hospital?" Esther asked. She tried to be just as sweet and sanguine as Miss Camille. She crossed her long tapering legs and inched the hem of her skirt just to the crest of her knee and wiggled her foot.

Esther laughed to herself at the sight of her own unfeminine, leather, running tennis shoes and arched them sexily. Then, she draped her arm over the back of her chair, hanging her hand casually over the end in a graceful decorum. She slumped down in the chair, hanging closer to him in feigned adulation.

Henry laughed unabashedly, squeezing tight the tiny body of the blond in his arms. The expression in her blue eyes had grown dark and mysterious, deepening with each serious inflection. Her wide eyes narrowed to two tiny sensuous slits as her full voluptuous mouth parted with each breath as she hung on to each word he uttered.

"Oh, Henry. You're too much for me," Esther cooed. "You see Camille. He treats all the nurses this way. Don't you, Henry? He's the most fetching single male around here. The girls flock from miles every day. Just like you have. Why, just this morning, several were waiting for him when he arrived." Esther paused a second, stifling her own laugh of hysteria.

Camille became disappointed and stiffened her upper body. A pout protruded on her cherry mouth, and her eyes widened in their defeat. "Is that true, Henry? I don't know if I like the idea of you seeing so many girls. Maybe just one. But not so many as all that."

"Now come on, Esther. You know that isn't true. I came in this morning, and no one was waiting." He gave Esther the evil eye. He appeared not to be able to repress his passion and ardor for this woman any longer. He took in a long whiff of her scent.

"Camille. You don't believe her. Now, do you? She is the original Mother Teresa up here. Why men don't dare even look at her, fearing spiritual retribution. She is a completely asexual being. Women aren't waiting here for me. You're the only one...lately."

"Well. Thanks a lot," Esther retorted, insulted fury shot toward Henry. "That isn't true, and you know it." Esther rose to her own defense, but she didn't altogether deny the idea of Mother Teresa. The vision even agreed with her. This wasn't the first time he called her by that name.

Melisa laughed to herself, not saying a word, watching the sparks fly from Esther to Henry and back again. They caught Camille helplessly in the middle.

"Camille," Henry said, staring down at her soft round bosom which was openly showing in the cleft of her red vee neck suit. "I have asked her out a number of occasions and what's her answer? No. She always says I'm not her type. But when my friends come in here to see me, she acts like I'm doing her an injustice even speaking to them. What do you think of that?"

Camille paused in long, quiet contemplation. Tiny folds appeared between her blue eyes as she thought about his question. There was no joking in her face when she answered.

"Henry, I think you'd better examine this lady more closely. Dear...she is giving you mixed signals and that...." She paused, studying Esther intently.

Esther became immediately uncomfortable. The longer Camille paused and stared at her, the redder Esther's face grew.

Camille primly stood up, kissed Henry affectionately on the cheek, picked up her red bag and announced, "Sugar. I have a meeting at 12:30 p.m. If I don't hurry, I'll miss it."

Henry looked shocked by both the disclosures and the exit of Camille and stood up too, groping for words.

"Camille...I...thought you were joining me for lunch."

"Not today dear...maybe some other day." She left abruptly, leaving a hint of her refreshing scent in the air.

Henry ran after her in a clumsy lope. His arms and legs flew awkwardly in his gangly stride, in an attempt to regain control of the situation.

On his way out of the nurses' lounge, he turned and glared back at Esther, remarking tersely, "Thanks."

"Henry, don't look at me that way. What did I do?" Esther replied, smiling innocently.

Esther gaped at the door for a long time after it closed, wondering if he was kidding or not about Mother Teresa. She ruminated about Henry, repeating every word he said and analyzed them. Shame on you. She told herself.

She still stared at the door after he left and when it opened slowly, the new nurse Tristina timidly peeked in.

"Come on in," Esther said, in as friendly a way as possible. She even motioned for her to sit down. The girl looked overwhelmed and sank into the chair next to Esther.

"Do you mind if I smoke?" Tristina asked, flashing a shy smile.

"No. If you don't mind being cooped up in this stuffy room."

"I don't think I've had a cigarette all day," she said, lighting one up. "The regulations are getting stiffer. They don't allow nurses to smoke in Atlanta in the hospitals now. They have designated areas outside."

"You came from a nursing home?" Esther asked with curiosity.

"Yes, but the conditions were horrible there. The Board of Health had to close it down.

"Why did they close it? The conditions must have been beyond belief," Esther questioned half-heartedly, not really wanting to know, but afraid not to.

"I worked there for almost eight months. The staff gave you a hard time if you helped the patients. If you fed them or bathed them, they ostracized you from the clique. No one wanted to work hard, so the nurses let the patients do their own care. Every month when they were inspected, that's when the tub baths were done...the beds were made once a week. The patients hoarded food in their beds...even mice nested there. Their food trays were barely washed. Remnants remained on the dishes from one feeding to the next. Patients stole from one another. Rats and mice ran over your feet at night when you passed out your medications. Even roaches. I got sick every night I worked there, but I wanted to help those lonely old people. They had no one." She glanced around the room forlornly saying, "I hope this place is better."

"Oh, you'll love it here," Esther said. "I promise you," She smiled to herself.

Esther returned to the hall to finish her medications. She spotted Mrs. Putnam enter Mrs. Shepherd's office.

* * *

Mrs. Putnam sat down heavily across from Mrs. Shepherd. She frowned at the piles of papers and left over decorations. "I'm sorry I have to bring you this news Florence. I've just gotten word myself this morning. The Company has put a freeze on wages and hiring for the present. It looks like the Veterans Administration has cut back the amount of money they allow for each patient's supplement of Medicare. The new contracts have changed, making financing for adequate staffing more difficult. These new nurses are the only ones you'll be getting for the next few months."

Mrs. Shepherd became speechless and studied Mrs. Putnam, wondering what she was up to. She didn't wait for a break but interrupted her.

"I thought you told me we were getting three more next week. These girls have been hanging on now for months, hoping for the staffing to change. They're not gonna be happy about this news."

"Ah...well...I don't think you should tell them right away. After all, you've just gotten two new nurses. If the others stay, the conditions will be much better than it was. Come on, Florence. Let them think they're getting new nurses. It'll keep the morale up a little longer. I may add it looks like Esther is working out well...doesn't it?"

Mrs. Shepherd let out a recalcitrant sigh and turned away, not wanting to let Mrs. Putnam see how disappointed she was. She knew the girls had worked hard, long past their endurance.

"I guess it'll have to be. We've had so many accidents up here. They never would have happened if we had enough staff. And I had to fire Shirleen. So, actually we only have one extra nurse."

"I know it's been difficult for you. We've sent in the Bleeding Hearts Team. By the way, they seem to be doing great work. Aren't they helping?"

"They're doing some work. But we need fresh nurses because Melisa is hurting more each day and needs to retire. I really think Esther is going to leave when her time is up. You know it takes time to train a new nurse."

Mrs. Putnam got up to leave saying, "I'm happy to see that we are in agreement. I'm glad to know you're trying to keep the peace here between your girls." Mrs. Putnam left the room without looking back at Mrs. Shepherd who was examining her schedule.

Chapter 21

Esther glanced at her watch, thinking she almost missed lunch again. Was she the only one feeding these patients? When she left Mr. Kroger's room, she stopped abruptly as Patrick Shaw wheeled himself toward her. She knew what he wanted and immediately dreaded the idea of getting him fixed up.

"Not now," she prayed.

He continued patting his stomach motioning for her to help him change his clothes and wash him up.

"What happened? I thought you could bathe yourself?" she said, hating herself for saying it. She ignored him and quickly slipped into the nurses' lounge to evade his demands. She didn't feel like washing someone else's patient again, even if he was Patrick Shaw.

Pangs of guilt gnawed at her. She decided she'd never become one of them.

The aroma of food assaulted her as she entered the nurses' lounge. Sally and Lyla glanced up at her from their pile of barbecued spare ribs, thick with a rich spicy sauce. They licked their fingers hungrily and ravenously chewed at the torn off morsels of meat.

Around the table, each nurse smiled or nodded at her. All their concentration fixed on the next forkful of food or the next outlandish tale. Their heads bobbed agreeably punctuating each sentence with, "I declare. Sure enough, Sugar," and, "Is that right?"

The nurses reminded Esther of a time in her past when she watched her great aunt's lunch at a family gathering. She remembered each story as being better than the last, and for a split second, nostalgia overcame her as she longed for her relatives' long dead prattle. She sat down quietly in the corner. Again, her loneliness taunted her. Then her stomach churned when she saw the plate of French fried onion rings which occupied the center of the table.

Sitting among them Mrs. Shepherd was voraciously ingesting her Chinese food. She dipped a huge egg roll into the tangy, yellow, mustard sauce, smacking her lips. She nodded her head and grunted in agreement to the conversation, too immersed in her food to offer a statement. Selysia sat there too, attacked a serving of barbecued pork, and alternately picked at a slice of cheesecake with her fork. She had covered her purple, polyester, silk blouse with a paper napkin jammed into the vee neck cleavage. Between bites, she exclaimed, "Uh huh...Uh huh...I'll tell ya, girl."

Esther smiled in response to their faces, wondering how to gently inflict them with the idea of cleaning up Shaw.

"Ladies," Esther said timidly, as they all looked up. "Shaw is out here wanting to have his shower. Who is assigned to him today?" she asked sweetly, as she glanced from one to the other. She secretly enjoyed their grimaces of disdain and frowns of disgust. They deserve this, she mused.

"Don't you know you're not supposed to discuss patients in the middle of lunch girl?" Lyla said, and then glanced at Mrs. Shepherd who seemed to be enjoying this interruption.

"I have him," Lyla reluctantly admitted. "Tell him I'll be out there in a minute...as soon as I finish lunch." She faced all the others with her eyebrows raised in arrogance. "You'd think he was King Tut around here the way he expects everyone to jump when he returns from therapy."

"Yeah, and he can't even talk," Sally said, still licking her fingers, laughing under her breath.

"Where did y'all get this wonderful lunch?" Esther asked, knowing the cafeteria didn't produce this kind of fare.

"Jewels went out for us," Mrs. Shepherd said, raising her eyebrows defiantly, "Didn't he ask you, Esther?" The others snickered under their breath.

"No. No, he didn't. I worked in the ward making beds. I guess he only took orders from the ones on his side of the floor," Esther answered with disappointment.

She stood up to leave saying, "Well, I'm going down to lunch now. Shaw is waiting to be cleaned up. It's 1:15 p.m., and if I don't go I'll miss lunch altogether. I'll tell Melisa that y'all are in here."

Esther left, irritated that the nurses weren't concerned a bit about the floor or who was covering. They relied on Melisa to take care of all the patients. She sighed again, witnessing their haphazard attentiveness to the patients, but at least Lyla intended to clean up Mr. Shaw. Others still waited to be attended to. She had already bathed two who weren't her patients. That was enough for today, she thought. She felt determined not to give in unless it became an emergency. No one helped her when she fell behind. She knew she stood out as a soft touch and reluctantly gave in after some begging. She always took pity on the patients and forgot about her own worries, regardless of whose patients they were. Someone once told her a big heart always stuck itself out there to get broken.

Once in the hall, she told Shaw Lyla would help him soon. He resisted, gesturing that Lyla wouldn't do it. Esther fended off his pleas, promising him she would check on Lyla. He retreated seemingly satisfied with her guarantee.

Passing Mr. Letters' room, she remembered his spirit. Good care depended on each nurse taking responsibility for her own patients. She had an idea.

After retrieving her lunch from the cafeteria, Esther joined the others in the nurses' lounge.

Karen, just to her right, ate out of her bag lunch, and still radiated the luminous glow of pregnancy. A permanent smile dimpled her cheeks.

"I'm wondering which piece of fruit to eat first." Karen lined up a peach, apple, banana, and bunch of grapes in front of her. "I hate having to watch my weight every meal. I'd love to pig out on fried onions and pork like y'all, but it gives me terrible indigestion. Oh, I almost forgot - cheesecake. I think it's been a month since I've had a piece of that wonderfully luscious dessert or any for that matter." Karen laughed at herself, tossing her head back happily.

The others laughed too.

Esther placed her lunch of dried out hamburger and old chocolate pie on the table.

Selysia took a large sip of sweet ice tea saying, "Oh girl. I was just the opposite when I was pregnant. I craved everything spicy. The more spicy the better. I loved those submarine sandwiches with hot peppers. I made my husband run to the store every night at eleven o'clock. It got my baby hopped up, but I couldn't help it. We had an Indian restaurant just down the street. Once a week, I insisted he take me there for curry. All night I broke out in a cold sweat from all those spices...but I just went back for more. And you know to this day Daphne, my youngest, hates spicy food. She says it gives her indigestion," Selysia laughed.

"Today is payday girls, and you all know what that means. Ha! Ha! We'll be busy tonight." They all laughed. "I guess I'll see my baby's daddy. He always gives me a bonus. And I don't mean another baby. I love that green stuff!"

Karen whispered to Esther, "Payday means an extra check for

these girls. Baby's daddy or not. Their friends and boyfriends show up with bonuses if you know what I mean. It helps them survive."

"That baby consumed through your blood enough hot food for a lifetime," Sally said.

Sally paused, sipping her sweet tea before continuing. "I'll never forget my baby girl, Lenore. Now she's grown and has her own chile. When I became pregnant we went to my grandmother's grave, down in the small town of Garrett, Georgia. We searched for that grave a long time. Overgrown in weeds and vines, the cemetery had been neglected and forgotten. The old church had burned down years ago, leaving only depressions of unmarked graves and weathered gravestone markers. Anyways, as I got close to her grave, Lenore kicked and turned inside my womb so hard, I had to stop walking and bent over from the thrust. I doubled over in pain. When I tried to move away, she kicked even harder. As I looked down, the edge of a tombstone lay right at my feet. When I pushed back the honeysuckle and brier underbrush, I saw my grandmother's name etched in the stone. From that moment, the baby slept soundly in my womb."

Selysia scrunched up her nose and said, "Ooowee...Jesus...Jesus. Don't talk about that grave stuff. Why I hate to talk about the dead like that. It gives me the willies."

"But that ain't all. I'm fixin to tell you the rest. If you give me a chance," Sally said, glaring around the room at everyone.

"I'll never forget this as long as I live. Two years later, my mama and I went back to that old grave site. It was still overgrown in vines and sticker bushes. We searched in vain for almost half an hour to find my grandma's. We were about to give up and leave when my baby, Lenore, squirmed free of my arms and ran directly to the grave stone in the far corner of the cemetery. She jumped up and down on top of it laughing at us as if she'd known all along where it was. To this day, my mother swears that baby resembles and acts exactly like her mother. It was the strangest thing I'd ever seen. I never knew my grandmother. She died before I was born.

Selysia covered her ears. "Don't talk like that girl. The spirits will come after you. You'll call 'em in, an they'll come to haunt you."

"Oh, Selysia! I don't believe in all that nonsense?" Sally said. "It was just one of those coincidences. But it don't have nothing to do with the supernatural at all."

"Yes, it does. I believe in the Holy Spirit too. Thank you, Jesus.

And in those other vile evil spirits. You need to pray immediately or else bad vibrations might come on you," Selysia said and promptly squeezed her eyes tightly shut.

"Thank you, Lord Jesus. Thank you, Lord Jesus," she said. Then she crossed herself several times just to be sure. "You can't be too careful these days," she said, wiggling her buxom body until her voluptuous breasts jiggled.

"Yes, I believe in spirits and ghosts. Many of my patients have talked about them too," Esther added.

She examined each contorted, contemplative face around the table. Their resentment had faded away after Selysia's comments. And yes, they appeared worried, all except for Selysia and Karen, who shook their heads in affirmation and saying, "Uh...huh."

"Yes!" Esther said again. "Do you remember Mr. Letters?" Esther watched them grumble in acknowledgment.

"Yes, Esther," Sally said with quiet reflection. "We all know he was your pet. You have your pets just like Melisa."

At that moment, the thrill of electricity surged through Esther's body when she realized it was perfect timing.

"Mr. Letters confided to me the Friday before he died that a huge blue light came into his room right here on the seventh floor. Right here. It floated in through his window and a voice came out of it saying it was Jesus. He said the voice told him it was his time to go home, and Jesus said he was waiting."

Esther smiled triumphantly, witnessing their huge eyes and gasping, open mouths. They all looked stunned. The nurses meditated pensively.

"He revealed to me he dreamt he saw himself dead. He saw himself flying up in the air overlooking his coffin, watching all his friends and relatives pass by. 'Imagine,' he said. 'Imagine seeing yourself dead and lying in the coffin you picked only three months ago.' The episode shook him to his soul. I believed him," Esther confessed in a soft tone of voice. The others shook their heads still in deep contemplation.

"He even whimpered and cried, clung to my hand for reassurance. 'Do you think the light was Jesus?' he asked. I told him I thought it was."

Esther heard Selysia in the background reciting prayers to herself, "Jesus...Jesus...Lord. Lord."

Esther ignored her and continued, "I was surprised myself that as sick as he was...not even able to walk. He didn't see himself as dying until he experienced that dream. Reality came home and from that moment on he talked of nothing else. By the end of that day, he expressed relief to be finally on his way to 'the other side,' as he put it."

Esther took a long sip of her tea, knowing every eye in the room still focused on her, waiting for more.

"I often wondered how he died that weekend. Chester told me no one fed him. No one came in to fill his tube feeding, and he starved to death. No one even gave him anything for pain."

Everyone at the table squirmed and voiced their outcry of revulsion at the idea. Mrs. Shepherd, in all her wisdom, didn't say a word. She narrowed her eyebrows and pushed her lips out in her contemplative manner. She shook her head, barely perceptibly, and Esther discovered an approving smile teasing at the corner of her mouth. Years of frustration reflected from those deep black eyes as they met Esther's. Yes, they all voiced their outcry except Sally.

Her expression changed from utter shock to wild-eyed defensiveness and even arrogance. Her great bosom heaved with her fuming emotion. Now all eyes riveted to her.

"I worked that weekend," she said curtly, hesitating as if grappling with some ordeal, as if pondering if she should relate what happened. "The floor was a nightmare. Two called in sick. Mrs. Grummand came in to work the other side, the side where Mr. Letters' was. She hadn't worked here for months and didn't remember how to find anything. I went in several times to suction him because he had become so short of breath. He barely hung on. We knew it would be any time. Henry told us on Friday. She ran and ran from one end of the hall to the other working every room. We both did. We called for the Bleeding Heart team, but they said they were swamped on the other floors. I don't know exactly what happened, but Sunday afternoon he died. She found him and called me over to see at 3:00 p.m. We were so pushed for time to keep the others alive that we just called his family, the morgue, and left the paperwork for the three to eleven shift. All weekend his body was shutting down. That's what Henry said. I filled his tube feeding Saturday morning and got lost in my work on the other side. We did everything we possibly could. He was dying. Henry said he probably wasn't able to digest the formula anyway. He belonged in intensive care. They expect us to do the work of five nurses. I've pulled every muscle in my body, and right now I'm going for disability and that's that. I have no choice. I have my children to think of and be able to take care of myself."

Esther knew now that neither Sally nor anyone else deliberately didn't feed Mr. Letters. She tried her best to do an impossible job.

Esther remembered her hospice patient's wife giving him too much morphine. Esther remembered her own nightmare of a case. Mr. Saunders suffered too with pain. His wife became distraught, watching him suffer, and ignorantly gave him a deadly dose of pain medication. She didn't know the extra dose of Morphine was deadly. Esther was blamed for not teaching Mrs. Saunders properly. Mrs. Saunders never admitted giving the medication. She refused to confess to the crime of murdering her husband. She didn't know how to get out of the situation. So, when the judge said accidental overdose, everyone felt relieved. Esther didn't think that little bit of morphine should have killed him anyway. The judge accused her as an innocent bystander. The administration could implicate her in some of the negligent cases here at Thornhill, but she stopped worrying about further incriminations long ago, knowing she was doing her best. If she worried about it here on the seventh floor, she'd experience a nightmare every day. God was their judge and jury. She sighed, shaking her head at the futility of it all.

Yes, Esther truly felt Sally's anguish and knew first hand about her anger and resentment. It happened to be their misfortune to have picked a profession where life and death met on a daily basis and sometimes they became caught in the extenuating currents. The key here was to have more nurses to carry the burden. A simple request, but they languished in a sinking boat miles from shore. The administration proved to be the abusive parent in this case. She felt beaten down. Sometimes she felt like giving up, giving in to the relentless onslaught of too much to do without enough time or hands to do a good job. She felt like hiding in the nurses' lounge with the others, avoiding all the misery of the patients. Thornhill had to be similar to the sweat houses of the early nineteen hundreds. At times, this work reminded her of the stories she had read in Dickens and other accounts. She never expected to be pushed beyond her ability like this.

Yes, for the first time, Esther saw Sally's strained face, her heaving chest, and her defeated spirit. Esther pitied Sally, and she pitied all the others too. She even pitied herself. They all reached up and groped for raw life, faith, and hope that the conditions changed, that their work grew easier and even tolerable. This idea became the only force that guided them on to the next day, and the next, and the next.

Esther knew in her heart the accidents, deaths, and neglect only stopped when the conditions improved. She too reached up and groped for Jesus's hand with all her heart. She searched all week for the key to the success of the floor and finally realized she had reached the core of this immense problem.

Esther reached out and tenderly touched Sally's shoulder for reassurance. She felt it tremble under the warmth of her hand, and then pull indignantly away. Anger still shone in Sally's eyes when they met hers, but Esther didn't really blame her anymore. Esther had come in here as the Miss White Goody Two-Shoes and fallen into their pit of despair. Now, she felt covered with the same blood that covered all the other staff. She had to find a way to wash away the misery. She believed in her heart it was possible with God's help, but she doubted it in her head.

Each nurse smiled in acknowledgment to what Esther said and left the room. All except Sally who sat shivering in her seat, and Karen who sat beside her, staring down at her plate, afraid to move. Esther knew the words reached Sally and all the others. She had accomplished what she intended to do.

"Well, Esther. I have one thing to say to you," Sally said gruffly. "I believe in ghosts too. I was raised on the philosophy of spirits. In Gray, Georgia, there's a river called Murder Creek. You know how it got its name? They say in the slaveholding days and for years later when a nigger acted up or disobeyed the law, the white men took him up to Murder Creek, weighed him down with concrete or stones, threw him in and left him to drown. Every full moon you can hear their screams for help. You can hear them whining, and calling all up through the tall Georgia pines. There were rumors of murders happening even in the sixties by the KKK in that area. I know it's true 'cause my brothers and I went swimming up there one summer just to see what the place was like. When we tried to stand up in the deep mud, we felt their bones under our feet. The bones of our dead ancestors restlessly swaying with the current, always moving with the tide of that river, their grave. My question to you is why should we be charitable to you white folks when some of these men here as patients at Thornhill were the same ones who persecuted my people in the thirties, forties, fifties, and even now?" An ancient boiling hate emanated out of Sally's eyes.

Esther didn't like Sally's anger directed toward her, but she felt determined to remain calm. She made sure her voice never wavered as she answered.

She glared straight into Sally's eyes with disdain, saying, "Because we took a pledge to uphold the rights of man and provide comfort to him regardless of race, creed, or national origin...at least that's the oath I took. I minister to all of my patients regardless of color, religion, or affiliation.

Esther continued glaring at Sally for a few seconds, but Sally's expression didn't change, and she fumed all the more, hating Esther with each word she said in retaliation.

Esther caught it all, thinking here it is, prejudice rearing its ugly head with full retaliation. She tried to remain calm adding, "The Bible says: 'Matthew 25, 35:40, For I was hungry and ye gave me food; I was thirsty, and ye gave me drink; I was a stranger and ye took me in. (36) Naked and ye clothed me; I was sick and ye visited me; I was in prison and ye came unto me. Verily I say unto you, in as much as ye have done it unto one of the least of these my brethren, ye have done it unto me,' Jesus said. Because it is spiritually, morally, and philosophically the only right thing to do. Did you forget that Letters was a black man?"

"No. No, I didn't forget he was black. I told you I did the best I could," she answered, hanging her head in shame.

"Prejudice is an ugly disease. It is a malice with serious consequences. It lingers, and twists, and devastates its victims until in its chronic state, it fully devours them, leaving them in agony, and paralyzing them with hate. You've got to put it all behind you and go on. Wash away all the anger and forgive your adversaries, Sally. We need to help each other, love each other, and try to make each day count. We don't have too many days left."

Sally's expression still appeared dejected. Esther hated Sally for her anger and for all the misery Sally caused her. It hurt Esther's feelings that even after the past four months, this woman still blamed Esther and every other white person for her own misery.

Lyla hung her head in the door and announced, "Miss Doddie needs to go to the BR and is calling for her 'Miss Sally.'"

She laughed at Sally's expression. Sally merely turned abruptly and left Esther and Karen alone in the lounge.

Esther sat in silence as Karen finished her lunch.

"I'm trying," she said softly.

"I know you are," Karen replied. "Just give her time."

Esther decided to cross over the dreaded demarcation line to the other side of the hall to help Sally. Standing outside of Miss Doddie's room, she overheard their conversation.

"Sally, I would like to get out of this bed and go to the BR. I hate to use that bed pan and you know it. I haven't been out of this bed for almost a week now."

"Look Miss Doddie, you are too heavy for me to lift by myself. The others are real busy. Now please don't fight me on this. I have more patients to finish as it is...."

"Well, that nice nurse Esther helped me to the BR yesterday for your information. Now, darling, I don't want you to take offense to this, but you have a mean, ugly monstrous wound inside of you that we can't see...but we can surely feel the extension of its tentacles. I know it because I've seen it before. Now come over here and let me give you a hug for all the wonderful things you have done for me. Let me try to do something for you. You work your heart out here and don't you think that I don't see it."

"Now Miss Doddie, you don't have to do that. Just get on this bed pan so I can go on and finish my work."

"No. You come over here and let me wrap my arms around you. I can't do much, but I can hug."

After several seconds of silence, Esther decided to stick her head inside the door. She was amazed to see the hulk of Sally's body caught tightly in the feeble bony arms of Miss Doddie. Miss Doddie's eyes were shut tight below her crown of miniature permanent curls. Her lipstick was drawn crookedly and bled into the many fine wrinkled lines around her mouth. She smiled warmly over Sally's back. Five or six tiny lace pillows surrounded Miss Doddie's head and body for comfort. She wore her new blue satin bed jacket.

She patted Sally's back saying,"You've been wonderful to me. I'll never be able to thank you enough. She held her in a steel grasp until Esther watched Sally's body give in and sink a little into that old woman's clutch.

Esther pulled her head back, knowing this is what Sally needed.

Out in the hall, Mrs. Shepherd hailed her saying, "Staff meeting at

2:30 p.m."

Esther glanced at her watch and realized it was ten minutes from now. She panicked, remembering all the work she had left to do, and hastened to her ward of men.

Chapter 22

Returning to the ward and anxious to finish her medications quickly before the meeting, Esther tried to rush past Mr. Kroger, who stood just outside his room in the hall. He stepped into her path before she was able to dodge him.

"I was looking for you. My arms are itching again. Can you give me some of that medicine you always give me?" he asked, as he stared timidly down at the floor. When she reached out to examine the bleeding spots, he didn't hold still for a second but paced back and forth in front of her like a nervous, agitated animal trying to get free of her grasp.

"Hey there. Stop for a second so I can see these places. Oh, my. Mr. Kroger, you have scratched your arms raw. As soon as I finish my medications in the ward, I'll bring you something for those scratches."

"Mrs. Culver. Do you believe in God?" he asked as if she had all day to stay and talk.

"Yes, I do Mr. Kroger. I believe that Jesus will save us and give us eternal life," she said hurriedly, trying to push past him and continue down the hall.

He expertly blocked her way again saying, "Mrs. Culver. Can I go home this weekend?"

"It depends if your wife will be there to take you. We'll have to call her to find out. I'll be back as soon as I give these medications." She pushed passed him quickly, hating to avoid him, but her medications were already late.

She unlocked her steel medicine cart and began to pour out the heart, pain, and muscle relaxant pills for each of the patients on the ward.

The area felt cold this afternoon, and she wondered if the weather outside had turned cooler. It was as if fall had arrived at the end of August, and the thought of it almost made her cry. Fall loomed over her, a climacteric, a great withering decrepitude of the landscape, the debut of old age, immediately taking away all hope for any chance to catch the final, lazy, blissful days of summer. What happened to them all? Where had all the days gone? She wasn't ready for summer to end. She wasn't ready for any more changes in her life right now either. She scanned the faces of the men around the ward and imagined some of these men's infirmities had arrived prematurely too, catching them by surprise.

Each one of the men in the ward sat patiently waiting in their wheelchairs beside their beds, waiting to go to the bathroom, and waiting to go back to bed. They were waiting for her. She became their life-line.

"Hey, Esther, did I tell you I'm going to see my son play football Saturday at Clemson? I'm just as proud of him as I can be. You know, I been in this job for over a month now, and I'm getting used to it. I guess I'm beginning to like work. I never did before...but now I think I changed my mind," Clay said.

Esther smiled up at Clay fondly. "I didn't know you had a college age son. How wonderful! I know you have a lot of work to do mopping these floors and stuff. I really need help getting these men in bed before our staff meeting. Can you help me again? Some of these men are so heavy, I'm afraid they might fall if I try to lift them by myself."

"Looky here, Miss Esther. Clay is strong. I'll help you any way I can. I gotta mop this hall so you just call me whenever you're ready," he offered, punctuating each word with a nod of his head. A huge smile circled the lower half of his long, thin brown face.

"Thank you, Lord," Esther said.

She needed to put Mr. Penderghost in the whirlpool tub as she promised that morning. He was waiting for her when she entered the ward.

"I'm sorry Mr. Penderghost. I'm so far behind today we'll have to skip your bath."

"Who am I? I'm nobody! What's one more day?" Mr. Penderghost said. "It's been so long I've lost count. I've never had one of those coveted whirlpool baths. I guess Mr. Martin is the chosen one, 'cause he's the only one to get in the tub."

"Please, Mr. Penderghost, don't be angry at me. Here are your medications." Esther held the tiny cup of pills over his head and poured his water into the special cup for his deformed fingers. "

"Just shove them in...would ya?"

"No. Mr. Penderghost. I won't. You must raise your arms to reach them. Don't you remember that's what the therapist said?"

"Yeah. But she isn't me either. I can't reach that high and you know it. Don't you?"

"Aaaaaaaaaaaa! Aaaaaaaaaa!" screamed Mr. Shuttleford, a patient in one of the wheelchairs just behind Esther. She immediately turned around to find Mr. Shuttleford sprawled face down on the floor behind her.

"Oh no!" Esther yelled. She hoped he hadn't broken anything and immediately ran her fingers across his arms and down his legs, but everything seemed all right. She realized he unbelted himself because she was sure he was tied when she left him only a few minutes earlier. Now, he screamed at the top of his lungs as he tried unsuccessfully to raise his head up from the floor.

Clay ran frantically into the room to come to his rescue along with Sally and Melisa. Clay looked shaken. "What happened Man? What happened?"

"Don't touch him until we can find Henry. He might have broken something," said Melisa.

"What were you doing, Mr. Shuttleford?" Esther asked, furious that he'd try to take such a chance.

He ceased his moaning for several seconds and said, "You told us to hold our urine until we could go to the bathroom...remember. I was just going to the bathroom. That's all."

"But you can't walk. You can't walk an inch. Did you forget about that? Did you forget that you can't walk anywhere?" Esther chided with dismay, as she surveyed his curled lifeless legs doubled up under him.

"I guess I did. I forgot that's all," he answered, and tried a painfully innocent smile. He struggled to lift his round pudgy face again, but couldn't. It remained pressed onto the floor. His greasy hair shot out in all directions. He groaned again in misery, unable to bear the excruciating pain. His face flushed red with each utterance as if all the retained, unendurable agony bulged out to an intolerable level, turning it red like an engorged fire in a wood stove, and when he hollered out, the sounds relieved somehow the pounding, burgeoning pressure from within.

"But I tried. I actually tried to fly," Mr. Shuttleford said after a few moments. "Maybe, I'll make it the next time. I almost made it."

They all watched silently as a yellow puddle grew larger on the floor surrounding him. No one seemed to realize he had actually held his urine momentarily, and if he was able to walk, he might have reached the bathroom in time. "Oh, I forgot again," he said with disappointment, squeezing his eyes shut tightly. "I went to the bathroom here on the floor."

Henry joined the crowd and bent over Mr. Shuttleford, examining his arm. Inch by inch he asked if this spot hurt or that spot hurt and each time Mr. Shuttleford yelled emphatically, "No!" Until Henry reached his collar bone. He let out his loudest cry and didn't stop.

"All right," Henry declared, shaking his head with remorse. "It looks like you've broken your collar bone. We'll send you down for an x-ray. Is anything else hurting you?" Henry's hair fell casually across his coppery forehead almost covering his eyes, gleaming like a ray of sunlight. Esther felt drawn to the tenderness he showed when touching Mr. Shuttleford.

"Nooooooo! I don't think so."

They all helped move him to the stretcher. "I'll call for transportation," Melisa said. "You'll have to write out an incident report, Esther," Melisa said and hurriedly left the room. It was time for the meeting to begin.

Esther still had to get Mr. Penderghost back to bed. She sighed in her weariness. She hoped she didn't get called down for the incident report. She had several now including finding Jessie Taylor's body. She only had twelve weeks left to work here, and the conditions seemed to be getting better all the time. More new nurses were scheduled to arrive any day.

"Clay," she called. He continued talking to Mr. Shuttleford out in the hall.

"Yes, ma'am. I hear you," he answered, as he entered the ward.

"Mr. Penderghost is the last one, but he doesn't have his board."

"It's all right, Miss Esther. I can just lift him back to bed in no time flat. Just you watch and see."

"He's clean for now. I'll check him when he's back in bed," Esther explained as she pulled back the sheets.

Clay lifted Mr. Penderghost and swung him around as if he were a load of hay and laid him deftly on the bed. His tall thin frame straightened up proudly. He smiled at Esther saying, "See? I told you I could do it."

"You young people have the world at your feet," said Mr. Penderghost. "Don't waste a minute or you'll end up like Mr. Shuttleford and me before you know it."

Thanking Clay for his help, Esther locked the medicine cart. Transportation had already come for Mr. Shuttleford to take him to x-ray.

She kept Mr. Kroger's medication on the top of the cart and

searched for him in the hall, but he was gone. She finally found him back in the nurses' station on the phone calling his wife.

The girls had already congregated in the nurses' lounge for the long overdue staff meeting. She hoped this wouldn't last long. She hated to make Mark wait and wanted to be punctual. He promised to pick her up early today and take her to her doctor's appointment. She felt thankful for that comfort anyway. She let her hand drop inconspicuously to that tiny spot of a lump right below her left breast, just below her heart. Yes, to her dismay, it was still there.

Chapter 23

Esther was five minutes late for the meeting, and Mrs. Shepherd had already started. The evening shift nurses changed their shoes by their lockers and noisily opened and slammed shut the metal doors.

The fetid, stuffy air in the crowded room surrounded her in a smothering swelter. Whiffs of mingled perfumes assaulted her as she leaned against the wall. She had endured the anxiety about her breast lump all afternoon. She already hated it. Her preoccupation with the growth possessed her now. She even imagined it a monstrous size, ruminating that its root had grown deeper than she palpated. She fought to hold back her panic. Did she wait too long to call the doctor about this hideous, monstrous lump?

Henry arrived and stood just behind her and as the room filled, he pressed his body against her back. She shivered as he exhaled his warm breath on the nape of her neck. The aroma of his perspiration mingled with his musty aftershave taunted her. His body pushing next to hers comforted her though. His presence behind her soothed her frazzled nerves more than she wanted to acknowledge.

Mrs. Shepherd continued to talk, "Come on in...there's room for everyone." She peered hard at each face around the table and then sighed deeply.

"Mrs. Putnam, informed me if anyone else is reported for abuse they will immediately be fired without recourse. Are there any questions? I hope not. I don't want to go through another situation like that again."

"I'm happy to inform you we have two new nurses. They will join us on the floor tomorrow. Some of you met them today. I've called this meeting to tell y'all that I'm counting on you to make their time here a positive experience. We all know the work is extremely difficult, but if they see it as tolerable...they'll stay. If they are overwhelmed at the very beginning, of course, they will quit, discouraged. So I'm counting on you to make their first weeks here good. If not enjoyable. We have the Bleeding Hearts to help us now. Be sure to call them when we is short. They know our patients and can help a great deal.

"Stand up, Violet and let the nurses who haven't met you see what you look like."

Violet Gray stood up and smiled at the others around the room.

Yes, Esther concluded, the conditions had improved here on the floor ever since Violet formed the Bleeding Hearts team. Ever since Jessie Taylor's death. Yes, ever since they fired Shirleen.

Henry groaned in Esther's ear, "How long is this gonna take?"

Esther motioned for him to be quiet, smiling to herself, thinking he was still Peck's bad boy. Always ready to leap ahead, always searching for an exit from this phase of life.

Mrs. Shepherd continued, smiling as if she had just won Miss America. "Whenever any of you see Violet up here go over to her and say hey. Make her feel welcome. We are all supposed to be working like a team. Cooperating with each other. Let's show the new nurses our best side."

Selysia fanned herself with an old magazine saying, "Whew. It's hot in here. We've all met her, Mrs. Shepherd. We know who she is." She chewed her gum with enthusiasm. "I hope this don't last all day cause I have to pick up my baby at the train station at 4:30 p.m. She's coming home from Smith College for a few weeks. She had to take a course in summer school. Sometimes, she brings home one of those white folk's children, and I don't know what to do about it." The nurses all laughed around the table and stared at Esther.

They hushed when Mrs. Shepherd scowled at them.

Esther laughed too, but Henry pinched her gently, whispering into her ear in the middle of the confusion so no one heard, "How about joining me in Bermuda this weekend? We're racing, and I'd love to be coming home to your lovely face."

"Stop that. You know I can't do anything like that." Esther hated him for tempting her. She wasn't available to flit around the world on a whim. She knew the divorce freed her now, but Henry's past shot up instantly as a huge yellow caution sign. She had to protect herself and stay stout-heartedly away from any relationship, even remain sequestered at home with her boys for the time being, as long as she remained so vulnerable. Her boys were the most important people in her life now.

She yearned to go. She desperately wanted to say yes, if only to escape this cloistered prison of the seventh floor. If only to gaze at something more enjoyable and pleasant like the white sands of the island. If only to have the wonderful memory to reminisce about when times became tough like now. She felt his body push closer and rub against hers obscenely.

She tried to pull away, but Lyla stood just ahead of her and said rudely, "Come on Esther, give me some air."

She tried to stifle the desire that rose up from her toes in gentle waves. Her desire turned into a kind of yearning for his warm gentle touch. The quest to love and be loved was the strongest impulse of man according to the great psychologist Jung she remembered. Now, she realized how deeply her own emotions and needs ran.

"Are there any questions or comments?" Mrs. Shepherd said in conclusion.

"Yes, I have something to say," Selysia said smugly. Her eyebrows shot up to her hairline. "What about all the injuries to the nurses and staff? What about the nurses' aide like me and the LPNs? We do the same amount of work that the RNs do only we don't get credit. Are these new nurses gonna expect us to do their dirty work for them? What's gonna happen to us? When are we gonna get a man around here to do all this lifting?"

The other staff echoed her remarks and voiced their own concerns to each other.

What about all the water pitchers they made her carry when it was their job and not hers, thought Esther. She decided not to say a word about it at this time. She only wished this day was over.

Mrs. Shepherd became mildly flustered, "Well, I imagine we have a system up here called 'team nursing'. That's when the RN is in charge of the patient for all the shifts and writes on the care plan. The RN or LPN decides when to discontinue treatments and give medicines according to the doctor's orders. The CNAs, aides and other auxiliary nurses aren't trained to decode these things, and we aren't protected legally for their mistakes." She glanced around the room as if hoping all the questions were finished.

Esther had heard enough and decided to stick her neck out. "I think we all know we don't have enough nurses to implement team nursing. Right now, that's a dream. Our biggest problem is anger. We are angry at the hospital for such desperate conditions, angry at the patients for all their demands, and angry at each other because we can't help any of these unpardonable problems. The demands for even the most mediocre care are not being met, and we know it. We can't improve it. The patients need someone to feed them and eating is the most elementary of requirements. We need to face facts here and see the reality of the situation. We need to stop denying the brutality and neglect on both sides. The demands far outweigh our ability to provide good care. So first, we must decide what the most important things are and be satisfied, accomplishing those things. Like feeding the stroke patients. Giving the medications to each patient and completing their treatments. When these necessities are completed, we must be satisfied. Then direct our attention to cleaning beds, baths, and changing the incontinent patients. Why can't the nurses on the evening shifts and night shifts do some of this bathing and bed changing? We have the same number of nurses they do. Some days maybe even less." She glanced around the table and watched all the faces nod in agreement.

Esther continued when she realized no one challenged her. "We get burned out when the work is far more than we can possibly do in a day, in a shift. Split it up into two or three days. If every patient is bathed every third day instead of every other we'd be saved...beds the same way.

The other nurses smiled and even marveled at the good sense of the idea. This gave them a feeling of relief from some of their guilt, Esther noticed. Yes, she witnessed the girls actually cared if they completed the work or not. They all cared deeply.

"Yes, Selysia said, beaming. "Let the evening nurses do some of this dirty work." Her smile gleamed broadly. She even sat up straighter. "They have the same number of nurses and staff we have, but they're only responsible for giving medications and changing the incontinent beds. They only have one meal too. Our duties include completing all baths, feeding two meals, and changing all the sheets. It's a breeze for them if you ask me."

Esther interrupted saying, "I've noticed the angry way people talk to these patients. It's so easy to answer the patients politely. If everyone used kind soothing words when they speak to the patients, everyone would be much happier. Merely asking, 'What can I do to help you today?' can improve a patient's whole day. We are the only people who communicate with these patients. The only ones who are around to help them with their problems."

Lyla glared at Esther skeptically "Well, that's fine for you. When I try to talk to these men, they curse me out. I just finished Mr. Shaw. He cursed me the entire time. Did I get any thanks? Not on your life."

Geraldine coughed spasmodically. Her red wig tilted to one side. "You can't say anything to these patients without receiving a whole lot of backtalk. They never want to do what you want. And furthermore, the night shift does some baths and beds already. So, I don't think we need to be expected to do anymore."

"And what about lifting?" Karen said with a worried, tired expression on her face.

Esther heard the echoes of, "Uh huh. Uh huh. Uh huh. She's right. I done broke my back already."

Esther reluctantly decided to divulge her source. "Ladies, don't be so worried. We have our own resources at our fingertips. I never have any trouble lifting anymore. I merely ask the housekeeper, Clay, to help me. He's so strong, he can lift anyone. I even taught him how to use the Hoyer Lift. No one is ever around whenever I need someone to help me." Esther said and watched them squirm. "Ladies," she said cynically, "if you treat Clay and Jewels with kindness instead of criticizing them, maybe they'll want to help you too. You put these men down. I see you killing your greatest asset...these strong men!"

"Oh, they won't help us," Lyla answered. "They never offered before. They'll just tell us to do it ourselves." Lyla jutted out her disgruntled chin.

"Well, that's all I have to say. Have it your way." Esther glanced at her watch anxious to leave. It was ten minutes past three. She was late again, and Mark waited for her.

She pushed past Henry, patting him gently as she reached for the door. She slipped silently out of the room.

As she walked past the nurses' station, the ward clerk hollered, "Esther! Esther! You had a phone call during the meeting."

"Was it the daycare center? Did they leave a message?" she asked.

"Yeah," the ward clerk smiled cynically. "He said his name was Mark...and he can't pick you up today. He said he was sorry. He said to call him at the office when your meeting ended."

"Thanks, Tom. I need to use the phone." She dialed Mark's number and glanced at her watch. It was 3:15 p.m., now. She only had thirty-five minutes to get to her appointment.

"Hello," Mark answered.

"What's the matter? I thought you were picking me up?" Esther said and sighed with frustration. Her heart pounded as she worried about how she would get to the doctor's appointment with her car in the shop.

"I'm glad you called," Mark said, tentatively, pausing for a few seconds. "This emergency has come up with one of our South American accounts. They've chosen me to fly to Rio for a week to take care of it. I can't believe they chose me. This is an honor. But the downside is the hearing for the boys contesting the will is scheduled for next Tuesday. I hated to do it, but I had to postpone it. This extra time will give them a few more days to prepare more of a case. It'll take away the advantage of surprise. I'll probably be away a week or more. This stock thing has gotten out of hand. I'm sorry. Look, Esther...take care. I'll call you when I get back." He hung up.

Chapter 24

"Can I give you a lift somewhere?" Henry asked, as he leaned down and whispered in Esther's turned away ear. "I overheard your conversation. By accident of course. I tried not to listen. It seems it's a good thing I did." He laughed heartily for this longed for, unexpected opportunity. "Face it, girl. You're stranded." A large smile returned her shocked gaze.

Esther didn't know what to do. Henry waited in the wings like a wolf. This time, however, she remained stuck, caught in a trap like a helpless mouse.

Esther surveyed the grinning, expectant Henry, whose chest puffed out more every second, as his added sense of control over the situation increased. His eyes gleamed with mystery, and his demeanor exuded overconfidence in the grand sweeping, orchestrated gestures of his arms.

"Mark promised to take me to a doctor's appointment. Then, pick up my boys from daycare. He's called to say his firm is sending him out of town immediately to take care of an emergency situation."

"Oh, I've heard that tune before. Face it! He's dropped you like a hot potato," Henry said with an unusual supercilious tone in his voice.

"No, you're wrong," Esther said in defense, shaking her head. "Mark has helped me a great deal in the past few months. His nephews are important to him. I believe him. He's left me stranded though. My old car is in the shop again. I need a ride to the doctors. Someone to pick up the boys from daycare and take us home." Esther glanced sullenly up at Henry.

"Are you prepared to handle all that? I don't know when my car will be ready. Not today anyway."

"Henry scanned Esther's face. A kind, thoughtful expression replaced his triumphant one. "I'll take you wherever you need to go for as long as you need me," he whispered affectionately.

"All right," she said finally. "Let's go, or I'll be late."

She slid gracefully into the seat of his vintage Jaguar as if this were an everyday occurrence. To her surprise, a small brass plaque with his name HENRY SEWARD was permanently attached to the tan dashboard. Yes, she thought, he has money somewhere or simulated money anyway.

"It was nice of you to offer. It's down on Washington St. The medical building. Do you know where it is?"

"I know the place. You look cold," he said and reached into the back seat for his old sweatshirt. "Here put this on for a few minutes. Until you get rid of that chill."

He turned up the heat, and it blasted hot stuffy air straight at her, but it felt good. It was unusually cool for the end of August.

"Why are you going to the doctor?" he asked with a sober, deadly serious glance. It was unlike him to be concerned about her well being, but she witnessed a sincere tenderness that lay just under the surface of his feigned masculinity.

She worried about how to explain this personal matter to him. Even though they talked freely about the body parts of the men and women patients, it remained pretty much a professional nature. Never anything personal, like this, her breast lump.

"Like what. It must be something special. Is it? Especially if you let me drive you. Especially since you conceded to jeopardize all those times you rejected my help before. It must be serious because it's out of character for you to ask for help," he said and laughed softly, chiding her reaction.

He pulled into the parking lot of the medical building.

"Do you want me to come up with you?" he asked without a glimmer of sarcasm in his voice.

"I don't know how long it'll take. If you don't have any plans or anything else to do, can you come back to pick me up?"

"No. I don't have anything else to do. What time are you scheduled to pick up your boys?"

"The latest is 6:00 p.m. They know I'll be late today."

"If you don't mind I'll come up with you and wait in the waiting room. Maybe they'll have some cute, single girls sitting around," Henry said with his usual taunting smile playing across his lips.

The return of his sense of humor relieved her tension somewhat, and she felt her ego bolstered that he felt interested enough to accompany her into the office. She filled out the new patient forms while he leafed through the sports magazines. She imagined having her breasts sliced off, leaving one of those butchered, massacre scars she had seen on so many women.

The nurse called her into the doctor's inner sanctum and then on to the examining room. Esther hated seeing strange doctors for the first time. Everything seemed so impersonal. A casual 'how do you do', and then he simply examined her breast.

Esther showed him the small lump about a half a centimeter in length under her left breast. The doctor measured it and maneuvered it completely.

"After you dress, please come to my office, and we'll talk about this," the doctor said impersonally.

"Well, Mrs. Culver, in my opinion, I can say these small lumps are benign cysts. They don't seem to be the type that becomes malignant. To be on the safe side, I think we need to give you a mammogram. This way we can see if there are any more. Usually, they disappear on their own. After the mammogram, we can decide if we need to have them removed or not."

The words benign cysts caught her off guard. Never once did she imagine that they were harmless. She had already prepared herself for the worst. Now the worst had come and gone. She breathed a sigh of relief. But suppose he made a mistake? Suppose she waited too long? Then what?

"What if you are wrong, Doctor?" she asked softly.

"Ha. Ha. Ha.," he laughed. Then, as if he sensed her nervousness about the subject, he replied pleasantly, "The cyst is free floating. I can move it around. The mammogram will show any tendency of the cyst to become malignant. If it grows rapidly, we will be able to see the progression. We still have time. It's very small." He smiled, indicating that her appointment was over.

Esther didn't want to wait even a single day. She wanted the cysts out now. She didn't want them to grow at all.

"I can see you're upset," Henry said with controlled emotion after they were sequestered in his Jaguar.

He pulled into Shoney's restaurant and said, "I'd like a cup of coffee. How about you?"

"I guess. It's only 5:00 p.m. So, why not?"

Sipping his coffee, Henry remarking gently, "Why don't you tell me? Maybe I can help you."

Esther watched the soft, tender expression in Henry's eyes grow warmer. He knew a lot about cancer. He treated so many cases up on the seventh floor.

"I didn't want to tell you. Now, I don't know what to do next."

He leaned toward her, calm and reassuring. "Go ahead. I'm listening. Sometimes talking to someone else helps figure things out."

"I have a lump in my breast. The doctor thinks it is a cyst, but he wants me to wait two weeks to see if it grows or not. I'm so scared about it. I've already waited two weeks for this appointment. What if he's wrong, and it's cancer? I guess all I can do is have a mammogram and wait. What do you think?"

Henry sat there in shocked silence. All the blood drained from his face, making it appear grotesquely artificial, like a Mardi Gras mask depicting death. She didn't know what to say. He sat there in that shroud of silence, all humanness gone. Immediately, she regretted confiding in him.

"Look. I'm sorry I reacted like this. The idea you might have cancer took me by surprise," he said cautiously.

"I don't know what to tell you. Is this doctor supposed to be good? Maybe I'll check around and see. I really don't know much about breast cancer. Most of the patients I see are men. If you had prostate cancer...I can answer any question you have about the subject." He laughed a little to lighten the mood.

"I shouldn't have told you," she said with sarcasm. "I used to talk to Mr. Letters. Now he's dead. I wish I knew what to do. I wish I knew if waiting were the right choice."

Henry dropped his head, ashamed, saying, "I'm sorry I reacted that way. I had a good friend die with cancer. Your confession reminded me of her. If anything," he said, and paused for several long seconds, "it hurts me to see you suffer with all these problems."

She relaxed a little and brightened as her eyes met his and held until she withdrew uncomfortably. She endured the same bewildering discomfort from his penetrating gaze she experienced her first day at Thornhill. She never forgot the episode. It came to mind immediately every time she saw him. Flustered, she glanced hurriedly at her watch and realized they only had ten minutes to pick up her boys.

Later that evening, she decided to make him a cup of coffee, not wanting him to leave the minute she put the boys to bed. The way he patiently played with her sons intrigued her. No one ever spent that kind of time with them before, rolling around on the floor, making animal sounds, and playing hide and seek, not even Mark. Henry's innate ability with children astonished her. He seemed as adept as he did with all the male patients, just one of the boys. She smiled to herself, seeing the unusually gentle expression on his face as he watched them romp.

She set his coffee on the captain's chest in front of him. He sat quietly on the sofa reading the paper. The evening seemed exciting, purposeful, even the way it should always have been and should always be as if there had never been a beginning or an end. She smiled thinking, what will Melisa and the others say?

She sat down in the stuffed arm chair. He leafed through the evening newspaper and didn't look up. She sunk heavily into the chair, tremendously relieved the day was finally over. Most important of all, the news she probably didn't have cancer turned into a wonderful surprise. Henry, who waited in the wings of her life, stepped up as if fate meant it to work out this way. She sighed heavily, loud enough for Henry to look up momentarily from his paper, smile, and return to what he had been reading.

She picked up her hot mug of tea and sipped. The hot brew soothed her frazzled nerves and seemed to flood its way through her weary body, relaxing all her muscles. The room had taken on a cozy evening atmosphere with dark shadows growing larger in the corners. Henry had fallen asleep behind the paper.

"Henry," she said softly. "Henry, you haven't drunk your coffee."

"Oh, I thought I had," he answered, raising his head and putting down the paper. "It looks as if Matt and Eric are settled for the night. I guess staying in daycare all day tires them out. Does their father pay any attention to them? They seem to be great kids." He stretched his long legs out across the room and yawned, raising his arms in a gigantic circle. She felt drawn to him.

She stood up and walked to the kitchen for something to do to try to repress her cravings. She took a long deep breath as she leaned over the sink. He followed her, placing his empty mug on the counter. She felt his sweet breath on the back of her neck and thought he planned to kiss her here in the privacy of her kitchen. He backed away awkwardly, returned to the living room, and nervously picked up the paper again.

"Hey," he said casually, "There's something I've been meaning to ask you all day. Did you tell those men to hold their urine and use their urinals?"

Oh. Here he is, she thought, the old Henry. Here to make everything right. This time she wasn't intimidated.

"It seemed like a good idea at the time. Don't you see? They're so desperate," she tried to explain, feeling at a loss for words. "I thought if they tried to hold their urine and use the urinals they might have more control over their life, their handicaps, and even their cleanliness.

The expression on his face grew more and more tentative. He backed away from her as if she were a little crazy. "These men have physical reasons why they are incontinent. It'll never happen. They'll be frustrated by trying."

At first, he appeared horrified. Then he brightened as if he witnessed her incredible vision.

"Don't ask me how I know. It was just an idea that came into my head. If it works, these men will have a second chance," she said softly. "I don't know why I did it. I knew I had to make them try."

"Well, I guess we'll see if you were right or not," he laughed, "I hope this ordeal doesn't cause a scandal. You have really stepped out on a limb here. The patients are upset about it. Pestering me about it constantly. Mother Teresa with freckles," he said and drew her to him in a gentle hug. "Well, I hope for your sake this new approach works. I guess they don't have anything to lose by trying. Next time, consult with me about your ideas first. Will you?" he laughed again.

He gently pushed her at arm's length saying, "Look, I've got to go. I'll check on the doctor in the morning and find out what options you have about that cyst. If I were you, I'd be worried too."

He leaned over, kissed her on the forehead, and left the kitchen with her following on his heels. As he opened the door, he whispered, "I almost forgot. Do you need a ride to work tomorrow? When will your car be ready?"

"Yes, I do. I've forgotten about my car with everything else."

"I'll pick you up at six. Will 6:00 a.m. give you enough time?" he whispered.

"Yes, we'll be waiting."

Chapter 25

"If you asks me I'll never get married again," Selysia said, flashing her taunting, mischievous smile. "Imagine waking up and seeing the same face every morning and going to bed with that same face every night. Nooooooo, thank you. I don't think I can endure that for a second. I need my privacy."

Selysia pried open her lunch container, allowing the tangy aroma of a beef stew concoction escape. Within seconds, all the faces looked up exclaiming, "What's that?"

Glancing down at her own hastily made tuna fish sandwich, Esther frowned with disdain. The sight of it brought back her recollection of Henry waiting in his car, tooting the horn impatiently, while they all scurried around her house, searching for toys. At the last minute in her panic, she misplaced her keys which made them all the later.

She apologized for the holdup and for the boys' exceptional crankiness. Matt cried the entire ride because she made him leave his favorite trucks at home. She had to, she told herself. The last time it took them almost a half an hour to find them at daycare.

Henry didn't say a word, only glowered irritably down at the wheel. His knuckles turned white from his tightly clenched fists. She regretted accepting his offer of a ride, relieved that her car would be ready that afternoon.

She studied her meager sandwich and took a quick bite.

Karen smiled weakly, wrinkled up her nose and questioned, "Uh huh. What's that smell? I can smell the sting of its spice all the way across the table."

Selysia shook her head back and forth with pleasure saying, "Ummm Huh. Lordy. Burgundy sour beef with onions and dumplings. Oh, it's an old-fashioned recipe of my mother's. I make a big batch of it, and then freeze it for the next week. I put away lots of meals in the freezer. When I get home exhausted from this place, which is just about every day, I don't have to cook." Selysia heaved her full breast and laughed easily.

Esther thought how smart Selysia was to be only a nurses' aide. Selysia's two daughters attended Smith College with full scholarships.

Karen's usually bright demeanor drooped wearily like a water starved plant.

"Are you all right? You don't look good today," Esther asked.

Karen glanced up timidly with her pale drawn face, but Selysia interrupted, "Hey. Esther! That wasn't a very nice thing to say. You don't look so good yourself," she smirked.

"Oh, leave her alone Selysia. Esther's right. I don't feel too good today," Karen answered. Malaise had settled around her usually lively brown eyes, giving them a distinctly foreboding expression.

"I'm tired. Too tired," Karen went on. "When I got home yesterday, I had to do all the grocery shopping. Since, our car is in the shop, I walked all the way home pulling the bags in our rickety grocery cart. Every few minutes, I had to stop and fix the wheel that falls off easily. I walked four blocks because Terrance has his papers due. He was too busy to help me. When I got home, I had to clean our tiny apartment and make dinner. He hasn't straightened up for weeks. Afterward, I fell into bed. You'd think he'd just pick up his clothes or something. Especially now when I'm so far along. After all, I'm the one making the money."

She paused, her mouth fell into a frown. "Ever since I got up this morning...I've been spotting...just a little."

Everyone around the table stopped chewing and fixed their eyes on Karen.

"Oh, you poor chile'," said Selysia. She sipped her sweet tea before saying, "You've got to rest now. Forget about cleaning and stuff. Just let it go. If he wants it clean, tell him to do it hisself. See that. Men wants you to do for them. What about us?"

Karen dropped her eyes with embarrassment. She glanced disappointedly down at her stomach, patted it, stroked it, and worried over it. Her white eyelet maternity smock, with a tiny Peter Pan collar trimmed in lace, flattered her, but seemed to accentuate her fragility. Her long tapered brown fingers trembled slightly when she reached for her sweet tea.

"I still have two months to go," Karen said. "I wonder if I'll ever make it? It seems as if it's been forever, and I'm exhausted. It's been so long I can't even remember the last time I felt good."

"Hush up, girl," said Selysia. "You'll make it. Don't say anything like that. You'll bring bad luck to yourself. Oh, you'll make it. We'll see to it. Won't we, girls? Don't get up anymore today. Just do our charts. The nurses will give the medicines. You just sit there and rest. I hate to do those old charts anyway. Now, we have to write on every patient every day. And I can't spell worth a darn. Your baby's gonna do fine if we have anything to do with it."

Heads all nodded in unison around the lunch table. Lyla stuck her head in and called Esther to the phone.

Esther took a quick sip of her sweet tea before getting up. She wondered who might be on the phone. She hoped her boys were all right.

"Ohhhh. I wonder who that might be," Selysia said jokingly, as Esther slipped out of the room.

It had to be Mark, Esther thought. It just had to.

The nurses' station glistened. The aroma of rubbing alcohol hung in the air like Selysia's pungent beef concoction, and Esther smiled to herself knowing Mrs. Shepherd made everyone wipe everything with alcohol now. Mrs. Shepherd had turned into an obsessive-compulsive perfectionist.

"Hello," Esther said expectantly into the phone.

"Hi. They took their time finding you, didn't they?" said Henry. Her heart sank on the one hand that it wasn't Mark, but she felt that old thrill surge inside her. She wondered at his remarkable change of humor from this morning.

"I called your doctor and got the facts straight. He says you have fibrocystic disease. Did he tell you this?"

"No. He didn't," she answered and wondered what he was doing calling her doctor.

"He says they aren't taking off the cysts with such aggressiveness as they used to. They made too many mistakes. But he's sure yours is benign. However, I've talked him into taking yours out next Friday. If that's all right with you. Outpatient surgery. He's scheduled a mammogram for tomorrow. You need to call his office and make the arrangements.

"Frankly, I'm surprised at his casual attitude about it. I'm relieved he's going ahead and taking out the cysts."

Already, she sensed his relief and even her own. She felt grateful to him, more than she was able to express. Tears rose up and crested in her eyes at the flood of emotion.

"Thanks," she said in barely a whisper.

"Hey, everything's going to be all right," he said tenderly as if he reassured himself too. "Will your car be ready? I'm down here in medical records dictating. I'll take you to get it this afternoon if that's ok. I apologize for this morning. I was in a lousy mood."

"It was hard for me to ask you for help. You upset me this morning. I don't want to put you out, but I do need your help," she heard her voice say in return. "I can easily get a taxi," she added, not wanting to repeat what happened this morning. Inside of her a small voice objected and told her to be grateful...you dope!

"No. I want to take you. I said I'm sorry. I'll meet you at 3:00 p.m."

She felt a new tenderness emerging in Henry. Surgery next Friday. She knew she had to have it done. There was so much to do this week with the mammogram scheduled for tomorrow and everything...surgery? Who is going to take care of her boys? Mark won't be back by then. She tried to phone him again, but his secretary said the same thing. He wasn't in and no she didn't know when he'd be back.

Esther returned to the nurses' lounge to finish her lunch. Karen bent over a pile of black charts, writing; her legs rested on a nearby chair.

Sally and Lyla sat side by side gloomily picking at their plates of food.

"What's the matter with you two?" Esther said, joking in a way she didn't feel.

"So, what did Mr. Henry have to say to sweet Esther?" Lyla said sheepishly, her usually pouting mouth curled up into a slipper of a smirk. "Ahhh, Hahhh. It seems ladies...Esther is Henry's latest, newest, bestest!"

"Now ain't that cute," said Sally. "Looks like you're no better than we are. Little Miss Goodie Two-Shoes is a sinner like us. An all that talk about Jesus ain't got you anywhere."

"All right! I'm a sinner too. I never said I wasn't. But not with Henry. Henry is just helping me until my car is fixed. That's all. I'm not one of Henry's girls," Esther said defensively, taking a long sip of her sweet tea and pouring more from her thermos.

They were all laughing. Laughing their heads off. "Henry's girl! Henry's girl! Henry's girl!" they yelled until Esther wanted to hit them.

"Lyla what about you? Whose girl are you? All I ever see you do is talk on that phone. Every time it rings, you are talking to Mr. Who Knows Who That Is," Esther said in rebuttal.

There was silence in the room for a minute, and they all dropped their heads, facing their plates, rapidly eating their lunch. I've hit a chord, thought Esther. Looks like I've hit a gargantuan nerve.

She bit into her sandwich with relish beginning to enjoy this turn of events. "No one's perfect," she continued. "That's just the point. Not one of us is perfect, and Jesus has come here to help us. If we turn to him, he'll surround us with his love and forgive us. That's why he died...to forgive us our sins. All of them. So what about you Lyla?" Esther said casually, watching Lyla squirm uncomfortably in her seat, her face ashen. Esther realized she had touched more than a soft spot in the usually tough-skinned, taunting Lyla. All the girls appeared shocked for a second, staring expectantly and sadly at Lyla. All the time Lyla sank deeper in her chair, burying her head in her chest.

What did I say? Esther wondered and decided to hold back for the present.

"Well. I would say you're exactly right about the Lord," said Selysia, trying to focus the attention on herself instead of Lyla who still cowered in the corner. "He's my main man. I go to him for everything. Ever since my husband Courtland left, and I had to raise my two daughters by myself. The good Lord has helped me every day of my life." She stood up, excused herself, and gracefully left the room.

Melisa entered and replaced Selysia in the gray folding chair. She clutched her chest. She poured some water from the pitcher in the middle of the table and took a pill.

"Well. What's going on in here? Ya'll look like you've seen a ghost."

She didn't wait for them to answer and continued. "I can't seem to get rid of this aching in my chest this morning. It must be this cold rainy weather."

"You all look so glum. I see Karen's busy working on the charts. Now, that's what I like to see...industry."

Sally broke in, "All you care about is how much work we do. You don't care about us at all."

"Yes. You never seem to notice how hard we work," Lyla answered, picking up her tormented head for a second.

Melisa glanced down at her juice smugly, ignoring their bantering and criticisms, and merely tilted her head away from their cries like an indifferent cat. She opened the foil lid, sipped the juice daintily, and slowly deflated from the on going declarations of injustice. Every element of her decorum was immaculate: her silver painted nails, crisp white uniform, and dainty gold earrings. Even with all her complaints of pain, she maintained a fussiness with her appearance. She remained an inspiration.

Esther examined her own nails self consciously. They were a wreck, cracked, peeling, and broken. Maybe she needed to take lessons from Melisa and spend more time on her own appearance.

Still, no one said a word about Karen or anything else that mattered.

"Karen's spotting blood so Selysia suggested Karen write up all the charts for us and stay off her feet," Esther said.

Melisa immediately turned toward Karen saying, "Oh, Karen dear, how horrible for you. Selysia is exactly right. You must sit there until you feel better. It's only a few more weeks and you'll see...that darling baby will make you forget all the misery you've endured." Melisa reached over and patted her arm.

"Thanks, Melisa," Karen answered, still disheartened.

Sally interrupted, "Hey, Melisa. Guess who Henry's new girl is?"

"Why, I couldn't tell you. I'd never be able to keep up with Henry in a million years," Melisa answered defensively and pulled an imaginary string off her blouse.

"Our dear, sweet Esther. That's who!" Sally said and laughed at Melisa's shocked expression. Sally enjoyed watching Melisa squirm in her seat.

Esther was fed up with their teasing. She endured their jokes and taunting long enough. Maybe if they knew the truth.

"I'm so sick of your ridicule about me and Henry," she blurted out uneasily. "I found a lump in my breast, and I'm supposed to have surgery next Friday. My car broke down again, and Henry offered to take me to the doctor and back home. I didn't have anyone else. He helped me out of the goodness of his heart. Mark is out of town. I haven't spoken to him all week."

"Oh, you must be scared to death," said Melisa. But the others merely appeared more disgusted and withdrew further into their silence. They immediately developed the narrow eyes and puffed out cheeks syndrome, revealing their indignant attitude. They hated it if anyone gave her an inch, and she knew it. She felt the stab as if it were a knife, wondering if they'd ever change. Hatred was an ugly thing. It's caused so much misery, she thought, trying to shrug off their slight, but she still felt the pain.

The door opened abruptly and Mrs. Shepherd burst into the room saying, "Uh, huh. So, this is where all my nurses are today and leaving those new nurses out there to run their butts off. What do you think this is the Geneva Conference?" She glared down at each one, raised her eyebrows, and pushed her snuff filled lips out in a disgruntled pout. "I'm not gonna let you slough off your work on others anymore. You hear?"

Melisa sat up straight and tipped her head to one side in resistance. "I beg your pardon, Florence. I just sat down for the first time in I don't know how long and found out that Karen's spotting blood from her poor, sweet baby. So, Selysia gave her all the charts to do, and I think that's a grand idea. We don't want any more problems around here than we already have. And Esther has a lump in her breast and needs next Friday off to have surgery. I think that's enough for starters."

Mrs. Shepherd's shoulders drooped wearily. "Well, that makes three. Sally wants four weeks off to have a hysterectomy and will probably need six or eight, depending on her condition. She slid heavily into the nearest chair. I don't know what we're gonna do with the staffing." She let her head fall heavily into her hands.

They all looked over at Sally and gave her their condolences. All except Esther who was thinking so that's what their attitude was all about. Esther still didn't feel any sympathy for Sally because of all her taunting.

Then Lyla, who until this time sat in the corner stewing in silence, stood up suddenly, frowned, shook her head violently, and cried out almost in a sob, "Bleeding. Bleeding. Bleeding. Isn't that all women do? Have babies, feed babies, lose babies, lose their man, and bleed their hearts dry. The tone of everyone's mood every day depends on one of those facts."

Lyla turned and stared at Esther too long, provocatively, like a wild animal penned up in a cage, showing her teeth, about to jump at the wire. Then she continued, the wildness still haunted her expression.

"When I'm on the phone, I'm talking to Garland Green. He calls me three or four times a day, but I can never call him. He's white and a married man. I'm an adulterous woman. If you want to know the truth. And this has been going on for fifteen years. No one knows but these girls. But I know the feeling because I have been bled to death. That's all I'm gonna bleed. God's cursed me, and that's all there is to it. Everyone's got children but me. Even skinny little Esther here. She got them two boys. Look at me. Now, just look at me. I ain't got nothing but this hard work to keep me busy. Even here the patients are bleeding me dry where I stand. All I am is a backyard sister to Garland Green. An he's been bleeding me dry for years. Bleeding me of every morsel of attention, and feeling, and strength I have to give. Then, he goes back to his Goody Goody Two-Shoes White Wife. Promises...that's all I get. He loves me for sure. I always say. We must have some kind of good love if it's lasted this long. All I do is wait and wait and wait for him to appear when it's convenient for him."

Lyla's neck tendons protruded like taught ropes as she stretched her chin indignantly and stared up at the ceiling. Her purple neck veins pounded from her emotion. She raised her hands up in the air as if in defiance, clenched into two tight defenseless fists.

"I had a baby once growing inside my body, bone of my bone, a flesh of my flesh, a tiny mite of Garland Green growing inside of me. All that baby did was kick and kick and kick inside my womb. All I did was bleed and bleed and bleed. The midwife waited and waited, put the knife under the bed and waited. I never had a minute of pain. Garland Green junior kicked and kicked until he kicked away his life right inside my womb, stuck in there. I guess he was never meant to see freedom on the other side. Hour after hour, I felt his baby kicks, flutter, and flutter, like an injured bird. Fainter and fainter they came until finally on that hot, blistering, July afternoon, they stopped forever. The afterbirth was first. He never had a chance. All these years since, never a day goes by when I haven't suffered the pain of that few hours. Girls, there are all kinds of pain. I think that sorrow is the worst. It eats at you until there's nothing left inside except an empty shell. All I wished I'd done was cut my stomach open with that knife under the bed and freed my Garland Green Junior. That's all it would have taken, an he'd be here with me today, my chubby-faced Garland Green. I'd have him here with his own children for my old age. But what do I have? Nothing. Yeah. Men come and go and never look back. Here, we are bleeding away our life. When our tears are gone...we is still giving our life's blood. I feel like we're just like Garland Green Junior kicking and kicking, as hard as we can, but there's just no freedom for us, no way out. We'll die right here in this giant womb of life never enjoying nothing." Lyla raised her long narrow face up to the ceiling and moaned and cried in a frenzy, flailing her arms, sobbing her heart out.

Sally got up from her seat on the other side of the table, hurried over to comfort Lyla, and hugged her repeatedly, saying, "Don't cry, honey! Don't cry, girl! Don't let him get that satisfaction."

After a few minutes, Lyla went into the bathroom and washed her face.

Esther felt again for her lump under her left breast, it was still there. She secretly hoped it had disappeared. Everyone's so upset today. She was surprised at herself for feeling anxious for Lyla. She wondered if she'd ever find someone to love her and her boys again. She knew exactly how Lyla felt. Women are left with the worries of the heart. Here we sit like so many pink, red, and yellow roses in a tapestry of black, mourning for those lost minutes of pleasure and spending a lifetime of regret if only to gain back just one. Every day we spend searching and yearning for security, for a home and family, a cozy collection of loving people to share the burdens of life. Where did all the people go? Her own parents dead. What did she do to deserve all this misery? What happened to the great dreams of little girls? Esther looked up only to see Sally crying for Lyla and hugging Lyla's scrubbed face to her again, trying desperately to take away the hurt. Sally caressed Lyla's cheeks with her large comforting hands, but there was no consolation for her. Her heart had been broken beyond repair years ago.

Melisa sat hunched over herself, bending down toward the center of the table. She hugged her arms to her aching chest, covered her mouth with her free hand in horror as if trying to stifle a scream. Her face grew redder, but her eyes turned mournfully away.

"What happens to the great dreams of little girls?" Esther said, shaking her head with her own disappointment. She felt as if the melancholia had reached in and grabbed at her heart, taunting her soul. She still tried to reject the truth that Paul had always loved Victoria. Had never loved her. Why didn't she see it?

Mrs. Shepherd shook her head moaning, "It's true honey! It's true," and then declared, "When I was a little girl, my life was going to be so different from my mama's. I wasn't going to have all those children my mother had. No, I was going to be free. I was going to get a wonderful job, buy beautiful clothes, and find one man to love me forever. That was before Scooter, the little boy next door, said come here let me show you something."

Mrs. Shepherd let out a long audible sigh, biting into her fried chicken voraciously. She shut her eyes tight and swung her head back and forth moaning.

They all watched every move she made, even breathing in with every breath of hers and breathing out too. After she finished chewing and taking a sip of her sweet tea, she continued, "The next thing I knew my tummy was growing, and when my mama saw the signs, she beat me. Then, she took me to the old, black midwife, and they planted roots. She laid me down on a black table in a dark room in her shed and put that red hot poker between my legs until the blood ran out into the green enameled bucket. I thought I was gonna die of the pain. I almost died from the loss of blood. After that, I never could carry a baby. At three months, the blood always flooded out in torrents as if a pipe had broken as if the devil himself had opened the gates of hell. Miscarriages, eight to be exact," Mrs. Shepherd stopped for a second, her chest heaved in unreconcilable spasms.

Finally, she confessed in her deep, hoarse voice, shaking her head furiously, "Rachel, crying for her children, can never be comforted. My daughter and son are my husband's children from his first marriage."

Sally silently stared down at the table, her large brown eyes narrowed with compassion, and she leaned forward as if to grab Mrs. Shepherd, but something stopped her. It was as if the torch had passed from one to the other and now it was her turn. Her eyes rolled up back into her head becoming huge, white saucers. It was as if she were pleading with a spiritual being beyond the ceiling, and her face turned away as if to hide the unreconciled sorrow underneath. Her perfect page-boy, coiffure split into two sections down the back of her head.

"Little girls think they know so much. I was just one more, pregnant at sixteen, dropped out of school to work. "I've been working ever since. Going to school at night and working during the day. I had great hopes for my daughter. I saved every penny for her schooling. But look at her...." Sally stopped, not able to stifle her disappointment. The sorrow welled up inside her, surging like the eruption of Vesuvius, a tempestuous storm embroiling all the pain of broken dreams, a failing that emerged as long, deep sobs.

"She's expecting her third. She couldn't afford the first. She has been going to school to become a beautician, but this baby is going to change all that. Then, she comes home to me looking for a handout." Sally angrily shook her head. "I've never had a chance to do anything I wanted for myself. Always...my life and my money is for those babies and now look at me. The doctor says all my muscles are pulled down there. All the lifting I've been doing with these patients has broken me.

My uterus is prolapsed, hanging out, down between my legs. But when they take that, they'll take all my nature. Like they taking out my heart. My man is gonna leave me for someone else. They always do. They like getting their babies or thinking they can. They never worry about how to take care of them."

"But you have your babies! You got your babies! Good, bad, or disappointing. Broken dreams or not. You got your babies to comfort you in your old age," yelled Lyla sobbing.

Esther fumed. Look at all these women, crying their hearts out, letting their hearts manipulate their lives. Letting their misfortunes hold them back.

"We've got to think better of ourselves and not give in to the men and their irresponsible demands," she heard herself say. "Make them help. Make them responsible. Say no to the Scooters and the Garland Greens of the world. Say no and hold onto your dreams as tight as you can in your heart, in your soul. Never give up. It's not too late for any of us. You have control over your life. We need to grab hold of the Lord and climb out of the pit of despair. Don't let those men manipulate you the way they want. Say no to them. Let them find someone else to suck all the energy out of like a vampire. They'll do it too if they can get away with it. They're all vampires."

"You have to look up into the face of the good Lord and say that I'm a poor humble servant and ask him...will you walk with me?" Esther said, looking not at them, but up at the ceiling.

"Will you help me walk a straight line? Will you help me to have peace in my life? Will you help me give up my old ways? There is power in the Holy Spirit and He'll surround you with his peace and protection. You can have it. All you have to do is reach for it. Reach out and grab it. Don't let the hormones of mother nature dictate what you want in life. Go for the big bowl of honey in the sky. Find yourself a God-fearing man who'll love you and respect you. We're all human. We need affection and love. Pray for God to send the right man to you. Rise above the mountain. Ask more of yourself. You'll find love, respect, and security. I know it and I believe it. The good you do to others will come back to you five fold. Read the Bible and believe it," Esther said with more conviction than she ever dreamed she had.

Lyla laughed hysterically through her tears, and when she regained her composure, she hoarsely cried, "There, she goes again. She's doing it to us the way she's telling those men in the ward to hold their urine.

Who do you think you are? We can do all the praying we want. That's not going to help. Oh, it's easy for you to say Miss Goody Two-Shoes. Miss Little White Miss. Yeah! That's easy for you to say. You don't have nothing to worry about. You'll find yourself another man. Look...already they're falling at your feet to help you." Lyla wiggled her tall, stick-like body, and swung her hand around to her hip. "Why there's Henry and Mark and who knows who else," she said and laughed too loud.

Esther took it all. She took the bantering on the chin. Then, she smiled with confidence and interrupted, "You forgot the Lord. I have the Lord on my side, Lyla. Those others aren't lovers. They're helpers."

The other nurses gazed from one to the other, laughing through their tears. Esther was determined not to be intimidated by their attacks ever again.

Lyla never let up in her assault and attacked her with venomous hatred. It was as if Esther represented all the white people who had ever crossed her.

Lyla allowed her pent up anger to rage on, "You don't know what it is to suffer. You can get out of here anytime you please. Just walk out that door and never come back. When you walk out onto the street, you're free to go. Not us. Not any of us blacks. We get looks from everyone. Questions from the whites saying, 'You try to better yourself. Well, I won't let you. Get out of my way trash! I'm kicking you off the ladder to where you belong. You can work for me, but don't try to overcome me," Lyla glared at Esther defensively.

Stress and strain haunted her bulging brown eyes. Distrust marched across her angry protruded face, forcing her lips into an ugly vindictive pout. She hunched up her shoulder and stuck it into Esther's retreating face. "And you know what? I'm leaving it there for all to see. That's my attitude, and I ain't changing it for anyone."

Esther simply retreated back against the wall. The others stared silently, mesmerized by Lyla's fury.

"You think everything is so easy," Lyla continued, still fuming. Now she was walking up and down the room. Her fury frightened everyone and no one was about to get up. She peered first at Karen, then Melisa, and then Mrs. Shepherd.

"Well, not for the blacks. I was a backyard chile and grew up in one of the shanties out behind the peach orchard behind the white Massa's house. Yeah! Me, my sisters, my mama, and my grandma all grew up there. An my daddy was one of the Massa's, and my granddaddy was too. So I'm almost three quarters white with black skin. The old black man who lived in the house always left when the Massa's man came by and took his pick from all my sisters. It just so happened that Garland Green took a shine to me and never let me go. Even on his wedding night, he came around to see what I was doing for twenty minutes or so. Said he had to be a gentleman to his bride the first night. I never had a choice, and neither did my mama nor my grandmama. We had no other money or way to get it...except working for them in their houses, cleaning, laundering, and taking care of their babies, things like that. When my mama died, we put her last two names on her tombstone in rebellion. To this day, her death note defied the dictums of the white fathers of Fayette, South Carolina, never to divulge your white heritage. The names of the two warring head families of our town stood out clearly on her tombstone--Thelia McBride Corday. Her final epitaph for all the people to see. It's the everlasting truth. It was funny how they never met each other coming and going. According to law, both men could have been her common-law husband, but when they died, she didn't get a cent," Lyla declared scornfully and looked away again.

A slight shiver covered her back. She reached down and smoothed the creases out of her white skirt.

Lyla glanced back again and seeing that everyone waited, she continued, only now her anger had vanished, and the tears fell.

"I went up to the law office of Billy Corday and said, "Hey brother! How about giving me a break on the legal fees since we're kin and all. He just looked at me in shock and laughed saying, 'No sir, gal. An if you know what's good for you, you'll keep that big mouth quiet. Your mother knew better than to put my name on her tombstone for all the town to see.' The truth carved in stone is the best revenge." Lyla blew her nose on some old tissue from her black purse.

"They don't do you like that in Tennessee," she continued. "There the law states all the children inherit from the father. Even the illegitimate ones. All the children stand up on that last day side by side and take their bows," Lyla said and laughed. "If I knowed it right, the whole town'd be at Mr. Corday's funeral."

Mrs. Shepherd, still emotionally flustered, took the opportunity to cut in, "Come on now...let's get back to work. You've been through a lot, Lyla. I know life's hard baby, but it isn't Esther's fault. Give her a break. You don't know what she's suffered. Everyone's suffered something." Mrs. Shepherd patted Lyla affectionately on the back, but Lyla pulled away.

Selysia stuck her smiling face into the nurses' lounge saying, "Where's everyone? Did y'all get stuck in here? I need some help."

Mrs. Shepherd waved her on. Seeing the expressions on each face, Selysia sighed, stepped into the nurses' lounge and closed the door. She stayed just beside the door in the hot, stuffy room, and punched Karen whispering, "What's going on?" Karen waved her to be quiet.

Sally stood up, swished her hips back and forth and said with a gleaming sarcastic smile, "Oh Lyla...you think you been through so much. You're not white...you're Ethiopian. One of those tall thin Ethiopians." She gently patted Esther's shoulder. The others glanced at each other's grim faces and burst out laughing.

Esther didn't laugh. She still felt indignant, as if all the animosity had been directed toward her, toward anyone white. The sins of the fathers passed down to the children. Her old hurts came back in waves from the hearing, the divorce, and even her mother's death from breast cancer. She guessed it had been simmering there, waiting for the appropriate time to emerge. All the old longings rose up and surrounded her in a smothering cloud of humiliation and rejection. "That's all right, Mrs. Shepherd. Maybe she has a right to be angry, but I do have my injustices too."

Esther faced Lyla. She wrung her fingers, and her body stiffened with vindication. When Esther spoke, it was slow and careful at first, with deliberation as if she were telling herself too.

"Esther, don't do that. You don't have to tell them your business. They don't need to know what you've been through," Mrs. Shepherd interrupted worriedly. Mrs. Shepherd shook her head hard and tried to reach out, but Esther waved her to be still.

"No, you're wrong. Maybe they do need to know it. Here, I'll give you more ammunition. I'm on probation for giving an overdose to a patient who died. There my secret is out. My Scarlet Letter," she said, looking around the room at the stunned faces.

"If you're going to tell them that much then tell them the whole story. Don't just leave them hanging," Mrs. Shepherd interrupted hurriedly.

Esther pushed her chair back against the dirty, cream colored wall and eyed each one of the girls who were gaping wide eyed directly at her. "You've given me a hard time here. Every day, I've worked here I've paid for it dearly...suffering with your criticism and rejection. I can't leave. I was falsely accused. The judge found me an accessory to the lady who gave her husband too much morphine causing his death. They claimed because I didn't teach her about the dosage, I was just a guilty as she was. They couldn't prove anything, so they said it was "accidental overdose". But my license was held until I work for six months with supervision on probation. Some of you have even tried to incriminate me here. Thanks to Mrs. Shepherd, I've survived that too."

Silence overcame the women as they contemplated deeply their own hurts and Esther's too. They hung their heads and turned away from her, ashamed of their behavior, all except Lyla and Sally, who smiled cynically as if they enjoyed Esther's misfortune. Esther didn't miss the other stab and knew they would never understand her position. Their lives were too far away to be able to see her point of view. They were always happy to see Whitey burn. She knew this for a fact now. She picked her head up proudly, knowing that no matter what happened, her relationship with the Lord will never change. From now on, she vowed to ignore their insults and stabs.

Finally, Selysia declared irritably, but with a slight smile curling her full Vermilion mouth, "Men! Men! Men! They're the root of all evil. I told my two daughters if they even think of a man, I'll take my switches to their bottoms until they are black and blue...even now. We've got to rise up and step out of our misery. Put it behind us. They've got to finish college and learn how to take care of themselves first. If they don't do it, no one else will. They can't rely on a man to take care of them or their children. I love my children and because I love them, I've made them walk the narrow road. I've kept a switch in my purse for the last decade. When they even looked astray, I brought out that switch and scratched their little legs, sometimes drawing blood. I don't think that's abuse. I think it's good sense. They've profited by it. They both want to be lawyers. They're smart enough to do it too. They have succeeded in landing full scholarships to Smith. I've never paid a cent for anything. They're the ones who've made their own way. Each one of us can do the same thing. It only takes hard work, discipline, and faith in the good Lord. Keep your eyes on Jesus. He'll lead the way. He'll help you make miracles happen for you. You must believe in Him," Selysia said emphatically.

Selysia was so filled with emotion that she turned away from their frozen stares. She brushed away a stray fallen tear.

Sally interrupted, "I'm gonna take that course in real estate I've always wanted to take." She stood against the wall, tall, and defiant. "I've wanted to do that for several years now, but I was afraid. I'm not gonna be afraid anymore. I'm gonna do it."

"Just do it after the operation please," Mrs. Shepherd interrupted laughing. "I can only take one catastrophe at a time."

Tristine, the new nurse, entered the room. "Melisa!" she said. "Admissions called and they're sending us a new patient for room 725. They said his name was Monroe Fawcett, er...Buster? They said he was returning from a nursing home with a severe infection. That's all."

Around the room, the eyes riveted on Melisa who simply put her hand to her throat crying, "I'll be damned. The good Lord has sent him back. He must not be too sick, or they'd have him up stairs." A big smile parted her lips with the first expression of pure joy Esther had seen in her face in weeks. Now that she thought of it since Buster left.

Chapter 26

The fetid air in the nurses' lounge smothered Esther. Abruptly, she stood up to leave. The others saw her leaving, but didn't say a word to her about her probation. Actually, she flinched in pain as they turned away from her with expressions of discomfort. All except Mrs. Shepherd, who examined her with concern in her eyes and even reached toward her in a gesture of consolation. Esther was too distraught to wait. Mrs. Shepherd bit her lip as if trying to decide what to do. The worry in Mrs. Shepherd's eyes showed her she crossed the line. She shouldn't have divulged her secret to them. She had opened herself for retaliation, exposed her deep dark wound, and this was something they had been waiting for, searching for, her Achilles heel. The room began to close in on her. She felt her claustrophobic tendencies rise up inside her, creating anxiety which quickly grew into panic. She walked as fast as she could to the door without running. What will they do to her now?

The cold air in the hall hit her hot perspiring face. She raced to the medicine cart and rapidly pushed it squeaking down the hall to the ward.

Esther saw Melisa running alongside a stretcher, trying to comfort a moaning patient. The red faced, ambulance drivers, wearing white shirts and black trousers, turned into the room Clay had just cleaned. Melisa's face reflected a terror Esther hadn't seen there before.

It must be Buster, Esther thought.

Melisa waved to her, motioning for her to come over.

"Esther!" Melisa whispered in a hysterical cry, covering her mouth. "Esther," she called again. Only this time, her voice was higher pitched, a mockingbird's outcry.

A pale, lethargic body, barely conscious, moaned back from the stretcher. Esther didn't stop but raced to the clean utility room for an IV pole. He'll need lots of blankets, she thought, pulling several off the shelf along with a gown. She wondered what they did to him in the nursing home. She grabbed some blue chuck bed pads and ran back to the room.

The two ambulance men moved him from the stretcher to the bed. With each bump he groaned. The nursing home had dressed him in a red, plaid, sport shirt and sweatpants, clothes she'd never seen before. None of the clothes Melisa sent with him were returned. Esther worried if he had bed sores or not, thinking of Mr. Markowitz's wound. No matter what remedy they tried, the sores never healed, they only grew larger and deeper.

"Kidney infection and a temp of 105 degrees," Melisa said pitifully. "Help me get these clothes off him. Help me check his back."

When they stripped him of his shirt and jacket, Melisa stood back and gasped at Buster's frail, emaciated body. Every rib protruded sharply in his chest, barely covered with a thin layer of skin.

Clay stuck his head in the room and acknowledged he'd get the scale.

"I'll hold him over while you check his back," Esther said.

"He's wet, of course. I couldn't expect anything else."

They both turned him on his side and pulled down the sweat pants below his buttocks. The two gasped at the open wound with white folds of dead skin layered like cobwebs over it, sloughing off the area around the sore. On the side of his hip, his iliac crest, a black oval scab of dead tissue, three inches in diameter, told them the story he hadn't been turned for days at a time. His skin burned to their touch, like a firing of the mass, a conflagration. Buster's body reminded Esther of a withering, dying Inferno inhabited by some raving, consuming monster, and they both knew if this infection wasn't subdued, he'd die.

"Go get Henry and come back if you can," Melisa said, groaning disconsolately.

"Just look at him. All they had to do was turn him even every shift. That's all." She looked down at Buster saying, "Now don't you worry. You're home now, and we're gonna take good care of you. Didn't they turn you at all?" Melisa's eyes filled with tears. "Didn't they take care of you at all?"

Melisa glanced up at Esther with pleading eyes. "There are people in this world who don't believe in God. How else can they let this happen? They have no fear of retaliation."

Melisa filled a basin with water and gently began to wash his tissue-paper, thin skin.

Esther left to try to find Henry, but she hadn't seen him all day. She remembered he was in medical records. She decided to phone him there.

"Hello," Henry answered after one ring. His voice sounded tired and deflated.

"This is Esther. They've brought Buster back, and he's practically dead...fever 105...barely talking...emaciated. It's just a pitiful sight to see, and Melisa's a wreck."

"I'll be right there!" He didn't wait for her to answer and hung up.

Esther hated leaving Melisa, but her men were returning soon. She still felt shaken from the sight of Buster but tried to suppress it. She grabbed Sally and asked her to help Melisa. She poured her afternoon medications for the men even though they hadn't arrived yet. She hoped Henry remembered she had to pick up her car. Now with Buster's problems, she didn't know.

She promised to put Mr. Penderghost into the whirlpool tub and hoped the others had tried to use their urinals. Otherwise, she had to fix all the attends on each patient. She collected her treatment supplies from the clean utility room and placed them at the bedsides, waiting for the patients to return from physical therapy. She felt calmer now. The tidiness of the ward gave her a sense of completeness and accomplishment as she gazed out the window at the three tall buildings of the city in the distance. Fayette, South Carolina, she said to herself. She never expected to be here, in a place like this. All the way from Hopkins Hospital to Thornhill. Maybe that's where God wanted her to be.

She only had two months left of her probation. She wanted to move back to Maryland. At least her friends were there, but her two boys wouldn't see their father.

At that moment, sounds of cynical laughter and the whirl of wheelchairs caught her attention. Peering down the long hall, she watched her rehabilitation patients, one by one, round the corner from the elevators and zoom straight for her.

First Mr. Marten, then Mr. Cristford, and then, to her surprise, Shaw picked up speed trying to catch up with the others in a race to the ward.

Screaming, "Whoopee." They threw their charts on top of the nurses' station counter, ignoring the complaints of the ward clerk. One of the charts slid too fast and flew sprawling to the floor. Pink, yellow, and white forms fanned out over the polished linoleum.

Loud curses and cries of retaliation from the ward clerk followed. He ran after them with his fist raised, while the chairs whirled past him with the riders curled up in a racing position, baring their teeth, competing for blood.

Esther laughed at their antics, loving them for it.

It seemed clear now. Even if she had cancer, what can she do about it? If she died, her husband will care for her children, whether she liked it or not. She had no parents or sister or brother to step up. Victoria may never have any children. She hated the idea of leaving them orphaned. It was the biggest stab of her life, but she realized finally, she had absolutely no control over anything. The fate of her life and her children's lives was completely up to God.

Clay strolled over to see her in his rhythmic gait, still moving the mop as if it were an extension of his body, whistling an obscure tune.

Esther smiled at the sight of a rolled up magazine sticking out of his back pocket, knowing when he entered an empty room, he'd take a few minutes to glance at the articles. One of the patients must have given it to him.

When Esther entered the ward, the men had already lined up at their assigned beds, waiting for their medications and vital signs. All except for Mr. Marten who flew past saying, "Help me. It's working." He flew into the bathroom and Esther followed him.

I can't believe they're controlling themselves, she thought. Can she possibly let herself imagine that asking them to hold their urine was possible? The idea worked for her and for them.

She ran into the bathroom and watched him use his urinal.

"What's going on?" she asked Mr. Marten, knowing exactly what he meant, bending over him to see if he needed any help, actually afraid to ask.

"That darned idea you had. I never expected it to work. But looky here. I held my urine just now. I held it downstairs too. I held it before lunch. This makes it three times today. I've been concentrating very hard. It's the hardest thing I've ever had to do, but it's working!"

Esther stood back awkwardly gawking at his smiling, boasting face. She impatiently waited as he continued to explain. Her heart raced. This was the grumpy Mr. Marten. She had already congratulated herself, but then she wondered if he might have done it all along. Even for the past five months since he'd been a patient in here. If only someone had directed him before. Or was it actually a miracle?

For the first time that day, she forgot all the misery she suffered. She felt light headed, pranced about as if she were walking on air. Yes, it worked. Her mother was right. Just listen to that small voice in the back of your mind. The one that tells you to look both ways before crossing the street. The one that tells you not to go out in a rainstorm.

The voice that tells you to watch out for certain people. The little voice of experience inside your mind knows more than you do. Her mother never told Esther where it came from or who it was, but only to listen to it and follow it. Even if you think you're on the wrong road. If it looks possible and good, go for it.

"Yes, this proves it," she said to herself and thanked God for it. Because the voice she listened to said to tell these men who were paralyzed, holding their urine meant living outside of the hospital.

"Mr. Marten, that's wonderful news.This means you can go home finally, as soon as you can use the walker. If you practice your balance and continue to hold your urine, you can go to the halfway house," Esther said, as she helped him wash up a little. He was even humming to himself.

"Now look," she whispered in his ear. "I want you to go around the ward and tell the other patients how hard you practiced and how the procedure worked. Maybe they will try with more concentration."

He grinned from ear to ear with pride saying, "Yeah! I'll show them how easy it is." He leaned over to her and confessed, "Mr. Cristford has been furious with you ever since you told him he was the one who had the control. See...all the time he's been blaming everyone else for not progressing faster...for not getting well sooner."

Yes, she thought, this was their secret. She patted him on the shoulder affectionately, and his appreciative smile returned her warmth.

Cries from the ward immediately interrupted their conversation. Mr. Penderghost hollered it was his turn for the whirlpool tub and not to forget him today.

She pushed the steel medicine cart into the middle of the ward and gazed around at each flushed face for a second. It didn't take her long to ascertain the situation. Over her shoulder, she witnessed Chester having a close heart to heart with Mr. Cristford. She watched them exchanging cups and knew for sure they didn't see her. No wonder they're so jovial today. She sighed heavily, dreading her confrontation with Chester. She thought he'd stopped drinking. She remembered him getting saved and giving up alcohol for all time.

"All right, Chester! I see you!" she said, glaring at him. "Maybe I should sample that cup you're passing around."

They jumped guiltily at being called out. The expression of dismay covered their faces. Chester merely laughed at her with cool detachment. Mr. Cristford, on the other hand, avoided her gaze and gulped a huge swallow, which twisted and contorted his face. A bitter potion, she concluded, at his expression. Serves him right. Immediately his face and especially his nose reddened, unmistakably flushed from the vasodilator alcohol.

"Ah...ha," she said to herself. She wasn't the naive person who witnessed this sort of exchange on her first day and didn't recognize it for what it was.

Without a moment's hesitation, Esther exchanged Mr. Cristford's medication with the cup in question, and after smelling its contents she recoiled from the pungent odor of pure liquor.

"Just as I figured," she said, shaking her finger at them both. "Haven't you learned your lesson by now?"

"I guess not," said Chester, smiling meekly. His smile appeared taunting this time, and they both knew Esther wouldn't turn him in.

"It's only a little snort," he added, cowering away from her admonitions. "Don't you think he needs something to calm his nerves?" Chester said, pointing to Mr. Cristford.

"Look, Chester," Esther said irritably, pulling his medications from the drawer in the cart. "I don't want to report you. But I'll have to if you don't stop this. I've decided to report you to Henry. Aren't you supposed to go to an apartment soon? I thought the social worker found a place for you to live."

Chester bent his head down ashamed. His red mouth twisted grotesquely. He stared down at his feet. Shifting his weight from one foot to the other, he carefully and deliberately unrolled the cuffs of his faded, worn, gray, plaid shirt.

"She has, Ma'am," he answered. "I'm supposed to go today. This was just a going away gathering that's all," he whispered timidly, scratching his whiskers and peering at her with intense knowing eyes. The look made Esther shiver at the worldliness of his gaze.

"Oh, gosh, Chester. I forgot you were leaving today," she confessed, her tone changing. She wondered if he'd be all right out on his own. If this kind of behavior was any indication, she doubted it.

"I'm glad you told me because I'm not going to be here tomorrow. I'm having some x-rays done. I'll surely miss you around here. If you need anything, just call us. We'll take care of it for you. I'm sure Clay or Jewels or any of us will be happy to help you out in a pinch," Esther promised. He had become a permanent resident here on the seventh floor, and the idea that he was leaving hit her harder than she imagined.

In the past four months, some of these men had become as close as family.

"So, can we have our little celebration? It's only Shaw, me, Mr. Cristford, and Penderghost?" Chester said, his eyes pleading for leniency.

"Penderghost? Is he in this with you?" She glanced back into the ward in time to observe all the faces staring wistfully and expectantly at her with innocent, upturned, cherub eyes, waiting silently for her decision. Their burdens had been forgotten for the present. How quickly they changed, she mused.

She scowled down at each face with determination not to give in, and declared, "No. No. No! I said no! Can't you remember what trouble you got into the last time? The entire floor got riled up, and Hudson died. Wasn't that enough for you?"

"Thanks, I appreciate the help," Chester said.

"Don't try to make me feel guilty about this. I can never give you the impression I condone this type of behavior. These men are on medications that will react poorly if they drink alcohol. You too. Don't you know that?"

Shaw grinned from ear to ear, his tongue protruded. She sighed in frustration at feeling caught in the middle. She slammed the drawer to the medicine cart as she carried Shaw his pills. He was one who she especially wanted to learn to hold his urine. He'd be so much happier, and so will everyone else.

Chester stubbornly refused to be moved by anything she said. Out of the corner of her eye, as she argued with him, she watched Penderghost and Marten in a huddle, passing another cup back and forth between them.

"You two men think you are so clever, don't you?" She ran over and grabbed the cup and smelled it, but there was no odor only water. She searched around for another one and found an empty cup in the back of Shaw's chair.

"You think you've fooled me. Well, I'm watching you every minute so get rid of the stuff. If they find this liquor on any of you, I'll be held responsible. I might even lose my job. Do you want that responsibility on your hands?"

The spectacle of her confession to the nurses earlier returned to her thoughts with an intense force. The visions of evil brewing in their vindictive minds haunted her. She shoved these immobilizing and paranoid ideas out of her head, knowing the nurses can get her on anything in this place. If they wanted to.

She needed to concentrate on performing her best job and getting out of here as soon as possible. She only had two months left. This was her only goal.

She ignored Chester and walked confidently over to Mr. Penderghost, whose face flushed too much to be from the heat of the room.

"Come on now, it's time for your whirlpool bath," she said softly. Turning his wheelchair in the direction of the showers, she briefly glanced back long enough to holler, "I'll be back in a few minutes. Get rid of the stuff. I"d better not find any inebriated patients in here either."

Grins expanded their faces from ear to ear, all except Mr. Penderghost who sat silently frozen in his chair, like a crestfallen child. His ragged bushy eyebrows drew together over-shadowing his disgruntled mouth. She laughed at the sight of him.

"Now, what's wrong with you? Why do you look so blue? You're getting your bath just like you wanted."

"Yes, that's right. I'm happy about that. But I'm missing the party. I'm missing all the commotion and celebration." The corners of his mouth pulled into a twisted frown.

"Oh, come on, Mr. Penderghost. I'll leave you in the tub longer and just think...you can fly today...take that ride on the lift," Esther said, laughing at his growling pout.

"Oh, I've never done that," he answered cautiously, his humor brightening a little.

She pushed him rapidly toward the shower room, hoping no one had taken her tub. Fortunately, the area appeared empty.

After Mr. Penderghost's bath, when they returned to the ward, the men were in the back corner of the room, in the shadows of the dim twilight. The group hung together in a wad of camaraderie, but a din of ruckus and loud laughter emanated from them. In the middle of the group, she saw Clay, leaning against the wall, evidently telling jokes of some kind, because every time he said a few words they laughed all the more.

When he spotted her entrance, they immediately grew silent, staring at her goggle-eyed with too wide gleaming smiles, and glassy eyes.

"Miss Esther," they all said in unison. "We all held our urine. Just like Mr. Marten here." They laughed hysterically, not able to stop themselves, enjoying the expression on her face. Mr. Marten hid a large bottle of mouthwash behind his back.

"I know you are all high on that booze, but I don't care anymore. If you tried to hold it you could. Mr. Marten did. This is your life, not mine. I'd appreciate it if you threw that stuff away." She glared over at Clay who also leaned against the wall, smiling just like the rest of them. She felt like giving up, but she knew she couldn't.

"I'm sick of all your fooling around."

"I'm sick of your fooling around," they mimicked her high, female voice.

Mr. Marten handed her the nearly empty bottle of mouthwash.

Esther grabbed the bottle from him and shook her head.

Chester shook the hands of everyone in the ward.

"Yes, this is my happy day. I never thought I'd make it out. I feel like I've been in prison or some kind of reclamation center for humans. God's called me again, and I'm heeding the call. No more booze for me. This is the last celebration," he said, smiling genuinely, exposing his broken teeth. All the time, he passed out packs of cigarettes to the men.

"You gotta find someone else to do your fetching for you. I'm fixin' to see my daughter and my granddaughter and stay with them awhile. The social worker found their phone number. I called my daughter yesterday. She said come ahead for a couple of days. I get my check every month. It's enough to eat and live okay on. I'll be free. Free as a bird flying in the sky. I can even sleep out under the stars if'n I want. They say I'm cured of that tuberculosis. They say I'm all right. If I take care of myself and don't drink, I'll be good," he explained in his rhythmic tone. He glanced at his watch as he walked over and picked up his suitcase. "It looks like my time is up here. They're kicking me out. Maybe the good Lord will find me a nice girlfriend, huh? Someone to fix me a little breakfast and get my paper. Someone to sit and watch the television with and pass away the time. Someone to turn over in bed next to at night and wake up to in the morning. Yeah. I think that'll be nice."

The others cheered him on saying, "Don't fall off the mountain. Don't get off the train! Keep your head up! You're our boy! We're counting on you!"

Chester lumbered out the door and down the hall in long strides giving way to his angular gait and waved to the cheers of the men. Shaw sat in the middle of the hall and stuck out his hand for Chester to hit as he passed by.

Esther felt a lump in her throat. "All right, men," she said, hoping this would be the last medicine today, "Laxatives. Who needs a laxative?"

Esther scanned the room, but the men laughed at her saying, "Can't you see, gal? We've already gotten ours!"

She pushed the heavy cart back down the hall, thankful this day was over. Echoes of their laughter followed her. Now, tomorrow was her mammogram and she'd find out if her lumps were malignant or not. She passed Buster's room where Henry and Melisa were talking with him. He already had IVs running. They waved her on. She slipped into the nurses' lounge to retrieve her things. She hoped Henry remembered she had to pick up her car. When she reached the elevator, Henry was waiting for her.

Chapter 27

A week later on Thursday night, the night before her surgery, Esther saw herself as alone in the world, more than ever. She glanced around her comfortable living room, letting her eyes rest on her grandmother's cherry, slant top desk which her mother passed down to her. She walked over to it and rubbed its chestnut-brown, time-polished patina, letting her fingers feel its satin smoothness, its rich familiarity. Beautiful pieces of furniture move across the generations in a way people can't, she thought sadly, missing her grandmother.

Esther remembered opening each of the tiny drawers with her baby fingers when she was a child and examining the contents as if they held prizes. One drawer held a broken figurine. Another drawer held pens whose points had bent into disuse. Another drawer held an old faded letter. Grandma said it was from her brother before he was killed in the war. At this moment, Esther felt happy that she memorized the contents of those drawers for special times like this when she needed reassurance that someone had loved her unconditionally. Esther drew comfort from the vision and experienced an unexplainable warmth from the love her grandmother lavished on her. She never became irritable or upset, only admired everything Esther said and did, even marveled at it.

Her boys tumbled on the carpet in front of her, laughing, and trying to catch each other's feet. Usually, she'd be upset by all the ruckus and be impatient to get them to bed, but not tonight. She watched them intently, awed at their perfection. She felt pleased that Matt carried Paul's exact blue eyes, her mother's perfect cherub smile, and her grandmother's square solid chin. She didn't see herself in that face, only the people she had loved and lost. Some days, for that reason, his appearance comforted her. She felt guilty she had to leave the boys in daycare all day, wishing she stayed home with them more. She wanted them to grow up in a loving home with both parents, but now they were already tainted, different, part of a divorced pair. She didn't know what having a father was like. A man who loved her and raised her up in his arms as if she were his perfect child. She didn't know what it felt like to have a man take care of her and her mother. She knew Eric didn't remember Paul's presence every day. Now he showed so many signs of irritability, aggression, and evidence of not being able to control his temper. She wondered if he had his father's impatient personality.

Some days, however, he played independently, acting out very sensible ideas, like Mark. She didn't know if his fussiness reflected his personality, like Paul's, or if it came from the effects of daycare.

The minute she sat down on the sofa, Matt and Eric surrounded her, wanting her attention. She grabbed a book from the table and read out loud to them, squeezing them tightly to her, never wanting to let them go. She wanted to give them the love her grandmother had given her. She wanted to make up for the time she left them in daycare, left them at the mercy of strangers. She felt a deep sadness that they didn't have a loving grandmother like her Nana. She wondered if she could ever make it up to them.

After she put her boys to bed, she sat down to write a few items in a letter to Paul, just in case something happened tomorrow. She thought this idea foolish, but visions of operation failure crept into her mind ever since she found out about the surgery.

The phone rang. She jumped up immediately, curious to know who would call this late.

"Hi!" Mark answered. "I've really missed you."

"Where have you been?" Esther asked, feeling her heart jump. She thought he'd forgotten all about her, caught up in Paul's wedding, and his trip to South America.

"I can say one thing. I'm happy to be home, finally," he confessed wearily. "It's a long story. They sent me to Brazil to take care of an old account. When I arrived, no one knew the reason for my being there. It seems that Mr. Connoly, the vice-president of the firm, sent me down there because I arranged the hearing for last Tuesday, contesting the will."

"Oh, that's terrible Mark. I didn't know they were so powerful."

"It seems they are," Mark answered. He sounded aggravated. "And that's not the whole story. Wait until you hear this. Mr. Connoly is the trustee of my father's will and trust. He is also my mother's right arm. He does whatever she wants. They didn't want me to contest the will before Victoria and Paul married. Somehow, they think if the hearing is after the wedding it will weaken my...ah...our case. It's a real mess."

"What do you think? Do you think we have a chance?"

"I've been asking around, and while I was in South America, I was able to do some research with all my spare time. It seems there are precedents on record where people have contested wills and won even with a child already born. We have a good chance without a child of theirs born, especially since your boys are his grandchildren. Yes, I think we have a good chance."

"I know this is a lot of work for you to do. I hope you don't get into any more trouble about it, but I know the boys will appreciate any help you can give," she said.

"If my guess is right. If we win, the boys will immediately receive an income...interest generated from the trust. You see he designed his trust so the final distribution will be to his grandchildren, equally and whomever they may be. Neither Paul nor I can touch the trust fund. However, since the boys will be heirs, their portion will increase each year as they age. I think that's the way it works anyway. When they reach twenty-five, they will receive fifty percent of their share. It's very complicated. How's everything with you? I'm sorry I missed your appointment. Is everything all right?" Mark asked as his voice changed from agitation to actual caring."

"I suppose you'll find out anyway. I'm having surgery tomorrow. Outpatient surgery. I'll only be in there one day," Esther confessed hurriedly, not really wanting Mark to come, and yet, she wanted to clue him in on what was going on. She was still angry at Mark for leaving and didn't want to be disappointed again."

"I'm sorry to hear that. What are you having surgery for?" I...a...I'm afraid you never told me," Mark answered.

"I didn't want to think about it myself. I have a cyst on my breast. The doctor is removing it tomorrow."

"Oh! Is there any chance it can be malignant? I never dreamt you might have something that serious."

"I'm worried now. I've tried to keep my mind off it. I have to confess I'm writing a letter to Paul in case something happens tomorrow. Can I ask you to look after the boys for me?"

"Yes, of course. Tomorrow's my first day back at the office. I have appointments scheduled all day. If I'd only known, I would have been able to help you. Saturday is Paul's wedding. I'm afraid I'm going to be busy all day then too. What are you going to do?"

"It's all right, Mark. I have someone helping me tomorrow. I only need someone to take care of the boys if something happens to me," Esther whispered, her voice dropping off.

"You know I love those two kids. I promise that if anything happens, I'll take care of them. Paul's their father. I know he will jump in and even Victoria. She is really a wonderful person." There was a long pause. "There's a call coming through on my other line. I'll call to see how you are tomorrow. Bye."

Esther hung up the phone, feeling oddly chilled. He said all the right words, but somehow she realized he wasn't the adoring Mark she imagined. He had changed. Ever since the divorce became final, his attitude towards her became more aloof. Before, he either visited or called every night. A week had passed since she'd seen him. This court hearing was fine for her boys' inheritance, but it had nothing to do with her.

Esther felt abandoned. Suppose she died during the operation tomorrow from some kind of accident. What will become of her boys? Hopefully, Victoria and Paul will raise them. By default, Victoria will get everything she had worked so hard to acquire, especially her children. Esther's head fell heavily into her hands. How did this happen to her? Why? Why God why?

Henry promised to take her to the hospital for surgery in the morning, stay with her, and take responsibility for the boys. She worried if Henry was as dependable as all that? This was a big order. She hoped he cared enough to follow through or get someone to help him. Even at the hospital when she told the nurses she was to have surgery, no one offered to help her. The blacks always stick together, she admitted. They wanted to be considered as equal, but only for the good things. Don't expect any charitable attention, she told herself. I guess they figured I don't need any help. Whites have magic. They can get anything they want.

Their reaction disappointed her. Especially after four months of working there. She hoped someone might volunteer to help. Maybe watch the boys for her, something, but they didn't. Only Henry.

She laid the white vellum note paper on her grandmother's desk and wondered where to begin. She had called Paul yesterday and asked if he'd take the boys for the weekend. It would have been such a help to her. To her surprise, Saturday was the day they were getting married. Under the circumstances, she didn't want Paul to care for her children anyway. How had she forgotten he was getting married this weekend? A lovely September wedding, she thought. How quaint. Had it shattered her? Was she ruined for any other fine glowing romance? Only time will tell.

Esther sighed and glanced around her living room. Each piece of furniture represented a too familiar object, carrying so many memories.

She remembered Paul loved the picture of a country scene hanging over her sofa. He said it reminded him of growing up on his farm in South Carolina. She wondered why he left it for her.

She tried to return to the letter she was writing, but for some reason, the words refused to come. What do you say to a man who deceived you, and you're about to give him the most prized possessions of your life? How can I expect him to cherish his sons when I'm gone? He doesn't cherish them now.

Suddenly, Esther remembered her mother sitting at the same desk, writing out a list of things for her to do the week her mother was in the hospital. It was only four years ago. Her mother found a lump in her breast just the way she found hers.

Esther remembered her mother sat up, poker straight, the day before the surgery in the exact same chair Esther sat in now. Her mother wore her fashionable, gray-flannel, Chanel suit with a yellow silk blouse. She had taken care of all her business at the real estate office where she worked and set up the apartment for her post operative stay. Her mother had her hair cut and waved in the most fashionable style, smooth and buoyant like Jackie Kennedy. She polished her nails blood red to match her new lipstick.

"It cost a little more for the manicure, but I think I'm worth it," she said. "Do you like it? I want to explain to you about tomorrow. If they discover the lump is malignant, the doctor will be forced to take off my whole breast. I have already signed permission for this to take place. If it is benign then we'll celebrate, and I'll be home the day after tomorrow. No matter what happens, I'll look like a million dollars for all the doctors and nurses. If I resembled death warmed over, I'd ruin everyone's mood including mine. So, do you like it Esther?" her mother asked casually, not caring if Esther liked her hair or not.

The day her mother had surgery was the last day Esther saw her mother genuinely laugh. It was the last day she joked about anything. When she returned from surgery, the doctor had removed both breasts. The lump was malignant and had already spread to the lymph nodes. One thing her mother was right about, she looked great, and her hair held its set for most of the week. The doctors, however, removed most of the nail polish in the operating room.

Esther's heart ached when she remembered those days. She recalled her mother coughing spasmodically just to get her breath. It was a nightmare. She prayed God wouldn't let her have cancer and die like that. It had only been four years since her mother's death, but Esther had repressed most of her suffering.

The phone rang, and Esther rose to answer it. "Hello."

"I was wondering if you're all right tonight? Are you nervous or anything?" Henry asked with concern.

"Yes, I'm scared to death."

"You know 5:00 a.m. is a God awful early hour. Maybe I should come over tonight and stay...spend the night. How does that sound?"

"Spend the night?" Esther answered, her voice cracked with each syllable. The thought that tomorrow might mean the end of her life too, changed her mind. Why not? God wouldn't mind if she was going to die.

"Sure," she said, casually. This was not her speaking only her voice. It didn't communicate the terrible thumping of her heart or the cold sweat on her forehead or the burning in the pit of her stomach. No, it didn't reveal her complex internal struggles. It seemed so easy on the outside. She was lonely and needed comforting right now. Suppose the lump was malignant. Then what? Henry will forget all about her. Henry will run off to his next conquest. She was a big girl now. She knew men didn't want any complications in their lives like cancer or children. Especially cancer.

She examined her tired face in the mirror. She was a different person from the young woman in the photo, the bride of Paul Culver, Southern gentleman. No, she looked thinner if that were possible. Her hair needed a new style cut, had for weeks now, but there wasn't money for beauty or for her boys' hair either. She cut their hair the old fashioned way, with a bowl. She thought they looked cute.

She brought out her suitcase and packed her makeup, clean underwear, pink robe, and gown. She didn't know what to expect up there in that stainless steel operating room. If the lump proved malignant, she knew they would remove her breast, but nowadays, they didn't excise the entire breast unless the cancer metastasized. They use chemotherapy and radiation instead. She examined her hair again and realized her hair would fall out with chemotherapy. She worried about managing her money. She had disability through the hospital. "God, please don't let this be cancer," she prayed again.

The doorbell rang. She forced herself to smile in the mirror, straighten her collar, comb her hair, and stand up straight, all rumination behind her.

She opened the door, and there stood Henry, slumped down, a little bedraggled, carrying his pillow, an overnight bag, a teddy bear, and several boxes of stuff. She laughed out loud.

"It looks as if you've prepared for a sleep in or an atomic bomb attack."

He examined her with a disgruntled expression and grumbled, "I don't know how long this siege is gonna last. You're not going to be in any shape to take care of things tomorrow night or Saturday. I figured I might as well bring everything I need." He pushed past her and dumped the bags and things on the floor next to the sofa.

He smiled sheepishly and pointed to the teddy bear and huge truck saying," I bought these for the boys. Are they in bed?"

"Yes and asleep I hope. I never expected all this," she answered, speechless.

"What did you think? Did you think I'd just drop you off tomorrow with two active boys and say 'so long'? Expect you to rise up from the anesthetic and be able to take care of them? What do you take me for? I take good care of my girls," he said and laughed exposing his two rabbit teeth. "I even brought several videos. How about Batman? Ha! Ha! I'm no dummy. These two square boxes represent three to five hours of peace and quiet. For me, that is." He coughed and sniffed his nose uncomfortably.

"I hope you're not coming down with anything," Esther said and reached for his forehead.

"Oh, it's just a sinus allergy of some kind. I've been nursing it for several days now." He waved her hand away. "Come on, you're the patient now."

He walked into the living room and took some of his things to the corner. He surveyed the sofa curiously and pulled the cushions off.

"Maybe you can show me how this thing works?" he asked with a silly smile.

She waited in silence for several seconds, realizing this meant he intended to sleep on the sofa. Relief filled her, and she let out her breath. She relaxed, knowing he wasn't going to compromise her integrity tonight, anyway. She shied away not wanting him to see her flushed face, but nothing escaped him.

"Hey, wait a minute. You didn't think I intended on sleeping with you?" He scanned her with his 3D eyes and raised his eyebrows into two quizzical points.

This caught her off guard, off balance. Yes, she wanted to sleep with him. No, she didn't want to sleep with him. What should she say now? Oh, he was an expert, she thought. He left it up to her now. He out maneuvered her. She wanted to sleep with him and even intended to, but she didn't want the problems or the hurt. She only wanted comfort. What would he say if she told him that?

"Please don't ask me that question tonight," she said finally.

His mood changed immediately. His step quickened. He quickly unpacked his things, hanging his clothes in the hall closet. Finally, he examined her face closely, saying in a serious tone, "I'm a guest here in your home. We've been through a lot together, haven't we? But you're still Mother Teresa to me. I hate to tell you that." He took a deep breath, increasing his chest size, and rising up to his full height.

"I know I'm so irresistible you can't keep your hands off me, but...." Slowly he let the air escape from his chest. She watched his shoulders sag and saw for the first time the desperation in his eyes.

"You're in trouble. I can't take advantage of your declined defenses. I know you. I know you're lonely and hurt by all that's happened. We're friends. I'm not gonna press myself or my desires on you when you are at your most vulnerable. What do you take me for? There are plenty of women who would welcome me into their beds. Not this way. You'd hate me later. I know you, and I'm not gonna take that chance." He reached out, pulled her to him, and hugged her with all the tenderness she needed and yearned for all day. He patted her head, stroked her hair, and sighed into her ear, saying, "I'm gonna hate myself in the morning."

They both laughed and she admitted, "I really appreciate your feelings. I didn't know what to expect when you wanted to come over. I'm a mess. This thing has really scared me."

"I know," he answered. "It has me scared too. My wife died of cancer."

Chapter 28

Esther woke up from the anesthesia to murmuring voices. Pain seared her chest in an unending assault, and she moaned from the discomfort. She tried to escape to the painless dream state of unconsciousness but couldn't. Her body felt cold from the shock of the anesthesia and surgery. She squinted her eyes in an effort to focus on what was going on around her. Unknown faces, with their hair covered with green scrub caps, entered and left her span of vision. Another nurse covered her with a heated flannel blanket and asked her if she remembered her name. All she said at the moment was, "Pain. Please get me something for the pain."

"Just press the button," the voice said kindly, as the face left her. "Morphine," the vague face whispered in her ear, "You're in the recovery room. Just press the button and the medication will be released."

Esther pushed the button, and to her surprise almost instantly an aura of wooziness surrounded her as she faded out of consciousness. The pain disappeared until she awoke again sometime later.

A familiar voice entered her dream acoustic fog saying, "It's time for her to wake up now, don't you think?"

The other voice called softly, "Esther. Esther Culver. Your surgery is over now. Everything's all right."

Esther felt for her left breast and discovered an immense bandage covering the painful area. She opened her eyes finally to see Henry staring down at her, bearing a concerned frown.

"Henry? What did they find?" she asked, slurring her words, and moving her tongue around her lips, trying to create some moisture from her dry mouth.

He grabbed her hand and said hurriedly, "So, you're awake after all."

He smiled his nervous teasing grin as if trying to hide something. His two rabbit like front teeth stood out from his face like two gleaming soldiers as he leaned down and whispered, "All the cysts were benign. No sign of cancer at all."

She closed her eyes and sighed deeply with relief. The words immediately erased the agony she suffered these past few weeks, and the dreaded picture of herself wasting away and dying like her mother.

Now, she knew God had given her a second chance. Silently, she promised Him she'd try to make the most of her life.

Henry's hand clutched hers firmly and steadily. His energy and warmth permeated up into her arm. The power of it raced through her body like some exotic, potent drug, until his all encompassing tenderness enveloped her completely. Feeling safe and cared about for the first time in months, she drifted off to sleep.

Somehow, Henry survived discharging her, retrieving her boys from daycare, feeding them, and tucking them into bed. Henry assisted her comfortably into bed as well, as if he had done this every day, and skillfully cared for the boys too.

The next morning, she awoke to the scampering of Matt and Eric, each, in turn, running in to check to see if she was awake yet. The burning in her chest had eased some. Now the discomfort was more from the tape than anything.

"Mommy's up," they hollered, racing in and out of the room. She hastily raised her hand in protest when they charged her, attempting to use the bed as a landing strip. The effort caused her to wince with discomfort, and when they saw this, they stopped immediately. They dutifully came over and kissed her on the cheek saying, "Are you better now?" Their blue eyes grew huge in their round cherub like faces. Their blond hair fell in thatches partially obscuring their eyesight.

"Yes, I'm better now," she answered softly, thankful she had them to give her something to live for.

She'd better get up, she prodded herself and feed them breakfast. She didn't remember Henry leaving the night before. She guessed he simply let himself out.

"Are you hungry?" she asked her boys who were imitating each other's cart wheels and performing acrobatics on the carpet, barely missing the bed with each turn.

"No!" they exclaimed. "Henry fixed us pancakes and orange juice. Henry fixed you something too."

She lay back on the white lace pillows, relieved, wondering if Henry treated all his girlfriends this way. She hoped he didn't ask for a great payment for his help. She hated to feel so indebted to him, but he had been wonderful.

He stealthily entered the room, blushing like a school boy, carrying a tray of breakfast choices: hot tea, pancakes, sweet rolls, and juice. A smile crossed his concerned face, and after he carefully placed the tray on the unfolded table next to the bed, he brushed his hair out of his sea-green eyes. Their depth always amazed her.

Matt and Eric scrutinized each movement he made as if they tried to memorize each action for a later date. The expression of adoration shown in their faces. They waited patiently for her reaction.

"Where did you get all the food?" Esther asked, surprised at his ingenuity.

He smiled broadly, not hiding his comical, lecherous expression. "Oh, I have my ways," he answered, glancing at the boys with a mysterious look. They sat up straighter and smiled little half soldier smiles as if sworn to secrecy.

"I suppose you do this for all your girls," she said, feeling defensive.

He turned his face away frowning from her barb. She wished she could retrieve her remark, but the carnage was done. His expression lost its unbridled joy. He began to hedge his remarks, awkwardly averted his gaze, as if self-conscious about his feelings.

She didn't mean to insult him. She felt scared of being hurt herself, that's all. How can she repair the damage?

"Oh, this is such a lovely assortment of breakfast food," she said, cowering into her pillow. "I don't know where to begin."

She tried to move over to the side of the bed, but the effort became terribly painful still. Henry lost his annoyance and leaned over to gently help her rise to a sitting position. He deftly propped all the pillows behind her, making her feel like an imperial princess, and proceeded to spread butter and pour syrup on her pancakes.

The aroma of his aftershave lotion, the pancakes, and sweet rolls filled her nostrils, overwhelming her with nostalgia, reminding her of the first Mother's Day Paul served her breakfast in bed, and other holidays when she and Paul were first married. She tried to repress the pain these memories evoked and attempted to see Henry in Paul's place. Underneath Henry's show of denial, she sensed an intense affection, a genuine caring beyond his professed friendship. There is passion under all his help, she told herself.

She examined him closely. His breaths came and went with deep inspirations and expirations in his immense chest. His wind sounded remarkably like the changing tide of the ocean. Waves crashing into the beach and foam floating out to sea. He cut her pancakes for her in delicate little bite size pieces, poured out her tea, and added the right amount of sugar. He scrutinized her every swallow, handing her the tea and juice at the appropriate times, saying cheerfully, "Here you go," and, "Just take your time."

He winced slightly when he examined her bandage, and even later when he removed the white tape to expose the three lines of black stitches. One of the incisions lay open at the end holding a drain. He expertly cleaned the incision with hydrogen peroxide and dressed it with a new gauze dressing.

When he guided her into the bathroom, his warm breath on her neck felt comforting for the first time. She hated to close the door on him. He merely smiled knowingly, saying, "It's all right. I'll be waiting right outside."

Later she noticed that a peculiarly pensive mood settled over him. No matter how much joking she pretended, she couldn't pry him out of it.

* * *

Later on that day, in the afternoon, he acknowledged to himself how worried he had been about her. He felt up tight all morning and didn't know why. Now he understood. The whole time he watched her pick up the cup of tea and sip delicately, he couldn't get the picture of Christiana out of his mind. There was something about the paleness of Esther's face and hands that haunted him.

He remembered how helpless he felt as he watched Christiana waste away. The chalky whiteness of her skin never left her body after the diagnosis. He always wanted to pour a pint of blood into her veins just to see the immediate pinking effect. Even after a transfusion, her cheeks refused to color. Her wonderfully delicate face, that he loved to hold in his hands, grew more transparent with each passing day. The whiteness of her skin appeared as if all her blood had evaporated from her body, leaving a shell resembling bone china. Sometimes, he'd touch Christiana and wonder if she was brittle enough to break.

When he poured Esther's tea and handed her the plate of cookies he placed on the table, he found himself wanting to do all the right things so she wouldn't get sicker. He was shocked that within hours Esther was reduced from a vibrant young woman to this frail resemblance to Christiana. At first, he approached her surgery as the casual helping out of a friend in need. He insisted this to himself over and over again. Esther was desperate and in need of help. An innocent gesture on his part and that was all. No strings. She was without family or friend. After facing his own frustrations in dealing with her boys and trying to fit her shopping, cooking, and cleaning into his own busy schedule, he realized how much responsibility she assumed in taking care of her boys by herself. He realized how complicated her life was. He saw the fullness of her life by comparison to his.

How did she persevere with all this work, he wondered? Getting them ready for school in the morning and occupying them in the evenings proved to be a full-time job in itself. She was all alone.

Unexpectedly, pangs of admiration for her taunted him. They tugged unremittingly at his heart. He felt a sense of confusion, she wasn't the free agent he envisioned her to be. He pondered why he hadn't seen her this way before, as the mother of her children instead of the object of his playful desires, an emotional temptress.

For the first time, he saw her vulnerability. Her meager attempts to put her life back together taunted his heart strings in a way no one else had in years. In a way, she reminded him of his own searching for some sort of stability. He saw her acting out his own fumbling attempts at putting his life back together after Christiana died, only he always chose the wrong path, causing him in the end to suffer even more pain.

He laughed for a second at himself, examining his own free wheeling illustrious past. He deliberately chose women who were loosely attached, party girls, women who will never become good partners. They were mere shadows of himself--slick, superficial women, lovers of unattached fun, donning dazzling, painted nails, scarlet lips, and satisfied with a day to day existence. They never wanted a permanent relationship--it was too boring for them, too confining. But he enjoyed their plastic nature...nothing heavy or real.

He knew in his heart he'd never find another woman as pure and wonderful as Christiana, so he simply stopped searching. He enjoyed the party life up to a point. Many nights, he admitted to himself, he joined a group just so he wouldn't be alone. He had always been too scared to invest enough emotion in a single individual to want to be with them on a regular basis. Not until Esther that is. Esther's solid strength slipped into his subconscious without him realizing it, and now it was too late. She charmed everyone on the floor including him. Henry saw himself as naked, exposed in front of her. His feelings hung out like so many bare wires at the end of a cable, unsheathed, vulnerable to any insignificant chiding on her part. He felt each joust of her humor as an intense jolt to his manhood. These sparks were new to him, and he didn't know how to protect himself yet. He didn't dare let on to her either. How could he? What if she didn't care for him at all?

He watched as she eased her presence into the lives of the patients, becoming an indispensable ally to them. She tended to them as a sister or mother. The men knew her days off and dreaded her absence. He found he hated her days off too. She didn't have to care for them, she merely conveyed to them an unspoken assurance that when she appeared, they had nothing to fear. Somehow she'd help them if they needed it. They relied on Esther and Melisa.

* * *

He listened as she read a story to her boys, and when they jumped up and ran off, he blurted out shyly, "I never told you I had a wife who died of Hodgkin's disease." He glanced away from her quickly, not wanting to see the hurt in her eyes. He was still too sensitive to speak about it, although, he didn't want to admit it. He feared she might ridicule his exposed pain whose root still lay unconsoled and unresolved deep within his soul.

She nearly dropped her cup and spilled the remanent of the tea on her robe. He reached for a napkin and quickly blotted up the accident.

"Oh, Henry. I'm so sorry. I think you said something about it before, but I was so preoccupied it didn't register."

She peered up at him steadily, examining him for scars that had eluded her before. "Life inflicts so many wounds on us undeservedly, doesn't it? How long were you married?"

"Only two years and six months. It happened so quickly. Those days seem to be a blur now. I was in medical school and trying to pass my second-year midterms when Christiana was diagnosed. After the shock of that first day wore off, if it ever did, her illness seemed to be a part of all the other illnesses I studied at the time. Only with hers, we experienced each painful change of symptom personally."

Henry paused and then stood up, straightening his legs into long stretches, trying to get the kinks out. He walked slowly into the kitchen, his head bowed in contemplation, and he returned with another pot of hot steaming tea. Without a word, he gently picked up her cup and filled it again. He picked up Esther's pink and green afghan and gently covered her legs with it.

He ran his huge hands hesitantly through his blond hair. He stood over her momentarily. He drew in a deep breath and sat down heavily next to her in the overstuffed sofa before continuing.

In a gruff, thick voice he confessed, "Before I knew it the struggle was over, and we had lost. All along we were so hopeful that we'd beat the monster--Hodgkin's Disease. We even called it the 'hedgehog' at times to lighten our moods. God wouldn't let this happen to us. Our love was so great He couldn't separate us. All the foolish little games we played didn't change the ultimate outcome. I don't think I really believed she'd ever die. When the day finally came, I was stunned and overcome with defeat. I quit medical school and ran from everything after that. Every reference to her or to those years was simply too painful to endure."

He stood up and walked arduously over to the French doors and looked out. The leaves on the Silver Maple tree had turned a vibrant yellow. Clouds sweeping the sky in obscure formations had grown thick and dark, bulging out in their need to unload.

Esther sensed how hard this was for him and waited silently for him to continue.

He looked back at her rather pathetically, as if every ounce of spirit had been drained from his body. She realized his vulnerability, loneliness, and how much he still suffered. She empathized with his pain because she had endured that same hollow emptiness and ache ever since her mother died. Sometimes even now merely seeing her children ignited the remorse she harbored that her mother will never watch them grow to manhood. Losing a wife, a lover, your heart's desire must be a terrible cross to bear, she thought.

Suddenly, she saw Henry in a different light. Why hadn't he said something about all this before? Why had he let her believe his main desire was to date, everyone and anyone? Especially now, with the HIV epidemic, this kind of thinking became suicidal. Maybe that was his intention–tempting fate.

She always discounted him as a partner because she thought him callous, superficial, and even macho, especially the way he yelled at her when she made a mistake, never dreaming of his sensitivity. She even thought him a woman hater. Now, she realized he had been running from his own tender feelings. His own deep, unreconciled, despair.

She reached out for him. He came back over to her and stood beside the sofa. She touched his arm. His firm muscles felt strong and resilient. His skin yielded soft and warm. His soul opened merely a crack. His face still turned away. The rigidness of his unshaven jaw disappeared. She watched his pulse pound in his neck. He gently sat down again next to her on the sofa with all the trust and beguilement of a puppy waiting for her next move.

She didn't know what to say or do. How can she attempt to console such a deep wound with her own injuries still so raw and exposed? She had little to give emotionally. Oh, it was so easy to give to the dying men and women on the seventh floor; they were so needy and required so little. It seemed all she had left was enough energy to pat her boys on the head and give them a hug at the end of the day. How can she ever begin to nurse the desperate need that Henry exposed? How can she ever measure up to a beloved dead wife?

God, you have really done it this time, she declared irritably to herself. I can't. I just can't fall in love with him. And I won't. We can be friends and build on that, Esther told herself finally, feeling relieved of the gargantuan burden. Here he sat unmoving in her living room, the stud of the seventh floor, the stud of Thornhill Hospital, maybe even the stud of Fayette, South Carolina.

She tried to evade his sideways glance, his forlorn expression. She let her eyes fall on her grandmother's desk in the corner and allowed memories of her grandmother's enduring love to penetrate her desperate heart. A small voice came into her head saying, 'grab him, hold him, comfort him, and never let him go.' But Esther rejected the words, too afraid to trust anyone else yet.

Esther glanced at her living room walls glad she had chosen the pale green against Paul's wishes. She wondered if there was room in her heart for another man. Henry's taste differed from hers in many things, and she wasn't ready for any compromises in her life.

"Oh, Henry. If words can penetrate your heart to take away your pain, I wish that. I don't know what to say." Esther reached out to him again. "I'll be here for you anytime you need to talk to someone. You can count on me," she promised, surprised at her own tenderness.

Esther stood up and walked over to the French glass doors and stared out at the misting rain. She felt thankful to have been able to keep the house after the divorce. It gave her some stability and a refuge. She wondered where Henry lived. What his home looked like. She realized she didn't know anything about him except how tenderly he treated the patients, and how he had come to her rescue in this emergency. But he always had a girlfriend. It might be fun to get to know him better, she concluded to herself, knowing full well he had already captured her heart.

Chapter 29

The elevator doors opened, and the machine heaved and readjusted its level, then belched her out like a cat spitting out a distasteful bug, giving her a second chance at life. The voices and actions of the people on the floor spun about her as rhythmically as a top, creating a certain velocity with its own life, discharging as it danced the mingled odors of diseased bodies, disinfectant, after shave, and paste wax. Together the sounds and smells were universal, affecting her instantly, stirring some innate instinct sleeping deep within her, an involuntary drive so strong she forgot her own plight. She felt goose bumps rise around every hair follicle all over her body, remembering that nursing to her was a drive which had become an addiction, a compulsion that she both loved and hated at the same time. It was her lifeline--the pulse at the center of her being. This obligation became so strong she even risked her life to satisfy her yearning to heal and comfort. They give so much back, she said to herself, not really understanding the dynamics.

She knew she craved the continuous satisfaction she gleaned from comforting her patients, as they balanced precariously on the pinnacle between life and death. There was nothing else on this earth that gratified her more, not her own children, nor her dearest friends, nor even the most intimate moments with her ex-husband. No, this feeling was not of this earth, but spiritual. Sometimes she gleaned, if only for an instant, the experience of touching that state of mind between the living and the grave. It was the core essence of life itself, the human spirit in its purest state. Without it, her life became empty, useless, inadequate. With it, she was overworked and overwhelmed, but deeply rewarded.

Immediately, her blood pumped faster, step quickened, and spirit picked up at the sound of Mrs. Shepherd hollering, "Jewels, where are those supplies I ordered?"

Buster calling, "Why is breakfast so late? Don't forget, I have to brush my teeth first."

Melisa hollering back, "Don't I always help you...now why are you giving me a hard time? Humph, it looks like this morning is already off to a bad start."

Karen resembled a spring chicken in her yellow gingham maternity top as she quietly leaned up against the dirty, cream colored wall in the nurses' station waiting for the night nurse to call everyone for report. Her spotting had stopped, but she remained on light duty. Even her hair had been pulled up into a ponytail tied with a yellow ribbon.

Henry waved to Esther from the hall, mouthing that he'd see her later, and then sheepishly disappeared around the corner to Mrs. Shepherd's office, his arms overloaded with patients' charts.

Clay painstakingly mopped the day room floor and emptied the ashtrays under the scrutinizing gaze of the manager of housekeeping.

Esther felt for her pocket and remembered the balloons she had slipped in there. They were left over from her son's birthday two weeks ago. She wanted to give one to each one of her patients this morning to cheer them. She asked a little prayer, "Please God, go with me today and help me survive all of this."

After report, Mrs. Shepherd called to her as she moved the medicine cart down to the opposite end of the hall.

"Esther, Mr. Kroger's mother is coming for him this morning. She's taking him home for a two-day leave of absence. Can you fix medicines for the visit?"

When she entered Mr. Kroger's room, he resembled a handsome man dressed in white Perry Como blend sweater over a red turtleneck. The symptoms of his odd schizophrenic behavior disappeared at a glance. Without the illness, he would have been an attractive and talented contributor to society. Oblivious to all that went on around him this morning, he stared out the window, caught in some fog or lost memory. He didn't even acknowledge her entrance.

"It looks as if you're ready to go on your holiday." She poured his water and handed him his cup of morning pills.

He examined her as if he didn't know who she was. After a few seconds, he recognized her and smiled.

"The treatments are finished. Didn't they tell you?"

"No. No one told me anything about it."

"You're completely finished. They'll wait to see what happens with your blood studies. For the time being, you can go home for a couple of days. Isn't that great?"

He slumped down on the bed. "I guess so."

I need to clean your port and put heparin in to keep it from clotting. It'll only take a minute.

Esther skillfully inserted the needle into the rubber end and injected the anticoagulant medication. When she pulled the needle out, she accidentally stuck her thumb. She repressed crying out.

She stared at Mr. Kroger wondering if he had any communicable diseases...Hepatitis C, A.I.D.S. Her eyes filled with tears. She bit her lip.

"When your mother arrives let me know so I can give her your medications to take with you. I hope you have a great time."

"I won't forget."

Melisa hung her strawberry blond head out of Buster's room calling, "Esther, can you give me a hand? I need to pull him up in bed. They've left him in an awful mess, and he's been like this for hours."

"I'll be right there." Esther pushed in all the drawers to the cart and locked it. She sighed, thinking she must take care of the needle stick right away. She ran to Buster's room.

"I haven't seen you since you had your surgery. Is everything all right?" Melisa said, finished with Buster's bath. She deftly pushed him over to his side, and Esther held him there while Melisa dressed his bedsore and rubbed his back.

"Yes, it was a benign cyst after all," Esther said. "I'm so relieved."

"You are very lucky, and blessed too. Especially after all you've been through," Melisa said. "He's a lucky man too. I've never seen anyone as sick as Buster was when they brought him in here. Most people in that condition die. Do you hear me, Buster?"

"I hear you. My fever just went out of control, that's all," Buster said, still weak and emaciated from the ordeal.

"No. That's not all there was. You had a kidney infection and septicemia. I wish you'd tell me what they did to you in that Crestview Nursing Home?"

"I told you they didn't do nothing to me. They treated me just fine."

"I know they didn't feed you. And didn't turn you, or you wouldn't have such a deep hole. And to think of all the months I turned you, and bathed you, and took care of your back just so this never happened."

"I told you over and over again, Melisa, they didn't do nothing to me. I just got sick that's all. Maybe I was homesick for this place. Maybe my body just got tired of all their stuff that's all."

"You were only gone a month, and they almost killed ya," Melisa said still rubbing his silky smooth skin.

"And stop rubbing that same spot over and over again. That hurts," Buster cried, clawing the air with his fingers.

"I'll tell you what hurts. It hurts me to spread your stiff legs apart to clean your privates. My chest gives me a fit every time. I can't help it. And these legs." She tried to pull his foot out from being twisted under his thigh, but couldn't.

"Esther just feel these retracted muscles. Another week, and he'd be permanently locked in a fetal position and none of us could break him loose." Melisa grabbed the can of baby powder sitting on the bedside table and spread a handful across his back. She brushed her white hands on his attends and placed the diaper between his legs. All this took less than a minute because she never missed making a movement count.

In the end, she squirted a glob of lotion into Esther's outstretched hand and massaged her own hands with another dab.

"I'm supposed to be on light duty all week. I'd hate to think of what would happen if Clay weren't here to help me lift the patients. Melisa, I stuck myself with Mr. Kroger's needle when I put the anticoagulation medication in his heparin lock. It still hurts." Esther sighed. "I need to tell Mrs. Shepherd and go to employee health."

"You must go right away. I'll tell Mrs. Shepherd."

"I heard Mr. Markowitz is worse?"

"Yes much worse. He hasn't talked to me all week. Not even a yes ma'am or a thank you. You know the way he tries to make you feel better for having to care for him. And he hasn't been eating either," Melisa said, shaking her head with worry.

"Did you tell Henry?"

"No, not yet. But I think I'll try to catch him today. I'll look in on Mr. Kroger and see how he's doing."

Melisa whispered into Esther's ear again, "I'll cover for you. I hate that for you."

"It was an accident. I was stupid. Not paying close attention when I cleaned his central line and injected the Heparin," Esther admitted.

When Esther returned from seeing the nurse, Melisa was waiting for her.

"What did employee health do?"

"She said I could ask him to have his blood drawn, but she didn't think it would make any difference. She said the statistics show the needle has to be covered with blood before anyone can be infected. Out of one-hundred sticks, only one nurse came down with the disease."

"Phew. That's all I'd need. Are you scared about it? I think I'd be a nervous wreck. I love taking care of these people, but when it comes down to it, I'm a baby when I'm sick. I'm telling you something. You just stick up for yourself. This hospital will try to get off the hook if they can and not be responsible for any of it. Look at me. I've given them the best nineteen years of my life. What do they care? Nothing. They're trying to squeeze me for all I'm worth."

Melisa examined her gloves closely for any tears to protect her from Mr. Markowitz's Methicillin-resistant Staphylococcus aureus as she put on her isolation gown.

"Every day we're exposed to all kinds of diseases: tuberculosis, hepatitis C, MRSA, A.I.D.S. and who knows what else. I learned a long time ago if you don't look after yourself no one else will. They can let me retire if they wanted to, but they just don't want to release me. I think Mrs. Shepherd is holding back my papers for some reason. I wish I knew why they haven't contacted me. Help me with him, will you?"

Melisa opened Mr. Markowitz's door and tiptoed in with Esther following her. Mr. Markowitz didn't even look in their direction. His respirations came and went in labored gasps. The heat poured into the room from the radiator, evaporating out any minute particle of moisture. The last person must have left the thermostat turned above seventy-five degrees, thought Esther, as she moved the lever back to seventy. She pulled a balloon out of her pocket, blew it up, and tied it on the bed rail. The yellow transparent sphere bounced gently against the bed, buoyed occasionally by a draft of air. Mr. Markowitz's eyes remained fixed on the wall opposite the bed. They were glazed over from not blinking.

Esther and Melisa nodded to each other, knowing it wouldn't be long for him now. He had made his peace so to speak. Melisa raised the sheets, and he was immaculate. The way she'd left him only a few hours ago. They turned him and replaced his limbs for comfort. He never said a word. Esther placed her hand over his forehead and rubbed for a second. He moved his head ever so slightly back toward her hand when she removed it. Dying is such a lonely process, Esther thought.

They stripped off their isolation gowns and held their breath until they reached the fresh air out in the hall. Esther hesitated and glanced back, wanting to feel again the undefinable peace she felt in that room. She imagined his soul departing his body, flying across the Serengeti plains of Africa. She pictured it zooming back to hover over the Swiss and French Alps, then soaring fearlessly over the great Atlantic ocean, returning for only a moment to watch his body breathe the last few seconds of life. In moments, his soul will be free at last from its cloistered prison and room 703, released at last from the terminal attenuation of his body from disease.

It didn't take her long to become distracted. Patrick Shaw wheeled his chair up to the medicine cart and irritably pulled on all the drawers. He appeared crazy. His eyes filled with fury.

She ran over to him and grabbed his hands. "What's all this about? All you have to do is ask. Look at you. You're drooling all over the place."

He pointed to his head, leaned over, and banged it against the cart.

"Do you want something for pain. For your head?"

He raised his stiff hands to his forehead and moaned, nodding yes.

Esther opened his mouth and didn't see anything obstructing it or causing the increased salvation. He grabbed a styrofoam cup from the medicine cart and pushed it into his mouth. She tried to grab it back, but he had already chewed it up and swallowed it.

She unlocked the cart and took out his box, carefully locking the rest of the cart again, but not before he grabbed another drawer and pulled it out, spilling the contents on the floor.

"Stop it! Stop it!" Esther yelled.

Shaw rammed into Melisa with his wheelchair and then crashed into the cart.

Melisa grabbed the chair and yelled to Henry who just returned from the nurses' lounge.

"Henry, we need you here!" Melisa attempted to push Shaw's chair toward his room saying, "We know you're hurting. That medication should help you real soon."

In spite of her caution, he careened the chair backward striking her knees. Henry intercepted, grabbed the chair, and nearly picked the chair off the floor in spite of Shaw trying to fight with his fists.

Henry shouted, "Give him two milligrams of Haldol, IM. What's gotten into you? Are you on some kind of drugs?"

"You're not gonna keep me here against my will! I'll teach ya," hollered Shaw. He tried to belt Henry with his left fist, but Henry caught it and held it.

Henry's face reddened from the strength it took to hold Shaw's hands. He turned toward Esther shouting, "No! No! Wait! He's delusional. He's psychotic. I wonder what's happened here?" Henry struggled to hold Shaw's shoulders, but there wasn't any controlling him. Thrashing his arms and head, Shaw tried to get free of Henry, while the others watched.

"Get Clay and Jewels!" Henry yelled! "I need some help holding him down so he won't hurt himself."

Esther didn't know what to do first, give the injection or go find Clay. She held her breath not wanting Henry to get hurt. Clay and Jewels pushed through the crowd of patients accumulating to witness Shaw's antics. With their help, Esther gave Shaw the injection.

Esther smiled sweetly to each patient in the crowd, as if nothing had happened, and motioned for them to move on down the hall.

"Esther! You'd better check on that man because there's something bad wrong with him," Doddie called out. She tried to speak with her hands, but they remained draped over the ends of the wheelchair's arms. Her legs remained frozen with arthritis, but there was nothing wrong with her mouth.

"All right, Doddie. You're right. There is something wrong with him," answered Esther.

The floor calmed down just fine until Esther stared into the face of Mrs. Kroger, a small thin, wisp of a woman dressed in cotton chintz who stood against the wall simply blinking her eyes quickly as if to get a picture of all that had happened. Her blinking reminded Esther of Mr. Kroger's blinking. Their skin resembled each other's too, fair, mottled with freckles, and flaking from dryness.

"I hope my poor boy hasn't had to witness this outlandish display," Mrs. Kroger said and scowled, heaved a disgusted sigh, picked up a bulging shopping bag full of clothes, and proceeded down the hall to Mr. Kroger's room. Her sturdy white pumps echoed every step as they hit the unforgiving linoleum floor. The noise rang out like shots in the silent aftermath of Shaw's psychotic break.

Henry jumped out at Esther from Buster's room saying, "I'm shot," and pretended to fall to the floor, pointing to the disappearing form of Mrs. Kroger.

"How can you scare me like that after all I've been through today?"

"It was easy. It was the perfect opening," Henry answered, smiling his old teasing joviality. "Come on, let's give Melisa a hand getting Shaw into bed. I'm hoping the medicine has worked."

"What's wrong with him, Henry? He's never acted like this

before."

"I don't know. I have my ideas though. If it isn't drug induced, then it must be organic. Something's definitely going on there." Henry stood in front of her and placed his hands over her head against the wall to afford them some privacy. He leaned his face down close to hers and whispered, "What did Employee Health say about Mr. Kroger's needle stick? Melisa told me."

"The nurse said it was a rare chance he had A.I.D.S. and that I was exposed, but if I wanted him tested, I should get you to order the blood work. I think I need to get permission from his mother."

"Good luck with that one. I don't know," he said thoughtfully. "I checked his chart. There isn't a record of anything like that mentioned. I can order it, but I don't have any grounds. You'd have to get her permission anyway, I'm afraid. Now, his wife won't mind. He may have contracted it from her the way she runs around."

Henry scowled and slumped a little. He took his arm down and patted Esther on the head. "Come on. Let's take care of Shaw."

"Henry, did you know Mr. Markowitz is close to dying?"

"Yeah. Mrs. Shepherd and I called his daughter last night. She said she'd try to come in to see him today. She probably will, but most of the families won't. They hate to get that last phone call. It means their big, fat, government check will stop. The one they've received all the time their relative is in the hospital."

"You say that all the time. I hate hearing it. It sounds so cruel, so inhumane, so callous."

"I hate it myself. It happens every day for me here. I don't think most of the relatives care a hoot for these elderly. They're glad to have them off their hands. Let the state take care of them, or the government, or whomever, but not me. I think it's an epidemic."

They turned into Shaw's room to find Melisa, Mrs. Shepherd, and Clay finishing tying the wrist restraints to the bed. Shaw's shouts had diminished to mere mumbles of unintelligible syllables.

"What do you think has come over him, Henry?" Mrs. Shepherd asked.

"He's too doped up now to do anything," Henry said. "I think I'll get some blood work on him. Maybe his electrolytes are off. I'll get a drug screen too. Who knows, maybe someone slipped him some crack or LSD. Anything's possible around here."

Mrs. Kroger angrily strutted out of Mr. Kroger's room and hailed

Henry and Mrs. Shepherd saying, "What on earth is going on here? For the life of me, I can't imagine my boy having that dreaded disease A.I.D.S.. What do you people think you're doing?" she said fuming. "He never had anything like that, and I'm insulted for him."

Mrs. Shepherd glanced at Henry and said, "I know it sounds ridiculous Mrs. Kroger, but our nurse stuck herself with a needle while cleaning his central line. This is just a precaution. We need your permission to test his blood. We want to protect him and the nurse. He has had so many blood transfusions. These times are precarious. It's only a blood test."

"No! You can't have the test, and even if he has it, I certainly wouldn't want to know about it."

Henry watched Mrs. Kroger walk the rest of the way down the hall in silence. Then he turned to Mrs. Shepherd saying, "I guess she told us. Didn't she?"

"I'm afraid this won't be the last we'll hear on this one. The Medical Director of the hospital is a friend of hers. I hope they don't find out about Esther's record and probation," said Mrs. Shepherd.

Chapter 30

Several days later, Mrs. Shepherd singled out Esther and Selysia from the nurses receiving report, motioning for them to come with her to Mr. Markowitz's room. She appeared weary. She scanned Esther's face and then Selysia's.

Her voice rasped in a low, deep whisper, "Now I know Melisa's been caring for Mr. Markowitz these past few weeks, but I'm asking you two to bathe him and make him nice for his daughter's visit. She's been here all night. I want her to see how clean and comfortable we're keeping him for her. I don't think Melisa can tolerate watching him fade away. She's suffering deeply from his death, especially since she's taken care of him for the past four years. His dying is hard on us all; he's family!"

"We have to make do again today. They pulled Lyla to the nursing home. The girls are short on the other side too. I've called the Bleeding Hearts in, but they started up on nine already this morning. They said they're very busy and don't know when they'd be able to get to us."

Mrs. Shepherd heaved a sigh again and confessed, "I don't know what we're gonna do if this keeps up. All this here pulling of our girls to the geriatric nursing home of the VA. Already, they're getting hurt. I don't know what to do. They're pulling staff from the other floors too."

Esther sighed. "Mrs. Shepherd you've got to say no to them. We have our own patients to care for and our own floor. Let them hire new nurses and train them like we have. Everyone's leaving the nursing home because they're so short. It's almost as if they want that to happen. And those Bleeding Hearts. Every time we need them, they seem to be on nine. I can't remember the last time they came to our rescue."

"I've told the Director of the nursing home how short we are. It don't make any difference. They only have one nurse now for thirty patients. All the floors help out, and even the head nurse. You're right! They need to hire new nurses. That's a fact," Mrs. Shepherd said. "I'm beginning to wonder about the Bleeding Hearts myself."

Esther poured Mr. Markowitz's medications and Selysia gathered clean linens and dressings. They both knew the procedures by heart: dressings, ointments, and what he likes. They knew his moods instantly and spoke about him as if he were their elderly grandfather. His name always entered conversations at break and lunch.

One day Lyla said, "Mr. Markowitz was a bit irritable today. Didn't want to watch TV. Said he was sick to death of hearing about crime and such. If you asks me, I'd be sick to death of everything if I were him. He's so polite about it all...all his suffering."

The new nurse Sakiko Smith said, "Mr. Markowitz wouldn't speak to me at all today. I guess he must be coming down with a cold or something. I gave him his pain medication, and I said maybe tomorrow you'll be in a better mood."

When they entered Mr. Markowitz's room, they were surprised to see Clay staring at Mr. Markowitz with a frightened expression in his eyes. He gingerly pushed the wet rag mop from one corner to the other when he saw Esther and Selysia.

"Mrs. Shepherd asked me to wipe up the floor just a little for his daughter."

The girls waited until he left the room before they began their duty of gently cleansing Mr. Markowitz's body, changing the linen, and dressing him like he was the Christ. They propped him up on the only good side he had left. Throughout it all, he never uttered a sound, except the labored, raspy breathing that continued to get louder and louder as if a monster were about to be released. The bed trembled with each expiration. The girls prayed that his next breath was his last, but it wasn't.

After they finished, his daughter entered and quietly tiptoed across the room, then settled herself in the chair next to his bed. She smiled slightly at them. Esther became taken with her likeness to him, the freckled skin, the red curling hair, even the tilt of her nose was identical to his. Esther spotted the pictures of his grandchildren on the bedside table, a girl and boy. The boy had the same red curly hair, freckled skin, and tilt to his nose. Genetics are sure something, she thought. For years, he didn't even know he had a daughter. Not until she searched him out.

Esther and Selysia left without saying a word to each other, merely caught up in the significance of this passing moment in time.

Esther followed Henry into Mr. Shaw's room.

"What's wrong with him, Henry?" she asked finally.

"I don't know yet. All the blood studies came back normal or normal for someone his age. I've ordered a CAT scan for him tomorrow. I'm sending him over to the University Hospital. I figured they'd be able to check him out better than we can." He examined her face, her lips, and her body.

"How are you doing with all this going on? We've got to get you out of this dark hole you keep falling into. I keep trying to save you, but you're slipping away from me at every turn."

Esther stared down at her feet embarrassed saying, "My stars are wrong this month or maybe this year. I don't know when it's going to end. I can't think about that A.I.D.S. problem anymore. I've given up. It's all up to God. He has my purse strings, and if I'm gonna die then there's nothing I can do."

"Don't give up like that! You've got to fight no matter what. You've got to fight. We can't just accept things like this. We can't!"

"What can I do about it? Nothing. If my tests come back positive, there's nothing I can do about it."

"You don't have it yet. I don't think Mr. Kroger has A.I.D.S. anyway. He would have died by now with his platelet count the way it is...so low. A.I.D.S. would have killed him immediately. He doesn't have the resiliency to even make antibodies." He reached out and rubbed her neck affectionately with his finger. He rubbed around her eyes, across her soft cheek, and then down her neck again. He glanced away lost in thought. The light in the room faded into the gray sky through the window, dreary, and dismal.

"How about dinner tonight?" he asked, glancing away. "Can you get a sitter? Can we go out just the two of us?"

He had such a vulnerable expression on his face it surprised her.

She tried to stifle a smile at his too serious expression, which seemed unlike him. She realized he wasn't mocking her anymore. His invitation proved completely serious. It bolstered her some. Gave her a feeling of hope that he hadn't abandoned her in the face of the possibility of her having A.I.D.S..

"I don't know if I can get a sitter or not," she answered apologetically. "My neighbor offered some time ago. She said she needed the money. I'll try to call her." Esther glanced up into his soft yearning eyes.

Mrs. Shepherd stood in the doorway.

"Esther, I'd like to see you in my office if I may?" she said curtly.

Esther and Henry stopped short, startled at the sudden intrusion.

Shaw hollered, "I told you that before, but you didn't listen."

Mrs. Shepherd entered the room and stood at Mr. Shaw's bedside.

"Henry, he hasn't changed. Do you have any clues?"

"I just told Esther I'm sending him for a CAT scan tomorrow at the University Hospital."

"I never thought this would happen to him. Every day there's another surprise," Mrs. Shepherd said and glared at Esther impatiently saying, "Come with me, please."

Henry went too, but Mrs. Shepherd said, "Not this time." Her tone felt so cutting and serious Henry stopped abruptly and stared at her with his mouth open.

Inside of Mrs. Shepherd's office, she gathered some papers and piled them up on the desk, clearing a place for Esther to sit.

"Esther, this is your file, dear," she said as she tapped her finger on the manila folder.

"I just had the pleasure of explaining your behavior to the Director of the hospital because of your needle stick from Mr. Kroger. His mother reported you. When the Director saw your probation problem, he was just furious. In fact, he wanted to fire you on the spot. That's where I've been all morning. He didn't care if you are a good nurse or not. He merely wants to be rid of the complication. You are supposed to apologize to Mr. Kroger and his mother about wanting him to have his blood tested. I know this isn't going to be easy for you," she sighed, shaking her head. "But you have less than two months of the probation left. I'd hate to see anything happen to your time."

Mrs. Shepherd moved her snuff from one side of her mouth to the other.

Esther remembered how much she had done for Mr. Kroger, bringing him out of his depression, encouraging him to participate in life, helping him progress to being able to go home in spite of his wife's philandering, and his mother's rejection.

Now the Krogers and even the hospital were being completely selfish and refused to have Mr. Kroger tested to settle the question in her mind and give her peace. Her own test would take three months for the virus to show up in her blood, and even then, the results might not be accurate.

"I'm sorry Mrs. Shepherd," she said. "I didn't think the A.I.D.S. test was so out of bounds. I thought we all needed to know if he has A.I.D.S.. For everyone's protection."

"I put myself out on a limb for you," Mrs. Shepherd said irritably. "I told him I'd be responsible for you from now on. You're a good nurse. I need you here to work." She shook her head as if in defeat.

"Look, Mrs. Shepherd," Esther said feeling hurt. "I didn't think it was so awful to ask him to give some blood. I've been giving my blood to all these patients ever since I came here. I'll be lucky to get out of here alive the way I'm going. I'm lucky Clay helps me lift patients, turn patients, and anything I need. He even keeps this floor cleaner than it's ever been. I really care about these patients. Doesn't that count for something?"

"I know you have, dear. You've worked very hard here. We all have. But you still have to treat these patients with kid gloves. I'm disappointed at their reaction too."

Mrs. Shepherd glanced away for a second, moving the snuff thoughtfully from one side of her mouth to the other, pushing out the pink inside of her lip. "Sometimes, we don't get credit for all the things we do." Mrs. Shepherd smiled to herself. "I had to talk mighty fast and take your side of it. Mrs. Kroger angrily waited outside the door still fuming. I hope he doesn't have that dreaded disease for his sake and for yours."

"I guess I should have realized how nervous he was about going home when he developed his itching. Instead, I asked him to be tested for A.I.D.S.. Thanks for saving me again. My life depends on it."

"I know dear. I know."

"There is something I've been meaning to ask you. I wanted to give Clay a special award or something to show how much we appreciate the extra help he gives all of us. Maybe a recommendation to his boss."

"That's a very good idea. Why don't you write a letter for us to sign? I'll give it to his department chairman. I'm sure it will pick up his mood. Give him some self-respect. I like the idea."

When Esther returned to her medicine cart for the afternoon medications, Melisa ran up to her grabbing her shoulders, hysterical, crying. "I can't believe what they're gonna do to my Buster. This is all Henry's fault. I just know it." Melisa's thin fingers dug into her shoulders, and her body trembled.

"The surgeon was here from the University Hospital and said he wanted to amputate Buster's legs. How can they do such a thing? He'll never live through it. He's too weak. It's an experiment. I just know it." Melisa clung to Esther like a scared cat. "You've got to help me fight them."

"I can't Melisa. I can't get into any more trouble. I'd like to help you, but Mr. Kroger's mother reported me to the administrator. Mrs. Shepherd stuck up for me, saved me from being fired. I have to be careful now. Not get into any more trouble."

"I can't believe that old woman reported you. After all, you've done for that man. I can't wait until I retire. What are we gonna do about Buster?"

The sight of Buster's twisted, emaciated, chicken legs scissoring at the knee joints from retracted muscles with unhealed ulcers at the contact points of the knees and ankles conjured up a vision of starvation and neglect. Maybe this was a good idea. If the operation didn't kill him, he'd get rid of the constant infection and uncontrolled movement.

"Come on Melisa, let's take a break. You look like you need a cup of hot tea."

"I do need to get a hold of myself. Don't I?" Melisa said dropping her eyes, ashamed.

In the nurses' lounge, Esther poured a cup of tea from her assortment of foreign teas. She produced some stale cookies from a hidden tin and spread them on a plate.

"Ummm. This tastes good," Melisa said. "I needed a break from all that out there."

"The surgery may help Buster. Stop the infection. Stop the scissoring. We haven't been able to heal any of his wounds no matter what we try. Without his legs, his body won't be drained by his immune system. It sounds horrible, but it may be genius," Esther said.

Melisa cocked her head to one side like a sea bird and glanced down across her nose saying irritably, "Maybe it'd be all right, but for the life of me, I can't believe it. This is not a good day for me." She crunched down hard on the stale oatmeal cookie.

The door pushed open slowly. Mrs. Shepherd poked her head in saying, "So I've found you at last...Melisa. Mr. Markowitz just died. Thank the Lord. I was hoping he didn't have to suffer through the night. Anyway, his daughter is out here. I'd like for you to help her collect his things and talk to her some."

"No, Florence. I don't think I can do that just now. I'm sorry about him. But he's at peace, and I'd rather just let it be." Tears brimmed her eyes and spilled down her cheeks.

"But you know her so well. She's hurting Melisa."

"Well, so am I. And now they want to amputate Buster's legs."

"I know. Henry just told me. His condition could improve. You can't tell. This way he has a chance to walk or get better. Please talk to her. For me. For all of us. For Mr. Markowitz?"

"All right. I'll go," Melisa replied, reluctantly getting up. She glanced back at Esther saying, "Thanks for the tea and sympathy."

Esther and Mrs. Shepherd watched her limp to the door, knowing she was doing what they felt incompetent to do.

Chapter 31

"The dinner with Henry last night had gone well, very well, in fact," Esther said to herself. She felt more optimistic about the future. She began to hum a tune.This was a new day. The brilliant October sky and brisk morning air invigorated her mood as she entered the hospital. With the memory of Henry's smiling, reassuring face the night before, the weight of all her problems seemed miraculously lifted from her shoulders. Even her endless worry about Mr. Kroger's needle stick seemed remote today, even hard to believe. She concluded, she felt too young to die. Henry was right. Mr. Kroger's condition remained too fragile to sustain or overcome an A.I.D.S. infection. The number of days she had left to work on the seventh floor was quickly decreasing.

On the way down the hall, she passed Mr. Markowitz's empty room. The sight of the wide open door reminded her of his passing. Already housekeepers scrubbed the walls, windows, and floors, eradicating any sign of disease, but the smell of disinfectant didn't obliterate the smell of Mr. Markowitz, and the agony he suffered in that room. Not for her nor for any one of the other staff. They prepared for a new patient's arrival.

Melisa joined her at the doorway. They exchanged sympathetic smiles, knowing Mr. Markowitz died well.

"We fixed him up nice for his daughter," Selysia offered.

"Yes, we did," Esther said, giving Selysia a hug.

Clay pushed the waxer back and forth in the room, soft polishing the newly waxed linoleum to ensure an excellent shine. With great affection Esther patted her purse, remembering the letter she typed to honor Clay for all the lifting of patients he so willingly performed for everyone. She reminded herself to have all the people working on the floor sign it. She wanted to see the expression on Clay's face when he read it.

Out in the hall, Esther overheard Sally and Mrs. Shepherd talking in the nurses' station.

"Please don't send me over to that nursing home today," Sally pleaded with Mrs. Shepherd. "I can't work there three days in a row. I just can't work there anymore. It's too hard and breaking me down. My back aches all the time now. I can hardly do the work here. Send Esther or Melisa. Are they too good to be sent to the nursing home?" Sally angrily glared down at Mrs. Shepherd, who stared out into space as if she hadn't heard a word Sally said.

"We all have to do what we have to do," Mrs. Shepherd said.

Esther quietly scanned the assignment sheet for the day and discovered her name absent. Mrs. Shepherd had assigned Melisa to take care of her patients, and Sakiko to the upper hall.

Mrs. Shepherd glanced up at Esther timidly saying, "I'm sending you to the nursing home today." Before Esther objected Mrs. Shepherd turned away, refusing any further discussion about the subject.

"Me!" Esther replied, "I've never worked there before. Can't you send someone else?"

"You're the only one who hasn't been there who is working this week. It's your turn."

Sally overheard the conversation and interrupted, "Yeah! I've been there twice this week and I'm not going back anytime soon." She left the station in a huff after flashing Esther a dirty look.

Lyla added her two cents saying, "My back is still throbbing from working there on Monday."

Mrs. Shepherd watched Lyla with an unusually cold indifference and backed slowly away, then added, "They need a lot more help over there than just one of us every other day or so."

"Uh, huh!" Lyla said in Esther's direction.

"Maybe, I'll like it. Who knows?" Esther said, shrugging her shoulders as she smiled at both ladies.

"If you'll have everyone sign this letter I'll pick it up when I'm finished today," Esther said to Melisa and gave her the letter she had written for Clay.

As she walked through the hospital tunnel, she decided to refuse to lift anyone without help. She must inform the head nurse immediately. Watching Lyla and Sally pop pain pills every morning after working at the nursing home, haunted her. She was determined not to let them treat her like a slave.

Esther strode up to the nurses' station and waited for the short black nurse with a bushy Afro haircut to turn around. Activity filled the area. Nurses laughed and joked with each other while standing around the chart rack.

A large, open ward across the hall housed as many as fifteen disheveled patients wearing wrinkled and soiled gowns. They sat in rows like an audience in a theater, tied into their wheelchairs, and stared forlornly at the TV in the corner. Their disheveled hair hung in long, straggly uncombed clumps. All their heads hung down and resembled the remnants of a dead winter flower garden. They weren't at all like the men on the seventh floor. Men sequestered there for rehabilitation. None like Shaw or Chester or Miss Doddy. These were the forgotten elderly, frozen in their state. Maybe if I work here for awhile, their personalities will emerge, Esther told herself with half-hearted optimism.

"Excuse me," she said trying to attract attention.

At the sound of her voice, all heads turned indignantly toward her.

"I...er...I'm Mrs. Culver. The nurse from the seventh floor," Esther said, shifting her weight self-consciously. "You can call me Esther, if you like. What do you want me to do today?" She smiled brightly and waited.

The nurse with the Afro smiled coolly at her and said, "I'm Mrs. Scott, the head nurse. We're so glad to have you help us. We're so short of help right now. Some days I don't know what we're gonna do. Thanks for coming. I've assigned you to the west wing which has thirty patients. You'll be there with Sara who is giving the medications today."

Mrs. Scott pointed to the petite, dark-skinned woman busily pouring pills into the cups. She appeared so tiny her arms weren't any bigger than Esther's wrists. Sara smiled at Esther, but when she turned her face back to the task of pills, her expression grew hard, her temples throbbed, and her jaw jutted out in a solid rebuff.

Mrs. Scott handed Esther a list of names saying, "If you bathe these seven patients, fix all the rest of the beds, and help feed at 8:30 a.m. and 12n., I think that will just about do it unless we have an emergency." She smiled sweetly. "If there is anything you need, just ask for help. Sara will assist you in whatever you ask."

Esther replied, "I hope I can do a good job for you. I'll need help lifting some of these patients. Who's going to help me lift?"

"Most of our patients can transfer by themselves or with a little help. Otherwise, Sara can help you," Mrs. Scott gave her a steely smile.

Now, Esther knew why everyone complained bitterly about the conditions here. After making rounds and assessing the patients, Esther realized all thirty wore attends, needed changing, and pushed to the cafeteria for breakfast and lunch. It took four trips in the elevator without help to get them to breakfast. Then, she observed many had to be fed. That was her job too.

"We never do anything over here except watch TV," a patient confessed.

She remembered the nursing home bragging about their crafts and parties. They even tried to bring in animals as pets for the patients. At the time, it sounded like Utopia.

Mr. Flock's two bloated legs resembled moon boots with his skin seeping fluid in places. Esther felt determined to notify the doctor about it. He needed a stronger diuretic.

Esther moved on to another patient, an emaciated skeleton like body who trembled and cried out in fear every time she touched the poor soul. She decided not to take this patient out of bed, knowing she couldn't walk or transfer, or support her own weight. She needed to be fed in her room in bed. When, Esther wondered, breaking out in a cold sweat? Too many...too needy for her to handle. An impossible task.

Fifteen minutes later, Esther stood in the cafeteria amazed she was able to get all these patients to the cafeteria so quickly. Altogether, she estimated there were more than one-hundred-ninety-nine patients there, but no one talked. The stainless steel counters set up along one wall were designed for cafeteria style serving. Staff collected one tray after another and carried it to the patients sitting at the tables. They opened packages of condiments, poured milk, placed bibs around patient's necks, and helped them to eat. It all had a cold institutional type sterility. Black cats and orange pumpkins decorated the walls in an attempt to liven up the atmosphere for Halloween. The sight reminded Esther to check her boys' old costumes.

A stab of excitement soared deep in Esther's stomach, knowing she had less than two months to finish, around the end of November, Thanksgiving. Maybe she'd make it after all. If she survived today, she felt anything was possible.

These patients resembled a wasteland of humanity. The light of their souls hid as if the tiny rays had been drawn inside for safe keeping, confined within a deep sphere at the center of their wasting bodies, waiting patiently for judgment day. Look to the fields of peace Esther wanted to cry out to these lost souls. Let go of these octogenarian trappings, crumbling like the Roman ruins. Let your soul shine brightly. Fly free toward the light. Fly free toward Jesus into his arms. Smile with joy. Where is all the joy? Don't look back. Look toward the fields across the river with the Prince of Peace. Esther remained silent.

Breakfast finished and back on the floor, she lined up her patients needing baths, one by one, outside the shower room, explaining, "Now, wait your turn. This one is first."

The men flew off the elevator and right up to her asking for help. "When I finish with these people I'll fix you. Don't you hold your urine? Can't you transfer to the toilet? " Esther asked.

"I haven't been able to do that for months," one patient admitted. He laughed a little to himself.

Esther scanned all the upturned faces watching her every move. They didn't intimidate her. "I'll get to you as soon as I can. One at a time. Try to hold your urine or use the urinals. That's what you're supposed to do."

"We can't," they all chimed.

She helped the first man into the shower, bathed him, and helped him dress in clean clothes.

"Thanks, gal! That's the first bath I've had in two and a half weeks," he said and sped away, leaving a cloud behind smelling of soap, aftershave, and shampoo.

With the line of patients waiting, she remembered the lady who needed to be fed in her room. When she reached the door, the lady's tray still sat on the table untouched. Esther tried to wake her. She sat her up to be fed, but she still slept. Esther went to the head nurse and explained the situation.

"Oh, she's been like that for a long time. Just do the best you can," was her response.

"I think the doctor needs to be informed about it so he can put down a feeding tube. And Mr. Frock needs a diuretic too because his legs are so swollen."

"He's been like that for several weeks too. Just do the best you can. These people are sick or else they wouldn't be here, girl. Why are you bothering us about them?"

"The doctor needs to evaluate their care. If he makes that decision, then it is his decision. I'd be happy to tell him myself," Esther said.

"Are you trying to tell me what to do?" Mrs. Scott said smugly, frowning with an ugly grimace. She slammed shut the chart she worked on and glared defiantly at Esther.

"No," Esther answered. "But I'm informing you of their condition and letting you decide if anything needs to be done or not."

Mrs. Scott raised her eyebrows defensively saying, "I can give you some more work if you want. Don't bother me with all these unimportant details. Don't you think I have work to do here?"

"Yes ma'am," answered Esther and returned to her line of patients waiting for baths.

A small lady with a wrinkled, whiskered chin and course features still waited in her wheelchair for Esther in front of the shower door. The others had grown impatient and left. Esther rolled the lady into the shower stall and helped her undress because of her left sided paralysis. The lady mumbled incoherently.

With difficulty, Esther helped the lady transfer to the shower chair but in the middle of the transfer she collapsed and Esther speedily swung her into the waiting chair, breathing a sigh of relief that she didn't drop her.

"You almost fell. Why didn't you stand when I told you to?"

The lady replied, "Uh huh. I thought so," to Esther as clear as a bell.

"All right Miss, when I say stand, I'll pull you up, and don't sit until I say so. Do you hear?"

"Uh huh," said the lady.

Esther straddled her legs, pulled her up to a standing position, swung her around, and leaned her into the seat. When she tried to push the lady to sit, the lady froze and refused to move. Without warning the lady collapsed, catching Esther off guard. She twisted her back while trying to keep the lady from falling to the floor. She pushed the lady's limp body into the waiting chair as a stab of excruciating pain settled in her lower back. Esther stood up straight attempting to work out the muscle strain as if it were only a cramp, but it didn't work.

When she pushed the lady out in the hall, the others still waited.

She glanced at the first one in line saying, "I'll be back, but you others had better go on and wash up for lunch."

They groaned, hardening their expressions, staring down at their wet laps.

"I'm sorry. I can't help it. You'll have your turns after lunch. Now go wash up the best you can."

She shook her head at them with dismay, leaning to the left and then to the right, trying to work out the continuous excruciating pain. She pushed the lady back to her room and rummaged around the bedside table for the lady's teeth. Esther smiled to herself remembering Lyla's tale of lost teeth in the nursing home. After an extensive search, the nurses found a pile of teeth in the drawer of a marauding demented patient. She left the lady watching the television which was blaring down from the wall.

Esther spotted Sara in the hall. "Can you give me a Tylenol? I've pulled my back muscles when that lady collapsed while I was transferring her."

Sara returned her gaze without expression as if she didn't hear her, but said, "We aren't allowed to give medications to employees. I guess you need to go to employee health." She turned away smugly.

Esther moved back down the hall, stopping at the next chair in line and said, "If we hurry, I think we'll finish before lunch." She tried not to let on to the patient about her pain, but the stabbing in her back kept on with a throbbing perseverance, a harsh warning not to continue.

"I'm afraid I can't do any more lifting today," she told the gentleman.

He smiled saying, "I can transfer pretty good myself. If you just spot me."

In no time, Esther finished his bath and pushed him out into the hall. Patients lined up at the elevator, waiting to be taken to the cafeteria for lunch. She thought if she hung on until her lunch break, she'd have time to rest before finishing the others, but she still had all the beds to change.

When the patients returned from the cafeteria, they seemed more comfortable, even less demanding. She slipped into the nurses' lounge and grabbed her lunch and purse.

"Mrs. Scott," Esther said softly, "I'm going to lunch. If I don't hurry, I'll be too late to get a drink."

"Girl! What do you mean? We are so short today no one is taking lunch. Most don't need lunch anyway. I suggest you continue to finish your work."

"I missed my break this morning because I tried to get everyone bathed. I'm a fast worker too. So I'm taking my break and lunch now because I need it. I've hurt my back, and if you want me to return and finish, you'd better let me go."

"If you insist. I'm remembering this," Mrs. Scott said, raising her eyebrows cynically and shaking her head.

Esther ran down the stairs despite her pain. She ran out into the long hall leading to the tunnel of the main building. She didn't stop until she reached the cafeteria, but it was closed. She didn't care and moved on to the concessions. The room appeared empty, although she fully expected to see Shaw there, but he was bedridden now. Leftover lunch trash covered the orange Formica tables. She didn't care and cleared a place for herself, just to sit for awhile, and escape even for a few minutes. She sat down, lit a cigarette, and settled back onto the hard plastic chair.

The nurses deliberately piled on the work. They perpetuated a lie. The discrepancy lay in the difference between the amount of staff needed to care for ambulatory patients compared with complete care patients. The difference here became too great.

Esther ate her lunch and realized it was 2:15 p.m., time to return. She stopped for a second at the gift shop, bought a bottle of Advil, popped a few pills into her mouth, and washed them down with the rest of her Coke. She laughed at herself. Now, she had to take pain pills just to go on with her day like Sally, Lyla, and the others.

When she returned to the floor, she rushed from room to room, changing patients and helping them into bed for their afternoon nap. She decided to bathe the last two patients in the shower like she promised.

Esther came to the final male patient who glanced down at his paralyzed legs saying, "I can't stand on my own. I need help for everything."

"All right. I'll get help, and we'll have you cleaned up in no time."

She approached the nurses' station where Mrs. Scott was checking charts.

"I need assistance transferring this last patient, Mr. Bloom. He says he can't support his weight, and I know I can't lift him. Is there anyone here who can help me?"

"Oh, come on. We're tired of all your complaining today. Go on and finish your work. He can stand. He doesn't need any help."

Esther's anger rushed to her face. She felt the throbbing pound in behind her eyes from her rage. "I'm not lifting him by myself. I can't."

Mrs. Scott's eyebrows narrowed, and her lips thinned in anger. "Sara," she called, "Please help this helpless little girl lift this man."

Sara turned and shot a steely glare at Esther, set her jaw, and reluctantly walked slowly up the hall toward the patient's room.

In seconds, Sara swung Mr. Bloom up to a standing position, took off his attends, washed him, dressed him in one stroke, and left with a smirk on her face. All the time, she never said a word.

Esther parked him in front of the television. Once in the nurses' station, she grabbed her purse and gave her report to Sara.

"I'm leaving," she told Mrs. Scott, "Sara's giving report."

When she arrived on the seventh floor to pick up her coat, the eyes of all the staff: Melisa, Mrs. Shepherd, Lyla, Sally, Violet, Selysia, and Jewels, followed her when she rounded the corner from the elevators. She walked slowly toward them, bent stiffly to the right, her face curled up in pain.

Without ceremony, she quietly said to Mrs. Shepherd, "If you ever send me there again, I'll quit on the spot." Esther walked into the nurses' lounge, returned with her coat, and left the floor.

Mrs. Shepherd didn't speak, only pursed her lips flat, puffed out her cheeks and squeezed her eyes shut like a reprimanded cat.

Chapter 32

The next morning as Esther entered the nurses' station, the staff huddled together in the corner with grave expressions covering their faces. She felt woozy from the pain medication she had taken earlier to help her navigate getting the boys off to daycare. She hated feeling out of control. She didn't pay too much attention to the group and walked past them into the lounge. Melisa followed her and pulled up a chair beside her.

"We've had some bad news today."

"What's the matter now."

"It's Karen. She's in the hospital bleeding. They took her in last night with placenta previa, the afterbirth coming first. When Mrs. Shepherd called the unit, they didn't tell her anything, but we all know how dangerous that hemorrhaging is for the baby."

Melisa appeared old and fragile. Tiny lines around her eyes and mouth had deepened since Esther first met her. She had lost her vitality. Maybe it was because of the chronic pain she suffered. Or maybe it was the unending labor with the dying patients.

Esther sat down hard on a chair, trying to sort out her concerns about Karen, Shaw, her needle stick, and her pain. But Karen's baby? Everyone had such hopes for her infant. It wasn't just Karen's baby but the seventh floor's. It represented a renewed faith in something positive, something reaffirming, and gave them strength to go on. The patients yearned for its birth as if Karen was a part of their extended family too. It reminded her of Lyla's little Garland Green.

"What happened?" Esther asked, dreading the knowledge of any more tragedies.

"I don't know. Karen worked over here in your place yesterday. We were so short. She didn't lift anyone. She helped me make a few beds. She said she was so tired of doing nothing. Said she felt so useless. I don't think anything caused it. It just happened. We've all helped her." Melisa stared up at Esther blankly, as if it were difficult for her to understand how Providence worked.

"Esther, you have to go see about her for us."

"She'll be all right. That's a good hospital."

"Sure. If she were white. But she's black and goes to the clinic at the University. Do you think they'll help her like that? I don't think so. They have too many."

"She's not illiterate. She's an RN, for God's sake! She's educated. Not one of the migrant workers. Someone's got to stand up for her. Is anyone with her?"

"Only her husband," Melisa said, pushing her hands into her white jeans pockets. "We've got to send someone over there to help her."

"I can't go," Esther said defensively. "I injured my back yesterday. Actually, I should have called in sick. I need the money too much to stay home."

"Yes, you can. What about all those men holding their urine? What about the ones who got better we never expected to walk? You've got to go. You're the only one and say a prayer for her and the baby."

"How can I help her if I can't even help myself? I'm never going to that nursing home again. I can tell you that. They treat us all like slaves over there. Something's going on, and I don't like it. The patients are suffering. The conditions are worse than they ever were here." Esther stood up to go, feeling dizzy. "I'm in rough shape today. This pain medicine is keeping me off balance."

Melisa frowned and held her fist to her chest saying, "You'll get used to the pain. We've all had to endure it." Melisa gently touched Esther's shoulder. "Think about Lyla and the others...Mrs. Shepherd. Do this for all of us."

At the mention of Lyla and Mrs. Shepherd, she was reminded of how lucky she was to have her two healthy boys. "All right. I'll go. Maybe she's already delivered."

"I'll call and find out. She doesn't have anyone here," Melisa said in a pleading tone. When Melisa left, her step sharpened and rose more sprightly than normal.

Esther gathered her purse and lunch, thinking she'd probably be over there all day.

At the nurses' station, she signed the leave of absence register.

"We called the hospital. She hasn't delivered yet." Mrs. Shepherd's eyes withdrew into tiny slits. She shook her head repeatedly, moving her lips as if having a conversation with herself. "You tell her we're all praying for her."

Mrs. Shepherd tore up Esther's pass saying, "This is part of your work. I'll take care of everything."

"Thanks."

"Esther," Mrs. Shepherd called from the station as she was leaving, "I thought you ought to know. Would want to know. Mr. Shaw has a brain tumor. It showed up on his CT scan yesterday. They don't give him much time. Maybe a few weeks." Mrs. Shepherd moved the snuff back and forth in her jaw slowly, with emotion, pursing out her pink inside lip flesh with a wild sadness settling over her face. A wildness Esther hadn't seen before.

When Esther passed through the entrance doors and didn't see Shaw where he always sat, she experienced a stab of grief. How did he have a brain tumor growing in his head, and no one diagnosed it before now?

All the way over to the University Hospital, she prayed Karen's baby lived. She was determined not to let the baby die.

When Esther reached the labor ward, her mood bolstered at the clean conditions of the hospital. The floors, walls, and stainless steel cart racks shined. The labor area was a large ward with ten beds separated by partitions and curtains at the entrance of each cubicle. Esther found Karen in the last enclosure. She didn't recognize her at first because Karen's cheeks were bloated, deforming her face almost beyond recognition. Her usually lively, large brown eyes disappeared under two puffy lids. Karen's condition had lapsed into toxemia. Esther picked up her arm to take her blood pressure. She slept undisturbed by all the moaning and crying of the other mothers.

Karen's forehead burned, and her pulse bounded rapidly in her wrist.

The monitor showed the baby's heartbeat and Karen's were too rapid. Her blood pressure was 90/52 – very low. When Esther rubbed the huge round abdomen, she felt a tiny jab from the inside. She smiled, feeling this new life.

"Karen, it's Esther. I've come to see about you for me and for all the other staff. We're all praying for you and the baby. Where's your husband? I didn't see him outside."

Karen smiled, opening her eyes. "It's so nice for you to come all the way over here to see me. My husband had mid-terms today and went on to class. He said he'd be right back." She smiled again. "I didn't expect to be here today. I hope y'all weren't too short of help today."

"No. They'll manage," Esther replied awkwardly, immediately feeling guilty about not wanting to come and help her. "Are you having any pain at all?"

"No, not really. Just a little cramping. Do me a favor and check between my legs to see if the baby is crowning. It feels so wet down there." She tried to reach, but with her huge belly, it was too far.

Esther opened the sheets to investigate the dilation of Karen's perineum and discovered a huge pool of clotted blood lying in the middle of the bed. She tried to stifle a gasp, but it escaped unrestrained.

"It's bad. Isn't it?" Karen said discouraged. "I knew something was wrong. I haven't seen a nurse for a while now. They're so busy. I'm feeling so tired. If I hold my legs open maybe you can see the baby's head."

"All right. I'll try. Push down! If the baby is close I'll feel it's head." Esther grabbed a flashlight from the bedside table and gloves. She watched helplessly as a huge maroon clot resembling a piece of calves liver pushed out and plopped onto the congealed blood between Karen's legs. Esther pressed with a gloved finger at the opening of the cervix and felt the soft spongy layer of the placenta give way to her gentle pressure, but she was unable to feel anything hard underneath like the head.

"There's no baby yet." She was right after all. Karen needed a section. She needed it immediately if this baby was going to live.

"No. I can't feel the head yet. I think I'll try to find the doctor. Is there one you've been seeing. Is there a name?"

"I can't remember it. He examined me when I first came in, but I don't know if he's still here. You know how they come and go with the shifts."

Esther ran out into the hall and down the corridor, searching the rooms for a doctor or nurse. She reached the delivery room where two nurses and the doctor worked busily with a new delivery. She waited for the right time to interrupt. The mother groaned, yelled, and the doctor pulled on the baby with forceps. Nurses stood by with an incubator. Esther panicked inside.

"Nurse," Esther called. Both nurses turned and one came over. Esther told them how urgent Karen's case was with the bleeding and all.

"We don't have anyone. This doctor has two more mothers to deliver. It's been a busy morning. They're waiting in the next two rooms."

"Don't you have a second on call? Her baby's gonna die if she doesn't get a section soon. She may die anyway. She's a nurse from Thornhill hospital. Her husband's a student at the university. She's lost so much blood," Esther cried.

The doctor delivering shouted, "Call Tracy and Bill Conner. They may be in class. Tell them it's an emergency. Call the OR. I examined her when she came in and hoped to stop the bleeding, but I guess the medication I gave her didn't work. Tell them to set up for an emergency section."

"Don't worry," The doctor told Esther, "We'll take care of her. Go back and stay with her. If her vital signs change, give us a holler."

Esther rushed back to Karen's bed. She slept so soundly Esther woke her up to make sure she was still conscious.

"I saw the doctor," Esther said. "They're gonna do a C-section. Don't you worry now." Esther said a prayer while she took Karen's blood pressure again.

Karen opened her eyes as Esther checked the color of her nail beds. She observed silently as Esther changed the messy sheets.

Karen stared thoughtfully at the ceiling saying, "You know I can't wait to put my baby in a carriage and stroll down to the park in the afternoons with all the other mothers. I'll sit there and talk about my baby's funny actions the way mothers do. She's gonna be so pretty. I'm gonna dress her so nice. Just as nice as any white folks baby. Even with designer clothes. Terrance will have a job by then, and we'll have plenty of money."

Karen groaned when Esther pushed her on her side to get the sheets out from under her.

"I already have a lovely crib and tiny sweaters for the winter months," Karen said talking to the wall. Her rich brown skin glistened on her back from the lotion Esther rubbed across it.

"What about your family? Have you called your mother or father?"

"Oh, they know it's just about time," Karen answered. "I talked to them last week. They live on the sea islands, St. Helena Island. We're Gullah blacks. I told you that before." Karen smiled broadly. "My baby's a Gullah through and through."

Karen's lips stretched into a frightened smile as she gripped the steel bed rail from another pain.

"Do you think it's gonna be ok? My baby?"

"Yes. Of course. Don't worry. You're both gonna be just fine. When I told the doctor you were bleeding, he said to call two doctors and take you up to the operating room right away. They'll be here in just a second. That's why I'm trying to get you ready so fast." Esther didn't want Karen to know the sheets were soaked with blood. She knew she'd need a transfusion of at least one pint. She wondered what was taking the doctors so long.

When Esther finished, she piled the linens on the chair, wanting to show them to the doctor when he came in to examine her.

"How are you feeling now. Are you woozy at all?"

"Can you find me a blanket. I feel so cold. I'm freezing here," Karen said, shivering from shock.

Esther searched for a blanket but didn't find one in the ward. She ran out into the hall and down to the delivery rooms where she heard voices echoing off the hard surface of the tiled walls.

The same doctor and two nurses, dressed in green scrubs, were in the other room now and had just delivered another baby who screamed his lungs out.

"Nurse! Nurse!" Esther called.

One immediately came over and recognized Esther. "Is there something we can do for you?" she asked. "Unless you are family, visitors aren't allowed in the delivery room."

"My friend is waiting for her section. Do you know when we can go up to the operating room? No one's been in to see her. She's still losing blood. I think she's going into shock."

The others turned and stared at her over their masks. The huge circular lamp radiated a harsh, too bright light which hurt Esther's eyes.

The doctor turned and said to the nurse, "Susan, why don't you go and take a look. We're all right here for the present. I thought I'd see those doctors by now. Check her for me while I finish up this episiotomy." He held his gloved hands straight up in the air to keep from contaminating them. The other nurse tied the strings of his gown tighter.

The nurse Susan stripped off her mask, gown, and gloves, deposited them in the trash can and followed Esther. She examined the sheets Esther brought to her outside of the cubicle. She checked Karen's vital signs and covered her with a warm blanket.

"Don't worry! We'll have you upstairs in a flash," she said, reassuringly.

The nurse glanced at Esther soberly saying, "Can you help me get her on a stretcher? We'll put her on now. I'll check if they're ready."

"I'm so dizzy," Karen moaned. "My baby isn't kicking anymore. Is everything going to be all right?" she said meekly.

"You're gonna be fine. And so is your baby," Esther said, trying to comfort her.

The two nurses slid her from the bed to the stretcher and pushed the stretcher to the elevators. The labor room nurse changed the IV fluids and returned to the nurses' station to call the OR again. Then she ordered two units of packed cells to go to the operating room.

She received another call and rushed back to Esther saying, "They're ready for her now. We can take her up."

"Thank you, Lord! Thank you, Lord!," Esther prayed.

The nurse took Karen right into the operating room, scrubbed her, and the anesthesiologist gave her the spinal anesthetic. In less than ten minutes, the doctor came and cut open her huge, brown glistening abdomen. Masked faces came and went, hanging intravenous solutions, giving her oxygen, and shouting orders to each other.

The doctor carefully pulled the baby out of Karen's womb by her arm and leg, hung her upside down and suctioned out her mouth.

"It's a girl," the doctor yelled triumphantly. The baby didn't cry. Its color was dark blue. It's tiny head flopped limply across Karen's deflated abdomen when he laid it down.

All eyes in the room fixed on the baby. The doctor reached out and cut the cord. Immediately, color flooded the tiny infant. Her chin trembled under the weak virgin whimper. The baby's cheesy, white head rose up simultaneously with the wrinkled legs as if someone had just breathed life into it like a plastic, blow-up doll. Around the room, sighs of relief heralded the moment. Murmuring from the staff resumed, directions to bathe the baby, sutures for the incision, and blood added to the IV line. The doctor began stitching up the great sagging womb.

"Praise the Lord! Praise the Lord," Esther said. Her heart still caught up in the tenure of the situation. Echoes of "Amen" filled the room with the squalling in the background, cries of the healthy newborn child.

Esther patted Karen's head saying, "I'm going to see if I can find your husband. It's his turn now."

"I'll never be able to thank you enough for all you've done," Karen said, grabbing Esther's hand.

"Seeing this healthy baby is all the payment I need. I know a lot of other people who will be very thankful too. This baby's also for them: Lyla, Mrs. Shepherd, and even Melisa. Everything's gonna be okay."

Esther returned to the seventh floor feeling so elated. It was only 1:00 p.m., and she figured it was too early to leave. When she entered the nursing lounge, Lyla and Selysia were just leaving.

Selysia raised her eyebrows sarcastically saying, "Humph! Why didn't you write a letter for me, Esther? I work hard every day too. Why didn't I get a letter of recommendation?"

"Yeah. What about me?" said Lyla. "Aren't we good enough for you?"

Esther didn't know what they were talking about. She examined their hurt faces blankly. "I was with Karen all morning. Did I miss something?" She paused for an interminable second. "In case you're wondering, Karen had a baby girl. The doctor performed a C-section because the placenta came first."

"Why did you go? That's my question," asked Lyla, pushing out her full lips from her curved fish like face. "I should have gone or maybe Selysia. One of us should have gone to help her."

"They asked me. That's all I know." Esther examined her hands trying to curb her mounting anger. "And maybe because I hurt my back working at the nursing home yesterday. Now, I know what you're talking about. They treat you like slaves over there. I told Mrs. Shepherd, I'll never go back."

Lyla interrupted sweetly, ignoring all the other comments, "Karen had a baby girl!"

Selysia smiled broadly too and said, "Karen had her baby. A girl. Wasn't she early?" She frowned for a second. "Oh, the nursing home isn't that bad. I like working over there. There ain't anyone to hang over you and check up on you. I like it just fine," Selysia said smugly, pretending to examine her Vermilion fingernails.

Lyla glared at Selysia with such ferocity that Esther had to stifled a laugh.

Lyla smiled snootily to herself as if slightly amused at all this charade, "I like the nursing home just fine myself." She paused for several seconds, her face lit up, "But that's so nice about Karen and her baby. It's nice to hear good news for a change. But you could've written us a letter like you did for Clay. We've been working here for years and Clay's only been here a few months."

"I'm sorry. I just wanted to show Clay how much we all appreciated his extra help. That's all. Make him feel cared about. How's Mr. Shaw doing?" Esther asked.

They examined Esther with renewed interest.

"Oh, that one," Selysia answered. "It serves him right to get a brain tumor. He's still a dirty old man. I felt sorry for him today and fixed him up nice and all. When he reached over with his restrained hand, he pinched the living daylights out of my arm. If I hadn't been here at the hospital, I'd a smacked him." She shook her head with dismay. "No, he ain't changed for a second."

The two nurses still hung around Esther nervously shifting their weight from one foot to the other. They followed her to her locker, and she wondered why. They watched every movement she made, when she poured her tea out of her thermos, and when she took her Advil.

"All right! What's the matter now?" she said glaring at them.

They both inhaled deep breaths. "You go first," said Selysia.

"All right," Lyla said, staring hard at her feet. "Remember when you told those men to hold their urine? If they held their urine, they could go home."

"Yes...that's what I told them. They are doing it too," Esther said as if hardly concerned. "I got tired of cleaning them up all the time. I thought at least they could try. I told them to pray and ask the Lord to help them."

Sally's and Lyla's faces shone with excitement. "We hate to admit this, but all the patients on the ward are holding their urine and using their urinals," said Lyla. "Even that old man from the nursing home. How did you do it?"

"No one can believe it. Even Henry's amazed," said Selysia.

"I told them they'd never be able to go home again if they didn't hold their urine. I told them they have control over their own bodily functions. Even the paralyzed ones. I told them because I thought it was the truth," Esther said.

Selysia interrupted, languishing her version of the story. "I heard about it before most of the others. The first time a patient told me I thought you were crazy. I thought you had gone off your rocker. I felt sympathy for the old ones, even with their complaining all the time. But I just told them to do what you said. I figured one more disappointment wasn't gonna kill them. It gave them hope and something to work for. We never dreamed you were right."

Esther's face lit up. The two followed her to the ward.

Mr. Wristman hollered, "It's nurse Good Body! Look at me. I'm beginning to feel like my old self." He pointed down at his long leg prosthesis and resembled a circus man walking on stilts. His knees proceeded each step. He no longer had to use the canes and strode up one side of the ward and down the other. "You knew what you were doing all the time didn't you?" he said and laughed until he became red faced.

"That's great. You are all doing just great. All of you," said Esther.

She returned to the hall letting Lyla and Selysia take care of their requests and entered Shaw's room. His limp body lay helplessly strapped to the bed. The sight shocked her. He spoke clearly now in his hallucinations which puzzled Esther because she had only heard his Jabberwocky and a few garbled words. She realized now that he always understood everything she said and could speak clearly if he wanted to. He carried on such a charade because the girls treated him so badly. She reached down and gently rubbed his red wrists where the restraints irritated his skin. He squinted his eyes up at her as if trying to clear blurred vision.

"Don't cry, girl. Everything's gonna be all right. Hop the table down to the floor. Book the sender into the door."

Esther sadly patted his bristled cheek and turned to leave just as Clay entered, pushing his broom.

"Hey, thanks for giving me the recommendation. My boss showed me the letter. She said you all nominated me for Employee of the Month." He grinned broadly at Esther and shook his head in disbelief.

"You deserved it, Clay. You've helped all of us lift these patients while still cleaning the floor. None of the other men help us like you do. Not one of them. Jewels, on occasion, will help. But not usually. Everyone signed the letter."

Clay glanced down at Shaw saying, "I'm gonna miss him. He and I joked all the time."

"Oh, he's an asshole!" the patient in the other bed said. They both laughed at him. His brown, beady eyes searched the ceiling and rotated from corner to corner anxious and paranoid.

Esther knew why they let his long white beard grow. "He's a mean one, Clay," she said. "When anyone gets close to him, he tries to kick and bite. He won't let them shave him either."

"He reminds me of a briar patch. If you get too close, he'll grab hold of your shirt or pants and never let go. When I'm washing the floor, I get tangled in his tight fingers as if they were thorns. And curse. Mother! He can curse the devil out of hell."

"Clay, Karen had her baby today. It's a girl. She's going to be just fine too," Esther said, smiling at him.

"How about that! A new life! I love my little girl. I give her everything she asks for if I can. And she loves me. I never thought she'd love me. I always ran from my ex-wife, avoiding her at all costs." Clay shook his head, laughing at himself. "Now I spoil my little girl."

"You know Miss Esther, I never told anyone this before. My mother died when I was only four." Clay hung his head down and gazed away from her, ashamed. "I'll never forget that day. A white lady took me off and said I was orphaned. From that day on, I knowed no family. I moved from one foster home to another."

"Oh no. I'm so sorry, Clay."

"I was a Mexican jumpen bean. No one was able to control me. Trouble followed me everywhere. Why did the Lord take my mother away? I was a baby. Just a little baby. Innocent. All I wanted was someone to love me and keep me close. That's all." He grabbed the aluminum bed rails and hung on as if he were hanging on for dear life. "Just someone to love me. A little boy."

"I can't imagine what it must have been like," Esther said, thinking of her two boys.

"It scares me when people die. All I see is my mama an all the years I wanted her back. When I grew up, I searched through my files and found I had a father. He's around." Clay huddled over in the corner of the room as if afraid.

He examined Esther's face saying, "Since I've been working here, I realized those babies are my family, and I their daddy. Before, I drank, smoked pot, and even used hard drugs. You know what I mean? I have steady work. It scares me when people die. Mr. Markowitz and Shaw here. I help these men 'cause I have no other family, and they have no children. That's why."

Esther smiled at clay, seeing a man for what he was. "I never thought badly of you, Clay. I knew you were good from the very first day."

"You did, Miss Esther?" Clay said surprised. He stood up straighter. "From the very first day?"

"Yes, the very first day," Esther answered.

Chapter 33

October seemed to pass unnoticed except for the change of temperature. Everyone pulled their heavy winter coats out of mothballs and complained when the thermometer reached an uncommon forty degrees in South Carolina. With Halloween in only two days, the girls arrived talking about their costumes and their children's parties. Their enthusiasm dimmed when they watched Mrs. Shepherd sit down heavily in the gray metal chair at the end of the table in the nurses' lounge.

The words "staff meeting" passed quickly from one person to another as they entered the stuffy lounge.

Neither Mrs. Shepherd's angry puffed out face nor her narrowed eyes hid her tentative expression, as she shuffled through the papers in front of her. She scrutinized each nurse as they entered the room as if solidifying a plan she had formulated for each one.

"It looks like we're in for a siege," Esther said to Melisa, who sat next to her.

"I can't image what on earth for," Melisa whispered.

Selysia sulked, wiggled her shoulders prissily, and tilted her head askew as she scanned the room with her impudent brown eyes. "I don't know why we need to have a meeting first thing at 7:00 a.m." Selysia yawned before continuing, "None of my patients have been set up for breakfast. This meeting is gonna put me behind."

The others grumbled in agreement, acting indignant about the change of pace.

"I hear you," said Mrs. Shepherd.

"All we do is talk, talk, talk, about all this work. It never gets us anywhere, much less more staff. I tell ya...I'm gonna finish my real estate course and will be finished soon. Then, I'm out of here as fast as you can say, Sally," Sally said. She leaned over and asked Selysia for something. Selysia dug in her purse and produced two Advil.

"I'm so tired and achy this morning. I don't mind it a bit if I sit here for a few more minutes," Melisa said. She smoothed the collar of her yellow check blouse and picked a fleck of dust off the sleeve.

"Ladies," said Mrs. Shepherd, "I'm not keeping you this morning. There are a few things we need to discuss. Thanksgiving is in three weeks, and we need to be thinking of the dinner. Sign up the dish you want to bring. I've decided to have it here on the seventh floor at lunch.

I've invited everyone who works here: housekeeping, supervisors, Henry, and the other doctors. I've even invited the Chaplain."

"Oh, who cares about those folks?" Lyla said. "I've never seen any of those doctors up here except when Shaw got that brain tumor. Anyways, what's happened to Halloween? Aren't we gonna have candy and wear masks."

"Ladies, let's calm down. I need to talk to you about the nursing home too," Mrs. Shepherd said, not meeting anyone's cold stare or acknowledging their irritated grumbles.

Silence enveloped the room. The nurses pursed their lips together as tight as clams, remaining stubborn and unyielding.

Mrs. Shepherd stretched and twisted her short neck slightly in resistance.

"I know each one of you has worked very hard over there. They're fixin' to hire more staff. During this shortage, they've asked me to send two nurses a day instead of the one we were sending."

"Florence," Melisa said calmly, "I don't know why you give in to them. They're using us. For once, they see we have good staff. They want to take our nurses away."

Mrs. Shepherd shot her a threatening glare. Melisa stopped talking and glanced down at her shoe saying, "Now I wonder what I stepped in?" Then she picked a leaf off the edge of her spotless crepe sole.

"Oh, I almost forgot. Karen has had her baby. It's a girl! We're so happy about it. We need to take up a collection for her so she can buy something nice."

Mrs. Shepherd glanced around the room, and her eyes fell on Sally and Selysia. Everyone relaxed some at the mention of Karen's baby.

"Sally, I want you and Selysia to go to the nursing home today. Now make us proud. You hear?" Mrs. Shepherd said and collected her papers. Fury glinted from one to another, warning her she had gone too far this time.

Sally stood up saying, "I can't go over there no more. You don't know what they want us to do? I'm still recovering from my surgery. I can't tolerate lifting all those patients. They need to get outside help like the other floors when they're short."

"I'm sorry about this," Mrs. Shepherd said. "I hope this shortage will be over soon too. We are sacrificing our staff here too. It's a burden on all of us."

Esther felt so relieved she wasn't picked. She decided to take another Advil and knew she was expected to do twice her usual amount of patients to make up for their absence.

Melisa hung back after the others left, whispering to Esther, "I wish I knew what this was all about. They've never pulled staff from us like this before. We need those girls."

Mrs. Shepherd motioned for Esther to come to the nurses' station.

"I just received a message that Mrs. Murphy wants to speak with you at 11:00 a.m.," Mrs. Shepherd said.

Esther tried to imagine why she was being called to the Director's office. The memory of Mrs. Scott saying, "I'll remember this," careened through her mind like an automobile of control. Was she being fired? She knew they squeezed all the life blood out of their young girls. Innocent nurses were tossed into the lion's den, the crucible at the heart of Thornhill, the Aeneid's Hades to endure incalculable agony by subjugating the injured and helpless. The administration didn't care what happened to the staff or the patients but merely waited to see which one's suffering surfaced first.

"Do you know why she wants me?" Ester asked.

"No dear, I don't. I'll go over there with you." Mrs. Shepherd said.

Esther returned to her medicine cart to catch up her medications. Stumbling into Mr. Shaw's room, she almost collided with a tall, thin man hovering over Shaw's bed in prayer.

"In the name of the Lord Jesus Christ, I pray for your soul to be delivered unto the highest most realm hosted by the Father, the Son, and the Holy Spirit. May your pain be small and your profound peace great. I pray you cross the plain into eternity with the Prince of Peace at your side, guiding you into the everlasting life. In the name of Jesus Christ, I pray. Amen."

The elderly man's face revealed sculpted angular cheekbones and a chiseled, square jaw. Tousled graying hair tumbled onto his forehead, and when he opened his eyes, he glanced at her.

He put forth his hand saying, "I'm Truman Uriel. I don't know why I'm here, except the Holy Spirit called me to minister to this patient."

"Truman Uriel! You must be a new patient on the other side of the hall," Esther said.

"I've been visiting the patients and praying for them. I'm here for a new heart. The University Hospital sent me here to wait for a donor for my open heart surgery. I served my country as a sergeant in Vietnam.

My heart is so badly damaged, they didn't want me to go home to Charleston to wait. I'll probably be here a few months." Creases wrinkled softly around his eyes and cheeks. His lips turned blue and skin became a translucent gray with each word he spoke from the exertion.

"If the Lord is with me?"

"How did you decide to come in here? Into this room I mean?"

"When you've been doing the Lord's work as long as I have, you understand these things." He smiled sympathetically, sensing her confusion.

"A long time ago, I realized I couldn't resist the Holy Spirit any longer. He tried to draw me into his work, but I was too busy selling insurance. One day when I was sleeping on the couch for an hour or so, the Holy Spirit dumped me onto the floor to get my attention. I knew immediately my life up to that moment had been a waste of time. I knew I didn't have a choice. He sends me wherever he wants me. So here I stand at your service."

"How did you know about Mr. Shaw?"

"I simply felt a strong instinct drawing me to this bed. He must have been a wonderful man because the vibrations felt very profound."

"He is. I can vouch for him," said Henry, his large frame blocked the doorway.

Esther bit her lip and experienced a surge of adrenalin at the sight of him.

Esther blurted out, "I don't know what you're talking about Henry. Shaw was a scoundrel! He drove us all crazy with his demands, his cursing, and his aggressiveness."

"Ah! That's what he wanted everyone to think. Especially the nurses and CNAs. He was very spiritual and helped many of the patients ask for forgiveness before they died," Henry said proudly. "If everyone knew he talked, he might have been discharged to a nursing home, not kept here on this rehabilitation unit. God needed him here. He supported the men in their last hours before death, helped them find salvation. They were afraid of ridicule with anyone else," Henry explained. "At least, that's what he told me. I respect him for it too."

"I believe you're right," said Truman. "There's always a reason why I'm called. This is the way the Holy Spirit works. I think I'll go lie down."

Henry smiled saying, "I'll be in to check on you in a few minutes."

After Truman left Esther said, "When I walked in the room, I watched him pray over Shaw."

Henry stared down at Mr. Shaw hard as he listened to Shaw mumbling continually to himself. The rebelling Shaw had been replaced by the clean shaven, cherub face of a man wearing a satisfied smile. "He's at peace now," Henry said.

"Hey, Shaw. Give me five," Henry said. Shaw's hand flipped slightly still attached to the restraint. Henry gently touched Shaw's palm. He frowned, blinking away his emotion.

"Where have you been all week? I've missed you."

"I had some business to take care of. I didn't know until the last minute. Family business," he said. "And how are you doing? Everything seems to be about status quo here."

Henry sounded remote as if all his emotions had closed down. Esther wondered what happened to him. He nodded toward Shaw saying, "It's amazing how every day he becomes dramatically worse than the day before."

"He's going fast."

"I know," Henry said as he slumped over the bed.

"Mrs. Shepherd sent me to the nursing home last week to work. Now I'm being called to Mrs. Murphy's office."

Confusion crossed his face. He leaned closer saying, "What happened?"

"It was a nightmare. They gave me thirty patients by myself. Many couldn't transfer or even stand without help. I injured my back when a patient collapsed while transferring, and I have been on pain medicine ever since."

"Go over there and meet with her. Be completely humble and obedient. You only have two or three weeks left. You don't want to aggravate them. Finish your time. Then, you'll be free," Henry said cold and hard.

He grabbed her shoulder with his massive fingers, shaking her slightly as if he wanted to shout something at her. Abruptly, he let go and held in his tempestuous emotions. "Don't give them any more ammunition, because they'll certainly use it."

The patient in the other bed yelled, "Kiss my ass! Kiss my ass, you bitch!"

Henry bent forward as if to kiss her, but he stopped halfway and reached awkwardly with his hand to brush several strands of hair out of her face.

"I'll be here most of the afternoon. Let me know what happens." Abruptly, he left the room.

At 11:00 a.m., Esther and Mrs. Shepherd walked into Mrs. Murphy's office. Esther wasn't surprised to see Mrs. Scott sitting on the other side of the room. Esther's blood pounded in her ears. Mrs. Scott had reported her.

"I think we should get right to the point," Mrs. Murphy said. "Why did you give Mrs. Scott such a hard time the other day when you were sent to the nursing home? When someone asks you to do a job, you're expected to complete it. Would you like to say something in your defense?"

"What was the complaint?" Esther asked nervously.

"I gave her an assignment. She acted very irritated about it. In fact, she said it was too hard. I suggested she give up her lunch and break to give her more time to complete all the beds and baths, but she refused. She said she was entitled to her lunch break and fifteen-minute break," Mrs. Scott said.

This is a setup, Esther thought. She scanned the room evaluating the two black women as they slowly and calculatedly reiterated the day and its complications.

"Oh dear. Did you jeopardize a patient just to go to lunch? That doesn't sound very professional to me. Most of our nurses work through their lunch to get their jobs done."

Those words sounded so self-effacing, expecting the nurses to work through lunch. Get a free half-hour of work out of the nurses who aren't paid for lunch breaks. Be wary and pay attention to what Henry said. Try to be humble, she told herself. They baited her. They wanted her to lose control, and she knew it. The only thing she did wrong was ask Mrs. Scott to watch her patients while she ate her lunch. Since they were short of help, that was not a crime.

Esther examined the chart on the wall. It listed all three floors of the nursing home and which floors had the largest deficit of nurses. The number sixteen at the bottom represented how many staff had resigned in the last three months.

Mrs. Scott continued, "Esther complained bitterly about lifting one of the patients. I have to admit she refused to do what we asked her." Mrs. Scott shook her head with irritation.

"Uh, huh," Mrs. Murphy said.

Esther sat up straight and peered at Mrs. Murphy saying, "I think you've gotten yourself in the strangest predicament with this deficit of nurses. I can tell you one thing, no nurse will stay on a floor staffed with only two nurses for thirty patients who need special, complete physical care. I work an extra half-hour every day to cover my lunch. I only get paid for eight hours and not eight and a half. I don't mind difficult physical work, but I need to eat several meals a day to keep up my strength. Otherwise, I get dizzy, hypoglycemic. My doctor warned me to eat several meals a day to prevent my sugar levels from falling. You're asking the wrong person to skip meals."

All the eyes focused on Esther. They squirmed in their seats. She knew she had them.

"It looks like your staff nurses quit because of inadequate staffing. The difficult working conditions force good nurses to leave. After I lifted all those patients by myself, I pulled a muscle in my back that's still painful. Many of the seventh-floor staff nurses have injured themselves, trying to give good care. You need to hire agency nurses to bring up the quota until you can get new staff. I don't want to jeopardize my health because you don't hire enough nurses."

Esther didn't care what Henry said. She had to get out of there. She didn't wait for their verdict. She left the office and never looked back until she reached the seventh floor. She heard Mrs. Shepherd's quick rustle and heavy footsteps walking behind her.

She didn't stop until she reached Henry who sat in the corner of the nurses' station for solitude, writing on his charts. She breathed a sigh of relief at the sight of his upturned, peaceful face welcoming her intrusion.

"Oh, Henry, I was right. The nursing home has lost sixteen nurses in the last three months." Esther dropped into the metal chair grateful for the rest. "They're making the nurses feel guilty if they can't care for all those patients when it's physically impossible. Those men are dying without the benefit of helping hands, without the benefit of love, or even comfort. Mrs. Murphy is laughing at us, Henry. Laughing at the fact she's fooling everyone. Why Henry? Why?"

Henry shook his head and sat there immobilized as if contemplating what she said. "I don't know," he said, slamming his chart shut. "But I'm going to find out."

He stood up and leaned closer to Esther whispering, "We're getting a new admission down on your ward."

"Oh, Henry! I can't take a new patient today. Send him to Melisa's ward. Tell them to wait till tomorrow."

"He smiled his teasing smile and continued, "It's Chester. They found him unconscious in a ditch, covered in leaves. He's all right. Only suffered from toxic alcohol ingestion and exposure."

"Chester? Will he be all right?"

"Yes. I suppose so. If he stops drinking."

"He'll be here for Shaw. He can help Shaw die with someone who cares about him," Esther answered, thinking maybe God has a plan for us after all. The thought of someone upstairs guiding our movements and rearranging our environment intrigued her. It seemed to happen exactly like Truman said. Chester returned to help Shaw. Maybe seeing Shaw die will influence Chester to stop drinking for good.

Chapter 34

Washed, clean-shaven, and smelling of a tangy after shave lotion, Truman Uriel sat stiffly hunched over his bedside table where he methodically and precisely anchored the strings of the mast halyards to his scale model of a clipper ship. Occasionally, he glanced at the patient snoring in the opposite bed.

Esther stood in the doorway, watching Truman's tedious attempts to complete the model. The pale, yellow glow of his light drew her to his room, the only illumination along the dimly lit hall. She was working overtime on the night shift to make extra money for Matt's birthday. The darkness and penetratingly eerie quiet depressed her.

She loved the hustle and bustle of the daylight hours, the melodious singing of Clay, the familiar scolding voice of Mrs. Shepherd, and the unending complaints and criticisms from the staff. She missed the sight of Melisa rushing down the hall and the soft tone of her voice. At night the floor seemed like a lonely, forgotten place.

"You're up early," she said.

He glanced at Esther without emotion. She heard no pleading in his voice, no furrowing brows, no sign of fidgeting anxiety she saw in the others. A tremendous peace surrounded him.

"Can't sleep," was all he said. He studied her in a benign sort of way. "They moved me in here last evening. I was in Mr. Chandler's room. He became psychotic and hallucinated all night. I couldn't sleep. I've been here twenty days still waiting for a new heart."

Esther gave him his cup of pills. A faint cold glow of the November morning lit up the horizon. "It's too late for a sleeping pill."

The moon appeared in the distance facing the faint glimmer of the rising sun. A thick fog hovered over the lake behind the hospital, reminding her of other country mornings in Maryland.

"Unfortunately, those pills don't work on me," Mr. Uriel said. "They make me groggy. I guess I'm homesick. My family lives in Charleston. I wish they'd let me go home. It's too far away to return in time for the heart transplant. My insurance ran out. This is the cheapest place in town," he laughed. A mask of disappointment covered his previously peaceful expression.

His heart problems were blatantly evident in his purple lips and gray skin. She wondered if he'd live long enough to receive a heart. She felt his desperation. His conversation caused his chest to rise and fall in laborious attempts to fill his negative oxygen supply. She heard the University Hospital sent its heart patients to Thornhill, knowing they would never get a heart. If he was called, he was their last resort. He became their experiment. She had her doubts that he'd be able to make it.

"The Holy Spirit is calling us all to feed our sheep. He helps us too. He gives us the strength to go on when we think all has failed. Salvation and judgment are up to God and the Holy Spirit. I'm merely a mortal man. I must depend on the Holy Spirit to guide me in the right direction," Truman confessed finally.

Truman sat back and laughed. "Sometimes life seems so futile. We work all our lives at one job or purpose when all along it's another goal entirely we're destined to discover. In the end, it's immortality I'm trying to reach. This life on earth is merely a prelude to the kingdom of the Lord waiting for us beyond the river."

"I think I was sent here by the Holy Spirit, only I didn't know it. Can it happen like that?" Esther said.

"Sure, it happens like that a lot. We end up in a place we never thought we'd be. We're helping people jump hurdles we recently struggled to jump." Truman smiled up at Esther. "Come over here and let me give you a blessing."

Esther stood in front of him closing her eyes. He stood up too and placed the palm of his hand on her forehead saying, "I baptize you with the power of the Holy Spirit and wish his loving kindness will surround you, keep you safe always, and give you strength to complete your journey. In the name of the Father, Son, and Holy Spirit I pray. Amen."

"Did you feel anything?" Truman asked.

"No. I didn't feel anything at all," Esther confessed.

"Well, I did," Truman said and smiled.

Esther waved goodbye. "If you need anything, just call me. Good luck," she said.

Three nurses called in sick and Esther panicked. Exhaustion engulfed her from working all night. She didn't want to work any more overtime, especially today. Henry walked into the nurse's' station and headed for his stack of charts with orders needing renewal. He looked haggard, and Esther thought he must have over-exerted himself last night. She laughed, hoping for his sake it was worth it. She knew today promised to be a tough one.

"Hey, Henry. How much will you charge us to work overtime

today as a nurse? Three staff have called in sick."

"Oh, leave me alone. That's not my problem and you know it. I have enough problems of my own."

It was already 7:30 a.m., and no nurses had shown up to take care of the sixty patients. Two night nurses still worked on the other side of the hall getting patients up for breakfast and physical therapy.

She called the Bleeding Heart's Team for help, but they had been called to the sixth floor. When the nurses found out they were assigned to the nursing home, they called in sick. She didn't blame them. Sally pulled her back muscles and was placed on the disabled list. Selysia ingested Motrin like it was candy, and swore she'd quit if they ever sent her there again. They are killing our nurses. She wanted to inform the Director of the hospital, but everyone said he didn't care. He was a wimp anyway.

Esther answered the phone. It was Melisa.

"Melisa, you can't call in. Mrs. Shepherd is on vacation and three called in already. I can't stay. I worked all night. You know Geraldine isn't going to stay and help. Even for overtime."

Esther spotted Geraldine walking slowly, slightly bent over, toward the elevator with her coat on. "Just a minute," Esther said to Melisa on the phone. "Geraldine, you can't leave yet. We don't have enough nurses in case there's an emergency."

"I can't help it. I have an appointment this morning." She waved her hand goodbye.

"Melisa, she's gone now. All right try to come in later. Maybe 10:00 a.m. We need you. I guess Paul can handle the boys. One day won't kill him. After all, this is the first time he's taken them since the wedding in September." As she hung up the phone, she wondered where her boys were. She called several times to tell him she'd be late, but no one answered. She figured he took them to his mother's house or to his new home.

She tried to suppress the panic welling up inside her aching body. Henry rounded the corner, coming from a patient's room. For some reason, the sight of him appearing so dismal bolstered her spirit. If he can survive all this chaos, so can I. The aroma of breakfast churned her stomach. She washed her hands at Mr. Kroger's sink and began another day.

"Mr. Kroger, can you help us feed some of these patients today?"

He had showered, shaved, and placed torn bits of tissue on the minute cuts across his cheek and chin. He sat in his chair stiff as a mannequin, in front of his tray table, waiting for breakfast, and for the world to come to him. The idea of feeding someone else flustered him. His eyes blinked furiously, his lips pursed in and out more rapidly than a strobe light, and mimicked the tremulous quivering of his hands.

"Oh, I don't think so. No. No...not today anyway." His hand tapped rhythmically, uncontrollably on the table in front of him. All the physical therapy in the world wasn't going to give him nerve.

Esther glanced at her watch. It was already 9:00 a.m. and she hadn't given any of her medications. She counted the patients she still had to feed.

"Henry, please help me feed Mrs. Monroe and Mr. Summerville. If you do that, I'll be able to feed the others and give them their medicines. No one from the Bleeding Hearts Team has shown up yet."

He stared back at her hard with his piercing blue eyes, as if he were drawing out her soul. She retreated uncomfortably from his gaze.

After a few seconds, he let his guard down saying, "No one can do all this work alone. Who do you think you are? I'll do Mr. Summerville. I'm not going near Mrs. Monroe. She'll have me move every object in her room just to get attention. I'll feed that new Mr. Spruil. He reminds me of another Buster."

"I forgot all about him. Thanks. I'll help you out one of these days."

He smiled at her with his large rabbit teeth gleaming in the fluorescent light. She knew he had been helping her all along that morning, feeding, changing, and transferring patients. Henry had backed her up.

Esther rushed to feed Mr. Green his cold tray. With his advanced dementia, she didn't think he'd mind. She was wrong. He spit out each mouthful with a vengeance. Hastily, she warmed his plate of pureed food in the microwave. She thought she smelled smoke. She ignored the idea, sure the odor was from the microwave. In the hall, a stronger acrid chemical smell permeated the air. It smelled like something was burning, but she didn't know from where.

She dashed up the hall and peered into each room, trying to identify the source. She stopped in front of Mr. Kroger's room. The area on the ceiling above his television filled rapidly with curling, billowing, invading gray smoke. The smell of burnt debris, resembling burning rubber, permeated the room. Flames licked at the ceiling tiles.

"I'm not leaving my room," declared Mr. Kroger. He sat in his chair, resembling a stubborn mule, struggling to get his breath. Esther grabbed his arm and pulled him staggering to the safety of the hall. He kept turning back, not wanting to leave. She pushed him toward the nurses' station, irritated at his resistance.

Terror stricken, Esther grabbed the phone and pressed 911. When the operator answered, she yelled, "We have a fire on the seventh floor at Thornhill Hospital. Electrical!" She hung up and called "Code Red," over the loudspeaker. "Code Red Seventh floor." The smoke seeped out of Mr. Kroger's room and rolled up the ceiling of the hall. She ran and closed his door. She raced to the next room. One of the patients had already gone to physical therapy. The other one was Truman Uriel. He slept soundly.

"Truman," she screamed. "Truman Uriel! There's a fire! Get up!" Esther didn't wait and pulled his body with his sheets wrapped around him gently to the floor, and dragged him down the hall to safety. She didn't wait, returning to the smoke filled rooms. The smoke billowed into a huge wall behind her, closing off the hallway.

"Henry! Henry! Help me!" She entered Shaw's room, took the scissors in her pocket, cut his restraints, wrapped him in a sheet, and dragged his heavy body down the hall, through the six-foot wall of smoke to safety.

Other patients stood at the end of the hall, sat on the floor or were in a group lying on the floor near the elevators. Strange nurses and staff arrived to help and guided the patients down the stairs to the sixth floor. She left Shaw and ran back. She rescued several other patients, including Chester and helped him walk down the hall to the nurses' station. He had declined so badly, he needed help keeping his balance.

At the elevator, she ran into Sally and Selysia who had decided to come in after all. She ignored their questions and shouted commands, "Sally, go over to the other side and make sure all the doors are closed. I think the fire is isolated here. If there's smoke get the patients to safety. Selysia, help me get these patients safely away from the fire. I sent Mr. Kroger to the nurses' station and told him to stay there. But I haven't seen him. Maybe someone took him down to six."

"I just came from there," Selysia said. "I didn't see him." Esther ignored her and dashed back into the smoke to Mr. Goffard's room. He still slept soundly on his bed. Smoke billowed in from cracks in the ceiling tiles like low swooping black clouds. She tried to rouse him.

Thick smoke took her breath away, burned her throat, and stung her eyes.

She wrapped her face in his Afghan, wrapped him in the blanket like a corpse and dragged him out of the room, down the hall, through the smoke to safety. She was sure he was dead by the way he thumped to the floor and didn't move. Why did this have to happen today of all days she cried?

Esther spotted Henry's long legs ahead of her carrying Mrs. Monroe who complained continually and insisted she was suing the hospital. Thank God, he's here, she thought as she pulled Mr. Goffard to the end of the hall. She felt his neck for a pulse. When Henry rushed past, he reached down and pinched Mr. Goffard's arm so hard he cried out and swung his fist up to strike Henry.

Henry let go, nodded to Esther, and ran back through the smoke. Relief flooded her when she realized Mr. Goffard was alive.

The lights darkened when the electricity failed, making it difficult to see the forms coming and going through the fog of smoke. She struggled to get her breath.

Firemen invaded the floor, trudging heavily like giants in their black coats. They shouted orders to each other, wore smoke masks, and carried extinguishers. Esther watched them enter and leave the smoke filled hall with tears in her eyes. She had forgotten how tired she was until now. She should be moving the patients to a safer area. Other nurses from other floors continued to assist the patients down the stairs. Some were still wrapped in their sheets. Looking around, she realized she hadn't seen Mr. Kroger for a long time. She worried about the others and speculated about where they had been taken. She hadn't seen Henry for some time either and scanned the forms coming out of the smoke for his long legs and arms, but he didn't return.

She felt the room spinning around her from lack of oxygen. Her nose and lungs burned as she tried to remember which patients were at the other end of the hall. To her surprise, Mr. Wristford came choking out of the smoke, wheeling his chair, with his face covered with a towel.

She grabbed him and asked if he had seen Henry. He shook his head no. He said he was the only one back there when the smoke became too thick to breathe. He didn't know what was happening because there wasn't any smoke in the bathroom.

Two firemen ran out demanding more smoke masks. The fire was put out with extinguishers. Foam filled the hall. Heavy smoke remained.

She sobbed, close to hysteria, and ran down the hall on the other side to make sure everyone there was safe. The patients appeared scared, all right, but they stayed in their beds with the doors shut, out of the smoke. Selysia and Sally followed her, trying to reassure her everyone had been counted.

Satisfied, she ran to the other side. Every door she opened produced an empty room. It amazed her how they were able to empty those rooms so fast. She knew Henry was the one who led or carried most of the patients to safety. Where was he? It had been too long. She was afraid to think of what happened to him.

Tears filled her eyes. Smoke filtered out through the windows. Thank goodness they had windows.

One of the firemen entered the thick, gray haze, pushing a stretcher. Holding her breath she followed him and grabbed a towel to cover her mouth. Fear gripped her as she dreaded the worst. Henry?

She struggled to breathe. Where was Henry? She lost her bearings and tried to find her way out along the wall. She knew no one survived this thick smoke. She was going in the wrong direction. She crouched down to breathe some oxygen near the floor. A strong hand grabbed her arm and pulled her back. It pulled her into the alcove in a corner of the hall by the telephone. The area was clear of smoke. She breathed deeply. The hand drew her closer until she felt embraced in the strength and warmth of Henry's chest. His arms surrounded her. It all happened too fast. She screamed.

In the split second of recognition and relief, Henry's mouth sought hers. Passion erupted to overwhelm them both. She struggled to be free, but he fought for her. He dug his fingers into her shoulders holding her, resisting her strength to pull away. Finally, she gave in, wanting his embrace, wanting his kisses, wanting his love, wanting to own him. She became dizzy, even faint, and pulled free, not understanding her hidden animal desires.

He had stolen this moment from her, taken her unaware. When she pulled away, it was just in time to see the firemen emerge from the still heavy smoke, pulling the stretcher carrying a covered body.

Gasping, she reached out toward the body, but Henry pulled her back. She felt the shaking tremble of his arm enter her arm. When he whispered the name Mr. Kroger in her ear, she felt a stab of pain in her soul. It was too much for her.

She broke loose from his clutch. Stumbling, struggling for air, she followed the stretcher. When she reached the head of the body, she angrily pulled away the sheet not believing what Henry told her. As if they had been children playing a game and he lied. Mr. Kroger still clutched his coat, hat, and a picture of him playing the piano at Carnegie Hall. Esther refused to believe he returned to his room, unafraid of the smoke and flames, for those few items. A certain peace converged indelibly across his still face. His blinking eyelids and pursing lips finally at rest. The hint of a smile had set at the turned up corners of his mouth.

They were all watching her now. The black coated firemen, with their dirt, streaked sweaty faces peered down at the frail Mr. Kroger laying in his tissue paper thin skin in his still corpse. She felt his death was all her fault. If only she'd gone back to look for him. If only she'd sent Selysia to search for him. If only....

The nurses on the other side of the hall huddled together. Their large eyes never blinked, silently observing her reaction. They knew Mr. Kroger was her friend. Esther's body sagged in defeat.

It was Selysia and Sally who finally came over and gently surrounded her with their arms and led her to the nurses' lounge for privacy.

The smoke began to clear and Melisa stood at the end of the hall, shocked at the scene. She observed silently as the firemen carried Mr. Kroger's body past her to the now running elevators. Henry's and Esther's stricken faces stared at her.

Chapter 35

After the fire, the floor remained in a state of confusion for several hours. Melisa stood near the nurses' station, watching the firemen clean up the messy foam floating on the linoleum floors. Walls, ceiling, and furniture grew a hairy black covering of soot from the smoke.

All these rooms will be out of commission for at least a week or more, she calculated. Mentally, she created an agenda for her next plan of action. The patients needed to be transferred to other floors until the unit could be repaired and redecorated. Mrs. Shepherd must be notified unless Esther had already called her. She worried about who notified Mrs. Kroger? Who pronounced him dead? She needed to find Henry.

The thought of Mr. Kroger dying in the fire closed her throat. Her knees shook uncontrollably, like teeth chattering from the cold.

She gripped hold of her package of new shoes so tight her nails cut deep creases into her palm. All the hours she spent with Mr. Kroger flooded her mind, and the pictures of his desperation flashed in front of her eyes.

Out of the darkness, Violet's hand gently touched her shoulder.

"I'm so sorry about this accident. The seventh floor was to be our next stop. When we arrived, smoke engulfed everything. Julie and I spent the last half hour taking patients to the other floors for safety. I've made a list for you of the patients and which floor they're on," said Violet. I know Esther was in charge. She was very resourceful. She and Henry emptied all the rooms filled with smoke. Esther lifted and dragged these patients with superhuman strength. She risked her life for Mr. Uriel. Racing back into that black wall of smoke, she dragged him out wrapped in the sheet."

Melisa nodded, trying to understand what happened.

"We gathered four patients from the alcove who Esther and Henry rescued. They were the only staff pulling the patients out of the fire and smoke. Sally and Selysia were checking on the others on the other side of the hall and trying to keep the rescued patients calm."

"I noticed Mr. Kroger walking around in circles mumbling to himself. He became agitated. I tried to get him to go down the stairs with us, but he kept calling for Esther. He pointed toward the smoke. Said she told him to stay there and wait for her. He promised me he would wait in the alcove for Esther to come out again. He kept walking around in circles whimpering, 'Where's Esther? She's coming out soon."

Violet's face flushed red; fear shot from her eyes. Her voice shook with a high pitched speech.

"When I returned to the alcove from the sixth floor, he was gone. I ran to the other rooms to look for him, but he wasn't there. I saw Esther at the edge of the smoke coughing, having trouble getting her breath, and still dragging Mr. Uriel. He was struggling for breath too. I took him still laying in the sheet down the stairs to the sixth floor to find oxygen for him. Get more medical care if he needed it. It was so confusing. I thought someone else must have taken Mr. Kroger off the floor, especially since he was able to walk. He must have slipped back through the smoke to find Esther and get his things. He must have gone back to his room, found his hat, coat, and picture, and became overcome by smoke." Violet's chin caught in a sob and tears splattered her face. "If only I had forced him to leave the floor. He'd be alive now. It's all my fault."

Melisa put her arm around her, "I know you did everything you could to help him. You trusted he'd wait for Esther to come out. You expected Esther to come out too."

But Melisa wanted to yell for God's sake why didn't you force him to go with you, tell him Esther was down there already, something or anything to get him to follow you. Melisa merely held in her emotions.

"Melisa," called Henry. His red eyes wept from the smoke. Gray and black soot streaked his white lab coat. His shoulders drooped like an old man as he motioned with his head toward the Director of Nurses, Mrs. Putnam and the Director of the Hospital, Mr. Forester, a short, balding man with a disagreeable expression crossing his face.

Melisa tried to compose herself. Patients' names and room numbers raced through her mind. She hated confrontations. She tried to stifle her guilt for spending the last two hours with Buster on the eighth floor. She never heard the Code Red alarm over the loudspeakers. The doctors had amputated Buster's legs and she wanted to make him comfortable. Her frail hand fluttered at her chest.

"I guess you all know what happened. Maybe you know more than I do," Melisa said feeling a deep ache in her stomach.

They continued to glare at her with grim, unsmiling faces.

"I suppose you want to examine the damage from the fire."

They appeared scared. They ought to be, she thought. After all the times she called and reported the faulty wiring, no engineer had come.

"Henry! You were here. You tell them what happened. Would you?" Melisa glanced tentatively at Henry.

Henry straightened his posture and led the way as they gingerly tip-toed over the foam covered linoleum, avoiding firemen coming and going.

Henry scratched his head seeing the burned out ceiling and wall for the first time since the smoke cleared and said, "I think the wiring problem started here behind the television. Esther was in here at the time, grabbed Mr. Kroger, and took him out to the main hall."

Remnants of the fire-charred blackened walls, ceiling, mutilated television, and the huge hole gaping into the room next door, gave testimony to the fire's destruction. Parts of the ceiling tile hung loose, melted from the flames, exposing the steel rafters and pipes. Crisp November air blew in through the broken window, circled the room unheeded, and created a heavy draft out the door and down the hall.

No one said a word. Mr. Kroger's locker door stood open. His suitcase sprawled across the floor with his clothes lying in charred piles amid the foam from the fire extinguishers.

The group continued to the next room where the hole in the wall resembled Mr. Kroger's. Blackened and smoldering beds had been pushed against the opposite wall. Melted plaster hung loosely around the burned out opening. An oily, black, sooty residue covered everything in sight.

"I'm not surprised by all this," Melisa said to the stunned faces in the room. "No, I'm not. For two months, we've been sending memos to the Engineering Department requesting repairs for these electrical sockets. Most of them don't work. The patients get shocked from some of the others. No one ever came to check on the problem. Mr. Kroger's plug hung out of his wall on a flimsy wire. There are about ten other plugs in other rooms. It was only a matter of time before something like this occurred. This wiring is so old anything is possible. We also have rodents. They could have chewed into a wire."

Mr. Forester cleared his throat and squirmed uncomfortably. "Who was in charge when all this happened?" he said.

"Esther Culver," Henry divulged with a strange indifference. Henry didn't take his scrutinizing gaze off the Director for a second. Mr. Forester flashed a knowing affirmation at Mrs. Putnam.

"Well, where is she?" Mr. Forester said, scanning the hall for her appearance. Then, he turned back to Henry saying, "I think you have exerted a commendable effort under the circumstances of this emergency." He grabbed Henry's hand and pumped it up and down with enthusiastic fervor. Henry's mouth dropped open with astonishment. His hand lay limply in the Director's firm grasp.

"I'd like to commend the lady if I may. Where is she?"

"I'll go get her," Melisa said. "I think she's in the lounge writing up what happened so she can tell Mrs. Shepherd exactly what the sequence of events were."

Melisa hurried up the hall, dodging all the cleaning men and the Director of the maintenance department. Firemen still collected their smoke masks and made lists of equipment they needed. Engineers arrived to evaluate the broken windows and structural damage between the rooms.

Knowing Esther and the others were in the nurses' lounge, trying to compose themselves and regain control of their emotions, Melisa lied to the Director. She heard Esther became hysterical after seeing Mr. Kroger's body, saying she was responsible for his death. She didn't want Esther to say anything to threaten her probation.

Esther, deflated and crying softly, sat at the table in the nurses' lounge. She gazed up at Melisa with swollen red eyes, hands trembling, and covered with soot, as she sipped her tea.

Melisa felt terrible for her. Selysia's usually spotless white uniform was gray with soot. Her longest fingernail had broken off into the quick.

"Melisa, you'll never believe this!" Esther said, tears filling her eyes. "Sally said the nursing home deliberately let their nurses quit and not hire new ones so their budget came in low. She saw an article in the Hospital Monthly about Thornhill's Nursing Home budget being twenty thousand below the allotted amount. The Veterans' Administration is awarding Mrs. Murphy, Director of the Nursing Home, a plaque for her excellent management practices. Can you believe that? She'll probably get a bonus too. She used us as workhorses so the budget had a surplus of money. We are being paid by the rehabilitation unit. The accounts of the nursing home are separate. We are suffering because she is using us as her skeleton staff." Esther exhaled.

"I'm going to report them."

"You will?" Melisa said and raised her eyebrows warning her to be cautious. Her head trembled slightly, and her hand fluttered at her chest. "Dear. The Director is out there and wants to see you. Don't get upset. He wants to congratulate you on your good work, evacuating the hall the way you did. He's out there pumping Henry's arm. Can't thank him enough for saving the patients."

"Oh," Esther said and stood up slowly. She tried to brush the black stains off of her uniform without success. "I don't know how I dragged all those patients to safety either."

Sally and Selysia said, "What about us? We helped too."

"Come out, girls. I'm sure he'd like to thank all of you. I'd like to thank all of you too. But Esther, I'm warning you to be calm," Melisa said with her hands fluttering at her throat.

Facing the Director, the three wiped the tears from their eyes and stood side by side in front of the nurses' station like three children waiting for a reprimand. They whispered to each other, "We need to tell him what's going on in the nursing home."

"So, you're the nurses who saved all these patients. I'd like to congratulate you on a job well done," Mr. Forester said as he moved from one to the other shaking their hands. You've prevented a disaster here, and we appreciate your help. We are extremely sorry about Mr. Kroger, but accidents happen." He glared at Esther for several seconds, anger crossed his face. "What do you think happened to him, girl? This isn't gonna look pretty for the hospital. Now is it?"

His change of attitude caught Esther off guard. She stumbled over her words. "I don't know. I'm still trying to figure out what happened to him. He was the first patient I brought out of the smoke."

"Don't you think we'll be sued for his death? Was there some connection between your needle stick and his death? This disaster? It's all very suspicious."

"No. I don't know what you are trying to insinuate. As I said before, he was the first patient I brought to safety. I had to go back to save the others. The ones who were bedridden and unable to talk. I told him to stay at the nurses' station and I'd be right back. He didn't wait. Evidently, he went back to his room," Esther said and started to cry again. "I'm sorry. I'm so sorry he didn't wait."

Henry rushed over and put his arm around her saying, "Look, I don't think this interrogation is getting us anywhere. It was an accident. The other nurses, Sakiko and Tarin, were sent to the nursing home this morning. Esther was the only staff. The others called in sick. The night nurses left and refused to stay. Selysia and Sally came in late after calling in sick. Maybe you should question Mrs. Murphy about why our nurses and CNAs are being pulled to the nursing home, leaving the seventh floor short, and today with this emergency, deadly short."

Henry stood his ground, strong, and defensive. "Esther risked her life returning into the smoke to pull out all the patients in these rooms. I pulled out eight or maybe ten, but she carried out the rest. I don't know how she managed it."

Mr. Forester stood back slightly. Surprised at their attack, his hands fidgeted at his sides, blood pulsed in his temples, face reddened, and he stammered, groping for words. He laughed to himself eyeing Henry from a different angle like an old calculating crow.

Esther continued crying, unable to control her sobs. Henry's face bulged with anger.

"For Christ's sake! Look at her! Maybe you should ask Esther how she managed to move eighteen bedridden patients single-handedly from their smoke filled rooms to the hallway where the others took them down the stairs to the sixth floor. I haven't heard any questions like that. She had breast surgery a couple of weeks ago, pulled a muscle in her back working at the nursing home, and is still on light duty. I know she carried them, dragged them in sheets, walked them because I watched her. There wasn't time to stop and complain. Trying to save everyone, she acted without thought to her ability or safety. She risked her life in that dense smoke. I carried about eight or ten. I've lost count. It was a struggle for me. It was a challenge to go back into the fire and smoke over and over again. We had to rescue the others left behind."

Mr. Forester squinted his eyes and observed the two contemptuously. His expression changed to a softer, warmer more concerned examination.

"Well, maybe I've been hasty in my accusations. Why didn't you tell me about the nursing conditions? I let the nurses take care of themselves." He touched Esther's shoulder saying, "Thank you for all your help this morning. All of you need to be commended." Abruptly, he nodded the conversation was over. He turned and left the floor, glancing with contempt at Mrs. Putnam running at his heels.

Esther coughed in deep spasms, bringing up black sputum. She returned to the nurses' lounge with the others following her. Cold November air blew into the hall in large gusts and followed the small group as if it were some lost spirit trying to find its way.

"I haven't called Mrs. Shepherd yet," Melisa said. "Maybe you'd like to call her, Esther. Would you like to make the call?"

"No, I don't think so. I'm going home. This is enough to do for two shifts. I wonder if they pay you extra for fire rescues?"

The others laughed at her saying, "Maybe we should be getting the bonus."

"I can't imagine how I carried all those patients to safety. I need to speak to Mr. Uriel."

"You did it all," Sally said in awe. "I watched you. Every time I brought out a walker you dragged a bedridden one and through all that smoke."

"We all did it. What made you and Sally come in after you called in?" Esther said.

"When I heard you were here by yourself, I knew I had to come and help you," Sally said. "We called in because I thought we'd be sent to that nursing home again."

"Sally called me, and I rushed around trying to get dressed. I felt this powerful urging and knew something was wrong," Selysia said.

"I never felt their weight. The patients seemed to cling to me as I walked. I never felt any pain either. With some I dragged, I ran as fast as I could, trying not to breathe in the smoke, holding my breath until I reached the elevators. Smoke billowed out of Mr. Kroger's room. I knew I closed his door when I brought him to the nurses' station. I didn't see Henry and searched for him. I thought he'd been overcome by smoke. I finally found him in the alcove where the stretchers were, in a small pocket of clean air."

They hugged each other saying the fire could have been much worse. Selysia rose her eyes toward the ceiling praying, "Thank you, Lord, for saving all of us."

Esther waited at the elevator to go to the sixth floor before she left and hoped Henry did the same to check all of them for residual effects of the smoke. Sally and Selysia were behind her.

"I didn't tell you I was called into Mrs. Murphy's office because I insisted I take a lunch break. Mrs. Scott reported me. I told her to stop pulling us and get agency staff. She merely smiled at me. She said we had plenty of nurses and needed to share."

"We didn't know you did that for us. You risked yourself for us," Selysia said.

"I was furious at them for making all those patients suffer. Why didn't you stand up to her? You have your licenses. I'm the one who has the most to risk."

Sally squirmed and said, "We have just as much at stake as you. Don't you know they'd fire us as soon as look at us? They don't care about us. Where would we be? We have friends here. Mrs. Shepherd gives us the hours we want. She helps us out. We'd be going against her. Don't you know that, girl?"

"Thanks for trying for us. It might have helped. Maybe now the staffing problem will improve," Selysia said.

Melisa called from the nurses' station, "It will be three days at least before we can bring the patients back. Get some rest. Mrs. Shepherd is coming in to help." She waved goodbye.

Esther strode wearily off the elevator to the sixth floor. She stopped at the nurses' station and asked where Truman's room was.

"You must be Esther," the nurse said.

"Yes, I am. How are the patients from the seventh floor?"

"That one. Patrick Shaw isn't doing too well. Henry's in there with him now. The others are doing pretty good. We are lucky we had these empty rooms. We were supposed to admit new patients today. The other floors had rooms too.

"What's wrong with Shaw?" Esther asked tentatively, not wanting to hear any more bad news.

"He has a brain tumor, doesn't he? I think it's just his time to go. They're in wards 623 and 624. You'll find them all together," the nurse said.

Esther didn't hesitate but rushed down the hall until she reached 623. They were all in the ward waiting for Shaw to take his last breath. Henry dozed in the corner with his feet propped up on the bedside table. Mr. Uriel was there too. Sitting in a wheelchair, wearing a nasal cannula for oxygen, he prayed silently while holding Shaw's limp hand. Death rales hung on his heavy inspirations and expirations sounding like a revving motor in a diesel eighteen wheeler. She had to turn away.

Esther touched Chester's rough calloused hand and examined his dirty cracked fingers. She squeezed it tenderly. "Are you all right?" she asked.

"Yes. I think I'm gonna be fine now. I've been through the fire, and I'm changing my tune. I'm quitting drinking and putting my life back together. I'm looking toward God now. I'm never looking back again." He gazed at Esther for a long time.

She squeezed his hand again saying, "I believe you, Chester. I believe you." This time she sensed something changed him. She wondered how many times God gave him a chance to start over. Finally, she understood God gave them all as many chances as it took. Even if He had to put them through the fire to get them over the mountain, He didn't want to lose anyone.

"Yes," Chester said as he peered mischievously at Esther. "You're the one. You're the one He sent to us to get this place back to normal. You done it too. I don't know how. It was only a matter of time for Shaw anyway. I saw it coming a long time ago. He slipped away every day right in front of our eyes."

"I don't think He just sent me," Esther said. "He sent all of us. It took all of us to see the light and help each other. It's taken you to help me. Truman to advise me and the others. Look here at Shaw. Believe it or not, he helped people reach out to the Lord before they died and not be afraid. It takes a leap of faith that God will save the soul and dying is all right. We have to put our soul in God's hands now. Live for him instead of waiting until the end and hoping he'll save us."

"Isn't that right, Truman? If we take the leap of faith now we can expect peace in our lives instead of all this suffering and pain."

"That's right. You'll have peace of mind in spite of all the suffering. Dying is a painful process of letting go of all our earthly possessions and relationships. The last of all is our body. For some, the parting is more painful than it is for the others. In that way we are free to embrace the life that is to come," Truman said stopping to get his breath.

Esther grabbed Chester's hand again and said, "Nothing can separate you from the love of God. Neither death nor life, neither angels nor demons, neither the present nor the future, nor any powers, neither height nor depth, nor anything else in all creation, will be able to separate us from the love of God that is in Christ Jesus our Lord. Romans 8:38. Suffering carries us along to be purified and sanctified in God's eyes. It's all part of being God's people."

Esther wished Henry was listening to Truman. She remained curious about his beliefs and didn't know if he believed in God or not.

"Truman," Esther said, touching his shoulder. "I wanted to ask you about the fire. What happened to me when I lifted and dragged all those patients to safety? Was the Holy Spirit helping me?"

"Tell me what happened," Truman said and glanced at Henry who still slept and smiled to himself. Chester leaned closer to listen.

"When the fire broke out, I received this surge of energy. More than epinephrine or adrenaline. I was given superhuman strength. I ran from room to room with a strained back muscle. I wrapped all the patients in sheets and blankets, pulled them to the floor, or picked up some, laid them on the floor, and dragged them out through the smoke to safety. Don't you remember me taking you too?"

Truman laughed and said, "I remember you dragging me off the bed in a cloud of softness, and before I knew it, you placed me next to the stairway."

"Yes, that's it. That's what I mean. A big cloud of peace surrounded me and helped me somehow."

"That's the Holy Spirit. He came to you to help you save those patients. To save us. The Spirit is with you. I think Chester is right. Maybe He has been with you from the beginning. Sometimes, we don't know these things. Having the Holy Spirit doesn't mean we are free from suffering, or heartache, or even strife. It means we need to trust in God to help us and guide us. After all, we have free will to do whatever we want, even though we know what God wants for us.

Truman scrutinized Esther and asked, "Will you touch my forehead with your hand?"

She obeyed and touched his cold, clammy forehead, laying her palm firmly against his skin. She felt more scared than any of them. Suppose she imagined all this power. Suppose there wasn't any power. She didn't feel special. She never experienced any current.

Truman closed his eyes and prayed, "In the name of the Father, Son and Holy Spirit, heal me with your strength, and might, and surround me with your everlasting peace."

Truman closed his eyes and soon fell quickly to sleep. A white light glowed around Esther's hand, around his head for several seconds, and then disappeared. Esther's hand trembled from the ordeal. She struggled to hold back the tears. She knew Truman had been healed. She knew deep within her soul, without a shadow of a doubt.

When she left the room a marvelous peace surrounded her, instantly calming her fears and sorrows. Why had this happened to her? What had she done to deserve it? Why now of all times, after all that happened? It felt too confusing, too frightening to think about.

She glanced back at Truman and Henry sleeping. Suddenly, she experienced an overwhelming exhaustion. Chester seemed oblivious to all the commotion. He sat quietly staring down at Shaw, breathing heavily with each one of Shaw's breaths. The heat from the room felt smothering. She wanted to scream. She wanted to run and leave all the suffering behind. Had she actually healed Truman? She never looked back after she left the three sleeping men, afraid it was all imagined.

As she passed the personnel office on the first floor, she realized her probation was almost up. She needed to get an accurate account of her hours. She sighed as she left the hospital, thinking of the past thousand hours that profoundly changed her life. Outside, the cold November air revitalized her as sharply as if she had been slapped squarely in the face.

It is true, she thought, the Holy Spirit is real. The glare from the bright sunshine hurt her eyes.

Chapter 36

Today was the Thanksgiving celebration . The morning started off wrong from the beginning. Esther left her house without the sweet potato casserole. She returned at the last minute and hated leaving her boys in the car while she ran back into the house. Her body ached too much to unbuckle them and drag them back for only a few seconds. Anything might have happened, she told herself.

The orange glow on the horizon reminded her again of the fire. Pangs of guilt from Mr. Kroger's death hung over her like a black cloud and weighed her down, using up her energy. She felt responsible for a man's death.

She nodded hello to several people she knew from the lab and the medical records. She had already suffered run ins with some of them and patched up hard feelings. Now a nod of hello meant they were all in this together. She smiled to herself realizing the hospital became an immense source of security for her. She needed to pick up her mood and smile for a change. Mrs. Shepherd gave her three days off in a row for the holiday. She couldn't wait.

Henry offered to bring the turkey. He wasn't going home to his brother's after all. She hoped Paul wanted the boys for the holidays but no, to her dismay, he actually refused, saying his mother wasn't feeling well. He would pass for this year. She felt rejected as if he spurned her all over again. She tolerated it though because it made the holiday simpler.

"Hey, wait up a minute," Henry called to her, sounding out of breath. "Where are you off to in such a hurry?" Henry said. "I tried to catch up with you a few minutes ago. You shot ahead of everyone and slid into the elevator before I reached you. Are you running a race?"

"No. I have so much to do this morning. That's all. I'm carrying this heavy dish of sweet potato casserole for Thanksgiving dinner. I didn't see you," Esther answered a little flustered.

"Oh, let me carry it for you," Henry offered, taking the bag out of her hand.

"This is heavy. No wonder you were running. How are you feeling today? Is your back better? If it isn't, go down to employee health. Maybe they'll give you something strong for it."

"Oh, I feel all right. I need the money right now and don't want to take any time off. I just want to finish my probation. The end is only a few days away. Anyway, how can they put me on light duty with so much work to do?"

Esther felt comforted by his concern. She retreated slightly, horrified at his disheveled appearance of a wrinkled shirt, unpressed pants, and loose tie. She wanted to mention his appearance when the tender expression in his eyes caught her and held her attention for too long. Her desires for him rose up inside of her making her feel dizzy. All her thoughts disappeared, being close to him now became all that mattered. She didn't care what he looked like.

"So what did you bring to the dinner today?" She asked quietly, knowing he was bringing the turkey. "Some great ancestral concoction for all of us to ooh and ahh over?"

"You'll have to wait and see," he said and laughed softly to himself as if he hid some prized secret. He examined her quizzically for a second, then grew pensive.

"Man, did you see the weather brewing outside today? We're in for a big storm. All the warnings are there. Unseasonably hot and muggy with a cold front plowing through. Just you wait and see," he said, agitated. "I don't like it. I tell you. I don't like it at all."

He stalked into the nurses' lounge and pulled up a chair.

"I guess that's the sailor in you coming out. Red sky in morning, sailors take warning. Red sky at night, sailor's delight. Or something like that," she said not really taking him seriously. She opened her dirty, yellow locker and placed her purse and sweater inside.

"No. I think it's sailor's fright at the wind's might. Don't you feel it? You're the one who usually senses these periods of disaster. Not me. This time it's me who's having the premonition of doom," Henry said as his face paled.

"I see. Well, if it's that bad you must pay attention to it. I think you should pray," Esther said with confidence and smiled brightly. "I always pray the outcome will be something I can tolerate and work through."

Esther didn't like the black expression of regret on his face. She tried to brush off his brooding as another mood she hadn't seen before, but she sensed a feeling of dread from the weather outside too. A distinct change of tide was coming.

She ignored the warning, though, because she anticipated a wonderful Thanksgiving. The Advil she took that morning had already taken effect.

Esther carried her dish of sweet potatoes to the clean utility room for the dinner. She placed her hot dish on the counter along with several others.

Mrs. Shepherd marched into the room, grabbing Clay's arm, Jewel's arm, and hollered to all the others who milled around in the excitement, setting up tables, and straightening the shelves.

"Now, I want this floor to shine especially nice today because Mrs. Putnam and Mrs. Murphy are joining us for dinner."

"Uh, huh! I hear ya," said Selysia.

"Who invited them. Those are the last people we want around here," said Sally.

"It's the big cheese...Louise," Jewels added with smug exasperation.

"This is our party...I thought!" Lyla added, sticking out her chin in a pout.

"I'm not finished," said Mrs. Shepherd, waving them to be quiet. "I've also invited all the other staff from the nursing home to bring a dish. What staff can get free of the unit? So I expect each of you to be polite to them and extend our hospitality. Do you hear?" She sighed heavily, pursed her lips together, and shook her head as if anticipating disappointment.

"I mean it. Tomorrow is Thanksgiving, and we have so much to be thankful for. Now stop complaining. Do you hear?"

They have twisted her arm, Esther thought. Yes, they are holding something over on Mrs. Shepherd. They are forcing her to say we are all one big happy family. They are forcing her to say she is on their side. What they did was wrong. It's not all right to squeeze the life blood out of the nurses, aides, and auxiliary workers. Mrs. Putnam and Mrs. Murphy successfully wedged her in the middle. Some kind of Thanksgiving this will be.

Esther wanted to run after Mrs. Shepherd and tell her to fight them. Tell her not to give up. For some reason, she knew Mrs. Shepherd didn't have a choice. Esther held her peace, not saying a word, and simply watched as Jewels acted out in his effort to smooth out all the ruffled feathers.

Jewels laughed, ignored all the disgruntled remarks, and said, "Let the merriment begin. Miss Esther, Mrs. Shepherd has asked me to say the prayer before dinner today. And now I is a Bible toting man. Me a Bible toting man."

"That's wonderful Jewels. I'm so happy for you," Esther said. He had come a long way from hating God for letting Jessie Taylor die so unjustly. Yes, we've all come a long way, almost a lifetime in a thousand days.

With her probation ending, she debated about leaving after all. If it weren't for her back pain and the strenuous work, she wanted to stay. The seventh floor had become her home away from home. Some of the girls meant a lot to her. They had become her family. She needed to get through today, and the next, and the next with her throbbing muscles. This was all she asked God for now.

She moved rapidly from one patient to the next, helping them transfer, bathe, and dress. All she thought about were her days off over the holidays and ignored the growing discomfort she felt in her back.

Esther entered the nursing station and slipped quickly past Mrs. Shepherd who was on the phone. She filled out the information sheet for employee health and placed it in front of Mrs. Shepherd. Shaking her head it was all right, Mrs. Shepherd signed it, but not without letting out a deep sigh.

Esther sat down in the small employee health office. The nurse practitioner examined her thoroughly and admitted she felt the tight muscle spasms.

"What are they doing to you nurses up there on the seventh floor? You're not the only one to have this same type of injury. I've had four this week alone. You are twisting where you should be side stepping," the nurse said and gave Esther a sympathetic look. "What happened to your A.I.D.S. needlestick? Did you ever find out if the patient has A.I.D.S. or not?"

Esther slumped down in her seat. "I've forgotten all about that. The patient's family refused to let me test him. In all the commotion, I suppose I forgot. He didn't have any of the symptoms so...."

"Where is he now?"

"It was Mr. Kroger. He died in the fire we had up there on the seventh floor."

"Was there an autopsy?"

"I don't know? I really don't know. I'll ask about the autopsy. I'm sure they tested him for everything." Assuming the test must be negative, Esther relaxed.

"I've written you a prescription for these strong muscle relaxants which ought to last for two weeks. I'm putting you on light duty for three weeks. That means no lifting of any sort. Do you hear?"

Esther answered reluctantly, "Yes," knowing she'd never be able to comply with the orders. No one will do her lifting for her except Clay, and he was on evenings now. She decided to take it one incident at a time. At least, she had some medicine now. Strong medicine. Tomorrow was Thanksgiving, and fortunately, she had three days off. Feeling like a wounded bird, Esther returned to the floor.

Her zest for life gone. The excitement of the dinner invaded every conversation. The nurses enthusiastically described their contributions to the fare. She scanned the utility room. Karen brought her darling new baby and everyone oohed and aahed over her. Clay stood in the corner watching everyone. Mrs. Shepherd sat at the head of the table. From the peaceful, serene expressions on all their faces, Esther thought we have so much to be thankful for.

At 1:00 p.m., the staff gathered in the large, clean utility room. Someone had hung orange crepe paper in festoons around the walls and applied orange leaves to the ceiling, walls, table, and on the paper tree in the corner. A gray and black turkey hung over the small utility elevator door.

Selysia danced around with her spicy dish of curried fried rice, slapping hands reaching for a taste. Clay produced four sweet potato pies he and his daughter baked for everyone. He talked about making them for days.

"The best in the entire city of Fayette, South Carolina," he vowed.

When Esther asked him for the recipe, he clammed up like a judge and refused to acknowledge her question, skipping as far away from her grasp as possible.

At the last minute, Henry arrived carrying a huge crusted brown turkey on a large platter and placed it in the middle of the table. The heat from the breast steamed up into everyone's face, imparting its nostalgic aroma of sage, thyme, and roasted dressing in time for everyone to conjure up and savor the memories from past Thanksgivings. For some, this celebration will be their only Thanksgiving dinner.

Mrs. Murphy arrived with a crate of beautiful apples and invited everyone to help themselves. As she thanked them for their hard work, she gave each a letter. The apples disappeared quickly.

Esther opened her letter immediately and read it. It was a carbon copy of the one she typed for Clay when she recommended him for an award. The staff became so gratified. They smiled with delight at the letter. Had they already forgotten about their life blood they sacrificed for the nursing home? Had they forgotten about all the fighting and crying they endured because of the difficult work? They walked around with their heads held high, proud they received a letter of commendation.

It took so little to please them. It became a letter of thanks in the face of the most contemptible work conditions. All the time, the administration knowingly saved money. Maybe she should write a letter to the president. What would he do?

In the end, no one cared because the people are dying anyway, the poor, and indigent. Doctors, lawyers, ministers, no matter what they were in their productive lifetime, now became wards of the federal government and forgotten for the rest of their lives.

Jewels stood in the middle of the room waiting to give the invocation and prayer. The staff gathered around and held hands, waiting for Esther. She stumbled down the hall and stuffed the letter into her pocket. She wedged between Henry and Melisa and grabbed each one's hand. Melisa's warm and soft one and Henry's cold and clammy one. She saw the same turmoil in his eyes that appeared there that morning.

"We've all seen a lot of changes up here on the seventh floor this year. Many of us have changed as well, said Mrs. Shepherd, smiling. "We've suffered through the bad times without enough staff to even feed all the patients once a day. We've even seen days when we were overflowing with nurses. We've grown closer than I've ever know a group of girls to be. We've formed the kind of friendships that grow when you come face to face with death and live through it enough times to try to understand the true meaning of life. We are thankful to the Lord for all these blessings. More blessings than I can name." She sighed deeply. "Now I've asked Jewels to say the prayer."

"Lord, we thank you for all the wonderful blessings you have bestowed on us and your unconditional love which surrounds us even when we've forgotten you are there in the wings of our life. All we need to do is call you into our heart, and you'll be there. Lord bless this food and our meager offerings of service that your name might be glorified. In the name of Jesus, we pray. Amen."

His rich voice echoed off the tile walls of the clean utility room, the stainless steel carts, the dumbwaiter elevator doors, and even the gates of heaven itself. He spoke as compelling as the beckoning Elijah. Even though every head bowed with eyes closed, the echoes of "uh huh," and Lordy, Lordy" mumbled under the breaths of several, all except Sally.

"How can you believe in all that malarkey," yelled Sally to all the misty eyes around the room.

It was Jewels who answered. "How can you not believe in God after working up here for any time at all?"

Esther waited silently in the shadows behind the line of people filling their plates.

Mrs. Putnam entered the room and hung back as she waited for her turn. Esther walked over to her and introduced herself.

Mrs. Putnam smiled and said, "Esther, I know who you are."

"This is the staff of the seventh floor here," Esther said, not able to control her fury anymore. "This is a very special group of people who have worked hard to develop ties and true friendships. We have come together and bonded through our misfortunes. Why are you allowing Mrs. Murphy to sabotage this strong working alliance? Go out and look at the patient conditions here. We take care of our patients and respect them. We are proud of our floor. Go look at the rooms and talk to the patients. Then, come back and have dinner. All the sheets are clean and patients bathed, scrubbed, shaven, and fed. This takes the cooperation of all the staff, not just a few."

Mrs. Putnam acted surprised and backed away from her.

"You've got to stop this drain on our nurses by the nursing home," Esther declared in as emphatic a tone as she dared use while confronting the Director.

"Let them hire their own nurses. Mrs. Murphy is causing all this neglect and abuse of the patients and staff. Mrs. Murphy is responsible for all the suffering going on over there. Don't you see that?" Esther realized she had lost control and raised her voice too loud. Her words reverberated around the room and the others stared at her in shock.

Mrs. Putnam inched farther away, out of the room, as if she didn't know what the else to do.

It occurred to Esther that Mrs. Putnam had no backbone. It must be Mrs. Murphy who called the shots. It all made sense now. Margaret Murphy wielded the power behind all the nursing problems. Margaret Murphy became the Simon Legree' of Thornhill Hospital.

The idea rushed into Esther's mind unannounced and startled her.

She stopped her thoughts immediately. She saw Mrs. Putnam as an oddity or even an imbecile. Esther's words became caught in her mind. She unburdened herself to the wrong person. Mrs. Putnam had absolutely no control.

She had to change her tactics. The reality took her by surprise. She gently took Mrs. Putnam's arm and guided her down the hall into every patient's room to show her what she meant.

At the end of the tour, Esther apologized saying, "I'm sorry I went on like that. I only wanted you to see what having a group of girls working together means to everyone. That's all I'm trying to say."

"Yes. I'm beginning to see the entire picture. I don't think you understand the pressures we're up against. Let's enjoy our lunch shall we?" .

When Mrs. Putnam finished going through the line, Esther helped herself to the coleslaw, mashed potatoes, sauerkraut, corn souffle`, ambrosia, collard greens, cornbread, and what was left of the curried fried rice and turkey. With her extra hand, she cut a piece of sweet potato pie. She vowed she'd try Selysia's curry dish first.

All the rooms became crowded with people. Some she didn't know. She wondered if the chair she saved was still available. Inching around the crowd, she found it miraculously empty.

Gazing around the room for Henry, she assumed he must have taken his plate to his sanctuary in Mrs. Shepherd's office. Or he may be eating his lunch with someone else. Esther ate her meal in silence as she listened to the others tell their tales of working in the nursing home.

Lyla told her story about the patient stealing all the false teeth. Sally told her description of the lady who collapsed in the middle of a transfer, and how she pulled her back out trying to keep the woman from falling to the floor. The story sounded very familiar to Esther, as she remembered her own injury. She wondered if that was the same lady.

"How can I forget?" Sally said. "It was the beginning of my back misery. I'll never forget that day." She abruptly stood up, stalked out, and irritably threw her plate and letter into the trash.

Lyla stared down hard at her hands with bulging, glassy, memory filled eyes, before getting up to follow Sally, without raising her head or saying anything in response.

Selysia withdrew a breath with such force when Sally bolted up and out that Esther felt the air rush by her. Selysia bit her lip and stared after Sally, as if not knowing how to get back the humor. Flustered, she jumped up and ran after the others, leaving her letter on the table laying open.

"Well, they all certainly left in a hurry," Melisa said coldly. "I never can figure them out. One minute they're happy as clams. The next they're bolting out the door just like that." She sighed deeply and stared with bitter remorse down at her hands. "You'd think Sally was the only one who has gotten hurt up here."

When she glanced back at Esther, she smiled sweetly as if nothing happened. "Buster's doing just fine with his stumps. They're sending him back here on Friday for physical therapy. He's doing so well the doctor wants to fit him with prostheses so he can learn to walk. I would never have believed it. How are you doing today?" she asked softly. "I haven't seen much of you lately. You look like all the life has been knocked out of you."

"Do I?" Esther answered slowly, as she picked at the almost empty plate with her fork. "How have you endured for nineteen years?"

"Now that you mention it. I don't know either. Actually, it's been twenty-one years. I asked them to do a count last week," Melisa answered. "I suppose one day took over the next until the years passed by me. My feet still throb too. If they'd let up for a few days, I'd feel a little better. My one clubfoot was corrected when I was a child, but now I have arthritis in it. I can't stand the pain anymore. The doctors have no cure for it either." Her hand flew up to her throat in desperation.

"The doctor says I have arthritis in both my feet, chest and my neck. Right here," Melisa said and pointed to the back of her hairline. He's documented this with x-rays. I've sent all the information to the medical board requesting early retirement. So far I haven't heard anything. I should be able to retire on disability. I know I'd be taking a deduction in payments. If I waited one more year, my payments would be several hundred more a month. I don't think I can wait any longer." She took a slow sip of her coffee and swallowed hard.

Esther felt her pain and knew Mrs. Murphy held up her retirement papers. The worst part was Melisa had no idea what was going on. Even after all these years.

"I think you should call in sick several times and see what happens. If you called in enough, maybe they'd believe you're really suffering. You never call in sick. Never. They don't believe you."

"You're right. I know I don't ever call in. I don't want to abandon the nurses here on the floor and make them suffer for my absence. I think I have about six or seven months sick leave," Melisa answered, lowering her eyes in contemplation. She laughed to herself. "

"Yes, that's it. You need to show them you're disabled. How are they gonna believe you're in so much pain when you appear every day and work like a slave with only a few complaints? They are humoring you by giving you those applications. Go to employee health several days in a row. Spend the afternoon in therapy and see what they say then. Maybe when Mrs. Shepherd can't depend on you anymore, she'd realize they need to do something else. The work conditions are better everywhere else. I've never worked so hard for so little money in my life. Yes! You can take six months sick leave. They'd have to keep our nurses instead of pulling them to the nursing home. You are the charge nurse too. You shouldn't have to do this heavy lifting. You should only have to do paper work."

"I think you're right, dear. I'll consider doing it," Melisa said and left the room, wearing a smile for the first time in days. Her irregular step appeared perkier, and her head rose proudly bobbing her shock of strawberry blond hair.

As Esther was about to leave the nurses' lounge, Mrs. Shepherd entered. There was a strange pensiveness about her, a holding back Esther hadn't seen before.

"I've been searching for you. Here you are still in this corner. I need to have a word with you. Come to my office."

Once in Mrs. Shepherd's office, Esther watched her push back the overflowing papers on her desk and open a file, her file.

"I've lost track of time. Things have caught up with me today," Mrs. Shepherd began in a tiny voice. She didn't look at Esther but rolled the snuff back and forth under her lip.

"Human resources called me this morning and told me your time was closed out today. I don't remember you telling me you were giving two weeks' notice. Here is your exit paper. I need your signature."

Mrs. Shepherd embodied complete composure now, not a sign of regret, or confusion.

"Notice! Time up! Exit paper! I didn't give you notice! Am I being fired?" Esther blurted out. "I'm being cut short."

Mrs. Shepherd stared solemnly into space.

"I haven't done anything wrong. Is this because I have been put on light duty? Because I have been complaining to everyone about the nursing home? I'll be short of time! I'll lose my license! I only have a few days left. Don't you know that?"

Mrs. Shepherd's brow furrowed deeply. "You didn't know about this? The business office told me you asked for your hours and said you'd be leaving. They thought you meant you were getting another job. Imagine my surprise when they told me. I thought you had more time." She smiled broadly, too big, too sweetly.

"I only wanted to know how many days I had left of my probation."

Mrs. Shepherd busied herself with shuffling the papers. She sipped her cold coffee. Her mouth distorted gruesomely at the taste, but she regained her composure, not once glancing at Esther. She let seconds pass without answering.

Esther waited impatiently for a reply. Her claustrophobia in close spaces began to smother her. Her hands grew hot, sweaty. Her head throbbed. When no reply came, she glanced at her watch. It was 3:00 p.m. She glanced up at the dirty air vent in the ceiling. Brown dust laden webs still hung down and waved continually from the blowing air. Can't she ever get that cleaned?

She's lying to me. The three days left of my probation is all that matters now. Esther saw the deceit in Mrs. Shepherd's eyes, in the way she moved the papers around, in the way she avoided Esther's gaze. They've told her to get rid of me before my probation was finished. I've caused too much trouble.

Esther decided to leave. I'll figure something out, she told herself. My record is perfect, and I've worked like a slave. I'm injured. Too much pain. I guess they've beaten me. I'll call the probation nurse and maybe she'll have a solution.

"Where should I sign?"

Mrs. Shepherd retreated some in her chair and examined Esther thoughtfully.

"I'm not supposed to do this. But if you work the evening shift today, tomorrow, and tomorrow night. You'd be finished before anyone knew it. Can you do that?"

"I'll try. If I can get someone to watch my boys. I'll do it. Then, I'll be completely finished." How can I be so thrilled about working two doubles and missing my Thanksgiving holiday, she thought.

She didn't miss the shrewd expression on Mrs. Shepherd's face.

Chapter 37

Entering the nurses' lounge, Esther trembled, as she imagined what she had to do, knowing she might injure herself permanently. Henry sat at the table, pensively writing orders. Nurses rushed in and left as they hurried for the report at the change of shift.

Henry examined her with concern. He put his pen down and turned toward her.

She watched his worried expression and puzzled about who he was, really. Yet, she shook her head with resignation, knowing he was the one person on whom she relied. How strangely peculiar it seemed to her now. How the path of one's life moved in twists and turns, creating an intricate maze, forming a definite direction toward a specific end without us ever knowing what the outcome will be. It was as if someone upstairs knew all the answers, and we are merely puppets in their hands.

"What's wrong?" he asked.

"They've done it. They've let me go."

Henry took her white hand as she sat down heavily in the chair.

"So much has happened here in such a short time. I don't know how I can leave. Leave all this behind. I've found my faith here. Faith to go on."

"Somehow the personnel office thought I was giving notice last week when I asked them to total up my hours. They have closed out my file as of 3:00 p.m. today. I've been let go with only three shifts left to work."

Esther pulled her hand away as if she didn't know him anymore.

"I only need three days, and my probation will be satisfied. Then, Mrs. Shepherd said she'd let me work this evening, tomorrow, and tomorrow evening to finish my time. A double on Thanksgiving."

"I don't understand any of this. There's a reason. You're getting too close. You've touched a nerve. They're getting rid of you." He stood up and put his arm around her.

"Go ahead and work. Satisfy the terms of your probation. We'll celebrate Thanksgiving with your boys when all this is over. I'm wondering if Florence had trouble covering for Thanksgiving, and instead of letting you off, she used this excuse to get you to work for her. I bet that's one of the reasons." He turned away, shaking his head.

"How can God let all this happen to me, Henry? How can he?"

Henry stared coldly back at her saying, "Esther. You might as well know. I don't believe in God. I don't believe that God helps us in any way. I believe we help ourselves. When we're dead, we're dead. Nothing else."

Esther gasped in disbelief. She stood up and backed away from him as if he were her enemy. Scenes raced through her mind. What about Hudson and Shaw and all the others? What about the times he sat for long hours with the patients until they died? No this wasn't true. If this were true she had misjudged him. He wasn't the man she imagined him to be. How did she not know?

Esther became too distraught to speak. She left the room without saying another word. She walked straight to the phone. She called Mark to see if he'd watch her boys while she worked. Paul refused to take the boys over the holiday which grieved her and brought tears to her eyes. She hadn't spoken to him for some time, but she was desperate. He hadn't called her since the hearing, and she used this as an excuse to call him. Maybe her sons were entitled to their part of the inheritance after all. She tried not to think about Henry's confession.

"Hello."

"Mark! This is Esther."

"What a pleasant surprise. Happy Thanksgiving girl! I've intended to call you all day, but I didn't want to disturb you at work."

"I hope it isn't bad news."

"No. In fact, I have good news for you," Mark said cooly. "The judge decided the case in your favor. Since your boys are Paul's only children and Dad's only grandchildren, they will share equally in the income from the estate." Mark sighed heavily and paused.

"What about you Mark. And your children?"

"The judge said the will was final. My father had the right to include or exclude whomever he chose. It seems old Dad composed an iron tight trust that no one can touch. Not even Paul. The income will go to Victoria and your sons and any other grandchildren. There is a discrepancy in the will which states all his blood grandchildren are entitled to be recipients of the trust, which includes my children if I ever have any. It looks like your sons are entitled to an income until they are twenty-one when the trust will give each twenty percent of the value of the trust in cash if they want it then. If there are more than five grandchildren the percentage is reduced. I'll come over sometime next week to explain the terms of the trust to you." He cleared his throat.

"That's great! I'm so glad to hear the news. But I've really gotten myself into a predicament. They've let me go three days short of my six months' probation. Mrs. Shepherd said she'd let me work tonight and a double tomorrow, Thanksgiving, to make up the shifts I need. I was wondering if you can take the boys for me."

There was a long pause on the other end of the line. "I wish I could, but I've already made plans. I'm sorry this has happened to you. At least she's letting you finish your time. I've been working closely on a case with Charlotte Pride, the new attorney in our firm." He paused for several seconds. Esther heard him breathe deeply and hesitate.

"If it were any other time. You know I'd be more than willing. I'm afraid the decision of this hearing has upset me. I've made arrangements to go away for a few days. I'm feeling rejected all over again. I don't know why he bequeathed his money to Victoria and not to Paul and me. Why don't you call Paul and Victoria," Mark added irritably.

"Thanks anyway. Paul has already told me he doesn't want them for Thanksgiving."

"I'm sorry. Look, I'll call you when I return next week. We can set up an appointment. Take care." Mark hung up the phone without another word.

The arriving nurses for the evening shift discussed their Thanksgiving day plans. She felt trapped and knew Henry was the only one left to help her out. Did she dare ask him? Her back ached more intensely than earlier as the muscle relaxants wore off. How can Henry not believe in God, after all that's happened? What about Truman? What about the others?

Esther hung onto the counter of the nurses' station praying for her pain to ease. She brightened slightly, thinking of her sons' new income. At least something good had come out of all this.

Henry sat with his back turned to her on the other side of the nurses' station. He must have come in while she was on the phone. She wondered if he had heard her conversation with Mark. Knowing his meddlesome curiosity, he probably did.

"Henry," Esther said timidly and stood close behind him as he bent over the desk writing on charts. He glanced up at her and smiled slightly. His previously old, wary-worn expression gone.

"I don't have anyone to take care of the boys this afternoon and evening, tomorrow and tomorrow evening. I called Mark and he can't.

Paul refused, so I'm really desperate."

"I have a surprise for you," he said with excitement dancing on his face. "Close your eyes."

He placed a thin sheet of pink paper in the palms of her hands and told her to read it, letting his fingers touch hers too long. "I knew you wouldn't believe me if I told you," he declared.

"Esther screamed after she read the results of the lab report. Mr. Kroger's blood test for HIV was negative.

"You ordered it didn't you?" Esther exclaimed, smiling down at his upturned face. The sea-green of his eyes dilated as she drank in their tenderness. After several long seconds, they reminded her of deep pools inviting her into their depths. "You never forgot about it, did you? She wanted to cry and hug him at the sight of such good news. But they weren't alone.

"Yes. Of course, I ordered it. What do you take me for? I wanted to order it before the accident, but I needed a legal reason. Yes. I'll take care of the boys for you. Tonight?" he said, smiling up at her with his two rabbit teeth gleaming in the light. She wanted to embrace him and never let him go. Instead, she squeezed his hand until the blood left his fingers. Abruptly, she dropped his hand when she remembered his confession. She felt betrayed all over again. Of all people, Henry didn't believe in God. She felt a scream rising up from the depths of her soul, panic closing her throat.

Slightly amused, he examined her rakishly from head to toe, as if he intended to possess her immediately, but all he said was, "Is it all right if I pick them up around 5:00 p.m.?" I've several things to take care of before I leave."

"Are you sure? You're the only one who can help me now," she answered. Her desires mingled with her fears. The combination churned her stomach like a green apple.

"After reading the results of the test, I think my bad luck is changing. Are you sure you can get them fed, washed, and put to bed?"

"I was able to do it while you had your surgery wasn't I?"

"Yes," she answered. Why did he have to tell me he didn't believe in God?"

"Yes, I suppose I can do it." He frowned, slightly indifferent.

"I was all boy once too. I think I know what boys like to do."

"There's something I've been wanting to talk to you about."

"Sure. Make it quick so I can get out of here."

"Henry, the nursing home has been pulling our nurses and other nurses from the other floors for the past three months. If that's the case why wasn't their budget lower than twenty thousand? For all those days. They should have saved even more money. Why are they so concerned about scrimping below budget? Most organizations are happy to make their budget." Esther's eyes met Henry's.

"I don't know. You definitely have a point there. In fact, I was planning to look into it myself."

"Do you suppose they were saving money and not telling anyone. Do you think they can do that? Give themselves bonuses. Or even have false employees? How can their conscience let them do something like that?" Esther whispered.

"I don't know. But I know how to find out. The Director of the hospital said he intended to investigate the situation. You can bet he will."

Esther leaned over and whispered into Henry's reddened ear, "I'll see you tonight at midnight. Go ahead and go to bed if you want. Thanks."

As she backed away a whiff of his taunting after shave caught her off guard and she hovered over him, drinking in the intoxicating aroma which characterized his essence. After she turned to leave, she glanced back to see him nod affectionately goodbye.

* * *

Henry knew instinctively what he must do. Esther was on the right track, and he sensed a cover-up. He'd know in a matter of hours if his hunches were true.

He picked up the phone and called the personnel department.

"Jill is that you? I hardly recognized your voice. How is everything going with you these days?"

"Oh, Henry! You are certainly the stranger. What's become of you? We're doing great now. If you hadn't helped us with the rent when they laid John off, I don't know what we'd have done," Jill Westin answered. She was the Director of Human Resources for both the hospital and the nursing home.

"I need a favor from you. I'd like for you to keep it under your hat if you can. This is rather important."

"Sure Henry. What are you up to now?" Jill chided playfully. "You're always sticking your nose into someone else's business aren't you?"

He laughed and admitted, "Yes, I guess you're right. This time it's just a little misunderstanding. Can you get me a copy of the nursing payroll for the nursing home and the seventh floor for the past three months? I know this is a big favor, but you won't regret it. I promise you!"

"You're asking for the moon. All of those records are kept by Mrs. Putnam in her office. If it's that important.... I can go into her office and copy them without her knowing it. You have good timing. As a matter of fact, both she and Mrs. Murphy are away this afternoon. I think they've gone to a conference or maybe left early for the holiday. I have so much to do. I won't be able to leave until late this evening."

"Yes, that's exactly what I want you to do for me. Please don't tell anyone will you?"

"Sure. Anything you say. I'll never forget what you did for us. Now don't be a stranger. You hear?"

"Thanks. Can you have this information by 4:30 p.m. today?"

"You don't want much do you?" Jill answered exasperated. "I'll do it right away. If anyone objects...I'll say it's for taxes, for the accountant. Come to think of it the Director's office called and wanted the same report the other day. Yesterday! I can give you both the copies of the records. I haven't been able to copy them for him because I've been too busy with the end of the year reports and everything."

"They did? That's great. Thanks for telling me."

Henry hung up and knew he had almost hit the jackpot. He worried about Jill getting access to the records and hoped Mrs. Putnam filed them in her office. He imagined they were intact. Suppose Mrs. Putnam suspected something and removed the files. Or possibly destroyed them. No. no. He told himself. Don't think of that now. It's against the law anyway.

* * *

Esther rushed into the nurses' lounge to get her pills before report. They are my salvation for the next two days, she thought. Her pain eased by the end of report. After scanning the schedule, she knew they needed her to work. The floor operated with a skeleton staff for the holiday. She had to forget the light duty. She knew they expected her to lift many of the patients. There was no one else to help.

Selysia came over and sat down beside her. The others waited in the other room to receive report.

"Listen, girl. I heard about you leaving. I came over to say I'm sorry. You're tough. You're a mighty tough cookie. We all appreciate what you've tried to do here. We are grateful you tried to help us stand up for what we believed. You inspired us to do our best work, but no one thinks they can win at it." Selysia shook her head with a resignation Esther hadn't seen before.

Selysia ran her fingers over Esther's disheveled hair trying to smooth out the tangles. Tears filled her eyes. She leaned over and hugged Esther saying, "You're the best white girl I know. I'm gonna miss you. I'm gonna pray that the good Lord makes everything work out all right for you. You'll see. He'll do it too!" She paused for several seconds and examined Esther sheepishly. "What I want to know is would you invite all of us blacks to your house to a party? Can you do that? Invite us to the white subdivision?"

Esther smiled and shook her head in disbelief saying, "Yes, Selysia. Of course, I can. You had to ask me that question didn't you?"

"Well," she answered shyly, "I had to know if working here made a difference in you. I had to know if we affected you as much as you influenced us."

Esther stared helplessly out into the empty room as scenes from the past six months streamed through her mind. "Yes," she answered softly, "all the difference in the world."

Selysia turned her head away to hide her emotion. "Listen, girl! Karen's working tomorrow to help you out since you have a bad back and all. Sally's gonna be here all evening. So if you need anything just ask her. She told me to tell you that. Good luck to you honey and come back to see all of us."

"Karen's working on Thanksgiving? For me? With me? And Sally?"

"They know you're hurting. They know you need help. How many times have you helped them? How many times did you bolster them? They haven't forgotten."

Selysia left the dirty, cream colored room, leaving Esther alone with her worries. Esther lit another cigarette, knowing she was missing report. She'd been here all day anyway and knew all the patients inside and out. She needed a few more minutes of rest.

* * *

Henry waited in Jill's office for her return. He had copied the assignment sheets for the seventh floor for this month and reviewed them while he waited. It appeared as if the nursing home pulled two to three nurses every day, even from the evening shifts, not only from the seventh floor but other floors as well. He uncrossed his legs and brought them down from where he'd propped them on her desk. He stood up to stretch out the kinks. He paced up and down in the room and realized his watch said 4:30 p.m. He needed to leave soon to pick up Esther's sons on time. He surprised himself that he liked them so much. He felt sorry for their situation of growing up without a father.

He examined the pictures of Jill's family sitting on her desk. He ached now for his own loving father who died five years ago. When he saw Esther's sons, they reminded him that he and his father were always at opposite poles. Growing up as a minister's son put him under the scrutinizing gaze of every cantankerous old biddy trying to save his soul. He evaded them expertly after a time and attributed his skill in this area to his early years. It was such a strange turn of events, he thought, as he reminisced over all those Sundays. He never understood what all the fuss was about. Why they all paid homage to God? His father spent his entire life saving the souls of the populace only to lose the soul of his own son. He tried to search for God. Whenever he reached into the stratosphere for help from God, he found nothing. No one ever responded.

A great icy current of air surrounded Henry while he stood at the window. He moved from one end of the window to the other, but the draft followed him. The memory of members of his father's congregation marching up to the altar to be saved overcame him. He heard the sounds of a choir singing Amazing Grace and saw the parishioners arms raised in pleadings as they approached the altar to be saved. He witnessed their deep emotion as they cried openly to God. He saw their suffering. He observed their agonizing desperation at life's frustrations all over again as if it were happening now right before his eyes.

He envisioned his father placing the palm of his hand on each bowed head saying, 'Come unto me all ye who are weary and heavy laden and I will give you rest. Accept this poor suffering sinner into the fold of your flock and surround him with the profound experience of your peace. In the name of the Father, the Son, and the Holy Spirit."

Still gazing out the window, Henry felt a great surge of emotion rise up inside of him, bringing tears to his eyes at the sight of his loving father. Then, he remembered Christiana dying and saying, "Henry, why don't you let Him into your heart?"

He recalled looking her straight in the eye and saying, "Who?" He hated seeing the hurt expression in her eyes. He became so angry at God, he refused to accept her faith or even God's existence.

He watched huge droplets of rain fall into the lake one by one, forming circles growing wider and larger until they touched each other. In minutes the entire surface of the lake formed perfectly round pockmarks of different sizes resembling the crust of the moon.

How was he able to open up now after so many years of misery? In the past, he argued there was too much to give up to change his life of running. Now he didn't really have a life anymore. All he wanted was peace of mind. He searched for it everywhere, but with God. Dare he take the leap?

He left the window and walked over to sit in the comfortable chair, thinking Esther is just one of those unusual people who have the gift of healing. It happened whenever she touched anyone. He saw it with his own eyes. Patients became healed maybe not physically or all at once, but emotionally a little each time. Yes, he believed in the healing. He still didn't believe in God.

How can he when Christiana died so cruelly? Never able to live a complete life with children and achieving old age. How can he with all the misery he saw daily on the seventh floor? Yes. He was a realist he admitted to himself. Life is in the here and now. He worried if Esther was able to accept him the way he was. Feeling sad, he stared out the window to the lake again.

Jill was lucky. She and her husband had it all. His intuitions were right this morning. There had been a storm for sure, but the thunder storm clouds overhead didn't compare with the storm which amassed and was about to explode on the seventh floor. Where will it all end? What will be left when the tornado finishes its devastation. Will he and Esther still be friends?

"Henry," Jill exclaimed, as she entered the office. "I didn't expect you to be sitting here waiting. Well, you're in luck. I found everything you wanted. I can't imagine what you're doing with these records, but I trust it's important."

"I think you've just saved my life." He examined the payroll she handed him and shook his head in affirmation as he scanned one sheet after another. The schedules displayed a full staff for each floor of the nursing home for each day for the last three months. Three nurses were assigned to work for each wing. This staffing was admittedly tight and expected each nurse to care for ten patients, but it was tolerable. "Yes! This is exactly what I wanted." Time had slipped away. Now he was late picking up the boys.

"Thanks, Jill! You'll understand why I needed these in a few days."

Taking a second before he left her office, he peered through the window, followed the outline of the lake to the tall buildings of Fayette, South Carolina, past the town to the billowing gray clouds filling the sky. He was thinking, You may lose many, but when You win, You win big, like now. Thank you. You out there.

Later that evening after he put the boys to bed, he sat down to examine the payroll reports. He compared the nursing home staff to the assignments of the seventh floor. Each day the nursing home pulled staff from the seventh floor. The payroll forms stated sufficient staff worked and were paid for their time. He needed copies of the assignment sheets from the nursing home to find out exactly where the discrepancies lay. He made a list of the employees' names and thought he'd ask Esther to check them out with the other nurses. If any false names appeared, the staff can identify them. He knew they hired no new nurses in the nursing home in the last three months.

He called Esther. "Hi, it's Henry. Everything went just fine. Your boys are in bed, sleeping soundly I hope."

"I'm so relieved to hear from you. I was afraid to call for fear they'd wake up and refuse to go back to bed."

"I have a copy of the payroll."

"How did you get that?"

"I have my ways. Let me give you some names to check with the other nurses. See if they have ever heard of these girls? For the life of me, I haven't. Cecile Post. Beatrice Carter..."

"Have you done it? Have you cracked the mystery? Have you discovered the root of all the evil here?"

"I think your insinuations are correct." He changed his tone and whispered into the phone. "You are more right than I ever imagined you to be." He returned his voice to a normal tone. "Ask if someone can find a copy of the assignment sheets for the past three months for each floor of the nursing home. I have the ones for the seventh floor. I'm finding it interesting reading. How's your back?"

"You'll never believe it, Henry. Sally came in tonight to work with me. Of course, she's getting comp time. She asked Mrs. Shepherd, and she said yes. Everyone has chipped in and lifted all the patients for me. All I have left to do is give my 10:00 p.m. medications, and I'll be finished. If anyone can get this information for you, Sally will."

"This is our chance. You've got to. If they get wind we're investigating the situation, they'll destroy every piece of evidence. It's evening and there'll be less staff. She can tell them she needs the schedule for the seventh-floor head nurse. Or something. Make up some excuse.

"All right. I'll be home about 11:30 p.m. Thanks for everything."

When Esther arrived home, Henry sat at her kitchen table pouring over the payroll sheets. He had compiled a list of nurses' and staff' names to check with their home addresses.

"I'm so exhausted," she said, as she dropped the brown envelope onto the kitchen table. "Here are the assignment sheets you wanted."

"Thanks."

Henry stood up immediately and pulled out a chair for her.

"Why don't I fix you a cup of tea to settle you down?"

"I think I'm gonna take my pills and go straight to bed. I hope you forgive me, but I have to get up at six and work another double," she said, sighed, and pressed her hand to her forehead. "I hope working these double shifts count. I'm getting a headache. They have to give me the hours I've worked. Don't they?"

He paled, thought for a second, and said, "Yes. If you work they have to calculate the hours and pay you. Unless they count it as volunteering."

They both gasped in horror at the idea. A grim silence permeated the room punctuated only with the sound of the dripping faucet.

Esther reeled and ran into the privacy of her room for shelter but found no security. She stripped off her uniform and hung another out for tomorrow. She jumped into the shower in an attempt to wipe away all the grime and stress of the seventh floor. Trust in God she told herself over and over. Don't panic. Trust in God.

Henry followed her into her bedroom but froze in the doorway unable to turn away. Esther turned and gave him a stern look as he reluctantly retreated back to his work.

After her bath Esther entered the kitchen, smiling to herself at the sight of Henry industriously moving his head from one page to another oblivious of her entrance.

"Do I feel better," Esther said as she pulled the pink sash on her robe tighter. She had wrapped her hair up tight in a white Turkish towel.

"I've been comparing the payroll sheets with the assignment sheets. In only ten minutes I was able to glean from the documents that the extra nurses never worked according to the nursing home assignment records. Every name has been faithfully recorded, including the wing where they worked. It's been clearly documented that these extra nurses were dummies receiving paychecks and not working. None of these nurses' names have been recorded in the telephone book. They don't have phones. I need to find out how their checks were sent, and who received them."

Henry smiled up at her shyly. His face glowed red from embarrassment at seeing her naked earlier.

"This is it! We've finally found the discrepancy."

He pointed to a list of names on the payroll sheet and the column showing the total amount of money they received from a check twice a month. He pointed out to Esther the assignments didn't include any of the dummy names of any of all three shifts.

"Henry do you know what this means? It means they were falsifying checks and embezzling money. I wonder if we can find the canceled checks?"

"That's it! You're a genius. Why didn't I think of it? Yes. Of course! The payroll department keeps those on file for the accountant.

Esther sat in the chair shivering more from the realization than from a chill.

Henry put his arm around her trying to comfort her, but tears ran down her cheeks.

"How can they do this and get away with it. All those months we struggled to complete the work, they laughed at us and raked in the money. People lost their lives. If they were able to do this, they won't stop at anything to ruin me or you or anyone else to cover up their sins.

"If we expose their scheme it has to be immediately and without any chance of failure. For our sakes. They've lied, and they will lie about anything to save their own skin. Who knows, maybe the Director is in on it too. We can't take any chances."

Henry sat down wearily, letting his long legs sprawl across the floor. He scratched his head and retreated deep in thought.

"We have to find those canceled checks tomorrow and find out where they are being sent and who is cashing them. It's our only chance."

"How are we ever going to do it?"

"You've got to do it tomorrow! I have a friend in the personnel office, but the checks will be in the payroll office or even the accountant's office. You need to go in with your time and say the amount wasn't correct. Or maybe you can get security to let you into the office."

"It's Thanksgiving Day. No one will be working tomorrow."

"That's right. I'll call my friend and see what she says to do."

"I don't know Henry. I think I'm too scared to invade their offices and steal the checks." Esther placed her hand on her forehead saying, "My head is throbbing. I have to go to bed. Tomorrow I'll try to figure this out. I've fixed the sofa up for you to sleep. Thanks for everything."

Esther stood up and left the room, leaving Henry excitedly comparing one page against the other.

Esther closed her eyes and drifted off to sleep. She was awakened when Henry's warm body slid underneath the covers beside her. She felt his hot hand gently caress her back, arms, and thighs. She dared not say a word, as she let every stroke of his hand sooth her exhausted muscles.

"I only want to be close to you," Henry whispered. "If you're wondering my A.I.D.S. test was negative too. Go to sleep now. We have the rest of our lives to satisfy our desires."

She turned over and kissed him softly on his cheek.

The next day she rushed through her morning medicines, baths, and transfers, and waited impatiently for a call from Henry. At 12:30 p.m., it finally came.

"Esther meet this lady, Jill, at the door to the accounting department. She'll give you a bag filled with all the canceled checks, and the files of the dummy nurses."

"How did you engineer that so fast?" Esther asked, wondering if she'd be watched. Her heart beat faster at the idea of possessing all those important documents. The schedules were one thing, but those checks were another ball game altogether.

"Never mind. Just do it. Meet me at the entrance. I'll be waiting there with your boys. We'll wait as long as it takes. We're lucky to have a good friend in the personnel department." Henry hung up.

Esther glanced around the nurses' station suspiciously, in hopes no one overheard her conversation.

"I thought you had Thanksgiving off," Melisa said, as she walked up to Esther.

"I did. I guess you didn't hear. They've let me go. Mrs. Shepherd let me work last night, today, and tonight to make up the last few days I needed to complete my probation. Why are you here?"

"I'm so sorry about that for you. I wonder how that happened?" Melisa said. "I came in because my husband went to his mother's. She and I don't get along as you know. I thought I'd look in on Buster. You know he is working with his prosthesis now and doing very well. I may add. I can't believe they've let you go. Well, at least they haven't fired you. But for all you've done for the unit, I believe they should have treated you with more respect." Melisa's hand flew up to her throat in disbelief. "I certainly hope they don't do that to me. They can you know. They can do anything they want. I'm really gonna miss you." Melisa looked older and slumped with sadness and resignation when she walked away.

Esther let out a sigh of relief at the empty hallway behind Melisa. She checked her watch and realized her meeting was only ten minutes from now. Karen walked toward her on the other side of the hall.

"Karen, I need to go down to employee health to get more medication for the weekend. Do you mind if I go now?"

Karen smiled warmly saying, "Go on. Before we need to give the 2:00 p.m. medications. We'll be all right here."

Esther's back still ached, and she leaned sideways favoring the pain. When she reached the third floor, she waited in front of the accounting room door, just as Henry said. Within minutes she heard the footsteps of a feminine walk in high heels. A tap, tap, tap echoed off the floors and walls which gleamed with fresh paint as bright as the newly waxed linoleum.

An attractive short woman, with blond hair, cropped conservatively around her ears, stopped in front of Esther, whispering, "Are you Henry's friend?"

"Yes," Esther said and smiled at the woman's caution.

She handed Esther a large, brown paper bag filled with files and canceled checks. The woman had placed some old clothes in the top to disguise the sack.

"You're a life-saver," Esther said. You'll never know what this means."

"Well, Henry helped me and my husband when we had nowhere else to turn. Whatever he wants me to do, I'll be more than happy to help." The woman smiled and patted Esther on the shoulder. Then she left, walking rapidly down the hall, disappearing the way she came.

Esther felt dizzy under the weight of the contents of the bag. The pain in her back stabbed incessantly. She raced to the elevator, down to the lobby of the hospital, pausing only a few times to get her breath. She didn't breathe easily, though, until she reached the front pavement and saw Henry's smiling face inside his black Jaguar.

"Mommy! Mommy!" her boys shouted simultaneously, very happy to have Henry's attention.

Henry glared at her wearily. "Come home soon. These little monsters are wearing me out!" They all laughed at his half-honest remark.

She kissed each of them and spoke a few words after handing Henry the precious parcel of evidence.

Two weeks later Esther returned to Thornhill Hospital to pick up her last check. Enjoying the crisp cool December air, she rapidly strode up the long avenue lined with live oaks that led to the entrance of the hospital. She missed the place, even in this short time, she acknowledged to herself as she scanned the garden filled with men for a familiar face. She felt disappointment at not seeing anyone she knew. She felt rested though, as the two-week break gave her muscles the necessary time to heal.

She hoped to see Henry sometime this morning. She had only spoken to him several times since that last night in her home when she worked for her time on Thanksgiving day. He had disappeared for the weekend saying he had some important things to take care of. When she tried to call him, he was always out or unavailable. Maybe she should have been more receptive to him. Maybe he assumed she didn't really think of him romantically. His absence hurt her feelings. She reached the covered portico of the hospital and stopped for a minute to watch all the people congregated in front of the entrance. A gray van with the giant black letters WTTG Ch 13 News painted on the side parked in the parking lot beyond the avenue of live oaks.

Esther stood behind the crowd of people trying to see what all the commotion was about. The angry expressions on the employee's faces and their loud vindictive voices told her something serious had happened. A black Buick police car waited at the curb with a policeman speaking into his telephone.

Another van with capital blue letters saying Channel 2 News, ABC Network, pulled up to the entrance, stopped, and two men, carrying black cameras and microphones, jumped out and pushed through the waiting line of spectators.

Voices grew louder. The employees screamed with raised fists at two women being led out of the door escorted by six FBI agents.

At the sight of Mrs. Putnam and Mrs. Murphy, Esther screamed, knowing Henry was successful in convincing the FBI and the local police of their crimes. Her own long suppressed fury boiled inside her. She wanted to throw stones too, but she held her composure enjoying the scene. She knew deep in her heart there was nothing anyone can do to these women to take away the horror, tragedy, and suffering their embezzling scheme caused the innocent patients and employees. Tears erupted in her eyes as the faces of the dead patients passed before her.

Searching for some message from the criminals, news teams jammed the microphones in front of the Directors' turned away faces, but they had nothing to say and pushed past the men. Towering above the animated crowd following the women, Henry strode forward, took the cameramen aside and gave them their coveted interview. Esther watched Henry's piercing eyes scan the faces in the crowd as he talked to the cameras. She felt their hot poker intensity captivate her all over again when they singled her out. She met his enticing gaze and realized how much she had yearned for his affection these past two weeks.

"Stop! Wait a minute," Henry yelled. "Get that lady over here. She's the one you need to interview. She's the one who first suspected the crime. She's the one who first complained about the desperate conditions."

All the eyes turned immediately on Esther. All the voices became silent as the people pushed her toward the microphones. Henry grabbed her and pulled her in front of the cameras saying, "She's the one you need to interview. Not me!"

Esther told the public how hard it had been for the nurses and nursing assistants to give excellent care when there wasn't enough nursing staff. She told them how it had broken her heart to watch the patients die while being neglected because of staff shortages. Two or three staff for sixty patients was neglect and abuse, not enough to feed, bathe, transfer to wheelchairs, and give medicines. We need regulations."

"We need volunteers to come in, feed patients, and just talk to them. Come in and adopt a grandparent. You'll be surprised how much they give back for just a little bit of time."

"It's 6:00 p.m. Turn the television to the news," Henry said and didn't wait for Esther, but raced over and switched the channel on the TV.

There's a late breaking story today involving Thornhill Veterans Hospital. The Director of Nurses Mrs. Putnam and the assistant Director of Nurses Mrs. Murphy have been arrested on the charge of embezzling funds, forging checks, and shorting staff at Thornhill Hospital. These women were given bonuses for staffing under the allocated budget. They claimed to have saved the government over twenty thousand dollars by understaffing and were given bonuses. Not only that but they falsified records and paid themselves for nurses and CNAs who were on the payroll with fictitious names. Our veterans were the ones who suffered the most." The news film of the two women being escorted by police into the police car filled Esther with satisfaction. She and Henry laughed as they watched themselves explain what happened.

Esther sighed remembering again all the patients who suffered at the hands of being short staffed. She prayed silently, "Thank you, Lord, for all your help."

Henry grabbed her to him and kissed her with all the passion he had ever felt for her. She clung to him a long time. Then, he led her to the sofa saying, "I have something to ask you."

She furrowed her brows slightly wondering what all this was about. She had good news to tell him too.

"Will you marry me?" he asked sheepishly again and caressed the side of her face with his finger. "I can't live without you. My life is empty without you."

"I don't know. You mean so much to me. I'm starting to get my life back together again. I care deeply for you." Esther didn't expect this. What should she say? If only she had some warning.

"Let's say, we'll see."

"No. I want you to say yes! I'm in love with you!"

"I'm too scared, yet."

"How can you be scared of me?"

"Henry, don't you understand. God helped work all this out. God helped with the expose'."

He sunk down in the sofa, shattered, disappointment covering his whole being.

"God again! I don't know how you can think God was responsible for this. We were the ones who smoked them out! Gathered all the files and information."

"You don't understand. He led us. He led us every step of the way. I was sent here to help discover all the crimes going on here. The Director of nurses from the University Hospital called me this morning and offered me a lot more money for my past experience. Mrs. Saunders' lawyer called me. She's the wife of the patient I took care of in Hospice when my license was suspended and I was put on probation. He said Mrs. Saunders notified him before she died of cancer that she gave her husband the overdose of medication because she couldn't stand to see him in so much pain. She asked him to find me and try to rectify the mistake. They've written a letter to the South Carolina State Board of Nursing Licensure explaining my license should never have been suspended. My life has taken a wonderful turn. There's blue sky ahead."

"I still love you and want to marry you."

"I can't believe you don't believe in God at all. Not the way you take care of those patients. Not the way you help people out." How can she explain her faith was the center of her life, and this will never change. Will he ever understand?

"I'm not saying no. I'm saying this gives us something to work on. I wish you believed the way I do. I'll pray for you and your belief. I want you to know you mean more to me than anyone except my boys. I need you desperately, and I feel love for you. We need to be together without so much stress. You were right the other night. We do have the rest of our life to see."

Esther tenderly touched his downcast face saying, "If only you believed. If only God revealed himself to you in some way. Your life will be so full and meaningful."

"Maybe he is. Maybe I'm beginning to see his power in our lives. But I really don't believe in the miracles you see."

Henry turned his head away like an impish boy and admitted, "I received my transcript from medical school yesterday. I only have three courses to take to finish my degree. I've been accepted at Emory next term to complete what I started. All these years I've regretted walking out on my degree. I've regretted leaving part of my life behind. My life is taking a new turn now too." He grabbed her to him and declared, "I'm never letting you go, so you might as well face it."

ABOUT THE AUTHOR

Barbara D. Duffey is a retired RN whose career spanned fifty years. During this time she worked at many facilities including Johns Hopkins Hospital, Veterans Hospitals, and the famous Central State Hospital of Milledgeville, Georgia. After nursing at the veterans' hospitals with the disabled and dying, she felt compelled to write this novel *Of Grace and Courage*. The plight of the veterans and their caregivers, their daily struggles, and their search for faith and immortality made an indelible mark on her conscience not to let their adversities be forgotten.

Barbara has two children, and two grandchildren, and lives on St. Simons Island, Georgia, with her pets. Her passions are writing, her faith, and helping those less fortunate.

Barbara's other published works include:

Banshees Bugles and Belles:
True Ghost Stories of Georgia

Angels and Apparitions:
True Ghost Stories of the South

Miracles From Heaven

Women of the Confederacy

Of Grace and Courage:
Thornhill Veterans Hospital